chef's kiss

chef's kiss

tj alexander

**SIMON &
SCHUSTER**

London · New York · Sydney · Toronto · New Delhi

First published in the United States by Atria,
an imprint of Simon & Schuster Inc, 2022

First published in Great Britain by Simon & Schuster UK Ltd, 2023

1 3 5 7 9 10 8 6 4 2

Simon & Schuster UK Ltd
1st Floor
222 Gray's Inn Road
London WC1X 8HB

Simon & Schuster Australia, Sydney
Simon & Schuster India, New Delhi

www.simonandschuster.co.uk
www.simonandschuster.com.au
www.simonandschuster.co.in

A CIP catalogue record for this book
is available from the British Library

ISBN: 978-1-3985-3060-7
eBook ISBN: 978-1-3985-3061-4

Printed and Bound in the UK using 100% Renewable
Electricity at CPI Group (UK) Ltd

For Kara, my favorite

chef's kiss

Chapter 1

Eight unbaked loaves of sourdough sat on the test kitchen counter, and Simone was working on the ninth.

She had come into work before the sun was up just for this: the culmination of many weeks spent perfecting her no-knead recipe. Each batch of dough had a slightly different ratio of bread flour to whole wheat, or salt to water. The doughs had risen overnight, and now they were nearly ready for the decisive bake. Simone could feel her excitement building, and in the quiet of the test kitchen, which was empty at this early hour, she allowed herself a pleased hum. She gave the ninth and final batch of sourdough its third fold-and-turn, then placed it gently in a parchment-lined bowl, where it joined the lineup. She frowned, giving the bowl a slight nudge.

There. Now all nine bowls were perfectly aligned in a neat row of stainless steel to match the rest of the sterile industrial kitchen. She jotted down a quick note to herself so she could keep them all straight—they were arranged from most bread flour to least starting on her left—and tucked the note in her apron pocket. Soon she would find out which recipe was the best of the lot. They just needed one last short rise before they went into the oven.

A glance out the window told her the sun was rising, too. Simone took a moment to sip her coffee and watch the peaceful scene unfold outside. From the top floor of the West Village office building, she could see the tiny triangular park across the street, the burbling fountain in its center lined with sleepy pigeons.

She took another drink of coffee. It was good—dark and strong. No one else on staff had the patience and know-how to coax the test kitchen's overly complicated espresso machine into producing it. Sometimes, she mused, hard work *did* pay off.

Though she was young—twenty-eight years old—Simone Larkspur had been aggressive in her career as a pastry chef, working long hours in restaurants of incrementally better quality and doggedly writing freelance articles for food and wine publications until she attained her dream job: recipe developer and writer for The Discerning Chef.

Most people had never heard of The Discerning Chef. It was a hybrid publishing company that put out a series of cookbooks and an eponymous magazine "since 1952," as their logo proudly proclaimed. Their material was aimed, supposedly, at chefs— whether professional or amateur, The Discerning Chef could never seem to decide. Simone had been working there for nearly three years, and she took such pride in her job that she couldn't imagine doing anything else.

Simone was considering whether she had time to cook herself some breakfast when she heard the test kitchen's swinging door creak open. She turned, wondering who else would be there so early, and found it was Delilah, the assistant to the editor in chief.

"She wants to see you," Delilah said in a tone that managed to be both firm and sympathetic. Her crisp shift dress and box braids were as precise as her gesture in the direction of the executive office. "You can go straight in."

"Me? But—" Simone gazed at her row of sourdough loaves. They needed to be scored and baked in about fifteen minutes. "Can I just—?"

"She's waiting," Delilah said, effectively destroying Simone's hopes of finishing up her task before facing her boss's boss. Delilah must have noticed the despair on Simone's face, because she added, "Everyone in Editorial is taking a turn. You just happened to be the first one here this morning—and, well, every morning. No need to worry."

In Simone's experience, when someone said you shouldn't worry, you should very much worry, and in fact, should clear your schedule to do nothing but. Still, if the big boss called, she couldn't dither. She squared her shoulders, stood at her full height (which, honestly, was not very tall), and marched to the executive office.

She tapped at the cloudy glass door and cracked it open, popping her head in to find the woman herself at her desk: Pim Gladly, editor in chief of The Discerning Chef for over thirty-five years, a giant in the culinary world. She was an occasional judge on one of those cooking shows that tortures its poor contestants with impossible, nightmarish tasks. She'd made several hardened chefs cry on camera. She was actually a popular meme, used primarily for reactions that required unimpressed judgment, though she refused to learn what a meme was.

Her eyes found Simone from behind an overly large pair of eyeglasses framed in red ovals. "Ah. Simone." Her gaze flicked down to her desk, where she seemed to consult a slip of paper. "Have a seat." She waved her hand toward one of the leather chairs opposite.

Simone perched on the chair and faced Pim with what she hoped was an earnest, serious look on her face and not anxiety-riddled terror.

"What did you want to speak to me about, ma'am?" she asked.

Simone had only spoken to her editor in chief a handful of

times, so tacking on the "ma'am" seemed prudent. Ms. Gladly tended to stay above the day-to-day workings of The Discerning Chef's operations, taking a more macro-level view of the business. This meant that, for the most part, Pim Gladly only came into the office two or three days a week, with the rest of her time occupied by her house in the Hamptons, her various boards of directors, her judging panels, and her seven purebred, wire-haired dachshunds.

She gazed at Simone across the expanse of her cluttered desk and said, "We're not making any money."

Simone blinked. "Oh." She waited for Ms. Gladly to continue, and when she didn't, she ventured to say, "Well, TDC has always served a niche market, and as long as we continue to provide that market with quality work—"

Gladly shook her severe pageboy-styled head. She continued, her voice lilting between a mid-Atlantic accent and a quasi-British one. "No, Simone. Actually, if we continue on as we have, we will shut down by next year. No one is buying our books. No one is subscribing to our magazine. No one cares about The Discerning Chef these days, not when they have cable television and the internet. We are a dinosaur," she said, lifting a paperweight from her desk and holding it aloft, "and if we do not act quickly, we are not going to be able to dodge the meteor."

She brought the glass lump of the paperweight back down with a heavy thud, making everything on her desk—and Simone—jump.

Simone stared at her. Her dream job was disintegrating like so much grated Parmesan in a hot risotto. Though her stomach hurt at the prospect, her head was already calculating who would be most likely to hire her after The Discerning Chef folded. *Gourmet*? *TasteBuzz*? That guy from culinary school who always seemed to be opening a new bistro every six months? She could make some calls. She disliked the idea of going back to work in a restaurant kitchen, where the pay was low and the nights were long, but it would cover the rent until she found something more stable.

But then the portion of her brain not occupied in revising her resumé came up with a pressing question. She decided to ask it aloud. "Why are you telling me this, ma'am?"

"Because." Pim Gladly stood from her desk and crossed over to the window, where she could fold her hands behind her tastefully khaki-jumpsuited back and gaze out on the little park opposite the office building. "It is now the mission of the entire Discerning Chef staff to get us out of this mess." She whirled on Simone. "You're all supposed to be the most clever, inventive minds in the business. Well, we're going to need every bit of it. We must pivot, and pivot hard."

Simone's mouth opened, then closed, then opened, then thought better of it and snapped shut again.

Ms. Gladly cocked her head. "Come on," she said. "Speak up. You clearly have something to say."

"Right." Simone cleared her throat. "It's only—I'm not sure how you'd like me to pivot. I write recipes. I think they're very good. That's what I know how to do, and I'm not sure I can do it any differently."

"They might be the best recipes ever devised in the history of the electric stove, my dear," said Pim with a snort, "but if no one reads the damn things, it doesn't matter how good they—or you—are."

Simone flinched. She had found herself thinking on exactly this fact many times in the last few months as *TDC*'s subscription numbers dwindled, but it did not make it any less painful to hear it with her own ears. If a dish is created in the forest, and there's no one around to attempt it themselves, is it really a recipe? Of course not. A recipe is only a recipe insofar as it is cooked, and Simone's recipes, according to the sales of The Discerning Chef's books and magazines, were not being made in any great numbers.

"Maybe this is something you should discuss with marketing

and publicity," Simone suggested. "It's kind of their job? They might have ideas."

Gladly waved a hand through the air, jangling the many metal bangles on her wrist. "Oh, them? I've fired them."

Simone's mouth fell open. "You what?"

"Fired them. It was only three people—four if you count the intern—which"—she tapped a finger to her chin—"I don't think we paid her. Maybe we should have kept her on, now that I think of it."

The marketing and publicity department hadn't contained any fast friends of Simone's, but she still spared a moment to feel sad for Patty, Nadine, and Jill (plus the intern whose name she'd never quite caught), who'd been so unceremoniously tossed down the garbage chute. Spine going stick-straight, Simone cleared her throat. "Ma'am, without a team of people dedicated to marketing or publicity, I'm not sure how we're supposed to get out of the hole."

"Those fossils put us in this hole," Gladly said, returning to her chair and rapping her knuckles against her desk. Simone frowned; the dinosaur metaphor was coming apart at the seams. "We don't need any more of *that* kind of help, thank you. It's time to start fresh, a clean slate. Totally overhaul The Discerning Chef as something"—she wiggled her shoulders—"hip."

Simone's heart sank.

"Youthful," Pim added.

Her stomach flipped.

"Urbane."

She shut her eyes. This wasn't happening. *Please,* she prayed silently, *tell me this isn't happening.* She tucked a loose strand of hair behind her ear and opened her eyes. "Ma'am, I'm not sure I know how to make TDC . . . all of that."

"Nonsense." Gladly waved a hand in Simone's direction, indicating, perhaps, her twenty-eight-year-old, overachieving, flour-dusted self. Her sensible cardigan with the little pop of personality in the enameled orchid pinned to the collar. Her glossy brown hair pulled into its sensible half-twist. Her millennial what-have-you. "You're just the thing."

Simone's discomfort grew. "The thing for what?" she asked.

"Our new direction." Pim Gladly held her hands up, making corners with her thumbs and forefingers, a little invisible screen in front of her. "I'd like you involved in our video-content initiative, Simone."

"Videos?" Simone floundered. "But—"

"Yes, I know, it's a wonderful opportunity for you," said Gladly. "Likely more responsibility than you could have hoped for, but I am certain you will rise to the occasion and make us proud."

"But, ma'am," Simone choked out, "I've never made a video. I'm not a YouTube star. I don't even know how to use Instagram!"

Gladly's eyes narrowed. "Are you saying that perhaps you're not up to the job?" She reached for a very expensive-looking pen on her desk and toyed with it. "That would be a shame."

Simone imagined that pen signing a pink slip with her name on it. Would Pim Gladly really fire her over this? She'd never been fired before, not from any job, let alone her dream job. Her stomach dropped even further. She wasn't sure she could bear that kind of shame. Her mom would be so disappointed. Her dad would probably be disappointed, too, if only to put on a united front, which had been the hallmark of her parents' divorce.

"Of course that's not what I'm saying," she backtracked. "Only—this isn't my wheelhouse. I studied at Le Cordon Bleu. I know food, and I know how to write about food. I don't have any experience in, in"—she gestured helplessly—"video content."

"Well, if that's your only worry—"

"It's not."

Gladly kept talking as if Simone hadn't spoken. "—then I have wonderful news. With all the money we've saved on marketing and publicity salaries, I was able to arrange for an expert to help train you and the rest of our video-ready chefs in the necessary particulars. He will also spearhead our rebranding and video launch."

Simone's brow furrowed. "But couldn't I just—"

"No need to thank me! This is really going to put you on the fast track, my dear." Gladly stood and held out her hand. Simone, dazed and unsure what else to do, stood and shook it. Gladly grinned. "Delilah will find some time to have you meet the new camera boy. Oh, and more importantly, our freshly minted director of social influence."

"Social influence?" Simone echoed.

"Social. Influence." The handshake ended with Simone's fingers feeling rather numb. "Excellent catch-up, Simone. Thank you."

Feeling very much like she was being dismissed, Simone walked out the door in a daze.

Chapter 2

S he was halfway down the hall before Simone realized she had just been saddled with a new project on top of all her regular work, and the topic of additional compensation had not been introduced. She sighed. Well, The Discerning Chef probably didn't have any additional funds if Gladly was telling the truth about their finances. She supposed she shouldn't rock the boat until she knew more about this video initiative—or whether she could get a new job. Something that didn't involve things like the completely meaningless phrase "social influence." Other people her age might be interested in that kind of stuff, but it wasn't Simone's speed at all. She probably wouldn't even be aware of half the things that happened on the internet if Luna wasn't always sending her memes.

Her phone pinged, and Simone fished it from her pocket to find that the ever-efficient Delilah had already scheduled a meeting for her. It looked like she'd be making the acquaintance of—she squinted at the other names on the invite—Francis Zhang and Chase McDonald in one hour.

Simone heaved another sigh as her fingertips flitted along her phone screen, adjusting her calendar to accommodate this upset. Her carefully planned list of tasks was shot to hell now. She slumped her way toward the test kitchen, moving by instinct, still absorbed in her phone. After suffering such a shock as the meeting with Gladly, she needed to concentrate on her sourdough loaves. It would soothe her. If she hurried, she could get them into the oven on schedule. She pushed her way through the swinging door with the jut of her hip.

Distracted as she was by her phone, Simone didn't notice anything out of place as she shuffled into the kitchen. It was only the noise (more of a yelp, really) that made her stop in her tracks, her head popping up. Her nose nearly grazed the metal shelving of a baking rack that was supposed to be ten yards across the room, situated against the far wall. Instead, it had been rolled right up to the entrance.

"Sorry, sorry, sorry," said the yelping voice. "They told me no one comes in here this early."

Simone's gaze left the baking rack and found the source of all the racket: a tall, *tall* girl wearing a flannel shirt, skinny jeans, and a baseball cap, a shock of tousled gold curls escaping from under the brim. She was big all over, actually, lanky in the limbs but broad in the shoulders, giving Simone the distinct impression that she was being dwarfed. But for all the looming the stranger was doing, she seemed to be trying to temper it with an apologetic smile and an "Aw, shucks" tilt to her head. She had very green eyes, Simone noticed. Troublemakers usually did.

"Uh," Simone said helpfully. She shook her head to clear it. "Yes, it's usually just Myra and me at this time of day." She looked around the empty kitchen. Myra, the elderly test kitchen manager, was nowhere to be found.

The only thing Simone saw was a huge mess. All the racks were moved from their usual places, stacks of pots and pans littered every counter, and there were dozens of ingredients strewn about like confetti. A gallon of grapeseed oil sat incongruously beside an oversized tub of sprinkles. An industrial-sized bag of flour nearly as big as Simone leaned against the wall, next to a pyramid of number-ten cans of crushed tomatoes.

And her doughs were not on the counter where she'd left them.

"M-my bread," she stammered, looking around wildly. "Where—"

"Oh, yeah, sorry," said the stranger. "Had to move them to make some space. They're here, safe and sound." She pointed.

Simone's eyes focused on the baking rack she'd almost run into. Her nine bowls of dough were arranged on the rack, three on each shelf. Her stomach dropped. "You *moved* them?"

"Yeah, like I said, I had to make some space."

"Each one is different!" Simone cried. "I was going to compare them once they were baked. How am I supposed to keep them all straight now?" All that work, down the drain. She'd have to start from scratch and redo the entire process.

"Uh, sorry." The girl paled. "They weren't labeled or anything. I just assumed they were all the same."

"They weren't labeled because I knew which was which! Until you moved them." She pointed an accusing finger.

The stranger held up her hands defensively. "Hey, I was just doing my job."

"Your *job*?" Simone stared. "Where's Myra?" she demanded, knowing the kitchen manager would not stand for this much reckless disorder in her domain. A little disorder, maybe, but not to this extent.

"She . . . retired?" said the interloper, making it more of a question. "I'm the replacement? It's my first day."

Simone nearly dropped her phone. "That's impossible. I just saw Myra. She never mentioned anything to me about retiring." Simone thought hard; had she missed the announcement? Had there been a depressing goodbye party with a paltry cake and a gold watch? Simone often skipped such things (mostly because of the offensive store-bought cakes—she would make one if someone just asked), but she was certain there hadn't been such a party for Myra. Come to think of it, she hadn't seen much of Myra since early last week, but it wasn't unusual for Myra to take a few vacation days around the beginning of autumn, so Simone had barely noticed.

"Did something awful to her back, I heard," the stranger said. "She's fine, just can't work like she used to. So, early retirement."

Simone sucked in a breath. Myra had been a somewhat ineffectual but calming presence in the test kitchen. She may not have always remembered to replenish the vanilla beans or keep the five types of sugars topped off, but she was maternal in a way that Simone appreciated. She'd always doted on Simone, especially when she was stressed, bringing her mugs of weak herbal tea and little plates of cookies that she baked when no one was looking (dry and a bit flavorless, in Simone's expert opinion, but still very thoughtful of her). Simone could've used Myra's particular brand of shoulder-patting at this very moment, and so it was a blow to discover this, too, had changed for the worse.

"I'm sorry about the mix-up, really," said the new, not-at-all-maternal kitchen manager as she swept her gaze around the room. She lifted her ball cap an inch and reset it on her head, giving Simone a glimpse of the buzzed side of an undercut. "Thought I'd have more time to rearrange things in here."

"Rearrange?" Simone asked weakly. The chaos of the test kitchen distracted her again. "What was wrong with the way it was?"

"I was told I needed to make room for some video equipment. It's all stacked up in that conference room down the hall. Shit ton of stuff. Need to find a way to make it all fit in here. Anyway. Hi." A hand that did not look totally spotless stuck out in greeting. "I'm Ray. The new kid."

"Ray?" Simone did not see any polite way around the handshake, so she took her new colleague's hand in what she feared was a limp, anemic grip and pumped it a few times. "As in . . . ?"

She wasn't sure how to finish that sentence in a way that didn't refer to older men who perhaps fixed up classic cars as a hobby.

"As in, that's my name," said Ray. She smiled wide, showing a mouth full of white teeth that were not completely straight.

Simone sized up this new threat to her well-ordered life. The girl—Simone thought of her as a girl, though she was probably right around Simone's age—had the air of a surfer forced to lope about on dry land till the next big wave. There was a solidness to her, a physicality that probably owed more to her height than her muscle. *She's got to be over six feet*, Simone thought, and felt the urge to mention it, though she tamped it down. Ray had undoubtedly heard every iteration of "Do you play basketball?" possible; Simone didn't need to add to the pile.

"Ah." Simone held Ray's hand stiffly in her own. It felt a tiny bit greasy, which made sense if Ray had been touching everything in the kitchen. Simone was desperate to wipe her hand on a kitchen towel but didn't want to appear rude—and didn't know where the kitchen towels were at the moment, anyway. "I'm Simone. Recipe development and baking column. Welcome to the test kitchen, I guess." She glanced around the ruined room. *Such as it is*, she almost tacked on.

"Yeah!" Ray's head swiveled as if taking in the room for the very first time. Her hand fell away from their handshake, and Simone distantly registered the loss of warmth. (*Hot hands,* she thought. *Terrible for incorporating butter into flour. Hands like that could never handle pie dough or biscuits.*) "Pretty cool. Much cooler than my last gig, anyway." She cocked her head. Simone was reminded of being eyed by a very large bird. Maybe a sort of hawk. "I still haven't had a chance to really explore. Do you think you could show me around the rest of the office? Help me get the lay of the land?"

Simone had never heard the phrase "lay of the land" sound so carelessly playful. She had already thought Ray might be queer based on the clothes and the hair, but the tone in her voice confirmed it. *Well, whoopie for Ray*, she thought. *Some of us have real work to do and don't have time to play tour guide.* She glanced down at Ray's hands again—just to try and figure out what kind of grease they had shared in the handshake, of course—and saw a rainbow-colored rubber bracelet encircling one of Ray's wrists. Oh. Simone felt a little silly for not noticing it earlier. Here she was, covertly judging this newcomer when the newcomer was clearly announcing who she was to all and sundry. Whereas Simone, who had considered the matter very seriously before deciding at age ten that she must be bisexual, didn't care to make a fuss about it.

Not that any of that mattered just then.

"I can't. I'm too busy." She spied her tub of sourdough starter on a nearby baking rack and grabbed it. "I should probably stick this in the walk-in, since I'm not going to have time to redo all these loaves today." She couldn't help the angry glare that accompanied her words.

Ray seemed immune to glares. "Let me do that for you." She smiled and reached for the container. "I'll probably be moving stuff around in there today, too, if I have time. Might as well put it somewhere safe now so I can fetch it for you later."

Perhaps it was petty, but Simone yanked her tub away from Ray's grasp before she could get ahold of it. "If that's the case," she said coldly, "I would rather store it myself. I have a mini fridge under my desk." She had been working off this same starter since she'd graduated from culinary school, and she was not about to hand her metaphorical child over to some stranger.

"Oooh, a desk." Ray crossed her rather nicely corded arms over her chest and grinned. "Must be nice. Best I can do is a shelf in the back where I can prop up my laptop, make some grocery orders."

Simone refused to be drawn into a conversation on the class differences within TDC. Myra had never complained about not having a desk. She had been quite content, perched on her stool at one of the four islands in the test kitchen, watching the staff and eating her dry cookies. Simone didn't see why Ray couldn't be happy with her lot, too. The test kitchen was Ray's natural domain, not the editorial bullpen.

"If you'll excuse me," Simone said, and swept out of the disaster zone with all the dignity she could muster. She immediately went in search of her boss—not Pim Gladly, though. Her real boss.

Chapter 3

Mikkah had been at The Discerning Chef since the beginning of Simone's tenure. Her palate was second to none; she could detect an eighth of a teaspoon of cardamom in a four-layer cream cake. She made the best pierogi that Simone had ever tasted, and she always knew where to put a comma. Simone admired her hugely and thought, in light of the morning's many concerning revelations, that Mikkah would be a stalwart ally. At the very least, her editor would lend her a sympathetic ear. They'd both worked shoulder to shoulder in the bullpen before Mikkah's promotion, and although she was technically Simone's boss, Simone felt they had more of a partnership than anything else.

She sat on the little pouf in front of the desk in Mikkah's office and awaited her arrival, a steaming cup of espresso on the side table as a welcoming volley. Simone had convinced the old Italian grinder to cough it up, and she hoped Mikkah would appreciate it.

When Mikkah arrived in a flurry of colorful scarves, Simone wasted no time.

"Did you know they want me to make videos now?" she demanded.

Mikkah unwrapped the scarves from her neck and held one finger in the air. She snatched up the tiny espresso cup and took a deep swig.

"Okay," she said, eyes bright. Caffeine had that effect on her. "What were you saying?"

"Videos," Simone repeated. "Gladly called me into her office first thing this morning to tell me herself. Are we not a *magazine* anymore? What exactly am I supposed to do?"

Mikkah sighed and collapsed into her office chair, spinning in a slow arc. Her hair, a pile of artful blond curls that Simone knew was only possible through the use of an expensive Swiss-made barrel iron, bounced as she moved. "We are still a magazine, of course. And the summer grilling cookbook is still in production. It's just—we need to work a little harder, do a few extra things. Like these videos."

" '*We*,' " Simone said, stressing the singular syllable.

"Well, you and every other fresh-faced young thing we still have employed around here. Gene has a nice beard, so he's in. Becca was tapped, too; she'll do fine. You'll blow them all out of the water, of course, just like you do with your written pieces." Mikkah sipped at her cup and furrowed her brow in thought. "Do you think Delilah knows how to cook? She's very pretty. Maybe she'd be good on camera."

Simone threw her hands in the air. "This is serious! You're asking me to do something that I've never done. This isn't my job! I don't know how to act on camera!"

"It's not acting. It's just presenting. How hard can it be?" Mikkah tossed back the last of the espresso. "Anyway, you millennials are already twittering every moment of every day. This will be second nature to you."

"No, it won't," Simone said, "because I'm not on Twitter. Or Instagram. Or Facebook, or—"

"No?" Mikkah's thinly penciled eyebrows shot up. "Why not?"

"Because it's a waste of time! I have better things to do than show people pictures of my lunch every day." Simone scowled at the corner of the office, which wasn't actually at fault, but she felt it was too unprofessional to scowl at Mikkah, who was still her boss despite how informal their working relationship had become over the years.

"It's not a waste if it helps you do your job," Mikkah said, waving a hand through the air. "And as for working on videos, don't worry about that. You'll be trained thoroughly by this Chase McDonald guy. He's supposed to be very good. Do you remember the Doggie Depot meme from last year? Hashtag woof woof winner?"

"No," Simone said flatly.

"It was everywhere."

"I must have been busy."

"Kids were dressing up like it for Halloween."

"I don't have kids. Or a dog."

"Well, that was him. The stores sold out of the little pink dog harnesses, if I remember correctly."

Simone slumped on her little pouf, in danger of melting to the floor entirely. She wished Mikkah kept real guest chairs in her office. Sitting on an oversized knitted mushroom made her feel like she was in kindergarten again. "Couldn't I just— I don't know—work behind the scenes? Do I really have to be on camera?" She hated to admit it, and she wouldn't except to herself, but Simone was not looking forward to being filmed and put on the internet. She was a fairly private person—see: her unfussy, unmentioned-in-polite-company bisexuality—and couldn't imagine these videos would allow her to maintain that privacy.

Mikkah shook her head. "Afraid not, kid. You're under thirty-five and you've got the cooking chops; you're going on camera. Nothing we can do about it."

Simone saw her chances of getting out of the extra work slipping through her fingers. "So you're all for this crazy plan?"

"I'm for anything that helps us get our numbers up." Mikkah looked at Simone, then softened. "I know you don't like being asked to do things that you haven't already mastered, but you can't be an expert in everything."

Simone made a noise that she would deny was a scoff; she would categorize it as an efficiently executed sigh. It was a noise she made when someone else had a point, but she refused to concede it.

"And it might do you some good to spread your wings, get out of your comfort zone," Mikkah continued. "Think of it as just one more way you can excel compared to the other chefs here. You'll see, you'll cook, you'll conquer."

"Any other platitudes you'd like to heap on me?" Simone grumbled.

"None whatsoever." Mikkah brightened. "Are you meeting with the new video guys soon?"

Simone checked her phone's clock screen. "In a few minutes. Hey, what happened to Myra?" she asked, remembering the second thing she'd come to complain about.

"Oh, yes, the poor thing." Mikkah shook her head. "Tore something in her back, decided to hang it up."

"And this new one, Ray?" Simone asked.

"Who?"

"The new kitchen manager?"

"Oh, yes, Rachel." Mikkah nodded and shuffled through the papers on her desk before finding a specific one. She tapped the name on the page with her fingernail. "Rachel Lyton. HR asked me to vet her on the chef side of the equation. Will she understand the difference if we tell her to order Thai basil as opposed to Italian? Does she know her cuts of beef? Can she tell a good avocado from a bad one? That sort of thing. She passed all my tests with flying colors."

"So she's really replacing Myra?" Simone cringed. "It's not just a temporary arrangement?"

Mikkah gave her an odd look. "Rachel is the permanent replacement, yes. Why? Not impressed so far? She's only been here a few minutes; she couldn't have done much to rub you the wrong way in such a short amount of time."

Simone held her tongue about the sourdough incident. She didn't want to admit that perhaps she should have labeled her bowls; she had plenty of excuses—she'd been in a rush; no one else had been around; she hadn't thought anyone would dare touch her station—but the fact was it had been a fatal error. "I just don't like coming into work to find some rando tearing apart the test kitchen, that's all," she said instead. "And we're sure she's qualified?"

"I should say so. Her last position was . . ." Mikkah consulted Ray's CV again. "Kitchen manager at Luigi's Tacos."

"Never heard of it," Simone said evenly.

"You wouldn't've. It shut down last month," Mikkah said with a raise of her eyebrows. "It was a fusion thing on the Lower East Side. Didn't make any money. I can see why. Italian tacos, bleh." She made a face. "Anyway, Rachel has years of experience. I have complete faith that she can keep the test kitchen clean, organized, and well-stocked. Maybe she's not the best judge of a restaurant's concept, but beggars can't be choosers in that business."

Simone's phone pinged to remind her of the imminent meeting with her new video overlords. She swiped the alert off the phone screen and sighed.

"Well, if Ray doesn't work out," she said airily, "I will keep my eye out for a kitchen manager who isn't so . . ."

"Charming and upbeat?" Mikkah suggested. "Experienced and, most importantly, available?"

"Tall," Simone said with a snit in her voice, and left before Mikkah could ask what the hell that meant.

Chapter 4

The meeting with the new video team began as meetings often do. They shook hands and introduced themselves all around.

"Simone Larkspur. Pastry." Short and to the point.

"Francis Zhang," said the new cameraman, "but please call me Petey. Everyone does." At Simone's quizzical look, he added, "Peter's my middle name."

"Chase McDonald, visionary and dream maker," said the remaining man, and Simone knew she was in for a very long meeting.

She sat at the table in the smallest, shabbiest conference room, which was currently cluttered with recording equipment, and eyed this McDonald character. He was young, Simone thought, probably no more than a year or two older than she was, which she considered very young to be in charge of the entire company's new direction. He was clean-cut in a sort of frat-boy way and wore a tailored gray blazer over a vintage T-shirt that read *Quinnipiac Debate Team Champs* above a rendering of a lightbulb, presumably to intimate thought and ideas.

"You did debate as a kid?" Simone asked as the other two took their seats.

"Huh?" said Chase, less than intelligently.

She pointed at his shirt. "The debate team? Were you on it?"

He looked down at his chest as if seeing his clothes for the first time, then laughed. "No, I collect these. It's vintage. This one came from a little shop in London, near Seven Dials. Have you been?"

"To London? Yes," Simone said, and she was about to describe the tasting she'd attended that had changed her entire outlook on phyllo pastry, but Chase cut her off.

"I find that travel broadens your horizons and lets your creative energy really flow. There's nothing better than getting out of your head for a month or two. I love sabbaticals. Well, I call them sabbaticals, but I'm still working, of course. I'm always working. Always thinking. Thought is the oil that greases the engine of productivity. Now, speaking of productivity—"

Simone met the eyes of Petey, who was seated on the other side of the table. The look they exchanged said plenty. It was nice to know she wasn't alone in thinking this Chase character was a real windbag.

Francis Zhang—Petey—was built along the same roundish lines as Simone. Simone liked the look of him immediately. He wore a faded T-shirt with a cartoon character on the front that Simone remembered vaguely from her own childhood, though of course she did not spend much of her time on something as frivolous as Saturday-morning cartoons, even as a child. As he noticed her noticing his shirt, he pointed to the picture on it and mouthed, *I watched it.*

Simone smothered a laugh.

Chase, who was still talking about his creative approach, clearly thought the laugh was in response to something clever he'd said, because he laughed along, too, and, without missing a beat, launched into a thorough explanation of his many-pronged plan. Simone avoided hearing the bulk of it by mentally constructing her weekly grocery list instead. It was her experience that men like Chase McDonald needed a chance to tire themselves out, much like an errant toddler, and the best way to get them to run out of steam was to smile and nod and not ask any questions.

But by the time Simone had reached the pasta aisle in her mental list (she needed a box of orecchiette), her ears picked up on something so outlandish, she couldn't possibly keep her peace. Chase McDonald was saying, ". . . and that's why you'll need to develop, say, a dozen new kale recipes, at least. Doesn't matter what they are, salads or smoothies or whatever, but if you can do that by tomorrow—"

"I'm sorry," Simone interrupted, blinking, "but a *dozen*? And why kale?"

Chase gave her an admonishing look, like he knew she hadn't been listening. "I just explained. SEO. People are searching for kale recipes, so we need to provide them."

"Yes, but the kale craze is pretty much over by now," Simone pointed out. A few years before, it had been pomegranates, which Simone had hated passionately. They were the least logical fruit ever conceived. If something was that difficult to open up, it should be allowed to keep its secrets, was her opinion. "And anyway, I'd rather write good, solid recipes that will stand the test of time. Isn't that the point?"

Chase shook his head. "Oh, Simone," he sighed, and Simone felt the skin-crawling sensation that meant she was about to be patronized. "No wonder your subscription numbers are down. You haven't been giving the people what they *want*. You need to look at what people are Googling before you decide what to write. All the successful platforms do it that way."

Simone frowned. "But if we do that, won't we be producing the same kind of content as everyone else?"

"Correct. We just have to do what works, same as what everyone else is doing." He smiled his real-estate agent smile. "A brand is just trappings. Slick production values, good editing. Francis here will handle that part of it." He waved a hand at him.

"I actually go by Petey," Petey said again.

"Whatever. At the end of the day, we are shooting for practical. Lucrative. Scalable. Uniformity." He tapped his fingertip against the conference table to punctuate each word.

Simone stared in horror. "That sounds like we're striving for mediocrity."

"Exactly!" Chase grinned. "Now you're getting it. We have to meet consumers where they are." He ducked down to rummage in the messenger bag that sat slumped on the floor by his chair, and Simone took the opportunity to look to Petey for confirmation that this nightmare was real. Petey shrugged in a textbook "It's a living" gesture. Simone despaired as Chase retrieved an iPad and began tapping along the screen. "I made a list of some keywords that we need to focus on. So, like I said, if you can come up with some stuff using these topics by tomorrow, we can start putting together a production schedule." He tossed the iPad onto the table, spinning it so Simone could read the screen.

She did so, her brow furrowing. "Sweet corn? Asparagus? Half of these things aren't even in season."

"Right, but it takes time to produce a video," Chase said slowly as if Simone were a misbehaving child. "So we need a few months' head start, and then once the video goes live, it'll be there in plenty of time for the next search crest. That's what I call the SEO wave, and we need to catch it." He mimed his hand into a little surfboard, riding an invisible sea.

"But the produce is going to look awful, because it's not in *season*," Simone stressed.

Chase shrugged. "We'll source some from, I don't know, Mexico or wherever."

That was not how seasons worked, but Simone wasn't sure this was the right time to explain hemispheres to a fully grown adult. "I like to advocate working with local products when possible," she tried instead.

"Well, that won't be possible anymore." Chase grinned. "We're providing content for a global audience, after all."

Simone flailed for a lifeboat. "But it usually takes me days—sometimes weeks—to develop and test a recipe. I can pull some old recipes out of our archive that use these ingredients, but I can't write dozens of new ones by tomorrow."

"Oh, when I say 'recipes,'" Chase said, making actual air quotes with his fingers, "I mean more like 'processes.' How to, uh, clean a cob of corn, for example."

"Shuck," Petey offered. "You shuck an ear of corn."

"Right, shuck, okay. Or something like, 'Ten Best Cheeses to Pair with Summer Squash.'"

"What does that even mean?" Simone asked. "There is no best cheese for squash. It's whatever the recipe— Or according to your personal taste—"

But Chase was not listening to her. "Maybe a few simple recipes. Tossing some things together with pasta or whatever. Meal prep, that's very hot right now. Besides, each video is going to be, like, three minutes."

"Three *minutes*?" Simone cried. "I can't cook anything substantial in three minutes."

"Calm down. That's the magic of editing. Right, Francis?"

"Petey," Petey grated out.

"We'll cut to each stage in the process so that the viewer will get the maximum amount of information in the shortest span of time. People are busy; they can't sit around and flip through a hundred pages of a glossy magazine looking for something to eat," Chase said.

"But aren't we trying to *sell* our magazine?" Simone's head spun. "How can we do that if we're catering to people this way?"

Chase made a vague gesture. "There will be trickle-down," he said, and explained it no further. "For now, let's concentrate on building out our video presence and raking in some sweet ad revenue."

He kept talking, but Simone was back to not listening. She couldn't listen and freak out at the same time.

Chapter 5

The rest of the meeting was a blur. Simone spent most of it focusing on not hyperventilating while Chase talked some more. At some point, he showed Simone her new Instagram and Twitter profiles, which she would have to fill with daily content, the very idea of which made her want to scream. When Simone finally left the conference room, her head was swirling in panic. Her feet took her back to the test kitchen, where, in the past, she had found some comfort in baking.

She had nearly forgotten that the test kitchen was under new management, as shaken as she was. When she walked in, though, she couldn't help but be reminded; everything had been rearranged and was now in its new place. And damn it all, her trained eye told her that it was actually going to be more efficient this way. Heavy containers were placed on the bottom shelves; small jars had been collected in clear plastic organizer compartments on the upper levels. Someone had gone to town on the label maker. Simone walked by the spice rack, touching each neat white strip: HOT/CHILES. WARMING/BAKING. DRIED HERBS. This system had been created with chefs in mind, vastly superior to the old alphabetical arrangement. In the heat of the moment, who could remember how to spell fenugreek, anyway?

"What do you think?" Ray came bounding out of the walk-in in a dense cloud of cold air. "Just got things the way I wanted out here."

Simone dropped her hand guiltily. "It's fine," she said, not yet prepared to award any points in Ray's favor. She brushed past the tall figure and headed to the far kitchen island. "Please don't mind me. I'm just going to throw something together." She noticed the rack holding the baking ingredients—flours, sugars, baking powder and soda, cornstarch—had been moved right next to that island. She stared at it for a moment.

"Yeah, Mikkah told me you usually use this workstation, so I thought why not move the stuff you probably use the most so you would have it close at hand?" Ray pointed to each island in turn. "Dried pastas and canned goods are stored closer to Gene's station now. He does a lot of the Italian food, right? Trying to make things flow, you know?"

"I see." Simone began pulling out her cutting board and knives, thoughts going to what she might bake to calm herself down. She wanted something savory. Comforting. Seasonal, since she might not get a chance to do much of that in the future. She winced at the thought and headed toward the walk-in.

Annoyingly, Ray followed. "What're you making?"

"Not sure yet," she muttered, and opened the heavy latch on the door of the room-sized refrigerator. Inside, she saw that Ray had already begun wrangling the many shelves and containers that supplied the test kitchen's chefs. The fresh herbs had been gathered upright in a large plastic bin filled with a few inches of water. Simone examined them closely before grabbing a bunch of velvety sage and a crisp bundle of rosemary. Why hadn't Myra ever stored them like that? It was a good idea; it would keep them from wilting.

The door hissed open and Ray popped her head in. "Need help finding anything? I moved some stuff around."

"Cheeses?" Simone asked curtly.

Ray pointed to a shelf at eye level. "Mild cheeses are there. I'm keeping the really stinky ones down there." She pointed to a lower shelf. "At least until I can build a little cave for them."

Simone looked over her shoulder at Ray. "A cave?"

"Yeah, like a wooden box, maybe lined with slate or tiles to try and mimic, you know, a real cave? I don't want the smells mingling. Plus they'll keep longer."

"Hm." Simone turned back to the shelves and took a cylinder of artisanal goat cheese sealed in plastic. She liked this particular dairy farm; their goat cheese was creamy, not chalky, and had a nice herbaceous tang.

"Once I start putting in the grocery orders," Ray added, "I'll label everything with the arrival date. Just to keep it all straight, make sure we're using things up before they go bad."

"You're letting out all the cold air," Simone said, not turning around. She could see Ray's reflection in the shiny, stainless-steel wall.

"Right." A chagrined duck of her head. "I'll leave you to it."

The door clicked shut, leaving Simone in the cold white-noise vacuum of the walk-in. She sighed. Seemed a fitting place for her today. She found the new home for the heavy vegetables on the bottom shelf and searched through the cardboard boxes of produce until she uncovered a beautiful acorn squash. There was a bushel of yellow onions; she took one of those as well, the size of a baseball. A couple bricks of European-style butter rounded out her armful of ingredients.

She returned to her island with her head down, determined not to let Ray or anyone else distract her from her improvised project. A picture of an autumnal galette flashed through her mind: warm and savory and buttery. Her hands found the flour and salt without any real effort on her part. This was exactly what she needed right now.

First, the dough. All the dry things in a large bowl. Whisk. A last-minute decision to add some hard cheese. She found a wedge of Pecorino in the walk-in and grated a few tablespoons into the flour, tossing to coat. Couldn't have enough cheese, was her thinking. Then the butter, cut from its European bricks into small cubes. Then, finally, the marriage.

Simone loved cutting cold butter into flour. There was something about it that made her think of chilly, faraway beaches in Nova Scotia. Perhaps it was the sandy texture of the end result. She retrieved her favorite pastry cutter from one of the under-counter storage fridges; it was best kept ice cold. The colder the butter stayed, the flakier the crust would be.

She adjusted the cutter over her knuckles and, like a common street brawler, began the process of subduing the chunks of butter into the dry ingredients. It was therapeutic, maiming butter. She imagined the bowl held all her frustrations. The expectations of the digital world. The fact that the rug had been pulled out from under her feet overnight. The new social media accounts that had been created for her that she was now expected to fill with insipid photos and corny captions. Her dream job morphing into something she had no interest in doing.

Chase McDonald's stupid, smug face.

"So what's it shaping up to be?" a cheerful voice said, shaking her from her vengeance-filled daydreams. Simone lifted her head to find Ray across the kitchen island, leaning over to peer into the bowl, chin propped up on her two fists.

"A savory galette," Simone said.

"Nice! I love a galette. It's like a pie without the hubbub. Or an open-faced Hot Pocket. Uh, a really big one. And round." Ray frowned. "Maybe that's not the best comparison."

Simone eyed Ray as she continued cutting in the butter. There were still a few chunks to deal with. "You bake?" she asked, and if her voice held a certain tone of disbelief, it couldn't be helped. Most bakers can sense the ability to bake in others. An intuition. Like calling to like. And Simone did not get a very strong baking vibe from Ray.

Ray didn't seem offended by her tone, just shook her head with a laugh, straightening to reset the baseball hat on her brow. For the first time, Simone noticed the Mets insignia on the battered cap. Obviously, Ray was someone who was well-versed in disappointment and struggle. Good. There was plenty of that to be found at The Discerning Chef lately.

"Nah, baking's not really my thing," Ray said, "but I've worked at enough restaurants to form some opinions on food."

"Well, opinions won't keep you fed," Simone said lightly, turning the dough out on the counter to be formed. She worked quickly; her hands were good and cool, but she still wanted to keep the butter from melting.

"Will you?" Ray asked.

Simone stuttered to a stop, wrist-deep in shaggy dough. "Excuse me?"

"Keep me fed?" Ray pointed to the pile of dough. "When it's done." They stared at each other a bit. "It's my backward way of asking, 'Can I please have a slice once it's ready?'"

"Oh." Simone quickened her hands again. "Uh, sure. Yes. I—I didn't plan on eating the whole thing myself." She laughed self-consciously. She had, in fact, planned on eating most of it herself. But Ray didn't need to know that.

The test kitchen door clanged open and other people started coming in to begin their kitchen work. Simone could hear Gene talking with Becca about the new video initiative. He sounded excited, damn him. *Everyone on staff must have heard by now,* she thought. And from the shape of their chatter, they'd already gotten their assignments from Chase. Simone tuned it all out. She couldn't deal with that right now.

"Excuse me," she said to Ray as she gathered the dough into a ball and flattened it into a disc. "I need to concentrate on this."

Ray smiled easily, too easily for Simone's taste. "I'll get out of your hair. Should meet the rest of the crew, anyway." She rapped her fist on the stainless-steel countertop and loped away, greeting Gene with predictable enthusiasm.

Simone responded to her coworkers' hellos with a wan smile and a bob of her head, indicating the dough needed to be chilled. She was already well-practiced in wriggling out of conversation. It wasn't that she disliked her fellow TDC chefs; she just liked working more. They were used to it by now and left her alone for the most part.

She kept at her galette. Hefted the industrial box of cling film onto the counter and wrangled one long sheet from it. Dough wrapped and chilling in the lowboy. Onions next. Sliced thinly, tossed into a pan over low heat with more butter, a sprinkle of kosher salt. Couldn't have enough butter, in Simone's view. It was like cheese in that way.

While the onions caramelized, she scooped the seeds from the squash and sliced the flesh into pretty crescent moons, then arranged them on a baking sheet. A drizzle of olive oil, plenty of salt, some pepper, the tiniest bit of harissa paste. Simple. Toss to coat, her hands becoming slick with the oil and spices. Into the oven at 425 degrees Fahrenheit for, oh, say twenty minutes, see how they look.

In the meantime, garnishes. Pluck the soft, rabbit ear sage leaves from their stems and fry them in the butter that the onions were cooking in, creating a little pool for them on the side of the pan with a deft flick of a wooden spoon. Let the sage's warm, savory smell infuse the butter so that the onions take on the taste, too. Take the crisped leaves out and drain on a paper towel. Pull a few sprigs of fresh rosemary through the fingertips, collect the little needles in a pile, and chop. Toss them in with the onions. Check their color. Golden, soft, melty. Good. Turn off the heat.

And wait.

Simone was very adept at waiting. It was one of the greatest gifts a pastry chef could be given: time that was her own, when every component was working by itself and she wasn't needed for anything. She gave the onions another little stir. They would be fine cooling in the pot in the time it took for the squash to roast and the dough to chill. Until then, Simone could sit on the little stool she kept at her island for just this occasion and work on something else. (Waiting, in Simone's opinion, shouldn't include sloth. Her ability to multitask and stay three steps ahead of schedule was the reason she could afford to spend part of her workday making a galette from scratch, after all.)

She was perched on her stool, clicking away on her work laptop, trying and failing to come up with a dozen video topics on the subject of kale, when Ray passed by, carrying a crate of lemons.

"Everything going okay?"

Myra had hardly ever interrupted Simone when she was working. It was a little grating. Plus, she still hadn't forgiven Ray for the sourdough disaster. "Are you going to check in on everybody every hour on the hour?" she shot back.

"No, just on the people who are making my lunch," Ray said sunnily. She poked at the packet of goat cheese on the counter by Simone's elbow. "You know what would go good with this?"

"The fried sage leaves that I've already made. Maybe a little chili oil," Simone recited, not taking her eyes from the laptop screen. "Some candied walnuts, if I have time. I haven't decided yet."

"I was going to say balsamic."

Simone glared over the top of her computer. Ray's grin did not abate.

"Balsamic," Simone repeated.

"A nice little reduction." Ray held her thumb and forefinger a hair's width apart. "Just the tiniest drizzle."

Simone flicked through her mental list of ingredients in the recipe she'd just created. Salty, salty, salty, spicy, fatty, savory, more salty. Okay, maybe a little acid wouldn't go amiss, but balsamic? Too strong, in Simone's opinion. "It doesn't need it," she declared.

"Well, sure, it doesn't *need* it. But it might *want* it. There's a difference." Ray's eyes twinkled. "Wanting is what makes life so exciting, don't you think?"

Simone's own eyes narrowed. She was fairly sure Ray wasn't talking about galettes anymore, but she couldn't be certain this was flirting. She was so rarely the target of flirting that it was difficult for her to know. Innuendo and subtle interest bounced off Simone like off a good nonstick pan. The last three people Simone had dated—if dinner dates at restaurants she had to review for work was considered dating—had not been the pursuers. Simone was a big believer in not wasting time and asking out the men and women who'd caught her attention forthrightly. Like an adult. And then, slightly less like an adult, ignoring their texts when the demands of work inevitably blotted out any interest she'd had in them.

"You can put some balsamic on your slice if you like," Simone said, unwilling to admit that the addition might actually be a pretty decent idea. "But you'll have to make the reduction yourself. I'm busy with this." She swept a hand at her laptop.

"Yeah? That's fair. If it's good, maybe I'll let you have a bite," Ray said with a wink.

Simone drew in a sharp breath. Okay, that was definitely flirting. She had never been winked at in her life! This was a place of *business*!

Her face must have looked as stormy as she felt, because Ray put both hands up in defense and backed away. "You know what? I get the feeling you work best alone."

"That would be correct," Simone said with ice in her voice.

"So I'll just . . . go."

"What a wonderful idea."

"And, uh—" Ray dug her hand under her cap to scratch at her mop of golden hair. "I'll cut that shit out. The winking and stuff. Didn't mean to make you uncomfortable. My bad."

Simone hid her surprise at that with a jerky little nod, then watched Ray mosey over to Gene, who was constructing yet another baked pasta magnum opus, laden with six kinds of cheese. The two began speaking animatedly, gesturing to the casserole dish where the foundations were being laid, and putting their heads together almost literally to examine the array of ingredients Gene was contemplating. As Simone watched, Ray gave Gene a friendly grip of his shoulder that turned into an arm slung around his neck. They shared a laugh, Ray's a loud, braying sound that made everyone in the room jump a little. Simone couldn't hear the joke from across the room, but the two seemed to be fast friends after only a few minutes.

She couldn't remember the last time she and Gene had laughed at something together. Had they ever? Simone wasn't exactly invested in fostering a strong bond with him; work was more pressing than being friends with the people you happened to work with, after all. Gene was useful for his knowledge of regional Italian recipes, and that was about all Simone knew of the guy. Did he have kids? She vaguely remembered him having kids.

Simone frowned (which was beginning to be a habit today) as she watched Ray and Gene pal around. Perhaps Ray was just one of those naturally outgoing people who attracted friendship and goodwill like a magnet. Perhaps she wasn't being flirtatious, just extremely extroverted. At any rate, Ray seemed to be just as interested in chattering away with Gene, who was a man, as with Simone herself.

Simone hoped that Ray didn't think her rude—or worse, homophobic. She didn't care that Ray was out and proud; today was just a horror show, and she couldn't take one more shock, including being the focus of the new kitchen manager's dimply smile.

The timer buzzed for her roast squash, and Simone busied herself with taking the pan of perfectly cooked vegetables out of the oven (slightly soft, just starting to brown around the edges) and getting the dough out of the fridge for rolling. Soon she was caught up in the familiar process of making something tasty, and all thoughts of Ray and the new video initiative and slimy little Chase McDonald left her for a few blissful minutes.

Oven lowered to 350. Dough unwrapped and slapped on

the countertop. Whacked with the rolling pin a couple of times to soften it up. Rolled into a circle, four millimeters thick. Simone contemplated her array of fillings. She could just pile them all in the center, but she felt like showing off a bit. Reminding everyone at TDC why she was really here: to make beautiful food. She built a bed of the jammy caramelized onions, then fanned out the crescent moons of roasted squash in a careful spiral. Dollops of goat cheese followed the spiral, one creamy island every two inches. A sprinkle of salt, a few cranks of pepper, a tiny bit of red pepper flake.

Then she folded the edges of the dough to create a flattened bowl that held all that goodness. She didn't strictly need to neaten the edges with a paring knife, but she did it anyway, cutting away the odd bit that didn't line up perfectly. Crack an egg into a small bowl, add a little water, whisk it up. A brush of egg wash on the dough, and the galette was ready to bake. Simone carefully took an already-hot sheet pan from the oven and slid her creation onto it, giving the bottom of the crust a head start in getting nice and crisp. Into the oven it went, already smelling delicious, like something you'd be served at a quaint B&B in the Vermont countryside during apple-picking season. Simone's mouth watered just thinking about it.

She returned reluctantly to her laptop and pecked away at her keyboard, trying to find any more recipes involving sweet corn that she'd already developed in years past, but the sharp, tangy smell of vinegar being reduced distracted her. Her head swiveled around until she saw a pot bubbling away at Gene's station, balsamic already thick and treacle-looking as he stirred it.

"Gene, does your casserole call for a balsamic reduction?" she called. It would be one hell of a coincidence.

Gene didn't take his eyes off the pot to answer. "No, but the new kid mentioned wanting some, and I said I could take care of it while my pasta bakes."

"That was nice of you," Simone said, teeth gritted tightly in her mouth.

Gene just smiled over his shoulder at her. "I do what I can."

Gene had never asked Simone if she wanted him to make a reduction for her. Everything Simone did, she had to do herself. That was the way she liked it, of course, because as skilled as Gene and the other chefs were, Simone trusted no one else to execute her recipes to perfection. *Ray must be quite a lazy person,* she thought, *if she couldn't even reduce some vinegar on her own.*

She'd have to keep an eye on that new kitchen manager of theirs. One more thing to worry about, she supposed. Simone sighed, turning back to her futile corn Google searches.

The galette was just right when she removed it from the oven precisely thirty-eight minutes later. She scattered the fried sage leaves artfully over the top, a beautiful deep-green color against the dollops of goat cheese. A quick sprinkling of grated Parmesan finished it off. It needed to cool for about ten minutes on the wire rack, but true to form (and with the help of finger-tips long desensitized to heat), Simone could only wait for five of them before cutting into it.

She chewed her first bite thoughtfully, her eyes drifting shut in bliss. The pastry was perfectly flaky and the squash and onions were so sweet. It didn't even need the candied walnuts; the crust that had developed on the roast squash was enough crunch. She was glad she hadn't bothered.

"Ooooh, am I still allowed to have some?"

Simone opened her eyes to find Ray sitting on the lip of the island across from hers, long legs swinging.

She swallowed. "Should you really be sitting on a surface we use to prepare food?"

"Wiping down all the countertops is next on my list. Right after lunch." Ray eyed the galette meaningfully. "Looks good." From behind her back, she produced a plastic squeeze bottle filled with a thick, black-brown liquid. "Might look better with a little of this."

Simone cut a thick wedge with two efficient strokes of her

chef's knife and plated it. "Here." She thrust the plate across the island. "You can put it on yours. I think it's fine as is."

"I'll try it both ways to compare," Ray said magnanimously, and hopped off the counter to grab the plate. She lifted the piece to her lips like it was a slice of pizza—no fork and knife for her, it seemed—and took a bigger bite than Simone thought was humanly possible.

"Oh my god," Ray moaned through a mouthful of food. "This is so good."

"Don't talk with your mouth full," Simone said automatically.

Ray swallowed before saying, "Yes, Mom," in a sarcastic drawl. She took another bite. "Mmmm. Mm!" Her wide shoulders waggled up and down in joy. The noises she made were bordering on indecent.

Simone pulled a face. "Okay, I know that's not technically talking, but can you not—"

Ray swallowed and said, "This is really good. Did you go to culinary school or something?" Her eyes danced as she began drizzling the balsamic reduction all over her slice.

Simone felt her hackles rise. "Of course I did! I studied at Le Cordon Bleu! They won't let just anyone walk through the door and start cooking at The Discerning Chef."

"I know, I know, I'm only joshing you." Ray took another bite, this time with the added vinegar. Her eyes popped comically wide. Somewhere deep in her throat, she made a high-pitched, urgent sound. She gestured to the slice, then to Simone, then to the slice again, still chewing.

"You think I should try it, huh?" Simone suppressed the urge to roll her eyes. "Fine. Give it here." She caught the plate as it was slid back to her and cut a tiny, balsamic-covered piece with her fork, then cut that piece in half so she wouldn't be eating any part that had touched Ray's lips. Kitchen hygiene was of paramount importance, after all.

She took the bite and held it in her mouth.

Damn.

It *was* better with the balsamic.

Simone chewed slowly, her eyes narrowing as she watched Ray's grin widen.

"What do you think?" Ray asked.

She swallowed. Patted her lips with a folded paper napkin. And said, with as much dignity as she could muster, "It's okay."

Ray spun in a circle, pumping a fist up and down in the air. "Yes! I knew it! Them's good eats, baby!"

"I'm pretty sure that's trademarked," Simone said, cutting another stolen bite with the balsamic while Ray was busy celebrating in the end zone. God, she thought as she chewed. It was *really* good. If she wrote this up tonight, could she make the deadline for the November issue? It would be the perfect fall baking project.

"Gene, come see what Simone made!" Ray called across the test kitchen. "It's so freaking delicious, I might die."

Simone watched as Ray bounded across the room in three long strides to grab Gene by the elbow, chattering away about the layers in the galette, leading him over to Simone's station to ooh and aah over the platter. Giving in to the inevitable, Simone drizzled more balsamic over the whole thing and consented to cut Gene his own piece. She expected Ray to crow about it, to boast about how the vinegar had been her idea, but she never did. She just caught Simone's gaze as Gene raved about the flavors and smiled, like they were sharing some kind of secret.

The urge to smile back was unexpected. Simone fought it down successfully, but it still gave her pause. It was very hard not to be annoyed by Ray's overly friendly good cheer, but she was finding it difficult to *stay* annoyed.

Simone brought another large forkful of galette to her mouth and chomped down on it. *This might be a problem,* she admitted (if only to herself).

Chapter 6

It was dark outside when Simone arrived home to find Luna in downward dog.

"Hey, lady, how was work?" her roommate asked without moving from her upside-down position. Her long royal-purple ponytail brushed the bright-pink yoga mat that she'd rolled out in the center of their living room. On the TV, a yoga workout video was playing on low volume.

Simone dropped her tote bag by the door and stepped out of her commute sneakers with a huge sigh.

"How much time do you have?" she muttered as she pitched herself into the IKEA armchair that they'd salvaged from the building's basement. (Simone had insisted on sanitizing it before bringing it into the apartment, of course.)

Luna levered herself out of downward dog and hopped into a forward fold. "I always have a minute to listen to you," she said, "but just a minute."

"Okay, hold on." Simone fished her phone out of her back pocket and thumbed over to the clock app. "Setting the timer for one minute. Starting . . . now." She let her phone drop into her lap and craned her head back to yell at the ceiling, "So The

Discerning Chef has decided to branch out into video and there's this horrible new Social guy who they brought on to do it and he wears T-shirts that make no sense and now I'm expected to do all these videos and I don't *want* to make videos; I just want to cook! And Pim Gladly threatened to fire me, I'm pretty sure, and my editor wouldn't take my side when I talked to her about it and on top of everything there's this new kitchen manager because the old one hurt her back or something and her name is Ray and she acts like everyone's her best friend and she has some ideas that are good but I can't admit they're good because she's already got a big ego—you can tell; she's like this very butch, out there, big, tall, loud . . . *problem*—and she winked at me—oh, and she's gay—"

"She told you that?" Luna asked, a rare interruption when they were on a time limit.

"She was wearing a Pride bracelet."

"Okay. Gay. Continue." Luna waved her hand.

"So she's out, which is fine, but I'm like, you know, whatever—and anyway I made it clear I didn't appreciate that—the winking, not the being gay, obviously—but then I thought maybe I hurt her feelings or overreacted and maybe she thinks it *was* about her being gay and—"

The timer beeped.

"Damn," Simone said, turning it off. "That went fast."

Luna came out of her pose and spun around to face Simone, hands on her hips. "Right," she said. "You spent about forty-five of your sixty seconds talking about this Ray of yours, so . . . just pointing that out." Her eyebrows flicked upward.

Simone frowned and slumped lower in her chair. "She's not 'my' anything. I just had a very stressful day is all. And—" She paused and thought. "This might start getting into 'Bitch, pay me' territory. Is that okay?"

Luna perked up. "I haven't eaten dinner yet, so yeah. That's okay."

"All right, give me a second." Simone rolled out of the armchair and went to retrieve a foil-wrapped slice of leftover galette she had brought home.

Successful long-standing roommate relationships are rare, especially in a city like New York, where tiny apartments and high rents can make even the mildest of tempers flare in a shared environment. Luna and Simone had beaten the roommate odds, staying together in their two-bedroom, one-bath on the top floor of a six-floor walkup on the Upper West Side for over five years now. In New York terms, that was practically a diamond anniversary.

How had their roommate arrangement lasted so long? They had two rules.

One: upon meeting for the first time to see the apartment, Luna O'Shea had shaken Simone's hand and said, looking her straight in the eye, "Do you have a problem with having a trans woman as a roommate?" A few strands of her hair, neon green at the time, worked their way out of her high ponytail and fell into her face. She blew a breath upward out of the corner of her mouth to get it out of the way.

"No," Simone had said automatically, because it was the truth. She rarely offered personal information, but she thought it only fair to add, "I'm bi, if that helps at all."

"Hm. Doesn't hurt, I guess." Luna had eyed her closely, then relaxed into a smile, shaking her hand in earnest. Her palm was as soft as room-temperature butter, Simone noted. "All right, then. It's always a crapshoot, you know, getting paired up on Craigslist. Some of those people are *straight*."

They had laughed at that.

So that was the first rule: mutual understanding. Solidarity, of a kind.

The second rule was written a few weeks after they had moved in to the apartment, when they were still new to each other and their habits had not yet been formed. Luna had been doing what would become her nightly stretches on the yoga mat while Simone tried to work on formatting an article she'd written, but she kept glancing at Luna in a way that made it obvious that she had something on her mind.

"What is it?" Luna had asked outright, catching her eye for the fifth time.

"Oh, nothing." Simone had tried to return to her work, but then said, "It's only, you're surprisingly good at that. The yoga stuff." She turned bright red. "Not that there's any reason you wouldn't be good at it! Just thought you look impressive is all."

"Okay . . ." Luna said slowly, going into Warrior Two.

"And, uh." Simone's eyes darted around for something else to grab onto. "And I really like those leggings," she said, pointing to Luna's activewear, which featured a swirling blue-and-white pattern. "Where did you buy them? Do you have to order them from some special place?"

"A special place," Luna repeated, not making it a question.

"Because you're tall! Not because you're—oh no, am I being offensive?" She clutched her face in her hands. "Please tell me if I'm being offensive."

"Okay, here's the deal," said Luna, snapping herself back to her full, not inconsiderable height, hands planted on her hips. "You've never met another trans person in real life before, I'm guessing?"

Simone shook her head miserably.

"That you know of," Luna added.

"Oh. Hm." Simone thought it over. "I suppose that's true."

"So you're really worried about saying or doing the wrong thing. Your heart's in the right place, but you're just"—she flapped her hand up and down, indicating the whole of Simone's deal—"in need of some guidance."

Simone sat up straighter on the sofa. "Yes, exactly!"

"And do you think," Luna said, with all her patience, "that it's fair to expect me to be responsible for guiding you?"

"Oh." Simone wilted back into the cushions. "No. It's not." (She knew this better than most. One of the reasons she had never bothered to reveal her sexuality in the workplace was because she didn't care to explain herself to any curious at best, belligerent at worst coworkers.)

"It takes a lot out of a person," Luna said, "holding your hand, telling you when you messed up and how to fix it. You don't want to hurt my feelings, which is sweet, but it does me no good to be in charge of *your* feelings. That's a whole 'nother job that I'm not even getting paid to do. Make sense?"

Simone considered this for a long moment. "It does," she finally said. "If I ever have questions, I will keep them to myself."

Luna groaned and shook her arms like she was trying to loosen up a tight muscle. "I don't want to completely shut you down and say 'Don't ask me about trans stuff or talk to me about your feelings' but I also don't want to get stuck being your Trans Rights Whisperer every time you need me. It's just so much work."

"What if I compensate you?" Simone asked. "Would that be fair?"

"Wow." Luna stared at her. "Your cisgender guilt is worth how much, exactly?"

"Hm." Simone's lips twisted in thought. "Maybe it should be a sliding scale based on how big of a pain I'm being. I don't make much money—*magazine jobs*—but I can bake. I'm very good at it. A batch of cookies for a quick check-in on preferred terms and stuff? A layer cake for something more complicated? You could set the terms, of course. You're the one eating the payments."

Luna tapped her fingertip against her lips. "And if I don't have the time or energy to talk with you?"

Simone shrugged. "That's fine. You can just say you're not hungry."

For a moment, Luna did not speak or move. Then, with a firm nod, she thrust out her hand. "You've got a deal, Larkspur," she said. They shook on it. "Now pay me, bitch."

Simone practically leapt to her feet. "I can whip up a chocolate mousse if you want," she said. "Would that cover me trying to pay you a compliment while sticking my whole foot in my mouth and being a complete doofus?"

"Does the mousse come with whipped cream?" Luna asked.

"Of course it comes with whipped cream; I'm not a monster."

They meandered toward the kitchen together so Luna could watch the mousse being made and Simone could ask, "So I should have left the word 'surprising' out of it, right? That's where I fell off the horse?"

"Yep."

"Got it." Simone began pulling milk and cream from the fridge.

Which was all to say, the second rule of the Larkspur-O'Shea household stated Pay Luna in Tasty Food and Baked Goods for Emotional Labor Including but Not Limited to Discussion of Trans Issues. Handing over a slice of the galette was in keeping with the pact they had made all those years ago. It was a good system, and it had worked for them so far.

"Oooh, what's in this?" Luna asked as she flopped onto the couch and started unwrapping the foil. "Do I need to heat it up?"

"It's okay at room temp, if you don't want to— Wow, okay, already eating it," Simone said as she watched Luna chomp off the tip of the slice. "It's fall vegetables and goat cheese, by the way."

"Mmmm!" Luna moaned. "I love this stuff on the top. What is that, balsamic?"

Simone could hear her teeth grinding in her mouth. "Yes. A little reduction."

Luna gestured to the chair as she chewed another mouthful, humming in a way that meant Simone should sit and go ahead with the talking. The foil crinkled in her other hand as she used it to catch the crumbs.

Simone tossed herself sideways into the IKEA chair and groaned, her legs dangling over the arm. "So. Ray." She closed her eyes. This felt strangely like the stereotypical sleepovers that

Simone had never had as a kid, sitting around gossiping. Luna was the only person she felt comfortable enough with to be anything less than completely serious. "I only mentioned her because it was so much on top of everything else that happened today. Maybe it's easier to complain about one single person than a whole host of company-wide decisions. And Ray is just so *chatty*. I really didn't need chatty." She stopped, remembering how Ray had made the distinction earlier about needing and wanting. "And I don't want it either."

"Doth the pastry chef protest too much?" Luna asked. "This is sounding more and more like a schoolyard crush."

"It is not a crush," Simone said, fighting to stay calm. "I'm enough of an adult to say that objectively, some people might find someone like Ray attractive. She's certainly very . . . personable." She said the word the same way one might say *contagious*. "But I am not interested."

"Sure," Luna said, not at all convincingly. "Makes sense."

"I have a lot happening at work that I need to concentrate on."

"Of course."

"Especially now that I'll be so busy. Which is totally unfair."

"Right."

Simone fiddled with her fingernails, examining her cuticles rather closely. "I just wish I could explain to Ray that, while I am personally not interested in being all buddy-buddy or whatever, it's not because she's gay. But I don't know how to explain that without disclosing that I'm bi. And even if I wanted to disclose that, which I really don't—"

Luna nodded. They had spoken at length about the pros and cons of being out at work. There had been a whole series of sweet crepes as a result. Luna was out. Like, way, way out—on Instagram and everything. But as she'd pointed out before, that was a personal choice.

"—on some level I know that would be kind of," Simone scrunched her nose, "cheating?"

"Ooh. Interesting word. What do you mean, cheating?"

Luna asked. Not for the first time, Simone thought her room-mate might make an excellent therapist. Too bad she had chosen a career as a virtual assistant.

Simone sighed. "I'm about to say something bad."

"Go for it. Safe space." Luna gestured to their living room with its struggling potted plant on the windowsill and kitschy pop art prints on the walls.

Simone took a deep breath and said in one big whoosh, "I worry that if I tell Ray I'm bi just to prove that I'm not being homophobic, it's cheating because it *is* possible to be bi and biased against gay people, and I know that because there have been plenty of gay people who have not been kind to me be-cause being bi is, like, 'Straight Lite' in their eyes or something. It would be really disappointing if someone at work thought that." She lifted her head and grimaced at Luna. "Does any of that make sense?"

"All right, you've got a few things going on at the same time here." Luna ate the last bite of galette and dropped the foil in her lap so she could hold up two fingers, one on each hand. She wag-gled one finger at Simone. "First thing: you're worried that Ray thinks you dislike her because she's gay, but actually you dislike her because she's making you all hot and bothered, which is upsetting."

"She is *not* making me—"

"Okay, okay, sorry. You dislike her for totally not-sexy rea-sons. Second thing." She made her right finger dance a bit. "You're feeling pressure to come out to Ray because Ray is ba-sically out, even though Ray being out has nothing to do with your own decision to disclose or not, and you're getting scared all over again about being judged and rejected by your cowork-ers, especially the gay one, because people have judged and re-jected you before. Yeah?"

Simone thought about the last girl she'd dated—gosh, was it really almost two years ago now?—who'd expressed surprise and displeasure months into the relationship when she found out Simone had not exclusively dated women and was actually bisexual. "I thought you were a *real* lesbian," she'd said. Simone had stopped responding to her texts after that.

"Yeah," she agreed, and groaned. "It's the crepes all over again." She chewed at her lip, anxiety overwhelming her. "Do you think maybe I'm just being too hard on Ray because I'm a bad, self-hating queer?"

"For what it's worth," Luna said, "I don't think you're harboring some deep-seated internalized homophobia. Biphobia? Anyway, if you were, you wouldn't be worrying so much about it." She reclined further on the sofa, stuffing a pillow under her sleek head. "The people who have that undealt-with stuff inside them are usually completely oblivious to it. That's the whole point of repressing." She brightened. "It's like how they say a person with anxiety can't be a psychopath!"

Simone scrunched up her nose. "Thanks?"

"It's a compliment. You're self-aware!"

Simone rolled her eyes and grabbed one of the throw pillows off the sofa, hugging it to her stomach as she thought. "So if I can accept that I'm probably not a supervillain," she said, "and that I can choose to not be out at work without being a horrible traitor—"

"And you aren't," Luna chimed in. "Remember the crepes?"

"—then the only real thing left to worry about is whether or not Ray thinks badly of me," Simone finished.

"Did she give you any indication that that's the case?" Luna asked.

Simone considered the incident with the galette. How Ray had wheedled a piece of it, had helped improve it, and had sung Simone's praises to Gene and anyone else in the test kitchen who would listen. Not exactly the actions of someone holding a grudge. "I don't think so. Hard to tell with someone that outgoing, I guess."

Luna stretched out on the couch with a happy sigh. "All right. So the real question is: How come you care so much about what this girl thinks of you? Hm?"

Simone threw the pillow at Luna's head but, having poor aim, only managed to bean her on the shoulder. Luna laughed as the fluffy projectile fell to the floor.

"I don't care what she thinks," Simone insisted. "I just want to make sure I'm being professional in my place of work. *Someone* has to be."

Luna nodded sagely. "Right. No winking for you."

"I'm not even sure I know how to wink." Simone attempted to shut only her left eye, but it felt exaggerated and awkward, not at all the quick, fluid wink that Ray had aimed at her. Her right eye kept squinting closed, too. "Am I doing it? It doesn't feel like I'm doing it."

"Remind me never to recruit you to help me cheat at cards," Luna said. Her phone buzzed, and she glanced at the screen with a sour look on her face.

"Guy from the gym?" Simone asked. She knew this character well. One date and he was texting Luna a lot of unsolicited nonsense, mostly pictures of his abs, which wouldn't have been so bad except one rogue dick pic had been snuck into the batch. Simone had clapped a hand over her eyes when Luna had tried to show her, declaring that a burden shared is not necessarily a burden halved.

"Ugh, yeah. I should just block him, I know, but . . ." Luna gave an expressive shrug that meant too many things.

"Tell me all about it while I cook dinner. That one piece of galette wasn't much," she said, and Luna brightened. They moved to the kitchen, taking up their usual weeknight places, Simone at the stove tossing together a quick stir-fry, Luna perched on the narrow counter, swinging her feet, and going through the entire list of Gym Guy's pros and cons. Simone was grateful—not just for the company, but for something to take her mind off work.

They ate their dinner in front of an On Demand episode of Lisette D'Amboise's cozy cooking show, *Home Kitchen*, where she visited various farms in the European countryside and then made elaborate meals using their artisan products. Lisette was Simone's culinary hero, a renowned French pastry chef who was approximately 155 years old and had been hosting cooking shows on public-access television since television was practically invented. Her gentle, wrinkled face filled the screen as she spoke in her trademark, near-indecipherable French accent. "Today, mon petit," she whispered, "I take you to Italy. A beautiful place with beautiful food. Come, let us cook." Then she turned and began hiking down a stunning Tuscan hillside in her impeccable Wellingtons, walking stick in hand.

Oh, to be Lisette D'Amboise's traveling companion, gallivanting around picturesque farmland, petting adorable piglets, collecting fresh eggs, and eating gourmet meals every morning, noon, and night. Simone sighed. Too bad she lived in the real world.

"Hey," Luna said during a commercial break, "just so you know, you're not a jerk for having boundaries. If you don't want to be winked at in the office, you should be able to say so, you know?"

Simone managed a smile. "Thanks." Part of the reason Luna had chosen to mostly work from home these days was because it was safer than navigating office politics; she knew what she was talking about. "That means a lot."

Luna turned back to the TV, where Lisette was visiting a farm and tasting some gorgeous cured pork. Simone tried to concentrate on the show, which she'd already seen a million times, of course, but something rankled in the back of her mind. Finally, after composing the lines in her head over and over again, Simone whipped out her phone and tapped out an email on her work account. It was just a quick message to Ray, who was now in the company database.

Subject: Today.

Message: I understand you are a friendly person. Please extend the same understanding to me when I say I am only interested in work when I am in the test kitchen. You are my colleague, and that's it.

She hit Send before she could overthink it. With a happy sigh, she was able to focus on Lisette masterfully crafting a carbonara. It was late, well after business hours, so she didn't expect Ray to see the email—let alone respond—until the next morning. Yet her phone pinged, causing her to jump a bit in her seat.

Ray had replied. Just two words.

Roger that!

Simone knew she should feel satisfied, but instead she felt something else, like a niggling tingle in her stomach. She put her phone away in her pocket and very seriously ignored it.

Chapter 7

Simone worried that her late-night email exchange with Ray might make things awkward around the test kitchen, but luckily that was not the case. When she arrived at work early the next morning, she found Ray was already there, hunched over a laptop at one of the kitchen islands and muttering at the screen.

"Hey, good morning," Ray said, eyes flicking up at Simone. Her smile was polite, if not exactly the huge grin of yesterday. "I'm glad you're here. Question: Do you care about which brand of almond flour we stock? I saw tons of Red Mill in the stack of old invoices the last kitchen manager left behind, but King Arthur's on sale this week."

"Oh, King Arthur is fine, it's a good product." Simone hesitated, then offered, "There aren't a lot of brand names I prefer over others. I can make you a list of the ones I do, if that would make things easier for you."

"That would be awesome." The smile became, somehow, even more polite. "That way I won't have to bug you with questions every time I'm trying to save the company five bucks."

"I don't mind questions," Simone said in a rush.

"Good." Ray's eyes crinkled at the corners. "I'll be judicious, then." It was all very chummy. Nothing even close to flirtatious, really. That was good. They could just have a normal working relationship. Exactly what Simone had asked for.

Not that she had much time to think about it, what with all the work she needed to do.

Simone cobbled together her lists of video topics and handed them over to Chase, who in turn handed them over to Petey the cameraman to fashion into a production schedule. (Petey seemed to be in charge of all the real work, Simone noticed. Chase insisted he was more the "idea guy," a stance that Simone could neither understand nor respect.) Petey's sprawling Excel spreadsheet made the rounds, and Simone deflated when she saw exactly how badly the videos would eat into her time. At least three days a week, sometimes more, her whole morning and most of the afternoon would be shot while she herself was being shot on film. She began mentally rearranging her schedule and realized she'd have to work late almost every day just to stay on top of her workload. It was the only solution, since she couldn't possibly come into work any earlier than she already did. Which meant she'd be getting home just in time to fall into bed. Which meant no time to cook dinner and hang with Luna. Well, it wasn't like she needed home-cooked meals and face-to-face interaction with other people, right? Her mom's voice chattered away in the back of her head: *You have to be willing to make sacrifices for your dream! Nothing comes easy!*

Right. This was supposed to be hard. Otherwise, it wouldn't be worth her time.

As the date of her first video shoot approached, Simone fought the waves of dread that lapped at her feet. It was just another assignment, she told herself. It may not be the one she'd have picked, but she was a professional, and she would get through this.

"I'll get through this, right?" she asked Mikkah during one of their many afternoon coffee-chugging sessions in her office.

Internal pep talks were all well and good, but it was nice to hear that her boss had her back.

"Like a champ," Mikkah assured her. "Like always." Simone was not exactly convinced.

She arrived at work even earlier than usual and triple-checked that all her ingredients and implements were ready. Ray was there, of course, because Ray was always in the test kitchen, but beyond a tepid good morning, Simone managed to avoid her. Ray had her own work to do, anyway. She flitted around the kitchen in relative quiet, it being so early in the morning. Simone was pleased to find that Ray eventually faded into the background hum of the workday, like the sound of the walk-in refrigerator motor or the buzz of traffic outside.

She and Petey had been set up and ready for almost forty minutes by the time Chase breezed into the test kitchen wearing mirrored aviators and holding a cold brew from the café down the block.

"Call time was ten thirty," Petey pointed out while adjusting the lens on his camera.

"Yeah, okay. This will be quick," Chase said, draining his cold brew with a loud suck of his straw and setting the empty cup on a counter. Simone frowned at it and placed it in the trash can that sat only two feet away.

This was going to be a long day, and not at all quick.

"Chase, maybe it would be a good idea to run through the game plan," she said, trying to get back on track. "I've never shot a video before, so I'm not sure exactly how you want me to act. Should I smile a lot? I read somewhere that I might need to smile a lot." She'd done plenty of research on her own, of course, mostly reading interviews with Lisette D'Amboise, who had once told *Life* magazine that learning to smile while cooking had been the most difficult part of her career. "More difficult than full puff pastry," she had said. "Much more."

Simone had taken this advice to heart, but Chase seemed less concerned about Lisette D'Amboise's words of wisdom.

"Nah, you don't have to worry about being likeable, thank God," Chase said through a yawn.

Simone blinked. "Excuse me?"

"What I mean is, you aren't going to be the focus of the video." He made a frame out of his hands and squinted through it at Simone. "We're featuring the food. You're an afterthought. Window dressing, really."

"Oh," Simone said, "I'm thrilled to hear it."

Across the test kitchen, Ray was sorting through a cart full of deliveries. She caught Simone's eyes and gave a wave, the universal gesture for *Don't mind me, pretend I'm not even here*. Simone frowned. She didn't like the idea of having an audience for this, even if it was only an audience of one.

Chase grinned widely. "Great. So for now I want to try shooting a batch of videos, hands-'n-pans style."

"Which is?" Simone asked.

"Which is what?" Chase returned.

"What is 'hands and pans'?" Simone said, refusing to shorten the conjunction like they were operating some roadside tavern.

"Oh, simple." Chase grabbed a cast-iron pan from the overhead rack and swung it onto the counter with a heavy thwack. Over his shoulder, Simone could see Ray wince from where she was messing around with the spice rack. Chase, oblivious, held his hand high above the pan as if miming a crane. "We do an overhead shot like this. Neat little bowls of ingredients over on the side here." He wiggled his fingers beside the pan to illustrate. "No narration, no faces, just your hands putting everything together." He pretended to stir something in the pan with an invisible spoon. "Mmm, delicious. We add all the chyrons—that's like subtitles, text on the screen—"

"I know what chyrons are," Simone said. (She completed the *New York Times* crossword on a regular basis; her vocabulary was no slouch.) Inwardly, she was glad to hear she wouldn't be appearing on camera past her wrists. Simone didn't care overly much about her appearance, but she was still aware that she was not some willowy blond supermodel. She was built along the same lines as a hobbit, confined to the realm of cute at best. Her chubbiness did not bother her, but even a neophyte like Simone knew that the internet was a platform for every Tom, Dick, and Harry to comment on it, and she didn't want to know what some stranger in Iowa thought of her.

"So the chyrons explain the steps in post," Chase was saying, oblivious to her annoyance. "Put some peppy music over the whole thing, badda bing, badda boom. The new concept of The Discerning Chef."

"And people will watch those?" Simone asked.

"Yeah, of course they'll watch them. People love them. You've probably already seen a ton of videos like this! Food Tutors? Cooking with Marla? They're all the same."

Simone shook her head. "I'm not really . . . into that kind of stuff." The fact that they were interchangeable made them even less appealing to her.

Chase tsked. Actually tsked! At her! "Simone, Simone, *Simone*, you have *got* to keep an eye on your competition. Or at least stay on top of industry trends. What cooking channels are you subscribed to on YouTube?"

"I don't really use YouTube."

Chase looked stricken. "You don't?"

Simone thought hard. "Well, sometimes my roommate sends me a video of a cat trying to eat a flower or something. Those are on YouTube. Sometimes. Other times they're just gifs." She watched as Chase's stare turned from surprised to disgusted. She went on the defensive. "Sorry that my career doing real work and cooking real food hasn't left me much free time to stare at a screen!"

From somewhere behind a baking rack, Ray snickered. Simone cast a glare in that direction; she didn't appreciate being laughed at.

Chase closed his eyes and pinched the bridge of his nose, like *he* was the one dealing with incompetent people. "Let's just run through the test video a couple times and see how it goes."

It had been decided well in advance that the test would be a fluffy French-style omelet. Easy, fast, and very few ingredients, therefore less waste. Simone could make a perfect omelet in her sleep, and literally had several times. In her younger days, she would sometimes find herself sleep deprived and starving after a long dinner shift, and would come home to a silent apartment in the wee hours of the morning with the intention to sleep first and eat later. Then, after crawling into bed and falling dead asleep, Simone would sleepwalk to her kitchen and start cooking eggs at the stovetop. She woke up halfway through the process a couple of times. She was very worried that she might burn the whole building down in her sleep, but the omelets were so good, she always forgot her fears after the first bite. After sleep-cooking a handful of times, Simone decided to always eat first, then sleep after coming home late at night, and the sleep-cooking stopped altogether.

She mentioned this to Petey as he helped her set up all the bowls and dishes of eggs and butter at her station.

He stared at her. "Seriously?"

"Oh, sure," she said. "This one time my roommate Luna found me cooking enough omelets for a party of six. I worked a lot of brunch shifts, so." She shrugged.

"So what did you do with six omelets?" Petey asked.

"Well, after Luna woke me up, we ate three omelets apiece and went to bed with really bad stomachaches." She tapped her fingers against her chin in thought. "They were well-cooked omelets, though, especially considering I wasn't conscious for it."

"That's hilarious," Petey said. "That really happened?"

Simone stuck three fingers into the air. "Scout's honor."

Ray walked by lugging two heavy canvas bags emblazoned with the logo of their grocery delivery service. She was wearing an apron of rich brown leather, pens and utility knives stored in its thin pockets. "You should tell that story in the video," she said. "It's funny."

Simone blinked. The leather apron was throwing her off. "Yeah, maybe."

"Dude, you look like a blacksmith in that thing," Petey said, echoing Simone's deeply embarrassing thoughts. "Maybe a serial killer."

Or perhaps not.

"Oh, this?" Ray hooked her thumbs in the apron's bib. "I love this thing. Never rips, never stains, and it's got a million pockets. I got used to wearing one at the butcher shop I worked at a few years ago. Figured I should keep at it."

Simone felt like she was being hypnotized by the sight of the leather stretching across Ray's lanky torso. Her own white muslin apron made her look so dowdy, like somebody's grandmother. Ray looked like she could fireman-carry someone out of danger, if need be.

"Simone? Simone."

Simone snapped back to attention, turning to Petey, who had apparently been calling her name for a while. "Yes?"

"I said, do you want to start with your story about the omelets? Ray's right, it's funny."

"Oh. Sure." She positioned herself on the far side of the island. "Should I just say—?"

"Quick reminder that you don't need to talk," Chase interrupted. "You can if you want, I guess, but it's not like we'll be recording any sound." He was over by the window, fiddling with some light meter thing. "No talking in the final video, remember? Just a soundtrack."

"Oh. Right." Simone busied herself with finding her favorite spatula in the utensil caddy. She felt silly for forgetting the very simple concept of this stupid video.

Ray set the canvas bags on the far island and started sorting through the contents, making piles on the counter. She didn't look up when she said, "I don't know, I'd rather hear Simone talk about her row of omelets than listen to some cheesy instrumental song. Wouldn't you?"

Simone darted a look at Ray. That sounded suspiciously supportive and—well, nice.

"*I* would rather stick to the plan," Chase said. He finally seemed satisfied by whatever his light meter was showing him, because he pocketed it and returned to the omelet station. "Okay, let's get started. And remember, we'll probably need to run through this a bunch of times before you get it, so don't get discouraged when you mess up."

"Maybe I won't mess up," Simone countered in a hopeful tone that suggested they could all try to be more positive.

"Oh, trust me, you will. Okay, Francis, I want you here, straight down, ninety-degree angle." Chase corralled the camera and its operator into place. Simone noticed Petey had stopped trying to get Chase to call him by his middle name.

"I think Francis is a fine name," she whispered to him as they took their places. "It's, like, old-timey, but in a good way."

"Sure," Petey muttered. "Good for people who want to be called Francis."

"Come on, people, I'd like to see some concentration. I know this is our first test, but let's try to treat it like the real thing," Chase chided. He took a black-and-white plastic movie clapper board out of the box of equipment and started writing on it with a black felt marker. He sure did love his toys.

"I didn't know those things were real," Simone said. "I thought they were just something they used in movies."

Chase looked at her askance. "They do use them in movies. That's where they come from."

"No, I know, I meant—"

"All right, let's have the professional run this show, okay? Places! TDC test kitchen, Simone video number one, take one! Action!" Chase stuck the clapper under the mounted camera hanging over the workstation and slapped the boards together.

Simone stared at him. What a little tyrant. Who did he think he was, Cecil B. DeMille? Simone wanted nothing more than to take her entire bowl of eggs and dump them over his head. He wasn't even aware of her angry gaze; he remained focused on the array of bowls and utensils on the workstation that Simone was very much not manipulating at the moment.

"When I say 'action' that means you can start," he said.

"Yes," Simone said coldly, "I am aware." She took a deep breath and picked up an egg, cracking it one-handed against the counter and parting the shell in her palm above an empty glass bowl. The egg yolk slipped free and was joined in the bottom of the bowl by the white.

"Cut," Chase barked. "What is that? What are you doing? You're supposed to be breaking eggs like a normal person. We want normal people to watch this video, okay?"

"This is how I crack eggs," Simone said.

"I don't care how you do it off camera. You need to do it with both hands right now. You'll confuse people if they see you doing that."

"I think that the average home cook will understand that as long as you get the eggs in the bowl, it doesn't matter how you—"

"You're giving people way too much credit," Chase said. "Viewers are stupid. You have to spell everything out for them. This isn't the time for you to show off!"

Simone flushed. "I'm not trying to *show off*," she said, although she sort of was. "And I don't think our audience is stupid."

"Hey." Ray popped up from behind Petey, who was staying well out of the conversation. "Maybe you could do a video that teaches people how to crack eggs one-handed. That might be cool."

"No one wants to know how to do that," Chase said, waving his hand through the air dismissively.

"I kind of do," Petey said from behind his equipment. "It looks awesome. Is it hard?"

"Not really, you just have to flex your palm—" Simone began, demonstrating with an empty hand.

"Okay! Stop! This is a video about omelets. Not about cracking eggs," Chase complained.

"Well, you do have to do one to make the other," Ray said, causing Petey to snicker.

Chase turned to Ray. "Who even are you? You're not one of the chefs they had me meet with. What are you doing here?"

"I'm Ray." She thrust her hand out, which Chase did not shake. "The kitchen manager."

"Oh, right. Rachel." Chase gave her a quick look up and down. "They told me you'd get us whatever ingredients we need."

"It's just Ray, actually," she said. "And yeah. That's what I do." Her hand retracted to hook into her jeans pocket instead.

"Whatever. Look, could you give us some space?"

Ray grinned, undaunted. "You sound just like my ex-girlfriend. It's uncanny."

Petey stifled a snorted laugh into the sleeve of his jacket. At Chase's glare, he said, "Sorry. Allergies," with a sheepish duck of his head.

Chase turned back to Ray with an imperious sniff. "I'm sure you have something better to do than impede my project, *Rachel*."

Ray tossed off a sloppy salute. "You got it, Mac."

"My name is Chase."

"Mister McDonald," Ray said in a cartoonishly bad Scottish accent.

Chase turned bright red in anger, his face lighting up like a bonfire. "That's not funny!"

Simone smothered a smile behind her hand. It was actually very funny.

Chase whirled on Simone with a glare. "If everyone's done messing around, maybe we can get some work done." He turned to his kit bag to retrieve his light meter again, and while he was looking away, Ray made direct eye contact with Simone and pulled a face that wordlessly said, *Can you believe this guy?* With that, Ray slouched away into the walk-in.

Slightly unprofessional, but Simone couldn't help but agree.

Chapter 8

After many long days of shooting video footage, and many more days of Petey editing the footage into bite-sized videos, Chase announced via email that Simone's first foray into the genre would be posted to TDC's YouTube channel. At least, that's what Simone thought the email said; it had been sent from Chase's iPhone, according to the signature, and the message was autocorrected so much that it was almost unintelligible: your frust vid scolded love later today. Still, Petey confirmed it when they ran into each other in the test kitchen, where he was preparing to film Gene putting together a pesto and Gene was loudly complaining about how he should really be getting paid overtime or something for all this extra work. Simone's video was scheduled to go live at 7 p.m. EST.

"After-work hunger traffic online," Petey explained. "People searching for food videos while waiting for their pizza to arrive, I guess."

A bleak outlook on their potential audience, but Simone couldn't think about that right now. Her anticipation bordered on a nervous breakdown. She tried to concentrate on her work—she was supposed to be writing up her recipe for the savory autumnal galette she'd perfected (balsamic reduction and all)—but knowing the video of her hands and her omelet would soon be online for the world to see was too much. Even though she still had her doubts about this whole video strategy, she wanted it to be a success. Otherwise all that work, as annoying and unfair as it was, would be for nothing. She had to crush it right out of the gate to prove to Pim Gladly and Mikkah and everyone else that she was capable.

She wanted to stop worrying about whether everything would be okay.

She made herself leave the office at a reasonable hour for once, even though it was torture, knowing that the video would go live in one hour. In thirty minutes. In five minutes.

Simone kept checking the time on her phone, wondering what might happen when the stupid thing was posted. Luna noticed and came out of a perfectly executed plow pose to grab the phone from Simone's hands just as the clock struck seven.

"You're making yourself crazy," she said. "And watching you is making *me* crazy. There won't be anything to see right now, anyway; the thing just went up. Wait until tomorrow, then you can check and see how many people watched it and how many comments it got."

"Tomorrow?" Simone cried. "But—"

"Don't make me hide this from you," Luna said, waggling the phone in her hand. "I swear to god, Simone, I will put this on a shelf so high, your short little self won't ever find it."

Simone sighed. Luna was right; it wasn't healthy to obsess over every video. If all went according to Chase's plan, there would be dozens, hundreds of videos. This first one didn't even mean much in the grand scheme of things.

"Fine," she said, resigned. "I promise to wait until tomorrow." She held her hand out. "Can I have my phone back now?"

Luna tapped the corner of the phone case against her chin, thinking. "Depends. How much was my heroic intervention worth, I wonder?"

"I was going to make enchiladas for dinner. Want some?"

"Oooh, the tricolor ones? That'll work." Luna handed back the phone. "Stay strong, Simone. Discipline!"

Well, if anyone could be disciplined, it was Simone. She cooked their dinner and served it at their tiny café-style table, listening to Luna chatter away about her day job as a virtual assistant.

"So then Tim says, 'I want you to book me into first class,' and I say, 'Timmy, we talked about this,'" Luna said, referring to the wishy-washy figurehead of a CEO she was supposed to be supporting, though to hear her stories, it was more like babysitting. "I told him, 'Remember Prague? You asked me to book you into first class then, too, and Finance wouldn't approve it.' And he's like, 'Ohhhh, okay, well can't you ask them to make an exception this time?' These guys act like they don't know company policy, it's ridiculous." She sawed off a piece of her enchilada and ate the bite off her fork like it was to blame.

"That is pretty bad," Simone offered. She could tell her roommate was trying to distract her from her phone, and she appreciated the effort.

By strength of will alone, Simone went to bed that night without once opening up YouTube to see how her video was doing. But it was a near thing.

The next day, Simone sprang awake at her alarm and immediately grabbed her phone to check the video. It took her a minute to navigate the unfamiliar territory of The Discerning Chef's YouTube channel—*probably should have bookmarked it or something*, she thought—but she finally succeeded in opening up her video's page.

Eight views.

Eight *total* views.

"There must be a mistake," she mumbled, thumbing around the screen. She refreshed the page. The number went up by one. Great. So now it was nine. Nine. Measly. Views.

Two of those were Simone herself. Another couple were

probably Petey or Chase, checking to make sure the video loaded properly. All in all, their hard work had netted a viewership of maybe five people.

Simone saw that her mother, who lived on the West Coast these days and tended to communicate without thinking of time zones, had texted her sometime in the night.

Saw your little video, honey! I think you did great :-)

Perfect. So one of those views was Simone's mom, which didn't really count. That brought the total down to four. Her heart sank. This was not good.

She dreaded going into the office and facing the team after such a disappointing showing, but she forced herself to get showered and dressed and into the test kitchen like always.

When Chase finally made an appearance, he made a beeline for Simone, an unconcerned smirk on his face.

"Hey, don't look so glum," he said, patting Simone on the back (a gesture she did not appreciate, and moved slightly away to keep him from doing it any further). "Long tail, remember? I explained this all before. It's a marathon, not a sprint. So what if no one watched your first video? You'll get better. Plenty of chances coming down the pipeline."

"It just seems to be an awful lot of work for very little reward," Simone said, not bothering to parse all of Chase's ridiculous clichés. "Maybe it's a sign that we should change tactics?"

"We stick with the plan. It'll all work out, you'll see." He fussily picked a piece of lint from his no-doubt expensive and vintage *Montauk: See You in the Surf* tee and pivoted out of the test kitchen to do . . . whatever it was he did all day.

Ray walked by, maneuvering a hand truck loaded with huge bags of onions. "Maybe he's right," she said. "Maybe it'll get better with practice."

Simone felt her anger bubbling to the surface. It had been on a low simmer for days, and now the pot overflowed. She turned to Ray and spat, "Maybe! Or maybe I will continue to be humiliated in front of all my peers, and for what? Because Pim

Gladly decided on a whim that we suddenly need to bring TDC into the twenty-first century?" She gestured wildly. "I am a chef and a writer. I am not a YouTube star! But that doesn't matter, does it? Because I just have to do what I'm told and accept it!"

Ray stared at her, then abandoned the hand truck against the wall. "Okay. Let's just sit. You're looking kind of shaky." Her big hand came to support Simone at the small of her back, gently guiding her to the nearest stool. For some reason, this touch didn't bother Simone like Chase's had. She took a seat in a little bit of a daze, astonished at her outburst.

"I don't usually—I'm sorry, I'm just stressed out, I guess," she said, stumbling over her words.

"I get it. It happens. Here, hang on." Ray disappeared around the corner. A series of familiar mechanical whirs and bangs floated to Simone's ears, and she frowned. That couldn't be . . . could it?

When Ray returned with a steaming cup of espresso, Simone's eyes widened.

"You got the machine to work?" she asked as she accepted the offering with all the appropriate awe. "I thought I was the only one who could do that."

"Sorry," Ray said with a laugh. "Didn't mean to get all up in your special thing. Should I take it back?" She reached for the miniature cup.

Simone pulled it tight against her chest. "No. My caffeine. Get your own. You can do that, apparently."

Ray smiled. "Already had mine this morning. Any more and my heart will explode." She crossed her arms over her broad chest and leaned the point of her hip against the counter. "Go ahead." She tipped her chin at the cup Simone still held. "Drink up."

Simone did, breathing in the heady aroma before taking a deep sip. It was good—strong and dark. Had Ray noticed she took hers black? Maybe it was just laziness, not wanting to bother with any milk. She sighed, chiding herself for even thinking that. Ray wasn't lazy; she could admit that now. Their new kitchen manager worked hard. The test kitchen had never been so spotless or well-organized. Simone looked around them with a stab of jealousy in her belly. *Must be nice to have a job you can do well,* she thought.

"I'm trying my best, but it's not good enough," Simone said, staring into her cup. "It's not fair. I never wanted to be an on-camera personality. I'm no good at it."

"I think you have a nice personality." Ray's grin was small and tentative. "And I mean that in a completely professional, work-appropriate way."

Simone ignored the heat in her cheeks that came with being the center of Ray's attention, however harmless. "You know my personality after just a few weeks, do you?" she asked. Her internal calendar reminded her it had actually been about a month, which was a surprise. Where had the time gone?

Ray gave a half smile. "I have a vague idea. Let me guess: You were an honors student? Did extra credit even when you didn't have to? Argued with the teachers when you got anything less than one hundred percent?"

Simone felt her flush grow. She didn't appreciate being seen so thoroughly. "I work hard," she said, fighting to keep her voice from rising into a defensive whine.

"I get that. I mean, it's pretty obvious. And admirable," Ray said.

Simone tried and failed to hide her surprise at that. "Is it?" She frowned and shook her head. "Most people don't think so." She ran her thumbnail down the side of the tiny espresso cup. "I know it can be a little . . . off-putting, the way I get wrapped up in work. I won't apologize for it, though. If I were a man, no one would bat an eye. The guys in the kitchens I've worked at were just as ambitious, just as brusque." She shrugged. "Maybe I'm not great with people, but I'm great at food. I know I am. But that doesn't seem to count for much right now."

Ray uncrossed her arms and instead propped her hands on

the edge of the counter behind her, leaning forward like she needed to stretch out her shoulders. "You don't have to explain yourself to me. I know what those kitchens are like; I've worked in enough of them. You do what you have to do to get ahead." Her gaze darted from Simone's to the floor. "Look, I don't have any good advice for you or anything. This situation sucks. Even Gene hates it, and that guy likes pretty much everything. He's like the human equivalent of a glass of warm milk." She shrugged. "I just want you to know that you've got people rooting for you."

Simone was so taken aback by this naked display of camaraderie, she couldn't manage to form any words for a moment. When she finally did, it was to deflect. "Yes, my mom is already sending me very supportive texts, smiley faces and all," she quipped, looking down into her espresso. "I'm sure with cheerleaders like that, I'm bound to win eventually."

Ray clapped her on the shoulder. "That's the spirit. You've got this. Just keep at it." She gave a cheery nod before returning to the onions and carting them away.

Simone watched her go, feeling a little warm. *Must be the espresso,* she thought, and took another drink from her cup.

The days dragged on. More footage was shot, more was edited. Soon another video of Simone's was posted, this time a how-to on prepping and sauteing kale simply in a tablespoon of oil with salt and pepper. Chase was confident that this was the sort of content that would really bring in the numbers. "No one cares about omelets anyway," he said, which hurt Simone, who did care about omelets quite deeply.

Simone readied herself as the video was scheduled for upload. Time to face the music. Again. She was not looking forward to experiencing this cycle every week.

The next morning, she seated herself on a high stool at her favorite kitchen island and booted up her laptop with a deep sigh. It was only her steely resolve that allowed her to go through the motions of calmly opening up a browser and logging in to the

YouTube channel to see the results of the video Petey had posted the day before. Simone closed her eyes as the page loaded. Call it childish superstition, but she thought that maybe if she tried hard enough, she could will the number of views to be higher this time. *Two hundred,* she thought to herself in a silent bargain to whatever saint watched over beleaguered bakers. Two hundred was doable. She would open her eyes and see the number "200" under the video—or possibly more, and it would be a nice surprise. With these low expectations, Simone opened her eyes to stare at the laptop screen. Her heart sank.

It was not two hundred.

It was a lot lower than two hundred.

After all that work.

Simone rubbed her eyes and groaned. A presence loomed at her shoulder, and from the low whistle, Simone knew it was Ray.

"Eighty-six, huh?" Ray made a teeth-sucking sound. "Bad omen."

"Yeah," Simone said into her palms, which she had applied over her face to protect her for the smallest moment from this harsh reality. "Maybe it's a sign. Maybe they should take me off the menu." She peered through her fingers to gauge Ray's reaction.

"Ha! Restaurant humor." Ray spun and sat on the lip of the counter, shaking the surface a bit with the added weight. Simone frowned, thinking that couldn't be hygienic, but decided not to press the issue. She was too tired.

"This took us a week to make," she said, dropping her hands at last. "What a waste of time."

"Hey, don't be such a downer, Mona," Ray said, long legs swinging. "You got some practice, at least. That's one positive."

"Mona?" Simone glared at Ray over the edge of her laptop screen. "Oh, no. Forget it. You're not saddling me with some silly nickname."

"Why not? Petey gets one, Mac gets one—kind of—and it's only fair you get one. Why? Don't you like it?"

"Mona is two syllables, same as Simone. It's not really a nickname if it isn't shortened; it's the same amount of work to say either way."

"Wow, you do not have a good understanding of what a nickname is for. It's not about ease of use." Ray laughed. "Come on, Mona, don't you think it fits you?"

Simone scoffed. "A forced sense of familiarity is not my idea of a good time either, thanks."

Ray seemed to think for one blissful moment of silence. "Sorry. If it bugs you, I'll stop."

One quick flick of those green eyes in distress and Simone felt like she was responsible for kicking a whole basket of puppies. "It doesn't *bug* me," she muttered, concentrating on her screen. "I just don't see the point. Do whatever you want."

"That's so Mona of you," Ray said, leaning over her workstation. "Mona Lisa. Working hard for the Mona. More Mona, more problems."

Simone pretended she wasn't listening, when in actuality, she was listening very closely and trying very hard not to blush at all the attention. She'd never had a nickname before. It was almost . . . nice.

She changed the subject and hoped Ray didn't notice. "Look at these comments! 'Wow, cooking kale in a pan, groundbreaking.' 'Are these tutorials for idiots?' Then this one's just one long curse word."

"See?" Ray beamed. "People left comments! That's something."

"But they're nasty comments!"

"It's the internet. Most comments are going to be nasty. At least, that's what I hear. I'm not even on Facebook." Ray cocked her head. "Forget those jerks, all right? You're trying new things, seeing what works. Don't give up on yourself yet, Mona. You've got to have hope."

"Sure. Hope." Simone shut her laptop with a click. "That's worked out so well, historically." Maybe if she was lucky, Pim Gladly wouldn't actually read the video reports. The threat of a pink slip loomed larger than ever. Simone sighed before going to the baking rack to grab some flour. This level of despair called for cinnamon buns.

Chapter 9

Winter rolled through the city with a freezing chill. The days became short, but work hours became long. Simone was at the TDC offices before the sun rose and stayed far past the time it set, just to keep up with her usual workload on top of the video project. It all began to blur together. There were moments where she caught herself making production notes in the middle of her choux bun recipe, or worse, dropping more kale ideas into an article about rooftop wine bars. In one memorable instance, she removed a picture-perfect blueberry pie from the oven only to realize she'd cut a YouTube play button shape into the crust as a vent. Clearly, she was burning the candle at both ends.

Not that she had anything to show for all her hard work. Her videos continued to be posted to the internet equivalent of crickets. At least today was a Friday, she thought as she sat at her desk, trying and failing to write bubbly, informative copy to accompany her recipe for rosemary and citrus shortbread. She looked away to give her eyes a break from the screen and stared instead at the little postcard taped to the wall of her cubicle featuring a smiling Lisette D'Amboise holding a platter of perfect croissants.

She brushed her fingers along the postcard. "Lisette, give me strength," she whispered, the same silly little prayer she always said when she was feeling lost. Hopefully no one had heard her. Simone glanced around and noticed that the entire open-plan area where she worked was empty. Not a single chef or copy editor or accountant was sitting at their desks. Simone checked the time on her phone. It was only 4:30. Sure, it was a Friday, but most of the staff had also been staying late to try and tackle their ballooning responsibilities. Where was everybody?

Well, if everyone else is taking a break, Simone reasoned, *I could probably stand to stretch my legs.* She made her way to the test kitchen for no other reason than it was a different place to be. It had, she was certain, nothing to do with who she was sure to find there.

Simone walked into the kitchen to see almost all of her co-workers had already converged there. Some were sitting at one of the workstations and some were milling around—mingling, Simone's mind supplied, the word was *mingling*—but everyone had a glass of something in hand. Gene was chatting with Kate from Legal while she laughed at something he said. Petey and Ray were talking animatedly over bottles of beer about some sci-fi show Simone had never seen. Even Delilah was there with a glass of red wine (a rarity, to see her away from Pim Gladly's side), listening intently to some gossip from a girl who worked in Finance; Simone didn't know her name. In fact, she realized as she took in the little crowd, there were a lot of staff members that she didn't know. Simone's work in Editorial kept her away from most of the other departments. For such a small company as The Discerning Chef, they sure didn't spend a whole lot of time bonding as a team.

Until now, apparently.

She gravitated toward Mikkah, the person she knew best. "Hey, what's going on?"

Mikkah turned to her with a wide smile. "Oh, Simone! You made it. Isn't it great?" She gestured with her drink, nearly sloshing a bit of what looked like a frothy cocktail made with egg whites. It was faintly pink.

Simone frowned. "Yeah. Great. What is it, exactly?" She looked around the room. Chase was nowhere to be seen, thank goodness, and neither was Pim, though that wasn't unusual. "Is it somebody's birthday?"

"Nope. It's Friday." Mikkah pointed at Ray, who had pulled a couple of guys from Legal into the conversation about the space-laser television show. "All Ray's idea. We have a ton of booze in storage—always getting samples to review, you know? And it was getting to be a problem, I guess, finding space for it all. So Ray said, Why not have a happy hour on Fridays? Give everyone a chance to let their hair down." She glanced at something over Simone's shoulder. "Oh, there's Gene. I need to ask him about sumac. Gene!" Mikkah slipped away, leaving Simone on her own.

Thankfully, Delilah took pity on her and smoothly wrapped up her conversation with the girl from Finance before moving on to Simone. She raised her wineglass in a salute. "Not a bad perk, huh? Why didn't anyone think of this sooner?"

"I guess we were all pretty busy," Simone said with an awkward laugh.

"We're still busy—busier, even." Delilah leaned in close, her voice dropping. "You wouldn't believe the hours Pim has me working. I don't mind the occasional text at five a.m., but lately it's just constant, you know?"

"Geez." Simone wasn't sure what else she could say. She couldn't imagine what it must be like to be at Pim Gladly's beck and call. The woman was eccentric at best, erratic at worst. "That sounds awful," she managed.

"You don't know the half of it." Delilah glanced around as if to make sure no one was listening in. Once she was satisfied their conversation would remain private, she said, "You know those little dogs she has running around all the time? The ones with the AKC names like 'Gladly's Great Romance' and whatnot?"

"Oh yeah," Simone said. She recalled seeing photos of the wire-haired dachshunds in some of Pim's magazine profiles. "They're super cute."

Delilah shook her head. "Not when you're the one responsible for picking up all seven of their poops on their twice-daily walk, they're not."

"Wait. She makes you walk her dogs? Can't she just hire a dog walker to do that?" Simone frowned, wondering when exactly Delilah was supposed to find time in her busy day to handle this on top of everything else.

Delilah made a wide-eyed, frantic hand gesture that meant *Yes! Exactly!* "She keeps saying her usual one is on vacation or something and she can't trust her babies to some stranger. Two months, this has been going on."

"Well, at least you get some fresh air and exercise?" Simone said, wincing even as she said it. "That probably doesn't help, does it?"

Delilah looked at her flatly. "No, it does not." She leaned in closer, holding her wineglass by the rim in her spread fingertips. "And the kicker is: I am allergic as hell. These dogs literally give me hives. I told Pim, 'I'm spending a lot of money on name-brand Claritin these days, and that stuff's not cheap!' And you know what she said?"

Simone's face crumpled. "Is it going to be really bad?"

"She. Asked. Me. For. A. Pill." Her hand slapped the countertop with each word. "She's got hay fever! And if I'm carrying these pills around anyway . . ." Delilah took a long drink of her wine, staring at Simone's horrified face.

"She didn't offer to cover the cost? Or at least let you write it off as a business expense?" she squeaked.

"Nope! Now she just hits me up for allergy medicine every time she sneezes. And I'm still picking up dog shit. I'll tell you what, this job is a scam."

"That's—" Simone couldn't find the words. "Awful." It didn't seem like enough. "Really awful." She supposed she should be counting her lucky stars that she didn't have a boss like that. Sure, Pim was technically everyone's boss, but still. Simone didn't have to pick up dog shit, at least.

"Well, it feels good to vent. Probably shouldn't make it a habit." Delilah sighed. "If people start thinking I'm gossipy, then somehow *I'm* the unprofessional one, you know?"

Something buzzed in the pocket of Delilah's skirt, and she fished out her cell phone with a sigh, staring at the screen. "Duty calls. Apparently Pim still hasn't figured out how to open PDF files." She drained her glass and set it on the counter.

"Good luck," Simone called weakly after her retreating figure. She sighed, realizing she was alone again.

Ray spotted her and slouched over. She'd stripped off her usual flannel shirt, leaving her in just a plain tee. Informal gathering and all, Simone supposed. "Hey, Mona! Can I get you a drink? We've got something for everyone." She gestured to the array of bottles lined up on the island: wines of all colors, liquors like glittering jewels in their fancy bottles, cans and cases of various beers. Simone took it all in, feeling a little overwhelmed.

"I'm not much of a drinker," she confessed. A glass of wine with dinner once every blue moon, a few sips of champagne when the ball dropped on New Year's Eve, and that was about it.

"That's cool," Ray said, not missing a beat. "We've got soda. Or, um, I can mix you up something without alcohol? A little mocktail?" She touched the caps of a few jugs of fruit juices as if sizing them up.

"Simone!" Petey appeared at her side, face flushed and smiling. He was wearing a novelty T-shirt featuring *American Gothic* with the human faces swapped out for Bugs Bunny and Daffy Duck. "Have you tried this yet? Ray made it at home." He lifted the brown beer bottle he held in his hand, plain and unlabeled.

"You made beer?" Simone asked Ray, unable to keep the note of concern from her voice. It sounded dangerous. And slightly illegal.

Ray shrugged, looking weirdly uncomfortable, which was

an unusual look for her. "It's just a hobby. I have a homebrew setup in my kitchen."

"It's so good," Petey gushed. "It's like the best beer I've ever had, and it's *free*. You have to try some."

"Simone isn't much of a drinker," Ray said, but not unkindly. Almost gently, like she understood tact all of a sudden.

"Well," Simone said, not wanting to be left out of the fun entirely, and actually quite curious about what Ray had created, "maybe I could try a tiny bit."

Like the sun breaking through the clouds after a long day of drizzling, Ray's grin lit up the test kitchen. "Yeah?"

"Want a sip of mine?" Petey asked, offering his own bottle.

"Uh—" Simone eyed the mouth of the bottle dubiously.

"Petey, come on, Mona isn't going to drink after you. Here, let me get a fresh one," Ray said, and bounded around the kitchen island to grab a full bottle and a bottle opener.

Simone watched her work the cap off with a practiced flick of the wrist. Had Ray noticed Simone's distaste for sharing food and drink that other people's lips had touched? It made her wonder what else Ray had noticed about her. She looked away at the thought, dropping her gaze to her shoes.

"Here." A paper cup half-filled with a golden, fizzing beer was thrust under her nose. Simone looked up again to find Ray being all sunny in her general direction. "Wasn't sure if you wanted an entire thing, so maybe just try this for now. Plenty more if you decide you like it."

"I'll have the rest if you don't," Petey volunteered.

"Thanks." Simone took the paper cup, raised it in a slight cheers, and took a sip. She so rarely drank, let alone drank beer, but she knew immediately that this beer was unlike any she'd ever had. It was so tart, it made the back of her tongue prickle like gooseflesh. It almost hurt.

Her eyes must have gone very wide in surprise, because Ray rushed to say, "Uh, so the first sip is going to really punch you in the face. Probably should have said that before you tried it."

Simone managed to swallow her mouthful with a gasp. She coughed, feeling very foolish. "What *was* that?"

"It's a sour ale. It can be an acquired taste," Ray said. Her brow furrowed as she watched Simone's face. "Try one more sip. The second one should be better, now that your palate has had some time to adjust."

"Really?" Simone looked into her paper cup. She wondered if maybe this entire thing was just a prank. She wouldn't put it past Ray.

Petey nodded furiously. "Yeah, it's true. Honest, it gets better."

Still, Simone hesitated. After one more beat, Ray reached for the cup. "Or, you know, you don't have to. It's fine if you don't like it."

"No." Simone jerked the cup out of Ray's grasp. "Let me give it another try." She steeled herself, shoulders back and spine straight, and took another tiny sip.

Flavor exploded across her tongue. The sour sensation was now a pleasant tingle on her palate, a serene backdrop for the bitter notes and the sweet ones. "Tastes of cherries," she said once she'd swallowed. "And tamarind."

Ray chewed on her lip, as if awaiting further judgment.

"It's good," Simone finally pronounced. She gestured at the open bottle still dangling from Ray's hand. "Can I have the rest?"

"You really like it?" Ray didn't even try to hide her pleasure. The sun was back out. She grinned broadly, pouring the rest of the bottle into Simone's cup with an unnecessary flourish. "Of course, drink up! Geez, I thought for sure you were going to spit it onto the floor or something."

"Don't be ridiculous." Simone took another sip, rolling the beer around in her mouth. There was something almost tropical in it, too, like mango or passionfruit. There seemed to be something new to discover with every drink she took. "I'd never spit on the floor; you just mopped. I'd spit in the sink."

Petey laughed long and loud at that. Simone wasn't sure why at first, then realized he was taking it as a joke. Ray smiled, and so Simone smiled, too, and soon they were all smiling and laughing together. She felt like she was actually fitting into their little coworker group, strangely enough. The experience was as new and surprising as that first taste of Ray's sour ale. Maybe it was also an acquired taste. She could learn to like it, given time.

"Seriously, though, man, this stuff is so good." Petey downed the last of his bottle and wiped his mouth on his sleeve.

"Is this the only kind you've made? Or have you brewed others?" Simone asked, remembering how polite conversation was supposed to go at parties. People liked to talk about themselves.

"Well," said Ray, "I did an imperial stout a couple months back that was a complete failure, and before that there was just a really simple brown ale, and that was okay, but what I'm really hoping to do is something New England style. You see—" She launched into a very detailed description of her homebrewing setup and the types of beers she'd attempted to make, and how some had failed and why, and what she had learned, and her subsequent successes, and whether she thought she should try her hand at a few saisons or double IPAs, and the merits of each, and what she'd like to try after that. Simone listened and nodded, but not in the way she'd listened and nodded to someone like Chase, who would be rattling on without saying anything of consequence. Her listening and nodding was encouraging, not just a ploy to get through the conversation faster. It was nice, she thought, to see someone so excited about something they loved, and Ray was a very excitable person.

"Man, you sure know your stuff," Petey said once Ray had finished. "I wish we could make a vid o of you just talking about beer. That would be fun."

Simone tilted her head in tentative acknowledgment. Couldn't be any less fun than the videos they were making with her hands and her pans.

Ray just laughed that loud, booming laugh. "Yeah, right. No one would watch that."

"I don't know," Petey mused. "Maybe someone would."

It was just one of those throwaway comments that Simone figured people said, especially when standing around in a group with drinks in hand. She thought nothing of it. The conversation turned to more mundane things, basic New Yorker topics like *Where are you from originally?* or *What neighborhood do you live in and what's the commute like?* She and Petey were New York natives, as it turned out, Brooklyn and Queens, respectively; Ray was from Indiana. Petey still lived in Queens in his family's duplex; Simone told them she lived on the UWS, where she'd roomed with Luna for years; Ray lived north of her in Washington Heights.

"We're practically neighbors," Ray said, even though they were at least a thirty-minute subway ride apart. "You should come by sometime, see my setup." She waggled her now-empty beer bottle in her hand.

"Yeah, maybe sometime," Simone said, just to be polite. That was what coworkers did, wasn't it? Say they should hang out sometime outside of work and then never actually make plans? That was fine, of course. Simone did not have a lot of free time, and she planned to use the bulk of it for catching up on sleep.

She finished her one beer, wished everyone a good weekend, and left the test kitchen feeling like maybe work wasn't so bad for the first time in a long time.

The feeling did not last.

Chapter 10

Less than a week later, Simone was sitting in the test kitchen at her usual early time, getting a head start on writing an article—an updated list of TDC's Recommended Must-Eats in New York. Ray had already clocked in, she knew; her leather apron was missing from its peg, though Simone hadn't yet seen its owner that morning. Must be receiving a delivery downstairs or something, she figured. She was busy trying to find a good synonym for "indulgent" when the door swung open. She was surprised to find Petey, not Ray, sweeping into the room. His eyes were glazed with a faraway look.

"Hey," she called to him as she pecked away at her laptop, "you're here early. I thought we weren't going to start shooting until after lunch."

Petey whirled and looked at her like he hadn't noticed her before that moment. He swiped the unruly fall of black hair out of his eyes and grimaced. "Have you seen it yet?" he asked.

Simone glanced up from her laptop's screen and stopped tapping away at her draft. "Seen what?"

"The video." Petey tugged her laptop out from under her

hands and swung it around to face him. "Here, I'll show you," he said, clicking away.

"Excuse me, I have actual work to do." Simone made a grab for the corner of the laptop's lid, but Petey expertly nudged it out of her reach.

"This *is* actual work. Look." He stabbed his finger at the Return button and swung the laptop around.

Simone frowned. A YouTube video was loading. It appeared, according to the date in the lower corner of the web page, to be one day old. As she watched, the video resolved and began playing.

Ray, of all people, filled the screen.

"Hey there, folks—or just Petey here, I guess I'm just talking to Petey—is that right, Petey? Should I just . . . ? Ahhhh, who's keeping track? We're all friends here." She was gesturing wildly around the test kitchen, wearing the brown leather apron she favored. It favored her, too, Simone thought.

Shaking her head, Simone concentrated. The video jumped ahead to show a series of jars and canisters lined up on one of the kitchen islands that served as workstations for the chefs. Ray was pointing at each in turn and babbling on and on.

"—so this one, you see here? This one is about one week old. You know how long brewmasters have been brewing, Petey? Oh, well, I don't know either. Yeah, back in the old country, you know, like Germany or whatever, or maybe it wasn't called Germany yet, but somewhere around there. Austria?" Ray looked up into the camera, an innocent look of surprise on her face. "Oh, we're making beer by the way. Did I say that yet? Let me do it again—"

But instead of letting her do it again, the video cut to a silly bit of animated text dancing and bubbling across the screen: Brew It Up with Ray Lyton! A tinny theme song played, jangling out a funky rhythm.

"What the heck?" Simone squinted. "This is ridiculous."

"I know," Petey said. "It was a joke. Just watch."

The video continued with Ray showing the camera—all while addressing Petey constantly and increasingly informally— her collection of homebrew projects. There were jugs of stout as dark as tar, IPAs the color of caramel, and sours made bright pink with fruit extracts. As Simone watched, Ray swung between showing off the jugs by holding them up to the light like a proud parent and explaining the process of fermentation in what could only be described as completely incorrect terms.

"That is not how yeast works!" Simone cried as she watched Ray stumble through the lesson, laughing all the while.

Petey shushed her.

The tiny video version of Ray stared straight into the camera and smiled. To Simone, she seemed to be larger than life, despite the small screen, like every particle of her outsized grin was filling the rectangle above the player buttons and overflowing to fill the whole room.

"So, what you're going to want to do is add the malt now. That's what's going to make it an IPA and not a stout or a lager or a pilsner, okay? I'm adding more malt than I would if I was making one of those; that's going to get the sugars up and you'll end up with a nice . . . you know." She threw her hands in the air. "A nice IPA! That's what we're making!"

A helpful cartoon graphic appeared at the corner of the screen waving a sign that said: *For an IPA, the ABV (alcohol by volume) should be between 6-8%.* Simone squinted. The cartoon was actually a crude drawing of Ray wearing chef's whites. If she'd been holding a pencil, Simone knew she would've snapped it in half. Ray was not a chef, even the cartoon version of her. She shouldn't be wearing those.

"Another thing that's going to give us an IPA," the Ray in the video continued, "is this." She opened a huge mason jar and showed the camera the dusty-looking vegetable matter inside, shaking it so the pieces bounced around. "You got to hop heavily. Lots of hops. Get that bitterness up, you know what I mean? That nice hoppy tang that a good IPA has. Listen, some are fruity hops, and if you like that, all right, but these are—what do you call 'em?" She stared off into the distance. Cricket-chirp sound effects filled the video's silence. Then Ray seemed to come back alive and the noise stopped. "New England style! That's the style we're doing. You can get these hops online."

From behind the camera, Petey's voice emerged, much to Simone's disbelief. "Where did you buy yours? Can you say the website?"

"Are you *talking*?" Simone cried. Petey shushed her again.

On the screen, Ray's grin became half-sheepish, half-feral. "Nah, I didn't go to a website. I've got a guy."

"A guy?" Petey asked.

"Yeah, my hops guy. I'm saying other people, the people at home, they can go online." Ray made a shooing motion at the camera lens. "Leave my guy alone. He's my guy, not yours. Get your own guy. All right, where was I? Oh, right, f—ing hops!"

The bleep was long and loud over the expletive. It was horrifying.

"She's all over the place," Simone murmured. Her gaze fell to the playback bar under the video, and her eyes widened. The video was over twenty minutes long and they weren't even halfway through. "Jesus, you let her ramble for that long?"

"Oh, I let her ramble much longer," Petey said. "This is edited way, way down. If you can believe it."

The volume of the video rose as Ray got more excited. She held up another jug. "Also, this is an ale, so the yeast should not be lagering yeast unless you're trying something really wacky." She stopped, her eyes going wide. "Ooooh, Petey, you know what we should try?"

Unable to take any more, Simone pressed pause. Ray froze on the screen with her mouth half-open and her eyes mid-blink in a very unflattering pose.

"This is everything we're *not* supposed to do," Simone said, whirling in her chair to face Petey. "It's loud, it's long, it's not done in an expert tone. It's definitely not hands and pans—she's speaking to you, for god's sake! You're having a *conversation*!"

"Yep," said Petey.

Simone flailed a hand at the screen. "None of the stages are prepped. There's no finesse, no expertise. It's like watching an unruly child jump from one piece of playground equipment to another!"

"That is true."

"And she cursed! She said the F-word, Petey! That's the worst one there is! Well, except—" Simone bit her tongue. This was a place of business, after all.

"You're absolutely right," Petey said. "We did everything wrong."

Simone relaxed a bit; at least Petey agreed with her. Then she squinted at her laptop screen and tensed all over again. Was that the TDC logo? "Petey? Why does the little icon look like the one on our official channel?"

"Um." Petey dragged his flop of hair out of his eyes once more. "Okay, so the thing is—"

Simone felt the blood drain from her face. "What happened?"

"I kind of accidentally uploaded it to the wrong place," Petey said in a rush. "I thought it was funny, so I was going to put it on my private channel and share it with some friends, but I made a mistake. It was late; I was tired. I didn't notice until this morning."

"You *what*? You have to take it down right now!" Simone began clicking frantically around the web page, trying to figure out where the Delete Video button might be. "Here, how do we do that? Quick, before Ms. Gladly finds out."

"She's . . . already seen it," Petey said. "I just came from her office."

"Oh my god! Petey, *no*." Simone felt her pulse racing. They were going to get fired. Ray and Petey would be thrown out on the street for this mistake. No more fun Friday happy hours. No more leather apron. No more anything.

"There's more. Look." Petey grabbed the attached mouse from under Simone's hand and used it to scroll down, then highlight something on the page. "You see?"

Simone looked at the number Petey's cursor had encased in blue. She blinked. She shut her eyes for several seconds, then looked again.

"Two point two million," she said under her breath. "As in, *views*?"

"Yes," Petey sighed. "Those are views. There's actually more; it takes some time for the system to update when the numbers are climbing so fast."

Simone stared at the laptop, then at Petey, then at the laptop again. This was a dream—it had to be. It was too bizarre to be real. "How is that possible?"

"I don't know! It must have gone viral overnight."

"But *why*?" Simone scrolled down the page in a frenzy. "Look at all these comments. There's so many." She squinted at the words on the screen. "Hold on. These are . . . nice."

"Yeah," Petey said, shifting from foot to foot. "They are, mostly. I was going to delete the video right away once I noticed my mistake this morning, but I wasn't sure if I should once I saw all that. It's the only video of ours that anyone's watching."

Simone scanned through comment after comment. The same sentiments kept popping up again and again.

This made my day!

Hilarious. Are there more like this?

Makes me want to have a beer lol

Is it just me or is this the hottest thing you've ever seen

Love home brew!!!

Love u ray

"Wow," said Simone. "Okay." The random person on the internet calling Ray hot was . . . something. It almost made Simone want to reach through the screen and demand an explanation. Super rational. Simone shook the thought from her head and concentrated on reading all the glowing comments. "This is really unbelievable."

Once in a while a petty comment from some know-it-all popped up, or something downright incoherent, but for the most part, it was just an endless stream of positivity. She turned to Petey. "Who else has seen this? Here at work, I mean. Obviously not . . . total. Because I know it's a lot." She gestured at the video's page.

"Well, Ms. Gladly has seen it for sure, like I said. Her assistant pulled me into her office to speak with her when I got in this morning."

"What did she say?"

"Delilah? Well, she was nice, but pretty firm. She said to go straight into the executive office and—"

"No, not Delilah! *Pim!*"

"Oh. Uh, she asked me what had happened. I told her the truth, that it was an accident."

"And?"

"And"—Petey sighed—"she got really quiet and said 'All right.' And that was it. I was dismissed. Uh, from the room. Not sure about whether I'm dismissed from my job yet. She didn't say."

Simone thought for a moment. "Where's Ray? Does she know?"

"Oh yeah." Petey pursed his lips. "Ray was next in line when I left Ms. Gladly's office."

Oh god. Simone couldn't even imagine the meeting of those two minds. Not to mention—"Has Chase . . . ?"

Before Petey could answer, the door to the test kitchen burst open hard enough to hit the wall. Chase stalked in, red in the face, his hair uncombed and hanging in his eyes. Simone noticed a wrinkle in his normally pristine vintage tee. Today's model featured the phrase *Welcome to Shenandoah National Park* with a little pine tree done in '70s burnt oranges.

"What the *hell* is this?" he barked, holding up his phone to show Ray's video playing at full volume.

Simone wasn't paying him any attention, though, because the door behind Chase swung open again to reveal Ray, looking even more dazed than Petey had, if such a thing was possible.

"Ray!" Simone left her stool and rushed over, ignoring Chase's indignant squawk as she brushed past him. "I saw the video. Petey explained what happened. What did Ms. Gladly say?"

"Well," Ray said slowly, "she didn't fire me."

"Dude, that's awesome!" Petey clapped Ray on the shoulder. "I guess this means we're good?"

"You are *so far* from good!" Chase roared. "This is a complete fuckup! We are trying to cultivate a *brand* here, not post stupid shit for laughs. From now on, Francis, all final cuts will be approved by me before you're allowed to upload. And *you!*" He turned on Ray with a snarl. "You're banned from all my video shoots. I don't want you in the room—I don't want you in the *building* when we're recording. You are not to go anywhere near a camera while the little red light is on. Do you understand, Rachel?"

Simone opened her mouth to say he really needed to calm down, but Ray beat her to it.

"You'll need to take that up with the chief," said Ray, "because she just ordered five more episodes of my show."

Chase stared. Simone could see an even deeper flush creeping up his corded neck and into his cheeks. Beside her, Petey made a small noise reminiscent of the *Ooooooh*s elementary school kids would make when someone had been properly dissed.

"*Your* show?" Chase demanded.

"Well, me and Petey's," she amended. "And Pim may have mentioned something about an executive producer credit for herself, but it was sort of a blur."

Simone watched with glee in her heart as Chase turned several shades of reddish purple before storming out of the test kitchen, presumably to have a word with their editor in chief.

She looked wildly to Petey and Ray, who both seemed to be sweating and panting like they'd run a marathon. Pim had that effect on people, she knew.

"Wow. So . . ." she said.

"So." Petey nodded to Ray.

"So." Ray pulled the ever-present ballpoint pen from its perch between her ear and her baseball cap. "Guess we should get to work."

Petey produced a small notebook from his back pocket and together, the two hunched over a kitchen island to start jotting down lists.

"Okay, so what's the next one? Maybe you brew something new from start to finish."

"Yeah, that's good. I've also got more projects I didn't bring in the first time. We can go over those, so that's one more video down. Hey, what about a tasting?"

"Oh, we could knock that out in an afternoon! Hey, do you think they'd give us enough money to rent a van? We could visit some breweries and sample theirs."

"God, that would be cool. Oh, and how about—?"

Simone left the intrepid duo to their brainstorming, slipping out of the kitchen and then heading back to her desk with a smile on her face. It was nice to see Chase get his comeuppance, not to mention how amazing it was to see what might be a real hit land in their laps. TDC might actually pull through after all, if Ray's luck held.

The whole thing was super weird, and Simone still didn't understand how such a silly video had gotten so popular, but if it let Simone off the hook from making more YouTube content, she didn't care. She only hoped Ray and Petey kept it up.

Chapter 11

They did keep it up. Better than anyone could have imagined, actually.

Working like racehorses, Ray and Petey managed to get their next video uploaded within the week. Views skyrocketed, subscriptions for the video channel climbed. There was even a small but distinct bump in subscriptions for *The Discerning Chef* magazine. Editorial was relieved. Finance was overjoyed. Payroll was practically doing backflips.

For his part, Chase slunk around the office, barking orders and working poor Petey to the bone to keep up with the official production schedule. Simone noticed the dark circles under Petey's eyes, and Ray wasn't looking fresh as a daisy every morning either.

"Hey, are you two at least getting paid for all this extra work?" she asked when she came into the test kitchen one afternoon to find them in the middle of filming another segment.

"Uh." Ray turned to stare at Petey. "I don't think so. Are we?"

Petey gave a shrug. "I think this is considered within my contract's scope, so . . . no?" But the topic was quickly forgotten. "We're losing the light here, Ray. Can we run through that last part one more time?"

"Yeah, sure." And Ray jumped into an extremely suspect explanation of malt like it was her job. Which, Simone supposed, it kind of was now.

Three million views. Four and a half. Six, then seven. The numbers just kept growing.

One of the new episodes trended on Twitter, whatever that meant. Simone only knew it was a big deal. Luna even texted the link to her with the message ??? Is this your crush? GIRL followed by a string of flame and heart emojis.

Simone texted back: Not my crush. And ignored the SureJan.gif Luna sent in reply.

Then a meeting was called.

This was, in Simone's experience, usually a bad sign. Meetings at TDC tended to be grim affairs, with Finance announcing cost-cutting measures or HR outlining newer, smaller benefits packages. Simone felt her dread morph into panic when she opened the meeting invite (which was unhelpfully titled "Staff Meeting") and saw that Pim Gladly herself would be attending.

She scanned the rest of the invitee list. It was basically everyone in the company, including Chase McDonald and Petey. All of Editorial would be there, plus the heads of other departments. But one name was conspicuously missing.

"Where's Ray?" Simone muttered as she thumbed down the screen. She read through the list again just to be sure. Yes, it looked like, for whatever reason, Ray was not going to be in the sprawling, mysterious staff meeting. Simone wondered what that could possibly mean. She checked the time and realized she didn't have any to spare these thoughts. She hustled toward Pim Gladly's rarely used personal conference room.

People were already gathering when Simone arrived, and, what with the size of the meeting, most of the seats were already taken. Simone chose to stand along the back wall with a few guys from Sales. She didn't know them but offered an awkward smile as they claimed their spots.

"Any idea what this is about?" she whispered to the one closest to her.

"No clue," he said. "Maybe we're finally getting sold."

Simone took a shaky breath. She hated not knowing things. It made her blood pressure go haywire.

Pim arrived, flanked by Delilah and a few finance people, and the murmur of the crowd in the conference room died down. Their leader took her spot at the head of the table, glancing to her right, where—of course—Chase had taken his seat.

You could hear a pin drop. Simone almost wished Ray could be there, if only to cut the horrible silence with a joke or an easy laugh.

At last, Pim Gladly spoke.

"So," she said, and looked over the top of her reading glasses at Chase, "it appears that every bit of advice you've given us, Mr. McDonald, every single shred of it, has proved the opposite of useful."

Simone's eyebrows winged up in surprise. This wasn't a staff meeting. It was a public execution. She should have made popcorn.

"Well, actually, I wouldn't characterize it like that," Chase protested, leaning forward.

Gladly consulted a sheet of paper in her hand. "I hold here the memo you shared with our editorial team when you were first brought onboard, your so-called six-pronged plan. 'Content should be uniform and branded across the channel,' it says here. Mr. Zhang?" She turned toward Petey, who had found a chair far, far down the table. "Would you characterize any of the videos produced by Ms. Lyton and yourself as uniform or branded?"

Why not ask Ray that question? was Simone's thought, and she was glad to see she wasn't the only one thinking it. Sweet, naive Gene spoke up from the other side of the table and said, "I can go grab Ray if you like, Ms. Gladly."

"Thank you, but that is unnecessary at this juncture. I would prefer to keep this conversation to our video team for the moment, as well as anyone who touches the project in an official capacity." Pim pinned Petey with her steely glare again. "Your answer, Mr. Zhang?"

Petey, sweat visible on his brow, now began showing red splotches on his neck. "Not really, no. They're not uniform or branded, not really."

"Hm, thank you. Moving on." Her gaze swung back to the paper. "Mr. McDonald then writes that 'Videos should remain short and sweet. The goal is to keep the majority of videos under the four-minute mark. Studies have repeatedly shown that this is the optimal amount of time for the consumer to—' Right, well, Mr. Zhang, how long would you say the average video starring our Ms. Lyton is?"

"I—I would need to check to be sure—"

"Ballpark, Mr. Zhang."

Petey hesitated. "Probably something like twenty, twenty-five minutes?"

"I see. Although the video that currently holds the title of most-viewed on our channel, called"—Gladly lifted a hand so Delilah could deposit another sheet of paper into it, then glanced at the printout there—"'Home Brewer Tries Ten Different Ales for Lunch,' clocks in at just a little under forty-nine minutes, is that correct?"

"Yes," Petey choked out, "but in our defense, we shot that on our lunch break."

"The Brew It Up videos are flukes," Chase broke in. "A few of them went viral, sure, but it's staying power that matters. I keep trying to explain the long tail to you! Smart content, filling the SEO gaps, upping engagement, that's what's really important."

"Ray is not a fluke," Simone found herself saying with more force than she'd planned. All eyes seemed to shift to her in consternation. Except maybe Petey's, which were wide and oddly hopeful. "Ray isn't a fluke," she repeated, softer this time. She hadn't planned to put in her two cents in this weird meeting, but it was too late to back down now. "I hate to admit it, but whatever Ray is doing is working." She waved a hand at all the pages spread before Pim Gladly detailing the latest channel stats. "Call me crazy, but if people are responding and our numbers keep going up, shouldn't we just . . . let Ray be Ray?"

"Like on *West Wing*," Petey whispered. "Let Bartlet be Bartlet."

Simone frowned across the room at him. "What? No, like in the real world. The one where Ray seems to be the only person here who knows what to do in front of the damn camera—pardon my French, Ms. Gladly," she said in one long breath.

Gladly eyed her from her place at the head of the long, sleek table. Somewhere in the room, a clock was ticking, though Simone didn't dare look for it. She stood under the terrible scrutiny of Pim Gladly's stare and waited for the verdict.

"Well." Gladly sighed. She tossed her hands in the air. "In for a penny and all that."

Simone let out the breath she'd been holding.

"But," Gladly said, raising a finger in the air, "I have some thoughts on how to best utilize our golden goose."

"Good point! We need to nurture Ray, make sure we're optimizing these new videos," Chase said, all smiles, like he had agreed to this from the beginning instead of fighting every step of the way. Simone looked at him with disgust. He sure knew which way the wind was blowing.

Pim Gladly glanced over at him as if he were an annoying gnat that had somehow been allowed into her conference room. "I was actually talking about using Ms. Lyton to train the rest of our video talent." Her eyes fastened now on Simone. "Beginning with you, I think, Ms. Larkspur. You could learn a lot from our breakout star, don't you agree?"

Simone's mouth dropped open. "Ma'am, I don't know if Ray's—uh—particular style would necessarily translate— That is, these videos are so unique—"

Gladly clapped her hands. "So it's settled! You two will work on developing a new video series as co-presenters. Some of Ms. Lyton's shine is sure to rub off on you. This can only be a success."

Simone felt as if her culinary soul were leaving her body. This could only be a *disaster*. Ray, training her? Being put in charge of Simone's videos and, by extension, her entire career? She felt like she was going to throw up.

Chase jumped in again. "I can have a few concepts worked out by next week. Talking off the dome here, but we can frame it as maybe a competition, the two of them versus each other on a weekly challenge. Competitive cooking is so hot, SEO-wise."

Gladly turned slowly to Chase, like his continued presence was a shock. "Actually, Mr. McDonald," she said, "I believe we should leave the ladies to develop the concept on their own. Ms. Larkspur is correct; we must give more creative control to the people who have proven that they can use it the most effectively." Her gaze narrowed at him pointedly. "You will, of course, assist in the production and offer technical advice and direction, but let's limit your involvement to more of the back-end for now, hm?"

Petey spoke up, though his voice was thready. "Um—maybe this is a good time to invest in our video production staff? I'm just one person; I can't keep up at this rate. Can we hire people to handle sound, lighting, that sort of thing? Maybe get more than one camera and a crew to operate them?"

"Ah. A sensible plan, finally." Pim Gladly turned to the head of HR and waved an imperious hand. "See to it, will you?"

Simone watched as Petey gave a small fist pump under the table. Well, at least someone was celebrating.

"Ms. Gladly," she tried again, "maybe Ray can teach me how to be a better presenter, but do we really need to work on a show together? Ray is not a trained chef, whereas I—"

Out of the corner of her eye, she could see Petey and Gene mouthing along with the words as she said them.

"—studied at Le Cordon Bleu."

"Won't that be an interesting contrast?" Gladly said airily. "Use that energy, my dear. I just know you'll come up with something wonderful."

The meeting ended, and so, too, did Simone's carefully ordered life.

Chapter 12

"So I have an idea." Ray pulled a pen from her leather apron's pocket and began tapping it rhythmically on the counter-top. "I think it'll be pretty funny."

"I don't *want* to be funny," Simone said with a bite in her voice. They were sitting in the test kitchen, trying to hold a meeting between grocery deliveries and visits from the oven re-pairman. Ray had taken the news about being basically put in charge of the video project all in stride, though Simone was still sore about it. "I want to be *informative*. I want people to actu-ally learn something. Entertainment is all well and good, but if someone can't learn to cook by watching me—"

"All right, okay, let me rephrase: the videos will be funny. I will look like an idiot, for the most part. You will look like the capable, badass chef that you are. Plus, it will be educational. How does that sound?"

Simone's eyes narrowed at Ray in distrust. "What do you mean, you'll look like an idiot? Why would you want to do that?"

"Trust me." Ray showed all her slightly imperfect teeth when she grinned. "It'll be worth it. Here's how it would go."

She stuck her pen under her ball cap, balanced on the curve of her ear, and gestured with both hands. "I'll bring in some food; I'll either make it here or bring it from home, I guess, and whatever it is will be a recipe from my mom's recipe box from, like, the eighties or nineties, right? Really grim. All the stuff I grew up with in the Midwest. Canned and boxed ingredients, lots of Jell-O, things that would probably be murder on your sensitive and professional palate."

"Okay . . ." Simone said slowly.

"Then you and I will taste them—"

"Oh, so you're trying to kill me?"

"Just hold on! So we'll taste them, and you'll be grossed out, and so will I, probably, but I will still try to defend the sort of essence of what I liked about it as a kid. Then comes the part where you get to show off." Ray planted her palms on the kitchen island, her eyes gleaming. "You see where I'm going with this?"

Simone frowned, but then her lips parted in realization. "I make it better?"

Ray slapped her hands against the counter and pointed at Simone. "You make it better! You redo the old recipe to make it modern and tasty and fresh and all the stuff you're good at doing."

The excitement was infectious. Despite how unfair the whole situation was, Simone could feel the creative itch at the back of her brain. "It wouldn't necessarily be about cooking the new dish with fresh ingredients, though I guess that could be part of it. I could take the old flavors you like and make something totally new with them." She thought about the wide range of possibilities. "Oh, wow, we could do some really cool stuff."

"And here's the kicker, to make it more interesting," Ray said. "You won't know what the dish is until I bring it in. Big reveal! You'll invent the new recipe on the fly."

"Oh." That brought Simone up short. "Won't that just make things more difficult?" Old worries swamped her. She didn't like the idea of possibly failing on camera and looking stupid in front of all of Ray's fans. "Maybe we should plan ahead, if only to make sure I have all the ingredients I need to make a new dish. I don't want to be hamstrung or anything."

Ray waved away this idea with the flap of a hand. "That can be part of the show, you and me figuring out how to rework things with what we have on hand, just like real people do at home. And don't worry; I'll make sure we've got at least the original components in stock. I'm the kitchen manager, remember? I'll handle the groceries."

Simone made a face, still unsure. "It sounds like there's still a lot of potential for me to look bad on camera."

"You won't. You're going to rock this," Ray promised, smiling. "So? What do you think? Should we give it a try?"

Simone sighed. Ray's smile grew. And somehow, the video appeared on the shooting schedule for the very next day.

Simone found herself at loose ends in the test kitchen right beforehand. Petey must have worked overtime to assemble a team like this so quickly. There was actual professional lighting and a boom mic and not one but two cameras positioned in front of her workstation, and the new film crew was buzzing around like the busiest of bees. There were so many new faces in the kitchen: Amir, the sound guy; Bridgette on Camera 1; Lin, who oversaw lighting; and Jake on Camera 2, and they all had a lot to do.

Meanwhile, Simone had nothing to do but worry.

"Ray, hey." She caught sight of her new cohost—how weird did that sound?—and beckoned her over before she could disappear into the walk-in. "Can we go over the game plan again? Rehearse our lines or whatever?"

Ray gave her a funny look. "There's no script, Mona. We're just going to go with the flow. A walk in the park, right?"

Have you met me? Simone fiddled with the collar of her blouse, trying and failing to get it to lay correctly underneath her apron bib. "I'm just worried that if we don't practice, I won't know what to say when it comes to the, uh, gross recipe."

"Who are you calling gross?" Ray reached over and, before Simone could protest, fixed her collar perfectly. "That's my Mee-Maw you're dissing."

"I'm not trying to diss anyone," Simone sputtered, frowning down at her collar. How come clothes never seemed to behave for her, but Ray could corral them without any issues? She gestured to the battered metal box with little roses and daffodils painted on it that Ray had brought in. "Is there a way I can talk about the Lyton family recipes without sounding like a jerk?"

"No, I think you need to drag Mee-Maw and Gram-Gram some more." Ray smiled and leaned her hip against the edge of the counter, arms crossed over her chest. "That would really establish your character."

"I'm not playing a character! I'm trying to—"

Ray looked over toward the crew, an amused tilt to her lips. Simone followed her gaze and saw Petey standing behind Camera 1, red light and all.

"Petey, are you filming this?" she screeched.

"Don't mind me," said Petey, flashing her a thumbs-up. "This'll make a good cold open. Keep going."

"Oh my god," Simone groaned into her hands. This whole thing was already a disaster. May as well hang up the apron and go back to being a sous chef at some hotel tearoom, Simone thought miserably.

"Hey." Ray scooted closer and nudged her hip against Simone's. "We're going to have fun, okay? Forget about the cameras—"

"Uh, please don't," Jake piped up. "You need to actually look into them."

"Fine. Forget about the *audience*," Ray said with a roll of her eyes. "Don't worry about who's going to watch this later or how the video will perform. It's just you and me talking, okay?"

"Okay," Simone repeated. It was hard not to look at Ray's relaxed posture and easygoing grin and not feel a tiny bit less stressed. She ran a hand through her hair and nodded. "Okay. Just talking. Let's do it."

Bridgette told them exactly where to stand, which was closer than Simone would have thought was necessary, but she went where she was directed, her shoulder brushing Ray's arm. The lights were so bright, but she took a deep breath and tried not to squint.

"All right." Petey's head popped up from behind the camera. "Action."

Simone stood up straighter and tried to figure out just how much eye contact was needed for the camera, but Ray had no such qualms, launching in like she'd been doing this for decades.

"Welcome to the first episode of Recipe Revamp, hopefully the first of many," Ray said, leaning over the kitchen island. "We're here to take the kind of food I used to eat as a kid, all the recipes I've got here"—Ray grabbed the little recipe box and gave it a shake—"in my mom's old collection, and Simone here is going to, uh—tell us what you're going to do, Simone."

Don't be awkward, don't be awkward. "I am going to take the bare bones of the vintage recipe, so to speak," she said crisply, "and transform it into something a little more—" She tried to think of a palatable word.

"Edible?" Ray laughed like a donkey.

Simone tossed her a pained look. "I was going to say modern."

"Right." Ray turned to address the camera. "So Simone is one of the recipe developers here at The Discerning Chef, makes a real mean pastry. I mean, if you could taste some of her food, folks." She laid a hand over her heart and closed her eyes. "It is so good. So fucking good."

Simone, not knowing where to put her hands or how to take the compliment, touched the countertop, then put her hands to her hips, then finally let her arms dangle at her sides. "Uh, thanks. Can we say fucking?"

"Don't worry," Petey piped up from behind the camera. "I'll bleep that part out."

"But." Ray's eyes popped open. "Simone here does have a

tendency to make things, let's say, a little bit fancy?" She focused her wide grin in Simone's direction.

"Or," Simone hurried to correct her, "you could say, a little more updated? Mature?" She stared up at the ceiling and stifled another groan. "We're making it sound like I'm a real pill, you guys."

"No, no, no, all I'm saying is that some of this food"—Ray picked up the old recipe box and shook it, making a small maraca sound—"is not great. Objectively. Let's be honest, growing up in the eighties and nineties, it was a dark time, food-wise!"

Now this was a topic Simone could speak to. She faced the camera. "A lot of ingredients that we take for granted in the supermarket today weren't available to the average person, that's for sure. In certain parts of the country, like small towns in the Midwest, for example"—she nodded at Ray, who pointed at herself with both thumbs—"they just didn't have access to certain ingredients, and even if they did, most home cooks didn't have the know-how or the time to use them properly. So, starting in the postwar years and into the decades when we were growing up, you'll see lots of family recipes from that era clipped from advertisements. That's because there was a rise in convenience products putting out recipes that people like your mom and grandmas relied on to feed their families. And there's nothing wrong with that!"

"But." Ray held up one finger.

"But," Simone said, a smile tentatively forming on her face, "maybe today we can do better." She clapped her hands together. "Okay, Ray. What did you bring in?"

"Petey, can you—? Yeah, in the lower fridge over there."

Petey abandoned his post behind the camera for a moment to dig through a lowboy, eventually emerging with a large Tupperware that had RAY'S PROJECT TOP SECRET scrawled on the lid in permanent marker. Simone watched as the container was deposited on her workstation with all the fanfare Ray's hands could muster.

"Oh, I cannot wait to show you this," Ray said, peeling away the lid.

Simone peered inside the Tupperware and tried very hard not to look too disgusted. "Okay. Uh, what is that? It looks like mush."

Ray tipped the container to show the camera the pounds and pounds of soft orange-and-white goo.

"This," Ray said, "is Yankee salad."

"We're calling that a *salad*?"

"Yes! It's a Lyton family classic," Ray protested. "On a hot day, a picnic or a barbeque, whatever, you see Aunt Fern pulling out a big old Tupperware of this?" Ray hugged the container to her chest. "Oh, man, you know you're in for a treat."

Simone pried the container out of Ray's grasp. "You know you're in for a ton of sugar, you mean. Seriously, what is this stuff?" She grabbed a tasting spoon from an apron pocket and poked around in the goo. "It looks so . . . lumpy."

"The lumps are part of its charm," Ray said. "Okay, ingredient list! You've got your cottage cheese, your Cool Whip—and it's got to be Cool Whip—one can of mandarin oranges, one can of pineapple pieces, and one packet of orange Jell-O powder."

A look of horror came over Simone's face. She was powerless to hide it.

Ray continued, "And then you just mix it all together in a big bowl and voila! Chilled orange, fruity, fluffy . . . thing."

"Okay." Simone took a deep breath to try and regain some of her composure. "And you eat this as a dessert?"

"Well, more like a side dish."

Simone sputtered. This was really too much for her to take.

"What? You never had something like this at cookouts with your family?" Ray asked. "Maybe called it ambrosia? With the little marshmallows?"

"I grew up in an apartment. I never had a backyard," Simone said, "so not a lot of opportunities for cookouts. Or marshmallow salads, my god."

"Oh." Ray shrugged. "Well, different strokes for different folks. Want to try some?" She nudged the container closer to Simone. "You need to get a sense of what Yankee salad is all about before you try to turn it into something restaurant-worthy."

Simone glanced helplessly at the camera. There was no getting around it. She pulled out another tasting spoon and handed it to Ray. Her own was clutched in her hand in grim determination.

They dug in.

Ray ate a huge heaping spoonful, her shoulders immediately wiggling in happiness. Simone took a much smaller bite and made a valiant effort not to grimace. It had been a very long time since she'd eaten this much processed food. The fruit definitely had a weird metallic aftertaste. She swallowed.

"Well, it's certainly sweet," she said. "And wet." *Think of something nice to say!* "I can see why little kids might enjoy this on a hot day."

"I still do. Is that trashy of me?" Ray licked her spoon clean, her eyes not leaving Simone's.

"No, no, it's fine." Simone felt her face heat. So this was why Ray's videos were so popular; it was impossible to be the focus of all that distilled charm and not feel a connection. Surely Ray's audience, all those people who left nice comments on the brewing videos, had experienced what Simone was now feeling: like Ray was someone you could easily spend hours with. Which, Simone realized, she was. "I mean, it's . . ." Simone trailed off, losing her train of thought.

Ray laughed. "You can say it! It's a little one-note."

Right. The food. Focus. "It's all one texture: soft, soft, soft. That, we can change for sure." Simone took another tiny spoonful and chewed thoughtfully. "The flavor isn't bad. It's a little fake-tasting with the Jell-O and the Cool Whip, but pineapple and orange is a good, classic combo. We can use that."

"So what do you think?" Ray ate another huge bite. "How

can we bring my aunt Fern's Yankee salad into the twenty-first century?"

Simone tapped her spoon against her lips. "So what's really grabbing me is the fact that the base of this is essentially cottage cheese. There's this German-style cheesecake that's made with cottage cheese instead of cream cheese. Mikkah taught me how to make it last year. It's really light and creamy, and I'm wondering if we can add orange and pineapple to that and make a Yankee salad–flavored cheesecake." She looked to Ray. "How does that sound?"

"Uh, *amazing*," Ray said. "Where should we start?"

The rest of the shoot involved Simone building her recipe off the cuff with Ray there to learn, ask questions, and help stir things. The traditional graham cracker crust was replaced with a sweet shortcrust pastry base, since, Simone pointed out, the cinnamon would clash with the tropical fruit flavors. The filling got a little orange zest and juice where normally Simone would use lemon. She dithered over how to incorporate the pineapple, not wanting to just toss in bits.

"I want the pineapple to have a really robust flavor. We're using canned pineapple like your recipe does since we don't have a ripe pineapple in the walk-in, but I don't want that tinned aftertaste," she said, staring at the Dole can in her hand.

"Can we concentrate it somehow?" Ray asked. Simone could tell from the look in her eye that this was a leading question to which Ray already knew the answer.

A surge of gratitude worked its way through Simone. It was like she was taking a test and knew all the answers backward and forward. It was actually kind of fun.

"Pineapple jam," Simone said, snapping her fingers. "We'll make our own jam and swirl it in. Cook out that processed taste."

"Maybe even throw in some orange juice so the pineapple doesn't overshadow it?" Ray suggested.

"Maybe. Or!" Simone gasped in delight. "I can make some

candied peel to garnish. Different textures! That's just what we need." She turned back to her cutting board to start cutting some peel away from the fresh oranges. "Candying peel looks really fancy and difficult, but it's actually super simple. You just need time," she said, knowing she was chattering away but not really caring.

Ray leaned over the counter to watch her work, chin propped up on her fists. "Admit it," she said.

Simone looked up from her cutting board, knife poised over a length of orange rind. "Admit what?" Her voice went high and tight.

"You're having fun," Ray said, a wide grin appearing on her lips. "This is like a trip to Disneyland for you."

Simone's mouth worked, trying to find the right words. It was true, she was enjoying herself. But she was starting to wonder if it was the work or the company that was making this dreaded task so much fun. She glanced up at Ray, at her sparkling green eyes and goofy smile, and decided this was neither the time nor the place to consider such questions.

"I admit nothing," she said at last, cutting the peel into strips as thin as dental floss. This was a show. This was all for show. "I'm just trying to improve the world, one Aunt Fern recipe at a time."

"Hey, let's get a close-up of Simone chopping?" Petey called, and Simone had to cover the jolt she felt at remembering that there were other people around, and it wasn't just her and Ray hanging out.

The crew took a break to give the candied peel plenty of time to set, and Petey ordered a small truckload of empanadas for their lunch. Simone tried to pitch in some money to help cover the food when it arrived, but Petey wouldn't hear of it, gently shoving her fistful of cash away.

"It's our first episode," he said. "It's a celebration."

"Yeah." Bridgette spoke with her mouth full, then swallowed. "Can't wait to see how it all turns out."

Simone watched Ray shove almost an entire empanada into her mouth. They were sitting shoulder to shoulder at the workstation, space being at a premium what with all the video equipment. This close, Ray smelled pretty good, especially for someone who'd been under the brightest lights in the universe for hours. Kind of woodsy.

Simone picked at the flaky edge of her pernil and pea. "Do you, uh." She swallowed; why was her voice so scratchy? Probably a symptom of talking to the camera all morning. "How do you think it's going?"

Ray held up a hand and covered her mouth with the other, chewing for a very long time. Simone waited. She waited so long she actually felt the urge to laugh.

"Why don't you take smaller bites like a normal person?" she asked, delighted by Ray's still-working jaw.

Ray finally swallowed the mouthful. "How am I supposed to restrain myself when it tastes this good? Here." She held out the remaining nub of the empanada. "You've got to try it. It's ham and cheese, but better."

Simone stared at the bit of offered food. Normally she wouldn't do something as unhygienic as eating a piece of food that someone else's mouth had touched, but . . .

She looked back up at Ray.

Screw it. It was a celebration, after all.

She took the piece of empanada, popping it in her mouth. Her eyes flew wide as she chewed. "Mmm!" She covered her mouth with her hand, not wanting to be rude.

"Right?" Ray laughed. "It's so good. Can I have a bite of yours?"

Simone found it impossible to say no.

After lunch, shooting resumed, and by the end of the day, they had a beautiful cheesecake filled with homemade pineapple jam and topped with little nests of candied orange peel set on a glossy rotating cake stand. Simone sliced into it, nervous about the reveal.

"I hope it turned out okay," she told Ray and the camera. "Obviously I've never made this before."

Petey let out a low whistle as Simone lifted the slice away from the cake stand. "Looks good from here," he said.

Simone gave the first piece to Ray, who nearly fell to the floor in rapture after taking a bite. "My knees!" she cried, really hamming it up. "Seriously, they've gone out right from under me. Mona, this is too good!"

Simone beamed as Ray demolished the whole plate. She took a bite of her own slice and contemplated the taste of it. "Maybe I could have added more vanilla to get that Cool Whip flavor to stand out more, but yeah. I think this is a pretty decent update to your family's 'salad.'" She used her fork for half of the air quotes.

"I don't see how it could be better," Ray enthused. "The orange, the pineapple, the creaminess, all the stuff I like about the original is there. But then you've got the crunch of that crust and the candied peel—I'd never seen that done before, that was really cool. And it tastes like real food!"

"It *is* real food," Simone said, eating another bite.

"We've got to get everyone in here to try this. Everyone!" Ray called, and the folks waiting in the wings—out of frame against the wall—appeared to accept their portions. The girl from Finance, Gene, Mikkah—even Petey got a slice. There was a chorus of praise, Ray the loudest among them.

Simone looked around wildly at the video crew. "So is that it?" she asked.

"Yeah, cut, print, cue theme song," Petey said, smashing his fork into the bits of crust that had nearly escaped him. "We got what we need."

The video went up the very next week, sleekly edited with cute graphics and a bubbly title sequence. Simone considered not watching it, but in the end, she couldn't help herself. She waited until the test kitchen cleared out at the end of a long day and watched the entire thing from start to finish.

It was weird, watching herself on screen. She looked different, sounded different. Not bad, just . . . strange. Especially when she looked at Ray. Simone clicked pause on the video, stopping it just before it ended. The miniature version of herself on the screen was staring up at Ray, and Ray was looking back, and they were sharing a whole host of emotions that ran the gamut from delight to relief. Simone still felt that. And maybe felt something more.

Total current views: 6.2 million.

"Fuck," she said into the quiet of the empty, dark test kitchen.

Chapter 13

Friday rolled around, and with it, the Friday afternoon happy hour. Simone walked into the test kitchen and headed straight for the row of liquor bottles Ray had arranged on one of the islands. She acknowledged the greetings from the small gathering of coworkers with barely a nod.

Ray hefted a wine crate onto the counter beside her. "Oh, hey, Mona, you're here a little early. Usually, you don't make an appearance until after we've all had a few."

Simone grunted and claimed a bottle of gin, not even bothering to look at the label to check the provenance. Desperate times and all.

Ray watched her fill a glass with ice from a bucket in swift, jerky motions. "Wow, going for the hard stuff, huh? Everything okay?"

"I was supposed to bake brioche today," Simone said, sloshing a hefty measure of gin into the glass and groping for the bottle of tonic water amongst the mixers.

"Yeah?" Ray pressed.

"I love baking brioche." Simone added the barest touch of tonic to her glass, then reached for the little platter of sliced garnishes Ray had set out. "I love that it's a pastry that acts like bread, or a bread that wants to be pastry. I love the eggs. I love the butter. I love the color and the smell."

"Brioche is tasty," Ray agreed, then gestured to Simone's beleaguered cocktail. "Hey, want me to mix you something? You're kind of lead-footing it there."

Simone wasn't listening. She was too busy squeezing about seven wedges of lime into her glass. "I have not baked any brioche today. Not a single loaf. Not a crumb. And do you know why?"

"Uh." Ray watched as she took a deep swig of her drink. "I have a feeling you're going to tell me."

Simone made a face at the gin's burn, wiped her mouth on one of the paper napkins Ray had arranged in a caterer's fan on the side table, then said, "I was too busy fielding congratulations and emails and meeting requests from every department, not to mention how much time I spent refreshing that stupid video page and reading all the new comments."

"Oh, Mona," Ray sighed, "you should never read the comments. It's not good for you."

"I know!" Simone took another gulp of her drink. "But I can't stop doing it! It's the exact opposite of what I need—" She caught Ray's eye and looked away swiftly. "And it's certainly not what I want, but I can't seem to keep myself from thinking about it. All the time." She stared out the window and sipped her drink.

Ray reached for a bottle of beer with a handwritten label that said RAY'S HOUSE PORTER and uncapped it with a bottle opener clipped to her apron strap. "Were they saying really mean things?"

"Hm?" Simone startled. "What, the comments? Uh." She thought back to the last one she'd read before slamming her laptop shut and stalking into the test kitchen.

My favorite part is when Ray says something cute and you can see Simone's brain stop working for like .002 seconds as she tries to process it lmao they are so in love!

"Some of them weren't very nice," Simone hedged.

Ray shrugged. "This is why I don't read that stuff. Once Petey tells me we're done filming, that's it. I don't even watch it once it's posted. Best to just keep moving on, you know?" She took a swig of her beer.

"Yeah." Simone shook her head. "I know. I should really stop." She took another drink, thinking of all the comments that had popped up on her Instagram that morning. Some people were calling the two of them Raymone, like they were a couple. Or a crime-fighting duo. It wasn't really clear.

Ray looked like she wanted to say more, but Gene pulled her into a conversation about noodles and starchy water, and all Simone got was a little beer-bottle salute before being left to her own devices. She looked into her glass and realized it was empty. One more wouldn't hurt, she thought, and poured herself another drink. That one also disappeared quickly, so she poured one more. It had been a long week, after all.

Simone usually looked down on people who tried to escape reality through the judicious application of alcohol; it was unhealthy, of course, but also unbecoming of a grown adult. There was something almost childish about drinking to forget, such a complete cliché, and normally she would look askance at such a plan. Which was why it was important to point out that Simone didn't plan to get drunk—it just happened.

Probably should have had something to eat, she thought hazily when the floor started rocking like the deck of a ship. Had she even had lunch? The day had been so busy, she must have missed it, which was unlike her.

Well, she was doing a whole lot of things lately that were unlike her—speaking out of turn in high-level meetings, starring in popular videos, posting daily to her Instagram account (and obsessively reading all the comments), pretending not to have a huge crush on Ray . . .

Ugh. What a disaster.

She took a seat on one of the high kitchen stools near the

wall and decided to stay there until the rocking sensation passed. It didn't.

"Hey, great job with that salad mess," said someone from Sales whose name might have been Mike. He clapped her on the shoulder before moving on, much to Simone's relief.

A few other people approached to congratulate her on the new hit video series. Simone managed to smile and nod her way through the brief interactions with what she hoped wasn't too ungainly a performance. Her whole face felt like it was on fire; it was always a dead giveaway when she drank, which was why she never did it.

Never say never, I guess. She caught sight of Ray across the room, chatting away with the new video crew. It was strange, having a real crew. Like a professional show or something.

Lin, the woman with a petite nose ring in charge of lighting, said something that made Ray throw her head back and laugh that obnoxious laugh. It was loud enough to startle a few people who were deep in conversation all the way across the room. Ray didn't even notice, just kept chattering away and gesturing wildly about whatever the crew was discussing. Simone hid her smile with another sip of her drink. Ridiculous. Just ridiculous.

Gene came over to her encampment by the wall and talked with her for a bit about how he hadn't had a day off in almost a year, and maybe now that Simone's videos were a success, they could all afford to relax a little. Simone wasn't sure if she was included in this hypothetical relaxing. All she knew was that Gene noticed her empty glass and gallantly got her another drink, which Simone couldn't figure out a way to refuse. She planned to just sip at it a little, just for show, but that didn't help her situation at all.

Gene drifted away at some point, and Simone thought it was a good time for her to make a quiet exit, but when she tried to plant her feet on the floor, the whole world swayed to one side, and she had to catch herself against the wall to keep from keeling over.

Okay. So she was drunk. No need to panic.

She slid back onto her stool and thought hard.

She would just . . . stay here. On this seat. Until everybody else left. Then she wouldn't make a fool of herself if she tripped or fell down on her way out. Simple.

Simone glanced at her phone. How late did people usually stay during these happy hours? She prayed her coworkers had lives outside of work—plans for the weekend, dinner reservations. Surely they would all have to leave soon.

Or she could just live on this stool for the rest of her days. Simone contemplated this option seriously. It was a fine stool, not too hard, and from her spot against the wall she had a view out the window into the little park across the street. She watched the pigeons scuttle around the fountain, looking for crumbs. *Not a bad place to spend eternity*, she reasoned. And it was better than making an even bigger spectacle of herself in front of her coworkers after the week that she'd had.

"Mona?"

Simone whirled away from the window, nearly unseating herself in the process. She only managed to keep from tipping over by reaching down and gripping the leg of the stool in one hand, her gin and tonic sloshing in the other. Ray was standing there before her, a look of concern in those bright green eyes.

"You okay? You've been hanging out here in the corner by yourself for a while now."

"I'm fine!" Simone said, carefully enunciating her words to avoid slurring. "I'm just . . . admiring the view." She waved her glass at the window.

Ray grabbed a stool from one of the islands and dragged it over. "Mind if I join you?"

"Um." Simone cast about frantically for some excuse. "Actually, I should be going soon."

"Yeah?" Ray cocked her head and took a seat next to Simone, beer bottle dangling from one hand. "Big plans tonight?"

"Oh, yes," Simone lied. "The biggest."

Ray stared in polite silence until Simone realized she was expected to share the details of her fictional plans.

"Well." She fiddled with her glass. "If you must know, I have two tickets to a show."

"Cool. Who are you going with?" Ray asked.

"My roommate, Luna," Simone said. It was easy to come up with that name when Luna was really the only person Simone did fun things with on a regular basis.

"Oh? And what are you going to see?" Ray asked.

Simone's sluggish brain went on the fritz. She tried to remember the names of any shows that were currently on Broadway, but the only one she could come up with was sold out for about six months in advance, and if she named that one, it would just make Ray ask more questions. "Uh . . ." Her eyes darted away. "*Cats*? Is that still running?"

"Simone." Ray leaned forward, eyes lit up in delight. "Are you . . . drunk?"

Simone made a noise that sounded somewhat like a stand mixer on high speed. "Only a little."

"I thought you didn't drink. At least—not to excess. You barely finish one beer, usually."

"These are extenuating circumstances," Simone said, or at least tried to. Her tongue tripped on "extenuating" and it came out a bit garbled. She tried again, and failed again, so she decided to return to sipping her drink.

"Are we celebrating?" Ray leaned against the wall, draping over the stool in a long, lanky jumble of limbs that Simone would have preferred to see walking away instead of getting comfortable. "Petey tells me the views on our new video are pretty good."

"They're *excellent*," Simone said with acid in her voice, dampened only by the slight slur. She swirled her melting ice in her cocktail glass. "I achieved exactly what I wanted. I can look forward to years and years of not baking brioche because making these videos is my life now. Hooray for me."

"Oh, you're *that* kind of drunk," Ray said. "Morose."

"I'm not m'roast." Simone closed her eyes, swaying a bit on her stool. Her stomach sloshed uncomfortably.

Ray's warm hands caught her by the shoulders before she could tip onto the floor. Simone looked up to see Ray was no longer smiling.

"Okay. I think we should get you home," she said.

"Noooo." Simone's gaze drifted to the center of the test kitchen, where a dozen or so TDC employees were still having drinks and chatting. "I can't leave my stool. I have to live on this stool forever."

Somehow, Ray seemed to understand. Her voice dropped to a whisper. "No one will notice, I promise. Here, if you put your arm around me—" She stood and manipulated Simone's arm for her like she was a living doll. "And we'll walk out of here all buddy-buddy, all right? Totally normal."

Simone let herself be guided to her feet, clutching at Ray's waist and feeling like her face was on fire. "This is embarrassing," she whined.

"Not as embarrassing as falling flat on your face in front of the entire staff. Come on, walk with me. Three-legged-race style, that's it." Ray laid an arm around Simone's shoulders, feigning casual contact when it was actually keeping Simone steady.

Simone wasn't brave enough to look up from the floor. "Is anyone watching?"

Ray's head swiveled. "Uh, Gene is waving goodbye. Bye, Gene! Have a good weekend!" Her hand left Simone's shoulder for just the moment it took to return the wave, then it was back. She leaned in close to Simone's ear. "Now laugh like I said something funny."

Simone gave a weak chuckle as they walked together across the kitchen and out the door. Once they were in the safe haven of the deserted hall, Simone let out a breath—and her knees gave out entirely.

"Whoa!" Ray caught her again, this time under her arms. "Took a lot out of you, huh?"

Tears rose to Simone's eyes. She was pretty sure her red-hot blush could be seen from space. It was bad enough realizing that she maybe, possibly, incongruously liked Ray as more than a coworker; did she really have to act like such a massive idiot in front of her, too?

"Please let me go," she said, mortified at how wobbly her voice sounded. "I'm fine, really, I don't need your help." She tried to regain her feet and proved herself a liar, slumping back into Ray's hold with a choked sob.

"That's debatable," Ray said diplomatically, "but maybe you *want* a little help? Wouldn't that make it easier?"

"Nothing about this is easy!" Simone shot back, defiant even with her red, wet eyes and all. She dropped her gaze before she could parse out the look on Ray's face. If it was pity, she didn't want to see it. "I'm so stupid," she muttered. "I—I should know better than to—" She swallowed and stopped herself from saying what she wanted to say. "Drink so much," she said instead.

"Listen." Ray's hands—so warm—found her shoulders again. "We've all been there. So you had a few too many; so what? It happens. As long as you get home safe, that's what matters."

Simone stared at her sensible, ugly chef's clogs and tried to blink back her tears. "You don't think any less of me?" she asked in a small voice.

"Are you kidding?" Ray threw back her head and laughed, that loud bray echoing through the hallway. "Mona, if you knew how many times I got wasted and barfed into gross trash cans on the platforms of the New York City subway system—"

Simone felt her gorge rise. "Maybe we could talk about that some other time," she said quickly.

"Right. Sorry. Come on, let's get going." Ray rearranged Simone back under her strong arm, guiding Simone's arm back to her waist, and together they made it to Simone's desk to grab her tote bag, then to the coat closet for their winter jackets, then to the elevator and out into the street.

Chapter 14

I take the C train uptown," Simone said, squinting into the distance at the station on the corner. She swayed toward it, but Ray held her firmly in check.

"Why don't we take a cab instead? It'll be faster," Ray said, and flagged one down with a loud, fingers-in-mouth whistle before Simone could protest.

"Ow." Simone rubbed at her ear. "Did you have to do it like that?"

"Sorry." Ray opened the taxi door and bundled her into the back seat, crawling in behind her. "I just don't believe in my ability to keep you upright in a crowded rush-hour train." Then, to the cab driver giving them the hard stare in the rearview mirror, "Hey, man, we're going to— Uh, Simone, what's your address?"

"Why're you coming with me?" Simone said. She was vaguely aware that she was still sniffling. "You don't have to come with me. I'm not a little kid." The back seat seemed nice and flat, and Simone was so tired. In her mind, this was as good a place as any to lie down.

"Is she okay?" the driver asked.

"She'll be fine!" Ray propped her back up. "Mona, come on. I'm not going to leave you all alone now."

"Because if she's going to throw up—" the driver said.

"She won't. Plus, she's got this." Ray held up Simone's oversized TDC tote bag. "I swear, nothing will get on the upholstery."

"I have to throw up in my *bag*?" Simone cried. "All my stuff is in that bag."

"You're not going to throw up! It's just my backup plan," Ray said. Her hand came to Simone's hot cheek and patted it a couple of times. Simone's watery eyes made the tortuous journey to meet Ray's gaze. She wondered if both Ray and the driver could hear her thudding heartbeat. "Now can you tell this gentleman where you live, please?"

Because she had grown up in New York and could direct a cabbie in her sleep, Simone rattled off her address including cross streets, and the driver at last pulled away from the curb.

New York taxicabs are murder on even the most stalwart of stomachs, and Simone usually felt queasy in them on the best of days. But the indignity of vomiting into her own bag like some nineteen-year-old club hopper—in front of Ray, no less—could not be borne. She simply would not do it. She closed her eyes and willed her body to keep everything on the inside. *Good advice,* she thought, and hoped other organs might follow suit, especially her dumb little heart.

"Doing okay?" Ray's voice was quiet. Her hand rested on Simone's, where it clutched at the black leather of the seat cushion. It took all of Simone's considerable self-control not to turn her palm over and thread her fingers through Ray's. *Such a nice hand,* she thought muzzily. All warm and wide and rough from hard work. A really good hand. It fit Ray nicely.

Simone tried to concentrate. She'd been asked a question and she needed to answer. "Sometimes I get carsick, riding in back seats," she said, surprising herself with her honesty.

"Jesus Christ." Ray's head thumped against the headrest. "You couldn't have mentioned that earlier?"

"*I* wanted to take the subway! It—" The cab hit a pothole, and Simone clamped her mouth shut, praying that she wouldn't get sick.

Ray's hand squeezed hers. "We'll be there before you know it. We're already at Union Square," Ray said. Then, a few minutes later, "There's the Flatiron. Making great time." For the rest of the cab ride, every few blocks, Ray would whisper the landmark or street number to Simone, letting her know their progress. It was weirdly comforting, as was the weight of Ray's palm.

Before Simone knew what was happening, she was snuggled against Ray's neck, hiding her face there and listening to the rumble of the traffic and Ray's steady voice. She might have even drifted off into something like sleep, because she missed everything between 42nd Street and Columbus Circle, coming to only when Ray said, "All right, we're here." The taxi came to an inelegant stop.

Simone didn't want to move, but she had to. She sat up and rubbed at her tired eyes, then noticed that Ray had levered her hips off the back seat to reach into her back pocket.

"Oh no," Simone said, "put away your wallet. I should pay for this. It's my fault, anyway." She dug through her tote bag, looking for her little coin purse where she kept her cash. She tried to remember how much money she had and hoped it would be enough; taxis were a luxury she could rarely afford on her salary.

"Don't worry about it. My treat." Ray pushed a handful of bills through the plastic divider's window. "Keep the change. One of those days, you know?"

The driver made a noncommittal noise, and then Simone was being pulled from the back seat and onto the pavement outside her building. She made a production of pawing through her bag for her keys, leaning against the decorative wrought-iron gate for balance.

"Okay, you escorted me home," she muttered. "Thank you. I'm good. You can go now."

"I'll make sure you get inside in one piece before I leave, how about that?" Ray plucked the keys from her slow hand and offered Simone an arm. "M'lady."

Simone scoffed, but took Ray's arm. She was still feeling pretty woozy, after all. Best to let the more sober person handle the lock and the front door.

The stairs were not fun—living on the top floor in a building without an elevator never was—but Simone climbed them slowly and steadily, refusing to even consider Ray's repeated offers to carry her.

"I'm just saying, we'd get there a lot quicker," Ray said, holding Simone around the waist as they navigated the third-floor landing.

"We'd both fall down the stairs and break our necks," Simone retorted. "I'm too heavy."

"I don't know; I'm pretty strong. I think I could manage."

Simone groaned. "Don't tell me how much you bench, please. I'm really not interested."

"Oh, you've made that super clear, Mona." It should have been a joke, but the way Ray said it—was it just Simone's imagination, or did Ray sound bitter?

Simone paused in the middle of the staircase, breathing hard, chest heaving. "I didn't mean . . ." She trailed off, clutching at the banister. And at the front of Ray's shirt. So Ray remembered the email Simone had sent the first day they'd met. Just colleagues, nothing more, that's what she'd said.

How could Simone go back on that now?

Ray's shoulder nudged hers. "It's fine. Just joking," she said, though Simone couldn't see how this was at all funny. "Come on, we're almost there. What's your apartment number?"

Somehow, they made it to Simone's front door, and Ray managed her key ring to unlock all three locks. Simone leaned into Ray's side with her eyes shut tight, praying that Luna was out and there would be one less witness to her drunken stupor.

"Hey, lady!" came Luna's usual holler through the apartment. "What's the good news?"

Simone stayed silent as Ray walked her through the narrow entry hall and into the living area. Luna tumbled out of her tree pose at the sight.

"Oh!" She looked at Ray, then at Simone, then at Ray again. "We have a guest?" Her eyes climbed Ray's great height. "And *what* a guest." She offered her hand, palm down, like Ray was supposed to kiss it. "I'm Luna. A pleasure."

"Hi, I'm Ray. I work with Simone at TDC." Ray shrugged, still supporting Simone. "Sorry, I can't shake hands. Simone isn't feeling well, so I thought I should make sure she got home okay."

"Oh!" Luna's hand retracted and instead splayed on her breastbone. "Simone, honey, what's the matter? Is it that flu that's been going around? Here, let me hang up your coat." She tugged Simone's winter jacket off and hung it on their coat rack.

Simone studiously refused to meet Luna's eyes. "I guess so."

"Uh, which room . . . ?" Ray broke in, and Luna rushed to show them the way to Simone's bedroom, playing the gracious host.

Simone knew her room was nothing special. Her furniture was cheap and sparse, her decor bordering on spartan. Besides the framed photograph of her and Luna at a New Year's party (a gift from Luna), and a tiny potted succulent that thankfully needed almost no care (a gift from her mom), there was nothing in the room to tie it to anyone in particular. It was the smaller of the two bedrooms in their apartment, which Simone thought was only fair since she didn't own as many clothes as Luna and therefore did not need the space for clothing racks or shoe caddies. Now, its smallness seemed very unfair—Ray filled it up to its brim so that there was nowhere to retreat. Simone gave a helpless moan as she was lowered to her crisply made bed. It was insult added to injury, the thought that Ray was seeing her room like this. If she had known Ray was coming, she could have tidied up a bit or rearranged some things.

"It's not usually this messy," she said, pushing her face into her pillows. "M'sorry."

"Messy? What the hell are you talking about?" Ray tugged at Simone's shoes and dropped them to the floor, two heavy thumps. "This place is pristine."

Simone sat up, face flaming. "Then what do you call *that*?" she cried and pointed an accusing finger at some unopened mail on her nightstand that she'd been meaning to sort through.

Ray blinked at the neat pile. "Wow. You're right. Your life is full of chaos. How do you live this way."

"You're making fun of me," Simone said, burrowing back into a pillow.

"It's just so easy, is the thing." Ray gave her a pat on the back before standing. "Stay there a minute. I'll be right back."

Simone listened to the sounds of Ray moving through the apartment, the quiet murmur of voices—must be talking to Luna. Simone's heart sank as she pictured it. If Luna hadn't already figured it out, she was sure to know by now that Simone was drunk as a skunk. The soft sound of twin laughter—Ray's deep chuckle and Luna's high, sparkling giggle—floated across the apartment. Simone curled into a tight ball. She wished she could disappear, just melt through the bed and go underground where no one would be able to laugh at her for being such a lightweight.

A soft thump and a click came from the direction of the nightstand, and Simone turned her head in time to see Ray placing a glass of ice water and a bottle of aspirin there. In the dim light of the bedroom, Ray looked so different. Daytime Ray didn't look half as worried, or as capable, or as gentle.

"Try and get some fluids in you, okay?" Ray said, doing that thing with her eyes that Simone figured could only be pity. "Do you want anything to eat? I could make you an egg-and-cheese sandwich or something. Diner food: good for hangovers."

Simone's stomach roiled at the thought. "No," she moaned into her pillow. "No food."

"Ever?" Ray's smile was watery. "That's going to be an issue, given our career paths."

A tear rolled from Simone's eye and dripped down the bridge of her nose. She sniffled, trying to stop it, but the crying was back in full force, it seemed. She hid her face in her pillow again and hoped Ray had the decency to ignore it.

Ray, of course, was not decent.

"Hey." There was that soft voice again, the one usually reserved for skittish forest creatures. "It's okay. Don't worry, it's fine."

"No, it's not," Simone whimpered. "God, I'm so stupid."

"You're not stupid. You had a bad day, and you got a little tipsy." Ray's warm hand touched her arm, a comforting weight. "I don't think any less of you for it, if that's what you're worried about."

"Yes, you do," Simone protested. "I definitely think less of myself, so you probably should, too."

"I don't. Simone, I—I think the world of you. Four gin and tonics and a bumpy cab ride isn't going to change that."

Simone sniffed. "It might have been five. I lost track."

Ray gave a low whistle. "Yeah, you need to drink some water, stat. Come on." She nudged at Simone's arm. "Sit up."

Simone followed orders, muzzily aware of how horrid her hair must look, all mussed and hanging in wisps around her face. She swiped some dark strands from her eyes and accepted the water glass. Ray had even brought one of Luna's metal drinking straws. Simone chased it with her lips until she caught it, then drank sullenly. The water tasted sweet on her sandpapery tongue.

Ray watched her as closely as one watched caramel coming together in a hot pan. "Finish that whole glass if you can, okay? And these are for when you wake up." She gave the aspirin bottle a jaunty shake. "Feel better. I'll see you Monday."

Simone let the straw slip from her open mouth as she watched Ray stand. "You're leaving?"

"Well, yeah." Ray lifted her cap and scratched at her scalp before resetting it. "I've got my own place to get back to."

"No plans?" Simone asked, curious.

"Well, I was supposed to meet up with a friend after work," Ray checked her phone, "but looks like that ship has sailed."

Because of me, Simone thought. "Sorry."

"No big deal. Kelsey will understand."

The part of Simone's brain that was still functioning was only doing so in the most basic sense of the word. All it understood was that Ray was here, in Simone's room, very near her bed, and that Simone didn't want that to change.

"Oh, here, let me straighten that out for you," Ray said, leaning over Simone.

Simone froze, not understanding what was happening at first and only slowly realizing that Ray was trying to rearrange the pillows that had gotten squashed against the headboard.

Ray tugged at the pillow that was caught under Simone's shoulder. "Can you lift up a little?"

Simone cursed inwardly. She raised her head a few scant inches, just enough to allow Ray to fluff up the pillows. It was also enough to bring their faces close together. Like, really close. Ray was completely preoccupied with her task, but Simone had nothing better to do than notice all the details of Ray's face that she never had the chance to see normally. There were little crinkles at the corner of her eyes, probably from all the smiling. And there was just the faintest mark—Luna would call it a beauty mark—right below Ray's ear on the left side.

And Ray's mouth. It was right there. Simone only watched it for a second, though, before it was saying, "All right, that should do it." Ray gave her a smile, gaze tracking back to hers. "I should be going." She began to pull away.

"You could stay," Simone blurted out. Her hand left the straw, leaving it to spiral against the lip of the glass, and reached out to grasp the cuff of Ray's flannel shirt. It was soft. Of course it was. "Here. If you want."

Ray's look was unreadable. Completely beyond the capacity of Simone's remaining brain cells. "Oh, Mona. I don't think that's a good idea."

That tone of voice made it sound like they were discussing criminal activity. Simone frowned. She just wanted Ray to stay. Here, in her room. In her bed, maybe. Oh. Her eyes flew wide. *Oh.* "I—I didn't mean—" she stammered. "That is—"

"You've had a lot to drink," Ray said, all patience. Simone felt about an inch tall. "You're just—just saying things. Stuff you don't mean."

Simone swallowed. Let go of Ray's shirt. Stared into her glass of water and told herself not to start crying again. How pathetic could she get? Like Ray was going to be swayed by a puffy red face and a clumsy offer to—what? Hang out and babysit a sloshed little loser? And now Ray was assuming this was all a really ill-advised proposition for sex, which Simone couldn't really say it wasn't, because how else could it be taken?

She set her water back on the nightstand with a click, then rolled over and pulled the covers over her head. Looked like she'd be sleeping in her clothes, because she was certainly not moving now.

"Okay," Ray said. God, this was awkward. In the darkness under the covers, Simone squeezed her eyes shut and let a few more tears fall in silence. "Keep drinking water. You'll feel better in the morning." A few footfalls. The light snapping off. Ray's quiet voice saying, "Good night, Simone," before the door shut with a creak.

"Night," Simone mumbled, unheard beneath her mountain of covers.

She was convinced she'd never get to sleep, what with her mind going a mile a minute, rehashing every mortifying moment of the last few hours. But even her legendary anxiety was no match for gin, and Simone was pulled into sleep faster than she thought possible.

She dreamed, which was unusual for her. In her dream, she was standing in the lobby of the apartment building where she'd grown up, complete with the old art deco mosaic flaking on the wall and the birdcage-style elevator that only worked half the time. Simone knew rationally that this building didn't exist anymore, that it had been torn down years ago to make way for shiny, soaring chrome condos with a bank and a Rag & Bone on the ground floor, but in the context of the dream, it made perfect sense that she was there.

She used to live on the sixth floor, the very top—no neighbors stomping above you, her dad had always said as a point of pride. Simone walked up to the elevator's gleaming gold lattice doors and pressed the call button. Nothing happened.

"It's broken," a familiar voice said from behind her. "Do you want me to fix it?"

Simone turned and saw Ray standing there, looking exactly as she had when she'd tucked Simone into bed: soft flannel shirt, soft eyes, soft smile.

"I don't think you can," she said, because even in her dreams Simone tried to be rational. "It's always been like this. And anyway . . ." She looked around the old lobby, which felt somehow bigger and smaller than it used to. "I don't live here anymore."

Simone blinked and suddenly she was at work, standing in the test kitchen, and Ray was there with her. Sure, of course; this was home, or at least the place where she spent most of her time. Same thing, right? Also, Simone was naked, which made less sense, but her dream-self wasn't actually concerned about the potential workplace harassment lawsuit. For once, she wasn't worried about much at all. She was too busy clinging to Ray's shoulders, because Ray was suddenly very close and those shoulders were so sturdy.

"Hey, you're not naked," Simone said, digging her fingers

into the soft flannel of Ray's shirt. That was unfair. This was a naked kind of dream.

Dream-Ray shrugged. "I guess you respect me too much."

Before Simone could parse the implications of that, she felt herself being lifted by those strong arms and deposited atop her stainless-steel workstation. Since this was a dream, she didn't make a fuss about sanitation. She could do as she pleased, and what pleased her was getting Ray closer. She buried a hand in Ray's wild curls and pulled her into a messy kiss.

It felt so good to be touched, even if it wasn't real. It felt real, in that moment. Simone could taste the cedar tang of Ray's mouth, could feel the brush of flannel on her skin. Her legs wrapped around Ray's narrow waist, rubbing against rough denim. In a move that seemed very true-to-life, Ray removed her baseball cap and set it aside on the counter, never once letting up from the kiss. Simone supposed that was all the undressing that Ray was going to do. Damn her paltry imagination.

Ray broke away from her mouth, panting. Her lips were beet-juice red and her eyes were sparkling with mischievous intent. "You know what I bet you'd like?" she said, and sank to her knees between Simone's spread legs.

Simone rethought her stance on her imagination. It seemed to be working just fine, actually. It certainly wasn't being stingy with the details. She could feel Ray kissing a line up the soft inside of her thigh, could feel warm breath over her skin, and definitely felt the first touch of Ray's tongue. She arched back on the cool metal of the countertop and made a thready noise of want as Ray licked over her, into her. Her hands reached for Ray's head but then stopped and hovered midair. Simone didn't want to be too needy, but then she remembered that this was her dream and she could do whatever she wanted. And what she wanted was to yank on Ray's hair until that smug face was buried between her legs. So she did.

Even in the fuzzy confines of a dream, Simone had the presence of mind to look down the heaving length of her body to see what effect this had on Ray. She found Ray staring back at her, eyes dancing with delight. Not breaking eye contact, Ray pressed the tip of that hard-working tongue right underneath her clit and gave it a playful flick. Simone cursed fluently and tossed her head back, not caring how desperate she looked, legs shaking where they were propped on Ray's capable shoulders, her hair a loose mess, her hand tightening in Ray's hair until—

Until she woke up with a jolt. Like a sweaty, hungover idiot.

Simone picked her head up off the pillow and blinked in the early morning light filtering through her curtains. Slowly, memories of the night before came to her in pieces. As did the memory of her dream.

Really? *Really?* Simone flopped onto her back and sighed. She hadn't even gotten to finish. Which was the least of her worries. Not that having a sexy dream about a coworker necessarily meant anything! Dreams were weird; she'd once dreamt that she was a goat herder at her old elementary school. It didn't mean she wanted to quit her job to raise goats, for Christ's sake. She had probably just had a dream about Ray because they were spending so much time together. It was probably a metaphor for how hard she'd been working lately. Her brain was just trying to tell her she needed a break!

Sure. That made sense. She only wanted Ray to go down on her metaphorically.

"Okay." She scrubbed at her sleep-caked eyes, trying and failing to banish the vision of Ray lavishing her with—attention. "This might be a problem."

Chapter 15

On Monday, Simone arrived at work wearing a pair of oversized sunglasses, bundled up in her best coat like Jackie frickin' O. Physically, she was completely recovered from her alcohol-soaked ordeal. Emotionally, she was still mired in the shame of her drunken misadventure and subsequent X-rated dream. Hence the sunglasses that hid her from the prying eyes of the world, at least a tiny bit.

She was dreading the inevitable moment where she would see Ray again. She invented a dozen reasons to avoid the test kitchen: she needed to sit at her desk and work on punching up the copy on a few articles; she needed a quick meeting with Mikkah to discuss how best to cook farro; she needed to double-check her grocery order for the week; she needed to—

Well, she *wanted* to avoid any more awkwardness. She just didn't think that was an option if she ever wanted to work in the test kitchen again. She pulled the sunglasses off her face with a sigh and tossed them onto her desk, rubbing at her eyes.

"Oh, Lisette," she sighed at the little postcard taped to her cubicle wall, "what would you do in my shoes?"

Lisette did not answer, obviously.

Simone tried not to be too disappointed. "Well, you probably only get drunk in that fun, classy French way," she said, "so you'd never be in my shoes to begin with. But if you were?" She studied the photo of her culinary hero and thought as hard as she could.

In three minutes, she was barreling through the test kitchen door. She caught sight of Ray, leather apron and all, milling around by the sink, sharpening a knife on a whetstone. Simone very bravely ignored the picture she made and definitely did not think about how Ray had starred in an actual sex dream of hers just a few nights ago.

"Hey!" she barked.

Ray's head popped up. That impossible-to-parse look was back. "Oh, hey, Simone. How are you?"

Simone stabbed a finger in Ray's direction. "What kind of cake do you like?"

Ray blinked. "Cake?"

"Yes, cake. You know, flour? Butter? Sugar? Eggs?"

"I know what cake is. You just put me on the spot." Ray put down the knife, which Simone felt was a good sign. "I guess chocolate?"

"Chocolate cake." Simone nodded. "What kind?"

"There's more than one?" At Simone's answering glower, Ray backpedaled. "They're all great, I guess."

"Okay," said Simone. She thought hard, her chin resting on her knuckles. The platonic (sigh) ideal of a chocolate cake that came to her mind was something rich, and dark, and indulgent, and complex. No fruit, no whipped cream, nothing between the taste buds and the flavor of chocolate. There was only one answer: a Brooklyn blackout cake. "Okay," she said again.

She went to her usual workstation and began assembling ingredients. Cocoa powder, bars of bitter dark chocolate, cream, cornstarch, powdered sugar: the pile grew and grew.

Ray approached with more caution than the test kitchen manager would normally display. "Are you . . . making a chocolate cake?"

"Yes," Simone said, her tone clipped. She buttered two cake pans with the ease borne of years of experience.

"Why?"

"For you to eat."

"I hate to look a gift horse in the mouth, but: Why?"

"Because you said it's your favorite."

"I'm going to sound like a broken record here, but—"

Simone stopped tapping her cake pans to distribute the coating of flour. "It's an apology. Do you want it or not?"

"An apology?" Ray's eyebrows went skyward. Simone ignored them and started measuring out sugar. "Mona, you don't have anything to apologize for."

"Sure I do." She readied her pink stand mixer with its paddle attachment and shoved a whole boatload of room-temperature butter into its bowl. "I drank too much, made you pay for a cab, ruined your plans, spouted a lot of nonsense—" She bit her tongue and shrugged. "So. You get cake. That's fair, isn't it?"

She reached for a box of baking soda, but Ray clapped a hand over it, arresting her momentum. Simone looked up at last to find Ray staring at her, eyes hard and serious.

Simone wilted somewhat. "Isn't it?" she said, unsure.

"You don't have to make me a cake," Ray said.

"Would you prefer a pie?"

"No, that's not what I—"

"Doughnuts?"

"Simone, listen—"

"It might take a while, but I can make some Danishes, if that's more your speed," Simone said in a rush.

"Can you stop offering me baked goods for one damn second?" Ray snapped.

Simone shrank back, her hand slipping out from under Ray's to hang uselessly at her side. Her eyes were wide as she stared at Ray. As far as she could remember, Ray never spoke in a raised voice.

"Sorry." Ray sighed, hands held up in a peaceful gesture.

"I'm just trying to talk, and you keep—" A shake of that tousled head, those warm hands perching on narrow hips. "You don't have to bake me an apology; you did nothing wrong. I helped you get home because it was the right thing to do. Friends help each other out. That's the deal. No reward required."

Simone swallowed around the thick lump lodged in her throat. "F-friends?" she asked, quiet.

"Oh." Ray had that hangdog look again. "Sorry. I meant totally professional coworkers. Who interact in only a professional capacity."

"No!" Simone said, far too quickly. "No, I mean, that's okay. Being friends." She ducked her head and concentrated on measuring out a level teaspoon of baking soda. "I don't have a ton, so you might need to refresh my memory: Do friends always rescue friends who are under the influence of juniper-based spirits?"

Ray laughed. "Yep." She held Simone's gaze for just a second before looking away. "And . . . friends understand that friends say all sorts of things they don't mean while plastered." Her eyes tracked back to Simone. "And friends will never bring it up again."

The weight of Ray's stare was as heavy as cast iron. Simone wished there was a way to clarify that when she'd offered Ray a chance to stay that night, it hadn't been tawdry or anything. Unless Ray wanted it to be tawdry, in which case they could discuss that. But they wouldn't. Since there was apparently nothing to discuss. That much was clear from the way Ray was looking at her, as serious as Simone had ever seen.

"That's very decent of friends," she said instead, and looked down into the mixing bowl, still pouring sugar on autopilot.

"Sure is. So, uh." Ray waved a hand at the stand mixer. "You can stop baking now."

Simone thought for a moment, then dumped the rest of the measure of sugar into the mixer's bowl. "I don't *need* to make you an apology cake," she said, "but I'd like to. At least, I'd like to make something. Oooh." Her gaze went dreamy and faraway. "What if, instead of a normal layer cake, I turn it into a trifle?"

Ray did not skip a beat. "I'm pretty sure we have a huge trifle dish in storage. You know, from the eighties? When people still made trifles?"

"Can you please reserve judgment on my trifle until after you taste it?" Simone shooed Ray away with her rubber spatula. "And find me that dish?"

In the end, the non-apology Brooklyn blackout trifle was spectacular. Chocolate was not traditional for a trifle since visible layers were so key to trifle-making, but even as dark as they were, the layers were distinct: slabs of lush chocolate cake infused with a tiny bit of instant coffee and soaked in coffee liqueur; a chocolate custard reminiscent of the blackout cake's traditional filling; a crunchy layer of black sesame brittle broken up into small pieces along with chocolate-covered espresso beans that Simone found in the cupboard; and finally, a layer of whipped chocolate mousse with chocolate curls on top.

"Wow." Ray dug in and didn't stop. "Wow, wow, wow."

"Good?" Simone asked, though she already knew from her own spoonful that it was.

Ray was already dishing out another portion onto her empty plate. "I am so lucky," she said, "that you keep feeding me."

Simone paused with her spoon still in her mouth. It hadn't occurred to her that she'd been feeding Ray fairly regularly, but she supposed between recipe tryouts and stress baking and, of course, making their YouTube show, Ray had been eating a lot of Simone's food over the past few months. It made her feel a little warm, thinking about it.

How annoying.

Petey popped up behind Ray, toting what looked like a shiny new camera. "Hey, is that cake? Can I have some?"

Simone shook herself from her thoughts. "It's a trifle. And of course. There's enough for the whole crew."

Good thing, too, as Lin, Amir, Jake, and Bridgette filed in at that moment. They all reached for plates and forks, the four of them chattering loudly. Simone watched them all and thought back to the time, not long ago at all, that Petey had been a one-man operation. Now that the team had picked up so much of the workload, Petey had become more of a director/editor type as the crew had taken over many of his old tasks, and Simone could see the difference. Not only did Ray's latest video look better, but the atmosphere in the test kitchen had changed. Where Simone used to spend hours and hours alone working on her recipes, the kitchen was now full of people, of chatter, of Ray's honking laugh as Petey relayed a story about a bad blind date he'd had that weekend.

That laugh used to set Simone's teeth on edge. Now she almost . . . liked it? She watched as Ray lent Amir a hand in hauling some equipment into the kitchen. Well, if she and Ray were friends now, it made sense that all of Ray's little quirks didn't seem nearly so awful anymore.

Simone's gaze lingered on Ray's forearms, where her shirt-sleeves were pushed back past her elbows. She probably *could* have carried Simone up those stairs; there was some serious definition there.

That was a totally normal thing to notice about a friend.

Simone helped clear the island to prep for their next Recipe Revamp video and hoped that no one noticed how weird she was acting. It was time to concentrate on work, not Ray's arms. By the time they were ready to start shooting, Simone had forced herself into her professional mode, her face an impassive mask.

Petey was making his final adjustments, calling for quiet on the test kitchen set, when Ray leaned in close and whispered, "You've got something on your face."

"What? Oh, the chocolate?" Simone's fingertips flew to her lips, scrubbing away. "Did I get it?"

"No, it's just—here, let me." Ray's thumb touched her cheek, a light brush against Simone's skin. Calluses, Simone registered faintly. Ray had calluses. She froze as Ray swiped at her cheek very carefully, very gently.

"There." Ray tried to smile, but something in Simone's own face seemed to dampen it. "Sorry, that was probably—"

"No, no." Simone almost smiled herself, but instead ducked her head and held a hand to her flaming cheek. "Thanks for getting that."

"And action," Petey called, and then it was back to work.

For this episode, Ray surprised Simone with something called Rainbow Chicken Salad, a name so inaccurate that Simone nearly had a fit.

"It's not very colorful," she pointed out as they poked their forks into the huge container of cabbage, scallions, a little carrot, diced baked chicken, and—Simone shuddered—uncooked instant ramen noodles that had been crushed into little crouton-like bits, all bathed in a simple vinegar dressing.

"The carrot adds a little," Ray protested. "And listen, at least this time, it's a salad that includes actual vegetables."

Simone ate a bite of the soggy mess and grimaced. "I get that instant ramen is flash-fried before being packaged up, so it's technically precooked," she said, "but why add that in raw?"

"For crunch," Ray said, as if it were completely obvious, and ate another heaping forkful.

They began working on an updated version, with Simone envisioning some properly browned chicken and fresh—cooked—ramen alongside an array of actual rainbow-colored vegetables rolled up in rice paper wrappers.

Normally while they were shooting a video, Gene or Becca would be in the background at the other workstations, quietly going about their business. It was just the nature of how the test kitchen was arranged that Simone's preferred island, the one farthest from the swinging door, was the best for video shoots in terms of light. And the rest of the work of putting out TDC recipes couldn't come to a standstill just for a video, so it made sense to keep the kitchen a working one during shoots. Simone was used to a certain amount of ambient noise behind her as the other chefs worked away at their own dishes.

The moment she heard the door swing open, though, she knew this would not be a usual amount of noise. Chase's fancy designer sneakers always squeaked against the kitchen tile, so she knew without even looking around that their erstwhile social guru had entered. Simone tried to continue on with her patter and ignore the unwanted interruption.

"So what we'll do is just cut these into matchsticks," she said to Ray, "and then it's as simple as—"

Chase appeared at Ray's side and slapped his—thankfully rubber-encased—iPad onto the countertop. "Let's talk about the production schedule heading into the new year," he said.

Ray groaned as the rest of the camera crew cried out in protest.

"Mac, you're in the shot," Petey said from behind Lin. "Get out of there; we're shooting an episode of Revamp."

Chase just rolled his eyes. "Sorry I walked in on your little side project," he said, "but this is important."

Simone tensed, watching Petey and the rest of her team carefully. Chase was still technically the head of the video initiative, but after the weird all-hands meeting where Pim Gladly had dressed him down in front of almost everybody in the company, he had been kind of a persona non grata around the test kitchen. Once in a while he would buzz by Simone's desk, making some inane comments about possible SEO opportunities or pushing her to read some buzzword-ish white papers he'd emailed around, but for the most part, Chase hadn't figured in much of their work. It was almost sad, seeing someone try so desperately to be relevant. Simone wasn't sure how Petey, who was clearly the real force behind their video production these days, would react to this stunt.

"Revamp isn't some little project. It's our number two most-watched series," Petey said, "though Gene's dinner party planning show and Becca's budget recipe series aren't doing too shabby either. Which you'd know if you actually looked at our numbers."

It went without saying what the number one draw on their channel was. Ray, Simone noticed, was staying out of this, leaning against a baking rack to watch the conversation.

Chase gave a scoff and started tapping away at his iPad. "Well, Francis, I have been looking at the numbers. That's why I'm investing my time into trying to improve production on Brew It Up. So, if I could just have a moment to do my job?"

What job? Simone bit her tongue before she could say the words that had collected there. She glanced at Petey, who clearly had even better self-control. He only looked like he was going to put up a fight for a moment, then sighed.

"We should break for lunch, anyway. See you in thirty, everyone."

The crew grumbled as they switched off their equipment and filed out of the kitchen. Simone thought about following them but decided against it. Maybe she was a little nosy, but she wanted to hear what was so important that Chase had to disrupt their shoot.

"I'm going to check the walk-in and see what vegetables we have," she announced to no one in particular, and made a show of puttering back and forth between the huge fridge and her workstation, piling up cucumbers and carrots and daikon radishes and red bell peppers. She only caught snippets of the conversation between Chase and Ray, but what she could hear was (predictably) just Chase talking.

"So for the spring, schedules will be laid out like—"

"And these are the topics I've vetted for the—"

"Sponsorship opportunities are the real moneymakers when you think about it—"

"Because based on our channel demographics, we skew like seventy-five percent female—"

"It's a great idea! Why are you so resistant to expert advice?!"

That made Simone pause in the middle of her extremely inefficient walk-in trips. She carefully placed a handful of fresh mint on her cutting board and said, in a way that she hoped didn't make her sound too interested, "What are you guys talking about?"

Ray glanced over at her, arms crossed in a textbook defensive posture. "Chase was just telling me about some ideas he has for future episodes."

"The girl means *brilliant ideas*," Chase insisted.

"Not your girl," Ray snapped back.

Chase gave Ray a weird look. "Okay. Whatever." He turned to Simone. "Did you know the first recorded instances of beer-making in the historical record were done by women? That it was considered a woman's job up until, like, nowadays?"

"Hm." Simone thought. "No, I did not know that."

Chase gestured at her, turning to Ray. "See? It's interesting! People don't know! That's why you should be doing an episode all about brewing's historical roots. We can even find some modern ladies making beer; you can't be the only one." He whipped out his phone and started typing. "You can interview them or trade recipes or tips or whatever—oooh, look, there's one right over the border in Vermont. She's on Twitter." He pushed his phone into Ray's face. "She's cute. We should get in touch with her."

Simone felt her heart sink for completely unrelated reasons. Probably something she ate.

Ray placed a single fingertip on top of Chase's phone and pushed it down. "I think I'll pass."

"Oh, come on!" Chase exploded. "This makes sense; it's on brand; it gives our channel a little shoutout to diversity—" The way he said it made it sound like a foreign word.

"I *said* I'm not doing it," Ray said, getting into Chase's space now. "You're not the one with creative control here, okay? So why don't you take your little phone and your little tweets and shove them right up your—"

"Hey!" Simone cut in, falsely cheerful and bright. She wedged herself between the two before she knew what she was doing. "Can I borrow Ray for a minute, Chase? I just remembered, we have this meeting—Ray, that meeting? We should really get going." She gave Ray a little nudge. Ray was unmoved, still staring at Chase with a challenge in her eyes. "You two can pick this up tomorrow, maybe." She looked up at Ray pleadingly. She wasn't sure what the issue was, but she was certain Ray shouldn't be talking that way to any coworker, even one as exhausting as Chase. The last thing she wanted was her cohost—her *friend*, she reminded herself—getting reprimanded for blowing up.

"Sure," Chase grated out. He talked a big game, but from the tremor in his voice, Simone could tell he wasn't used to being yelled at. "Tomorrow."

Chapter 16

Simone practically frog-marched Ray out of the test kitchen and into the first safe place she could think of: a conference room that was miraculously empty. Ray went without much resistance, though Simone could feel the tense muscles under her fingers where they were guiding Ray by the arm. Under other circumstances, she might have allowed herself a moment of reflection on said muscles, but Ray's quiet obedience was alarming enough to keep her focused on the task at hand.

"Okay." Simone shut the conference room door and whirled on Ray, arms crossed over her chest. "What the heck is wrong with you? I get that Chase is a jerk and all his ideas are usually terrible, but this one is actually pretty good."

Ray ignored the dozen or so perfectly decent chairs that surrounded the conference room table and instead hopped up to sit atop the console table under the picture window. Staring out at the busy avenue below instead of looking at Simone, Ray said, "Look, I just think there are plenty of other topics we can cover."

"But the history of women in brewing—that's important, Ray!

What's the industry breakdown for brewmasters these days, ninety-nine percent male?" Simone padded over to the window, her clogs muffled on the carpet. "You could show all our viewers that it doesn't have to be that way, that it never used to be that way. You're a direct descendant of those women, and I think that's really cool."

"Yeah." Ray lifted the Mets cap and scratched a hand through messy hair. "Um—the thing is . . . "

Simone waited, but the sentence never continued. She frowned. Ray normally ran her mouth a mile a minute; silence did not become her.

Maybe Simone was getting through. She pressed on. "Think about the whole culinary world, even. Men still dominate. We're lucky to have a platform like this—and run by a woman, too!" She flung a hand in the general direction of Pim Gladly's office. "You should be proud to represent all the ladies in the industry who are working their butts off."

Ray blew a long breath out. "Okay." She turned from the window and looked Simone right in the eye. "The thing is, I'm not a lady."

Simone threw up her hands. "Right, okay, I get it, you're very butch. Not ladylike in the least. But, as a woman, you should really—"

"No, Simone, you're not getting it." Ray gave a short little laugh, then sobered. "I'm not a woman. I'm nonbinary."

Simone stared for a moment. She understood the words, of course, but her mind was having a difficult time matching them to reality. "Oh. But—" Her eyes widened. "Oh! Oh my god."

Ray shrugged. "Yeah."

"I'm— But—" Simone groped behind her for a chair and sat heavily down into it. "I didn't know."

"Yeaaah, that's why I'm telling you."

"Uh." Simone shook herself. *Get it together, Larkspur.* "Okay! I mean, that's great."

"Is it?" Ray said doubtfully.

"Well, I mean—it's cool. I mean, *I'm* cool with it. My roommate is transgender," she blurted out, then closed her eyes and scrunched up her face with regret. "I didn't mean for it to sound like that. Like, 'Oh, I have one transgender friend.' I know lots of trans people. What I meant was— Argh! That sounded really stupid, didn't it?"

"A little," Ray said, grinning broadly now, "but for what it's worth, this is the cutest reaction I've ever gotten to coming out."

Simone made a face. Cute? Kids were cute. Poodles were cute. "I'm not being cute! This is serious!"

"Yeah, I know." Ray swallowed and looked away. "It's kind of my whole, uh, life. And career."

Simone dropped the anger and that thread with a sigh. Bigger fish. "Sorry. I'm sorry. If I had known, I wouldn't have said"—she waved a hand as if to indicate all the air between them that might hold their conversation—"any of that. Before." She paused. Her mind was racing. This was a lot to take in. She abandoned the chair and started pacing along the length of the conference room. "I want to be supportive, okay? What can I do? Do you want me to talk to Chase, tell him we should do some other video instead? I won't mention why if you don't want me to, I can just—"

"You can stop and breathe," Ray said. Simone did so, halting in front of Ray's seat on the console and taking a huge breath, in through the nose, out through the mouth like Luna's yoga videos. Ray watched her, half smile still making an appearance. "And you can start using they/them pronouns for me, all right? I've been using them outside of work for a while now, and I guess it's time to let everyone here know, too. So, like, instead of saying 'She is our kitchen manager—'"

"I know about pronouns!" Simone said, standing at attention like she was being called into service. "I can do that."

"Yeah?" Ray's eyes twinkled. "Learned that from all your trans friends, huh?"

Simone frowned. "You're making fun of me."

"I am. It's really easy."

"I'm just trying to—" *Do right by you* sounded too intimate. "Do the right thing."

"I know. That's what's so cute." Ray stood, stretching their arms over their head and giving a long gusting sigh, like a muscle had just loosened from a cramp. "Kind of nice not to be the one freaking out during one of these talks, to be honest. Your anxiety is really calming, did you know that?"

"I'm not freaking out," Simone protested. "I was just—it's an adjustment, is all." She chewed her lip as she chewed this over. Ray was not a woman. Ray was nonbinary. That meant they didn't identify with any gender, right? Or with more than one? Was it okay to ask? What would Luna say? Probably that it was really personal and Simone should mind her own beeswax. She glanced over at Ray, who was adjusting the fall of their leather apron now that they were standing.

This had to change things, right? Now that Simone knew?

So why was she still staring at Ray's shoulders like she always seemed to do?

"Oh, um." She forced herself to look away from Ray's shoulders and at their face. "Do you have another name that I should start using, too?"

"Ray's fine. Thanks for asking." That lopsided smile returned. "Most people don't."

Simone's lips parted as realization dawned on her. "Is this why you hate Chase calling you—I don't want to say it's your legal name; that makes it sound like it's official or something."

"Deadname," Ray supplied. "Or just my outdated name. It's not the worst thing in the world for me to hear it, personally, but it is pretty annoying. I've been going by Ray since I was, like, fourteen. Anything else just sounds weird."

Simone's thoughts went to all the times Ray had pushed back against Chase's insistence on using their outdated name, or the label of *girl*, or a thousand other tiny things that must have been pretty annoying as well. "Why didn't you say something sooner?"

Ray's lips twitched in a way that Simone knew meant she had said something kind of silly. "I wanted to. I guess I kept putting it off because, you know, it could suck." They sobered. "I need this job, Simone. I really do."

"Oh. Right." Simone flushed. She knew better than most what was at stake in being out, especially at work. How had she forgotten that?

"Speaking of which, I should probably go apologize to Chase." Ray sighed. "I don't want to get fired over something so stupid."

"Can I do anything to help?"

Ray fiddled with their fingers, working away at a hangnail. "It would be nice if you could help me make it suck a little less," they said. "Just—I don't know—have my back if things get ugly."

"Of course! It would be my pleasure," Simone said, then thought better of using the word *pleasure* in this context. "I mean, it's the least I can do. But it'll be fine! We're in New York City, for god's sake. Everyone here at TDC is cool."

"Everyone?" Ray raised an eyebrow.

"Well, obviously not everyone, but—I mean, even Chase wouldn't dare to— You're our biggest star," Simone stammered. "No one would be nasty to you—not over this, at least. Right?"

"Let's hope not," Ray said noncommittally. "At any rate, we'll find out soon enough."

Simone tried to inject a little optimism into the discussion, even though it wasn't her strong suit. "So you're going to come out to everyone? That's exciting. Have you thought about how you want to do it?"

"Yeah, sort of." Ray scratched their nose. "Petey kind of knows already, I think, though we've never talked about it. Should probably take him aside after work today, maybe get a drink. He can tell the rest of the crew for me; I don't need to make a speech or anything."

"But do you *want* to?" Simone pressed.

Ray barked a laugh. "Fair question. No, I don't want to either. Not really my style, gathering everyone together for the important announcement." They made jazz hands to illustrate. "I just want this to be as chill as possible."

Simone considered this. "So I shouldn't bake a cake?" she asked. "Every occasion should at least have cake. Otherwise, it's just a meeting, to paraphrase Julia Child."

Ray shook their head and grinned. "I don't think we need a cake. Honestly, this isn't a big deal. At least, I don't want it to be. For me, nothing's changed, you know? Same person." They swept a hand down the long length of their torso. Simone's eyes followed the motion helplessly. "Same me."

"I get that." Simone nodded eagerly. "I swear, I really do. I might not always say the right thing, and I may not understand everything perfectly right away because I'm cis, and I'm sure I'll mess up the new pronouns at first—"

"This isn't really inspiring me with a ton of confidence," Ray said with an amused tilt of their head.

"But I will try," Simone finished somewhat weakly. "I promise."

"That's all I'm asking you to do," Ray said. They looked at Simone with those sleepy surfer eyes. "Hey, Mona?"

Simone felt her face heat. She wished that look meant more than it really did. She wished, very briefly, that she could see it across the short expanse of a pillow, where it belonged. "Yes?"

"Thanks," they said. They glanced down at the floor, then back up again. "You're a good friend."

Friend. Right. Simone swallowed hard on the lump in her throat. "No problem," she mumbled as she followed Ray's bouncing gait out of the conference room.

Chapter 17

Simone didn't mean to slam the door when she came home that night, but it happened anyway. She didn't bother waiting for Luna's usual greeting, instead shouting into the apartment, "Ray came out to me today!"

Luna popped into view at the end of the entry hall, her head tilted to the side as she put in a shiny, dangly earring. "I thought Ray being gay was, like, confirmed?"

"Not as gay." Simone let her tote bag fall to the floor. Her coat followed. It was a testament to her rattled state of mind that she couldn't be bothered stowing them away in the hall closet. "As nonbinary."

"Oh," said Luna. She finished with the left earring and started working on the right. "Neat!"

"Is it?" Simone asked wildly, echoing Ray's earlier disbelief.

"I think it is." Luna regarded her closely. "Don't you?"

"Of course I do. I'm one hundred percent cool with it. Obviously." Simone marched past Luna and threw herself into the armchair. "But when sh— I mean, they. Damn it. When they told me, I acted like a total weirdo. She must—they! They must think I'm— Argh, why is this so *hard*?"

"Yeah," Luna drawled, "Ray coming out must be *so* hard on *you*." She ducked back into her bedroom with a roll of her eyes.

Simone called after her, "Of course it's harder on Ray; I know that. But I've been so used to thinking of . . . *them*," she enunciated carefully, "in a certain way, and this just took me by surprise. This whole pronoun thing, especially. Ugh, even in my head, I can't seem to get it right." *She would be so disappointed in me*, Simone thought, and then hated herself for thinking in the wrong terms again. She grabbed a pillow and screamed into it in frustration.

When Simone finally emerged from the pillow, she saw that Luna had reappeared, having replaced her workout clothes with a light-gray sweater dotted with sequins of the same color, sleek black pants, and low-heeled boots. "You look nice," she said, her own problems momentarily forgotten. "Going out tonight?"

Luna flitted around the apartment, scooping up her purse, her phone, and her lip balm. "Yeah, I'm going with some of the girls to see Willow's show. She did the costumes for this off-off-*way*-off-Broadway thing, and we all wanted to be supportive." She looked at Simone with a gleam in her eye. "Hey, why don't you come?"

Simone curled further into the welcoming embrace of the armchair. Willow and the girls were Luna's best friends, a close-knit group of trans women she'd met online and through community meetups. Simone had hung out with them a few times and liked them all well enough, but after the day she'd had, she wasn't sure she was up for it. "Oh, I wouldn't want to intrude—"

"It's not an intrusion," Luna said. "I want to hear more about this juicy new development, for one thing. And don't worry, you won't be the only cis person there. Aisha is bringing her wife."

Simone sighed and peeked over the top of her pillow. She *had* been busy with work lately; she'd barely had a minute to spend with Luna at home, let alone get out of the house with her. She missed her friend. She missed being forced to have fun.

"Will I even be able to get a ticket to the show tonight? It's kind of last-minute."

Luna laughed. "Trust me, it will *not* be a full house. It's *Jekyll & Hyde*, but as a musical set to nineties pop songs. And apparently the lead cannot hit any of his notes."

"You're really selling it."

"Come on, just throw on some cute clothes and have fun for once! We can dish about Ray on the way."

Simone raised an eyebrow. "Free of charge?"

"You can owe me some brownies. Now let's see what you have in your closet," Luna said, taking Simone by the hand and pulling her toward her bedroom.

Within twenty minutes, Simone was wearing the tartan sweater dress and thick, warm tights that Luna had picked out for her, and they were on their way downtown. The subway was mercifully half-empty when they caught it—the perks of going out on a Monday night. They snagged a free pair of seats and settled in for the ride.

"So?" Luna nudged Simone with her shoulder. "Big day for Ray, huh?"

"Well, kind of. I was the first person at work Ray told, but—" She paused and tried to get it right. "But they said they were already out to their friends and all that." Simone glanced around, nervous about hashing out such personal stuff in public, but the few people sharing the subway car with them were either occupied with their own conversations or had their headphones stuffed in their ears. She kept her voice to a safe whisper anyway. "And I'm happy for them, totally. But when we first met, I made it clear I didn't want us to be anything more than coworkers, and Ray has respected that. Then that thing happened on Friday, when Ray brought me home—"

"Yeah, are we ever going to talk about how drunk you were?" Luna asked, crossing her legs and leaning against Simone's side. "I'd never seen you like that before."

Simone looked away, face growing warm. "Ray told you that

it wasn't the flu, huh?" She had avoided the subject all weekend, too ashamed to tell Luna the whole story.

"I managed to work it out on my own. You smelled like a distillery, after all." Luna made a face. "Ray just confirmed my suspicions, and only because they were afraid you might get worse and need to go to a hospital or something."

"Oh, come on, it wasn't that bad," Simone said. "I'd had a rough week, I drank too much. It happens, or so I'm told." Funny how she was echoing Ray's own comforting words now.

"Tell that to Ray." Luna took a compact mirror from her purse and checked her lipstick, but her eyes kept darting to Simone's face. "They were super worried about you. Like, about-to-call-in-the-Marines-level worried."

Simone scoffed. "Don't be ridiculous."

"No, I'm serious. It was kind of sweet. I made some joke about mother henning, but Ray just laughed it off." Luna cocked her head. "Guess that should've been 'non-gendered parental henning.' Or something."

"Oh." Simone frowned. So they hadn't been laughing at her? Luna had been poking fun at Ray? That made her feel slightly less embarrassed, but knowing how concerned Ray had been for her made up for it in spades. Her stomach flipped at the thought. "Okay, so we talked about how much I drank. Can we please focus on the real issue?"

"Which is?"

"What happened earlier today at work." She launched into an explanation of the chocolate trifle and how Ray had declared they were friends.

"Aw, that's sweet," Luna said. "Did you bring any of that trifle home?"

"No, the crew ate it all. Focus! Ray said we were *friends*," Simone keened.

Luna squinted at her. "And that's . . . bad?"

"No! But—" She fidgeted with the wrist strap of her purse,

a sequined clutch borrowed from Luna's stockpile. "What if I don't want to be friends?"

Luna opened and closed her mouth in a way that suggested she was trying to think of a tactful way to say something. "I get that you're super focused on work," she finally said, "but having a few friends can be a good thing."

"I know *that*. What I mean is—" Simone stared up at the steel ceiling of the subway car. "I think I may have, possibly, at some point, maybe started wanting to be more than friends with Ray."

"What!" Luna almost fell off the bench seat. "So I was *right*?"

"Can we please stick to my imminent heartbreak and not who was right about what?"

"I'm just saying, let the record show I knew it from the start," Luna crowed. Then she sobered. "Wait, what do you mean by imminent heartbreak? What's the problem?"

Simone sighed. "The thing I said about only wanting to be coworkers. I knew I was starting to feel an attraction toward Ray, but I can't take back what I said. Now Ray has let me know they're nonbinary, and I've never been attracted to a nonbinary person before—except I guess I was attracted to a nonbinary person all this time. And still am." She covered her face with her hands and groaned. "But I can't tell Ray I like them because, I mean, they're dealing with enough right now. It would be kind of weird to make a move right after they came out to me, right? Isn't that weird? She would—they, argh!" She gave a frustrated flail of limbs against the hard, unyielding subway car seat. "This is too hard!"

"Okay. Stop." Luna held up a hand. "Close your mouth."

"I swear, I'm trying with the pronoun thing, it's just—"

"No, I mean this is our stop." Luna pointed out the window. The train was rolling into Lincoln Center.

"Already?" Simone rushed to make sure she had her purse secure and her scarf around her neck, stumbling toward the door while Luna glided through it like an unaffected swan. "You weren't kidding about how off-Broadway this show is."

"It might be more accurately described as non-Broadway," Luna admitted as they both swept through the turnstiles and left the station. The air was bitter cold when they reached the street, and they both buttoned up their coats against the chill. "Seriously, though, prepare yourself. This show is probably going to suck."

Simone walked faster to keep abreast of Luna as they made their way down the sidewalk. "Remind me why we're subjecting ourselves to this again?"

"Because we're here for Willow, and she worked hard, so we have to be nice about it, okay?"

"Okay, okay, I can be polite," Simone said. "It's pretty awful, though, don't you think? That Willow and a bunch of other people put in all this time and energy for a thing like this?"

Luna gave her a funny look. "So it's not going to win any awards, so what? They can't all be winners, Simone. She's having fun doing it." Simone was about to argue that they should at least all *try* to be winners, but Luna stopped and gestured up at a sign above a doorway. "This is the place."

"Are you sure?" Simone squinted at the sign. She'd been expecting some offshoot performance space around the opera house, or maybe a studio of some kind. "This is a bar."

"Apparently the owner is the director's cousin or something." Luna waited with her purse held primly in both hands until Simone jolted into motion and opened the door for her. "Thank you, madam."

Technically, the show wasn't being put on in a bar. Technically, it was being put on in the bar's back room. Simone paid $10 to the bored girl at the door to said room, who stamped her hand with a smear of ink and handed her a pink paper ticket. Luna showed the girl her printed email confirmation and received the same.

"You get one free drink at the bar. Beer, wine, or well. But you have to use it now; it's no good at intermission," the girl said.

"Always a nice sign when the production wants you to get buzzed before the opening number," Luna whispered to Simone.

Simone gave Luna her drink ticket. "Go for it. I think I'll stick to water for, oh, I don't know—the rest of my life?"

"We'll see how long that lasts. Your crush makes beer for a living," Luna pointed out.

Simone groaned. "Don't remind me."

"Of alcohol? Or your crush?"

"Either. Both."

They headed to the bar to get Luna two vodka sodas (extra lime) to double-fist before entering the back room. There was an actual pool table in the middle of the floor, and the audience's folding chairs had been arranged around it, probably because it was too heavy to move. They were a few minutes early, but only a handful of other people were milling around or claiming chairs.

"Luna! Luna's roomie! You made it." A tiny wisp of a woman with strawberry-blond hair rocketed into Luna and wrapped her up in a hug. Luna gestured frantically with her sloshing glasses of vodka soda, and Simone obligingly took them from her for safekeeping.

As she watched the two friends, something inside Simone braced for all the human contact she would have to endure tonight. *Calm down*, she told herself. *It's just a small group.*

With her now-free hands, Luna hugged her friend in return. "Simone, you remember Lily?"

Lily gave Simone a cheerful wave and then pointed to some seats to the right of the pool table. "Aisha and Ruth grabbed some spots there. Not *too* close to the action." She grimaced as if thinking about the perils of sitting in the front row, where the hapless performers would be able to see their reactions—or lack thereof.

Simone stayed on the periphery when Aisha and her wife rose to greet them, too, and while everyone was chattering away,

Willow popped out from behind a curtain at the back of the room to say hi. She was dressed all in black and looked very cosmopolitan with her blond hair pulled into a twist.

When Simone complimented her on her outfit, Willow laughed. "I'm doing double-duty as a stagehand tonight. Wait, no, triple. I'm on props, too." Another stagehand dressed in black called out for Willow from across the room, and she gave a wave in return. "I've got to go. Thank you all for coming," she said, flashing a smile at everyone before taking her place behind the curtain once more.

Another woman walked in, drawing gasps from Luna and her friends.

Lily was the first to rush in for a hug, which seemed to be her usual M.O. "Sara! I haven't seen you since you got your new face."

"Sara got FFS a few months ago," Luna told Simone.

"You look uh-mazing," Aisha put in, pulling her wife along to form a protective circle around Sara. "What did you get done again?"

Sara ticked off her fingers. "Forehead, nose, and cheekbones. I thought about getting my lips done, too, but I don't think they needed it." Her smile was tentative, nervous but sweet.

A chorus of agreement burst forth.

"It looks fine!"

"Especially with everything else."

"I think you look great," Simone offered, edging into the circle.

"You look like *you*," Luna declared.

"You think so?" Sara blushed a faint pink and fanned at her eyes. "Oh my god, y'all are going to make me cry."

Simone watched as Luna's friends continued fawning over one of their own. She had almost forgotten, as focused as she was on her own stuff, that there were a few million people in this city all starring in their own story. It kind of put things in perspective.

Her phone buzzed, and she fished it out of her pocket to see an alert from the group chat from work. It had been Petey's idea to set it up as a way for the entire video crew plus Ray and Simone to keep each other updated on projects, but clearly it was also fulfilling a role outside of work as well. Hence Jake's ping to the group to make sure they saw a viral video of an extremely small dog trying to walk in a deep snow drift. As Simone watched it, Ray responded with a series of cry-laughing emoticons and a heart. Simone stifled a laugh.

Maybe it was worth all the social anxiety after all, to have people in your life who you actually enjoyed being around. Not just in group chats but here in some scuzzy bar's back room. Simone smiled to herself as she put away her phone. Luna caught her eye and gave her a questioning look, probably wondering what the dopey expression was for.

"I'm glad you brought me," Simone told her in a quiet voice.

Luna gave her a friendly nudge with her shoulder. "Anytime, Larkspur."

Then the lights started flickering on and off in what Simone guessed was an approximation of the usual signal to take their seats. Their group clambered into the chairs that had been saved by the judicious application of Aisha's and Ruth's coats and bags. Simone found a spot between Luna and Lily and finally handed off the drinks.

The lights went down and a fog machine started spitting a sad puff of smoke along the stage area that was marked off with blue painter's tape. A remixed version of Ace of Base's "All That She Wants" began blasting out of hidden speakers. From the corner of her eye, Simone saw Luna down a good half of one drink. Yep, this was certainly going to be something.

Simone watched a caped and top-hatted Jekyll—or was it Hyde?—cavort in front of the small audience, failing to carry even a fraction of a tune. She wondered how it must feel to be Willow, waiting behind the flimsy sheet that served as a backstage curtain to help bad actors with their quick-changes and fix their hilariously cheap wigs. Simone couldn't help the sticky sensation of secondhand embarrassment swamping her stomach.

"At least the costumes look good," Luna whispered to her while the chorus of scantily clad Victorian street urchins subjected them to a horrific rendition of "Livin' La Vida Loca."

"Now all the ladies in the house!" screamed the urchins, pointing to a cluster of women in the front row. Bewildered, they mumbled their way through one line of the song. "Now all the men in the house!" There weren't many. Two or three sad voices tried their best. Simone clutched her purse tighter in her lap. Luna had been right; they couldn't all be winners. But did they have to be bad in this particular way? How heteronormative could you get?

The intermission seemed to take ages to arrive, and when the lights finally came up, Simone found herself exchanging wide-eyed looks with the group.

"What, and I mean this sincerely, the fuck?" Aisha whispered.

"This is really bad," Lily said with a worried glance at the curtain. "I'm trying really hard not to laugh. And I don't think it's supposed to be funny."

"The second half should be shorter," Luna said. "That's something. Drinks?" She held up her now-empty cups.

They all filed out of the room to join the crush of regular patrons at the bar. Loud laughter and conversation enveloped them. Simone busied herself by playing with one of the damp coasters on the bar while waiting for her glass of ice water.

"Hey." Luna elbowed her lightly in the ribs. "You okay? I know this isn't exactly Shakespeare, but you look like the play personally insulted your mom."

"It's just—" Simone gave an unsure shrug. "That part where they made the women sing and then the men—"

Luna's eyebrows winged upward, but she didn't say anything, just waited.

Simone hesitated, then said, "I hate that there wasn't a place for Ray to sing."

Luna's face melted into the sappiest of expressions. "Aww!"

Heat came into Simone's cheeks, and she ducked her head. "Well, it was also rude for them to assume those people in the front row wanted to sing the lady part. Or that those other people were guys! The whole thing is flawed; it's only natural to be rubbed the wrong way."

Luna flung an arm over Simone's shoulders and hugged her into her side. "You got mad on your nonbinary beau's behalf. And you're starting to see all the weird gender pitfalls out there! My little girl is growing up."

Lily wriggled through the crowd on Simone's other side. "Simone's got a beau?"

"A *huge* crush," Luna stage-whispered. "She's ready to burn down this production to defend their honor, and they're not even here."

"Okay, all right," Simone said, shrugging off Luna's arm. "Let's not get ahead of ourselves. I'm just trying to be a better friend to Ray." She sighed, accepting her water from the bartender and tossing a dollar on the bar top because only a monster didn't tip. "Or at least try and get—*their*—pronouns right. Ugh, how am I supposed to get over this stupid mental block?"

"Okay, can I give you a piece of advice?" Luna signaled the bartender with a little wave of her empty cup and a smile, and he must have remembered her from before, because he went right to work on another vodka soda. "I get that you're frustrated, but don't let Ray hear you moaning about how hard it is to not misgender them. No one wants to feel like a burden."

"That's true," Lily put in, nodding. "It's super annoying."

Simone thought about this for a moment. "I don't want to be an asshole, sure," she said, "but I also don't want to slip up at work either. How can I nail this pronoun thing?"

Ruth squeezed in beside Lily. "We should practice."

Simone blinked. "Practice?"

"Yeah." Ruth gestured down the length of the bar, where her wife was trying to get the attention of one of the bartenders. "When Aisha came out, I just had to practice. It takes time, and you might still mess up, but that's okay. We can practice what to say then, too."

"Exactly. You just stop, correct yourself, and then keep talking," Lily said.

"That's it?"

"That's it," Luna confirmed from Simone's other side. "Same as you'd do if you misspoke any other word. Don't make it a big deal. If you do, then Ray feels like they have to reassure you, and then it's all about you and your feelings." Luna's hand made whorls in the air. "Make sense?"

Simone nodded eagerly. It sounded like a plan, and she loved plans. "Can we start practicing now? How does it work?"

"We just talk about Ray," Luna shouted over the noise of the bar. "They're not here, so it gives you lots of chances to refer to them by their pronouns."

The girl at the door to the back room started waving a flashlight over the crowd, the beam sweeping over the tops of their heads.

Simone grimaced. "I think we're supposed to take our seats for the second act."

"Right. We're good friends. The best. Once more into the breach." Luna downed the rest of her drink. "Then afterward you can tell us all about Ray to get in some practice."

Lily gave a whoop. "I can't wait to hear all about this hottie of yours."

Simone felt her cheeks get warm again as they all made their way to the back room. "Thanks, I guess," she said, but despite her grumpy tone, she was kind of touched that Luna and her friends wanted to help.

She found her seat in the dark and spent the next four musical numbers thinking up tidbits of information about Ray that she could share when it came time to practice. She thought

about how tall Ray was, and how handy it was to have someone who could reach the stuff on the high shelves in the test
kitchen. How they wore that butcher's apron so well. How loud
they laughed, and the way Simone could hear it down the hall
sometimes.

It occurred to her that, besides baking, Ray had become her
favorite topic. She smiled to herself, glad that the rendition of
the Backstreet Boys' "Everybody" she was currently being forced
to hear had been made a little more palatable.

Chapter 18

In the days that followed, Simone found herself nervous but excited to be the best ally possible to Ray. A thrill went through her the first time she was able to use the right pronouns at work, just like she'd been practicing with Luna and the girls.

"Have you seen Ray?" Petey asked her one afternoon in the test kitchen.

"Not since lunch," she said, looking up from her bowl of meringue. "They said something about going to the greenmarket to look for pencil asparagus." Winter was coming to a close, and the first bundles of spring vegetables would be appearing in the farm stands.

"If you see them before I do, tell them I need to go over our production calendar," Petey said. "We're going to try to get approval to shoot some footage at breweries upstate. You'll be coming, too; we can do a special episode of Revamp."

"That would be awesome," she said. "As long as I can sit up front in the passenger seat so I don't get carsick."

"I think we can swing that."

Simone was surprised to find she was looking forward to this. "Thanks, Petey. This should be fun."

Petey shrugged. "Don't thank me, thank Ray. It was all their idea."

Simone allowed herself one silent, internal cheer. It was going so well! As slow as The Discerning Chef could be to catch up with modern times, it was nice to see that the staff were all on the same page when it came to Ray's coming out. She smiled down at her mountain of fluffy whipped egg whites.

"Ray mentioned that you were going to talk to the video crew about—" Simone paused, not sure how to phrase it.

"Ray's pronouns and stuff? Yeah, I told the guys." Petey climbed up on a stool to watch Simone work. It was getting to be a habit for the team, one that Simone was surprised to find didn't bother her. "Maybe I shouldn't say 'guys.' Bridgette and Lin might not like that. What's a better word? Group? Team?" He scratched his chin. "This gender stuff, man." Then, eyes widening: "Should I not say that either? Aw, geez, I say 'man' all the freaking time!"

Simone almost laughed at his deflated look. "Glad to know I'm not the only one who's overthinking this."

Petey gave a sheepish shrug. "I'm trying to be a good bro. Sibling. You know what I mean." He waved his arms a little. "I'd never really heard of nonbinary people before. Ray kind of had to explain it to me, how there's a spectrum and some people don't fit in the *man* or *woman* boxes. And now I'm seeing all the weird ways things are gendered, you know?" He leaned forward on his stool. "Like, did you know the shampoo they sell to women is more expensive? And you get less of it? Even though it's the same stuff as the men's shampoo?"

"Yes." Simone sighed. "I'm very well-acquainted with the Pink Tax."

"How come we can't have just one kind of shampoo that everyone uses?" Petey asked. "Hair is hair, right?"

Jake passed by with an armful of what looked like electrical cables. He didn't say anything—he was a pretty quiet guy, from what Simone had seen of him so far—but he raised both eyebrows at Petey in a way that made it clear he'd heard this comment and had some Thoughts with a capital T.

Petey caught the look and frowned. "What?"

Jake pointedly flicked one of his short dreads off of his forehead.

"Ah," Petey said. "Point taken." He turned back to Simone, letting Jake continue on with his cabling. "Okay, so there are different kinds of hair, fine. What I'm getting at is, there's no such thing as man hair and girl hair. Once I started thinking about how stupid it was to separate stuff like that, I couldn't stop noticing it everywhere." He looked very serious. "Simone, is this what being woke is?"

"Maybe." Simone folded in some cake flour. "At least, a tiny bit. I'm pretty sure there's more layers to get through."

"Well, it's exhausting," Petey declared. "I would like to go back to being completely ignorant, please."

Simone looked at him sharply. "Do you really mean that?"

"No. 'Course not." He let loose a long, expressive sigh. "Guess it's only fair that I get a taste of what Ray's got to deal with all the time."

The door swung open and Ray swept in, lugging two heavy bags of produce, leafy green tops poking out. "What do I have to deal with all the time?" they asked.

Petey spun on his stool. "This gender bullshit! It's rough out there, man." He paused. "Should I still call people that, by the way? I can't figure out if it's bad."

Ray set the bags on one of the unoccupied islands, a thoughtful hum on their lips. "I think it depends on the person. I like it, but then again, I tip more toward the masc side of the spectrum."

"See?" Petey nodded sagely at Simone. "There's a spectrum."

The door swung open again. Chase strode in, preoccupied with his phone. "Spectrum? Are we talking light meters?" he asked.

"Nah." Petey waved a hand in Ray's direction. "Just, uh—"

He paused, seemingly realizing that he wasn't sure what to say and who, exactly, he could say it in front of.

"We're talking gender," Ray said, saving Petey from his dithering. They busied themself with unloading the bags. "I'm nonbinary, by the way. I asked the team to start using they/them pronouns for me, so if you could do that, too, I'd appreciate it."

Simone marveled at how casual Ray sounded, like this didn't faze them at all. Well, they'd probably had a lot of practice. She looked over at Chase, her teaspoon of vanilla frozen in midair as she waited to see his reaction.

Chase tore his attention from his phone. His eyebrows were winged high on his forehead, and his lip curled slightly. "Okay . . ." He drew out the word like it was taffy. "And did nobody think to inform me of this before now?"

"Uh." Ray carefully placed a bundle of delicate asparagus on the counter. "No? Why—?"

"I am still in charge of this project, even if everyone acts like I'm not," Chase said. "Sharing relevant information with the technical crew and your costar and only telling me as an afterthought is . . . Well, where do I even begin?" He used his phone to point at Ray. "I don't appreciate being treated like this."

That jolted Simone into motion. She dumped the vanilla into the bowl and set down the spoon. "Ray told us first because it happened to come up. They're telling you now out of courtesy. Their gender isn't relevant to the project, so why would you need to be told at all?"

Chase whirled on her. "Because! Ray is our top content producer! Has anyone even considered how this will come across in video?" He turned back to Ray. "You're not going to bring it up on the show, are you?"

The produce bags were empty, so Ray began rolling them up for storage. "I'm not sure," they said, concentrating on their task. Simone idly wondered if they'd ever made a Swiss roll; their technique was tight enough. "I figured if it came up, it came up.

Like if Simone ever referred to me in the third person. Which happens more than you'd expect in conversation, actually."

"Maybe we could work it into our intro," Petey said with a shrug. "No big deal."

"Yeah." Simone flashed Ray a small smile. "I could start with sharing my pronouns at the top of Revamp, then you could take a turn. Do you think the others would want to start doing that in their videos, too? We could make it a normal thing across the board."

Ray's whole posture softened and relaxed, but Chase cut in before they could open their mouth to respond.

"Listen to yourselves," he scoffed. "You're making these stupid plans without even consulting me. *Again*."

"If you have a better idea," Ray said, "go ahead and share it."

Chase flipped his mirrored sunglasses up to rest atop his head. His eyes were ugly little beads sitting in his doughy face. For whatever reason, he only addressed Petey. "Look, I don't have a problem with—" He stabbed his phone in Ray's direction. "Whatever that is. Gay, straight, black, white, purple, I don't give a shit, okay? But a lot of people—a lot of *sponsors*—do."

"Excuse me!" Simone said. She felt her blood rising. Ray was not a *that*. "You're way out of line, Chase."

"No need to get emotional. I'm only stating facts," he said, brushing Simone aside with a gesture of fingers. He still only looked at Petey. "We have to think about TDC's audience. Right now, we have a broad appeal. Broad appeal equals money. I'm in the middle of a couple negotiations for product placement. Do we really think we should endanger that?"

"I think," Petey said slowly, "that you're asking me and not Ray or Simone because you expect the only other guy in the room to agree with you. But I don't." He slid from his stool, hands balled into fists. "We let Ray be Ray. That was the plan. I say it still is."

Simone could have cheered. Instead, she very unemotionally watched as Chase turned a bright fuchsia and stormed out of the test kitchen, nearly knocking over a baking rack and muttering not-so-subtly under his breath, "Fucking fat-ass pussy."

Simone fumbled with the ties on her apron, ready to doff it and go after him for that crack. "Oh, he did *not* just call you—"

"Let him go," Petey said, sighing a little shakily. He looked like he could use a glass of water and a handful of almonds. "Man, I do not like conflict. That was— *Oof.*" In the blink of an eye, Ray had crossed the kitchen and wrapped Petey up in a fierce hug. "You okay, bud?"

"Yeah." Ray's voice was tight as a bowstring. "Just—thanks. You did good."

Petey's shorter arms patted at Ray in return. Their height difference meant that Petey was almost engulfed. "Aw, least I could do, man. That guy sucks."

"Mona, come on, you too." Ray lifted an arm in invitation, and Simone's breath caught. "Everyone gets a hug for being the best."

"But I didn't really do anything," Simone said, fingers stilling on her apron ties. "I shouldn't be rewarded for the bare minimum of decency."

Petey offered his arm, too. "Shut up and get in the group hug, Larkspur."

Simone relented, stepping around the island and tentatively allowing herself to be drawn into the hug-huddle. It was a little strange, being this close to other people. She normally wasn't much of a hugger. Ray smelled nice, she noticed (and not for the first time). A little like cedar. And Petey smelled a bit of fear sweat, but he'd earned it in a heroic ordeal, so she didn't really mind.

"I never would have asked you two to go to bat like that for me," Ray said in the weird quiet of their little cocoon, "but I'm glad you did."

"Hey, ride or die, man," Petey said. "We got you."

Simone wasn't sure what to say, so she just squeezed the two of them tighter and hoped that communicated her agreement.

Ray squeezed back for one head-spinning moment before untangling themself from the knot.

"Okay." Ray gave a lopsided grin, composed and easy once more. "Back to work, I guess."

Petey snapped his fingers. "Oh, we need to finalize that proposal for the trip upstate. Can you look at some dates with me?"

Simone left them to their plans, fading into the background once more. She finished up her meringue quicker than she normally would, tossed it into the oven, and went to seek out Mikkah. She wanted to tell her boss about what had happened, maybe set the wheels in motion for some kind of disciplinary action against Chase. He couldn't get away with saying those horrible things, not in a place of business. Simone wouldn't let him.

She ran into Mikkah in the hallway outside her office. Her editor had a Starbucks cup in one hand and a harried look on her face. Simone didn't even have a chance to greet her before Mikkah spotted her and shook her head.

"Whatever it is will have to wait, unfortunately," she said. "I just got called into some emergency meeting."

"Emergency?" Simone's brow furrowed. "I don't think I got that invite." She checked her phone just to make sure she hadn't missed it.

"You wouldn't have. It's leadership only. Just us muckety-mucks." Mikkah glanced at her wristwatch. "Got to run. We'll talk later?"

Simone nodded, and with a smile, Mikkah bustled off down the corridor in the direction of the executive conference room. At TDC, an emergency could mean anything from a delay at the printer to a typo in the amount of chili powder a recipe called for. Whatever it was, Mikkah and the other bosses would handle it. And once they were done, Simone would have time to talk to Mikkah about Chase.

Deciding to return to the test kitchen, Simone thought that at least she'd have time to cook a quick lunch for the crew while the meringue baked. They deserved a little celebration for their win over Chase. Simone could hash out the details of his punishment—and hopefully, his firing—with Mikkah later. It wasn't like they needed Chase; TDC's video channel was doing just fine without his direct involvement.

She whipped up a batch of meat-and-potato Cornish pasties—cheese and onion instead for Bridgette and Amir, neither of whom ate meat—humming all the while. While they baked, Simone used the time to rework some of her upcoming articles and recipes. One of the great things about the Recipe Revamp format was she didn't need to do any prep for it, so unless she was due to be on camera, she could concentrate on the rest of her workload.

She was finally getting into the groove of her new schedule, juggling everything fairly well. Even these feelings for Ray. All she had to do was leave them to braise on the back burner for a bit, where they could simmer away without bothering anyone. Maybe one day the stew could be served, but she doubted Ray would want to order that particular dish when the menu was so . . . varied.

Simone decided to stop that metaphor before she got too confused. Ray needed the support and understanding of a friend right now; that was all Simone could be for the moment. Simple as that.

Simone was so wrapped up in her work—or rather, her thoughts—that she didn't notice Gene until he was right at her elbow.

"Hey, have you seen this?" he asked, startling her terribly.

"Jesus." She put a hand over her racing heart. "Seen what?"

"HR just sent out this company-wide email," Gene said. He was scrolling slowly down his phone. "I can't make heads or tails of it."

Simone clicked out of the article she was very much not working on and opened her email instead. If it was a message from HR, she figured it must be something regarding Chase's earlier behavior. Maybe Petey or Ray had gone to speak to them before Simone had a chance to meet with Mikkah. The test kitchen had been empty for the last hour or more, so her theory made sense.

Eager to see just how badly Chase had been disciplined, Simone opened the all-hands email with the subject line ALL STAFF - PLEASE READ.

The message began: The Discerning Chef has always been an inclusive, equal-opportunity employer for professionals from a variety of backgrounds.

Ha! Take that, Chase McDonald.

However, it continued. Simone's eyes skipped ahead. In an instant, her heart sank. She reread the next few sentences just to be sure. It didn't seem possible, but there it was in black and white, straight from the HR department.

However, it has come to our attention that certain individuals are pushing the boundaries of professionalism and using our welcoming environment as a platform to force personal, intimate details of their lives onto their coworkers. This is harassment and it will not be tolerated. Nor will any form of political rhetoric be allowed on TDC's video platform. We strive to create wholesome, family-friendly content for a multitude of people, and that mission remains unchanged. Furthermore, any verbal attacks on staff will be dealt with immediately. Going forward, the Director of Social Influence will approve all stages of video content, especially prior to upload, to ensure that the material is in line with our policies and those of our parent company.

Simone was frozen. She felt sweat gathering under her arms, rage building in her chest. This was all backward. Harassment? Verbal attacks? If anything, Chase had been the one doing those things. Political rhetoric? *Family-friendly?* They were talking about Ray's gender like it was some kind of horrible plot to destroy America.

"Sounds like there was some kind of kerfuffle, but what do I know? No one ever tells me anything around here." Gene was still talking, though Simone barely heard him. "You okay? You look a little peaky."

She pushed her stool away from the workstation, standing abruptly. "I have to go." She was so flustered, she didn't even bother removing her apron, just shoved her phone in the bib pocket. "Gene, when that timer goes off, can you—the oven?" She didn't even wait for his response as she flew through the swinging door and down the hall to Mikkah's office.

"Did you know about this?" Simone demanded. She had her phone in her hand, open to the offending email. "Is that what your emergency meeting was about?"

"Simone, nice to see you, too, please come in," Mikkah drawled, not even looking up from her laptop. "Have a seat. Take a load off." Like it was all a big joke.

Simone's patience was disappearing like salt into boiling water. She remained standing. "Whatever Chase McDonald told you all, it's not true. Ray never harassed him. The only thing they did was tell Chase to use the correct pronouns."

Mikkah closed her laptop with a sigh and folded her hands on her desk. Despite the fact that she remained sitting while Simone stood, Simone felt very small under her gaze. "So Rachel never told Chase to 'shove his phone up his ass'? He was very specific; hard to believe he made it up out of thin air."

Simone gaped. "But that was— They had that argument *weeks* ago. And Ray apologized already. If anyone was slinging around verbal abuse today, it was Chase. You should've heard what he called Petey."

"Yes, Chase said there would be accusations thrown around to try to muddy the waters." Mikkah sighed. "I don't want to get into a he said/she said fight here, Simone."

"I'm not muddying— Mikkah, come on, it's *me*." They were supposed to be partners. Fighting on the same side. "You know me. Why would I lie?"

"Why would Chase?" she retorted.

"Because he's obviously pissed that Ray and Petey have taken over the video project," Simone said, gesturing wildly, "and now he's trying to use Ray's coming out to twist it into something it's not. For god's sake, all I suggested was that we start sharing our pronouns during video intros. That's hardly throwing a Molotov cocktail through a window!"

"I would refer you to the email from HR," Mikkah said, light as anything. "It's not personal; it's just business. We have bosses above us, too, you know. If the shareholders aren't happy, none of us will be happy, because we'll all be out of a job. Do you want to be out of a job?"

"But—" Simone struggled for words. "But you can't say you're inclusive and welcoming in one breath and then in the next tell Ray they can't be out if they want to be."

Mikkah made a pushing motion with her hands, as if this problem were an invisible pile of stuff she could just nudge off her desk. "No one is telling anyone that. We are only saying that there are editorial standards that we all need to be held to. Gene isn't going on camera and telling everyone about his penis, for example." She laughed.

"That—that isn't the same thing at all." Simone couldn't believe what she was hearing. Mikkah had always seemed so easy to talk to, so levelheaded. Maybe Simone just wasn't explaining it very well. "When the Brew It Up videos started taking off, we said we'd let Ray be Ray. Don't you think we should stick with that plan?" Simone asked, echoing Petey's earlier argument.

Mikkah gave a little *hmph*. "I don't think we should give anyone special treatment, regardless of how popular her videos are."

"*Their* videos," Simone said. "And it's not special treatment. Ray's just asking to be treated like everyone else is. If people were calling you 'he' and 'him,' you'd want them to address you correctly, wouldn't you?"

"You're being absurd," Mikkah said. "No one would mistake me for a man." She fluffed her shoulder-length curls. "And anyway, no one else in this company has asked us to completely change our language and bend over backward to accommodate them."

Simone pointed accusingly. "Aha! See? Accommodate *them*! You're already using that language. It's no different."

"I said 'them' to illustrate a hypothetical person," Mikkah said, getting louder now, "not the actual woman who stocks the groceries in our test kitchen."

"Ray isn't a woman," Simone shot back.

"Her driver's license would beg to differ!" Mikkah screeched. "I cannot believe you of all people are buying this asinine argument! What, anyone can just make up what they are? And we have to accept that? It's ridiculous. I could claim to be a man or a horse or a stapler," she said, holding up the stapler from her desk set, "and it wouldn't make it true!"

Simone stood frozen, her mouth open in shock. "Oh my god," she said slowly, "you're transphobic."

Mikkah put down the stapler. "That is a radical accusation, Simone, and I will not tolerate it. I'm simply pointing out that the truth still matters."

Simone's hands balled into fists at her sides. "You think Ray is just *making this up*? Because it's so fun and easy to be nonbinary? Are you nuts?"

Mikkah looked strangely amused. "Sit down, Simone. My goodness, the drama." She sighed. "We're not like—like those *gays*; we should be able to speak to each other like adults."

Simone saw red. And orange, yellow, green, blue, and purple.

She very deliberately placed her hands on Mikkah's desk and leaned forward. It was like she was watching herself from the outside, knowing she was acting in a way she never had before. Almost like a dream.

She spoke clear as a bell. "You are the only straight person in this room. And I am so glad I never told you before, because people like you don't deserve to know me."

Mikkah went as white as a sheet of uncooked phyllo. "Now, hold on—"

"No, *you* hold on." Simone straightened to her full height. It wasn't much, but it was what she had. "No one gets to talk about Ray like that. Not if I have anything to say about it."

She swept out of Mikkah's office, letting the door slam shut behind her.

Chapter 19

Simone returned to an empty test kitchen. Ray's leather apron wasn't hanging on its peg, so they had to be around somewhere. She checked the walk-in—no dice—and was about to send a message to their group chat when she heard faint voices coming from the back storage room. A quick press of her ear to the door told her Petey was inside, so she knocked.

"Come in?" Petey called, sounding unsure.

Simone pushed open the door to find the entire video crew inside the crowded room, some standing, some using the huge cans of tomato sauce as seats. Ray was noticeably absent.

"Did you see it?" she asked, shutting the door behind her.

Petey nodded glumly. "Total bullshit. The whole thing stinks. Don't worry, we're not going to let them get away with this."

Lin smacked one fist into her opposite palm. "Gender expression is protected in New York. I know; my brother's a lawyer. What they're doing is illegal. Ray could totally take the whole company to court."

"We have to document everything," Amir said. "Get everything in writing if we can."

"That might be difficult." Simone sighed. "I . . . kind of just yelled at my boss." She was still shaking. "She said some awful things, but it was all during a verbal conversation."

"So write it all down right now, while it's still fresh in your mind," Lin advised. "Email it all to HR right away so we can start a paper trail." She glanced at Petey. "Or we can go straight to Pim Gladly."

"Yeah, if she's actually in the office for once," Petey snorted.

"We don't involve Pim until we have more proof," Simone said. She shook her head. "I can't believe this. Ray is their meal ticket. Why are they making this so hard?"

"It's funny, the ways people will cut off their nose to spite their faces," Amir mused. "Prejudice is a hell of a drug."

"It's not funny, it's stupid," Bridgette countered.

"I'm texting my brother to see if he thinks we have a case," Lin announced, tapping away at her phone.

Simone pulled out her phone, too. "I'll start writing down my notes for HR."

"Does anyone want to ask me what I want to do?"

Simone turned to see Ray standing in the doorway. No one had noticed their entrance. They looked horrible. Their ever-present Mets cap was missing and their hair was a mess of curls, like they'd been tugging at it. Tense lines marked the edges of their tired eyes and pinched mouth.

"Ray." Simone stuffed her phone back in her apron. "Are you okay?"

Ray reached for the bill of a baseball cap that wasn't there, sighing when they realized they didn't have that to fiddle with. "I just got reamed out by HR," they said, "so I wouldn't bother writing to them if I were you."

"But you don't understand." Simone gestured to the small assembly packed in the storeroom. "We're going to help you fight this thing. Mikkah made some big mistakes when I talked to her just now. If we just—"

"We're not fighting anything," Ray said, loud enough to

startle Simone into silence. Their eyes fell to the floor and stayed there, their jaw working. When they spoke again, their voice was quieter. "HR told me I had to apologize to Chase, and I did."

"What?" Petey yelped. "But you didn't do anything wrong!"

"I know," Ray murmured.

"This is against the law," Lin insisted. "They can't treat you like this."

Ray shrugged. "Well, they are." They crossed their arms over their chest, staring down at their shoes. "I was an idiot to think this would go well."

"You don't have to take this lying down. We can get a lawyer, we can—" Simone grasped Ray by the arm, surprised when they flinched away. She dropped her hand and stared at them, but they still wouldn't raise their eyes. "Ray, don't you want to stand up to them?"

"What I *want* doesn't matter," Ray said. "I need this job. I can't jeopardize that. Not now."

"Fuck this job," Jake said, breaking his silence. After holding his peace for so long, he seemed to explode. "Seriously, fuck it. While we're at it, fuck the way only white people get to be on camera, and it's just us Rainbow Coalition members behind the scenes."

Simone was taken aback slightly, but when she thought about it, she realized Jake was right. TDC's staff was overwhelmingly white. Besides Delilah, Jake was the only Black employee. And Simone was pretty sure that the video crew contained the only other people of color in the whole office.

Jake gestured to the group. "There are other jobs, right? We don't have to stay here and take this."

"We can all walk out," Bridgette said with a nod. "Demand they let Ray be out for real, or we all quit."

Simone's chest felt tight. Working at TDC was her dream job, the only thing she really cared about. Was she really willing to give that up for Ray? She looked over at them, hunched and miserable, and knew.

Yes. A million times over, she would. Because her job was far from the only thing she cared about anymore.

But before she could voice her agreement, Ray spoke up. They picked up their head, eyes blazing.

"No," they said. "I appreciate you all trying to help, but—no. We're not going to do anything, okay? We're going to go along with whatever they say, and we'll let Chase run the show, and we'll just keep our heads down and stay out of trouble."

Every word was like a knife slipped into Simone's heart. "You can't be serious," she whispered.

"It's my life. My career," Ray said. "My decision. You don't have to like it—god knows I don't—but please"—they looked at each person in turn, ending on Simone—"respect it." They turned and left the storage room, leaving behind a frisson of ozone, like the air itself was fraught with a storm.

"So that's it?" Lin asked. "The revolution's over?"

No, that couldn't be the end of it. "Let me talk to them," Simone said, and hurried after Ray.

The test kitchen was still empty, but Simone shivered as she passed through a patch of cold air—the walk-in must have just been opened. She unlatched the heavy door, biting back a gasp as the freezing cold slammed into her. Whorls of mist danced around the dark space, and in the thick of the fog was Ray, standing with their back to Simone, hands braced on a high shelf, forehead leaning against a box of bitter melon.

"Hey." Simone had to speak up to be heard over the whirring of the walk-in motors. "What's gotten into you? This morning you were giving us hugs for standing up to Chase; now you want us to just stand aside while everyone walks all over you?"

"You're letting all the cold air out," Ray said, not turning around. "It's wasteful."

Simone stepped in and closed the door, sealing them inside the freezing room. She shivered and rubbed her hands briskly up and down her upper arms for warmth. Her breath was a light mist hanging in front of her face; she could see the answering puffs of Ray's floating toward the upper racks.

"I don't get it," she said, advancing on Ray while sidestepping boxes of citrus and pallets of eggs. "How come you're giving up? Aren't you angry about this?"

"Of course I'm angry!" Ray spun around, teeth gritted, tears standing in their red-tinged eyes. "I am *furious*, Simone! I am seething with rage, and I want to set fire to this fucking kitchen or dump rat poison in all the food or do anything but let them get away with this—but I *can't*."

"Yes, you can." Simone stepped closer. She was almost toe to toe with Ray now, could feel the heat rolling off their body in the freezing room. "You have to. It's not just about you." She thought about what Jake had said. The company needed changes, big ones. And lots of them. "Think about the people who come after you, Ray. You have a chance to make this a better place for them."

"Right, so it's all on me," Ray scoffed. "Well, I'm sorry I'm not up for playing the hero."

"You don't have to be a hero! I'm just saying you have options. Like getting a good lawyer."

Ray barked a harsh laugh, a single tear tracking down their face. "And how am I paying for this lawyer? In what universe is my measly salary enough to cover something like that, huh?"

Simone blinked. "I don't know; we could all chip in—or there's always pro bono—"

"And what happens if I bring a lawsuit? You think everything's going to be hunky-dory here at the office while it goes to court?" Ray was shouting now, hot breath bathing Simone's face in steam.

"There are laws, Ray. You'd be protected from retaliation."

"*Listen* to yourself!" Ray tugged at a fistful of their sandy curls, their voice marinated in frustration. "You live in this world where things are fair, and people follow the rules. That world doesn't exist for me, okay? You think they won't make my life hell in all sorts of creative ways? You think they won't figure out some excuse to fire me the minute they can get away with it? Wake up, Mona! We're not all living perfect little princess fairy tales!" This last was snarled out right into Simone's face, leaving her breathless.

"I-I'm not—" she stammered. "I w-wasn't—"

Ray waited, not giving her an inch, not softening at all. Simone could feel the ice in the air seeping into her veins. Was that really how Ray saw her? As some high-and-mighty perfectionist? They didn't even realize the lengths Simone had gone to for them, how she'd finally come out in the face of Mikkah's vitriol. And if Ray was throwing in the towel, Simone was on her own to deal with that fallout. Her whole being hardened at the thought.

This was why she never got close to people. They always disappointed.

When she at last found her voice, it was an old one, cold and distant. "At least I'm not a coward," she said.

A flash of pain appeared in Ray's eyes, and it should have felt gratifying, but Simone only felt despair. This wasn't what she wanted. Especially not when the pain turned to disgust.

Ray ducked their head. "I have work to do," they said, and brushed by Simone, slamming their way out of the walk-in.

Leaving Simone very cold and very alone.

"Don't cry," she muttered to herself. She pressed her freezing hands to her hot eyes. "Don't cry, don't cry." Breathe in, breathe out. She told her racing heart to calm down. It was over. All of it. Especially any chance of Ray ever— No, best not to even put a name to it.

Ray had made their decision, and nothing Simone said or did would change their stubborn mind. Fine. Good. Nothing for it but to get back to work. If she still had a job after that blow-up in Mikkah's office. She checked her phone, but there were no new messages. At least she wasn't getting dragged into a meeting with HR, too. The best she could hope for was a chilly silence between her and her editor. *Ignore what happened,* she told herself. *Just focus on your work. That's what you're good at.*

She took a few more deep breaths, the chilly air biting at her lungs, before she felt composed enough to leave the safety of the walk-in. As she cracked open the door, she heard Ray's voice booming cheerfully through the test kitchen. The crew had set up their equipment and were actually . . . filming?

"Today we're making some stout," Ray said into the camera, baseball cap jammed back on their head, pencil tapping against the countertop. "Now you've got a lot of different kinds of stout. You've got your oatmeal stout, your dry stout, your milk stout . . ." They sounded as jovial and upbeat as always. Like nothing had even happened.

Simone shut the walk-in door and crept to her station, intent on cleaning up the now-cold pasties and meringue and getting out of there as fast as possible. She couldn't stand hearing Ray talk like everything was normal. Had Ray's friendly demeanor always been an act? Perhaps Simone didn't know them at all.

Maybe the person she thought she had feelings for—maybe that Ray didn't exist.

Chase was there, too, and the sight of him sitting on one of the high stools with his arms crossed, like he was a king viewing his subjects, made Simone's blood boil. He called, "Cut," and turned to Amir to say, "Can we get some better lighting on her left side, please?"

"Their left," Amir corrected, already adjusting the lights.

Chase ignored him. "Little more. Great. And action."

Ray didn't do anything except start from the top with a smile plastered across their face, repeating their script like a broken record. "Today we're making some stout. Love a good stout. Now you've got a few different types of stout—"

Simone kept her mouth shut only by biting the inside of her cheek until it hurt. She packed up her food and left the test kitchen before she could get pulled into a tasting or something in Ray's video. Unlike some people, Simone wasn't about to pretend like everything was fine.

Chapter 20

Work became a lonely place. Simone was fighting a cold war on all fronts at The Discerning Chef. Mikkah was only speaking to her through curt emails, and only about work-related matters like deadline reminders (as if Simone had ever missed a deadline). The video crew was much more subdued, especially now that Chase was popping in and bossing them around whenever his whims dictated. There wasn't much laughter or chatter, and definitely no group lunches in the test kitchen.

Simone came in, did her work, and went home, end of story. In many ways, it wasn't much different from how Simone had operated before Ray had joined the company. But whereas she had been fairly content with her life before, she wasn't now.

She missed the jokes. She missed the chatting. She missed the Friday happy hours, which had come to an unceremonious halt. She missed everyone sitting around, eating her food and exchanging stories.

She missed being Ray's friend.

Ray wasn't being rude to her or anything; in fact, they were polite to a fault when Simone came in early in the mornings.

They said hello, asked her if she needed anything, offered to fetch things from the walk-in or the storeroom. Simone, too, was courteous, thanking Ray for their offers of help, assuring them that she had everything she needed. It was like they were back to square one, almost: strangers dancing around each other, on the edge of tipping over into enemies if one of them looked funny at the other.

Simone had told Luna the whole story over a pan of lemon bars, and Luna had been sympathetic to her point of view, but even she didn't give Simone a break. "You don't know exactly what Ray's dealing with," she'd said with her mouth full of sharp curd and sweet crust, "just like they have no idea what you're dealing with on the Mikkah front. Just apologize. Tell them you're sorry and that you'll try to be more supportive."

"I *was* trying to be supportive," Simone had countered, "but it didn't matter. Why should I even try when it just blows up in my face?"

Luna hadn't had an answer for that. She just stuffed another lemon bar in her mouth and rolled her eyes.

The weeks dragged on like that. Until the date of the planned road trip upstate was imminent.

Simone was dreading the trip. What was supposed to be a fun getaway for the crew in an idyllic setting was now a minefield. How was she going to survive being trapped in a van with Ray and Petey and everyone else for hours and hours, let alone feign enthusiasm during the on-location shoots? She knew the latest episode she'd shot with Ray had been stilted and wooden. Ray had been their usual charming self when presenting her with some strawberry pretzel concoction, but Simone hadn't been able to match their energy, only barely managing to turn out a strawberry panna cotta with a crushed pretzel topping. Not her best work.

She was in low spirits when she arrived outside the TDC building on the morning of the trip, dragging her overnight bag behind her. The van Petey had rented was double-parked right outside, and the crew was loading it up with their luggage and equipment. Ray was lending them a hand, and as Simone approached, she saw Ray pause in their lifting and hauling to unzip their hoodie and shrug out of it, leaving them in only a thin T-shirt. Simone looked away. It was so unfair, the way her stomach still flipped at something as simple as seeing Ray's bare forearms.

"Anything I can do to help?" Simone asked the group as she came to a stop behind the van, where the back doors were open, and piles of stuff were being arranged and rearranged.

"Nope, think that's the last of it. Here." Ray grabbed her overnight bag without even asking and slung it into the van, the last piece of the Tetris puzzle. "What do you say, Petey? Time to hit the road?"

"Let's do it." Petey tossed Ray the key with the rental-car company fob. Ray caught it one-handed. Apparently, it went without saying that Ray was going to drive. "Does anyone need to go to the bathroom? Do it now, because we're not stopping until we're out of Pennsylvania," Petey said.

"Geez, Dad, are you going to make me pee in a roadside ditch, too?" Bridgette grumbled, and Jake barked a laugh.

Simone smiled tentatively as she rounded the van. Maybe this would be a good trip after all. It might give them all a chance to relax away from the weird atmosphere of the office. Plus, Chase wasn't coming—apparently, he didn't do road trips or motels.

"I call shotgun," Lin said, popping open the passenger door.

"Sorry, sport." Petey pointed at Simone. "Mona's got dibs, remember? She gets carsick."

Simone glanced at Ray, who was hesitating by the driver's side door, keys dangling from their hand. She was sure they weren't looking forward to sharing the front seat with her for the next four and a half hours.

"Uh, that's okay," Simone said. "I can sit in the back. I'm sure it'll be fine." Squishing in with everyone wouldn't be ideal, but at least it would spare her the awkwardness of sitting next to Ray.

"You should sit up front," Ray said, not looking at her. "Better safe than sorry."

Jake slammed the back doors shut and gave the van a double tap with his knuckles. "Whatever we're doing, let's do it quick before we get a ticket."

"Yeah, that is not in the budget," Petey said as he climbed into the last row of seats in the back. "Come on, folks, get in and buckle up."

Simone turned back to stare at Ray over the hood of the van. "Really, I'll be okay in the back, I'm sure."

"You weren't okay in the back of that taxi." Ray tugged open the driver's side door with more force than Simone thought was necessary. "Just take the damn seat, Mona."

Simone stiffened at the mention of her drunken misadventure; that was not the sort of thing she wanted the rest of the crew to know about, and she cast a glance back at them to see if they'd heard. Luckily, they were all preoccupied. Lin had already given up on sitting shotgun and was wedging herself between Petey and Amir in the back. Reluctantly, and with a stone weighing down her stomach, Simone climbed into the passenger seat and shut her door.

"I can navigate," she said, pulling her phone out of her tote bag and opening Google Maps. It would be nice to have a job to do, something to focus on.

"After the tunnel, it's pretty much a straight shot until we cross back over the New York border." Ray started up the engine and checked all the mirrors. "I can handle it."

"Great," she said through gritted teeth. She shoved her phone back in her bag and let it fall into the footwell with a loud thump. "I'll try not to bother you, then."

Simone glanced at the rearview mirror, watching the rest of the team chatting away, sharing a bag of corn chips, laughing at the way Lin was struggling to find her seatbelt's buckle. It was like they were in their own little world. She wished she could be back there instead of stuck up front.

Ray sighed as they pulled the van into traffic and headed for the Lincoln Tunnel. "I didn't mean you should sit in silence for the whole ride."

"Well, I don't have anything to say." Simone looked at the mirror again, worried that their tense exchange might have drawn the others' attention, but no one seemed to notice, too wrapped up in their own goofing off.

Ray's hands were tight on the wheel. "Yeah. Same."

Bridgette's red head popped between them. "Hey, can I put on some music? I have a great road trip playlist."

"Uh, sure," Ray said. "Hook it up."

Simone didn't really keep up with new music, so when Bridgette's songs started playing off her phone and everyone in the back seat began singing together in one loud chorus, she wasn't really sure what to do. She didn't know the words and certainly didn't know the dances that apparently accompanied some of them, if Amir's seat-bound moves were anything to go by. She watched the rest of the team's antics in the rearview with a little smile. It was good to see someone was having fun, at least.

She looked over at Ray, whose entire concentration was on the bumper-to-bumper traffic leading up to the tunnel. "You don't know the words either?" she asked. "I figured you'd jump at the chance for a sing-along."

"Not really a fan of my singing voice," Ray muttered, trying to change lanes and groaning when no one would let them in. "I did choir as a kid. Soprano. Doesn't really fit me these days."

"Oh. Sorry." Simone turned to stare out her window at the sea of cars and concrete.

They drove in silence through New Jersey. Well, Ray and Simone were silent; the back seat was hopping. Then they hit Pennsylvania and the monotony of the scenery—trees, trees, and more trees—combined with the early start time meant that everyone in the back seat eventually dozed off. Simone grinned as she turned around to see that Petey, Lin, and Amir had fallen like dominos, each against the other's shoulder with Petey on the end, leaning up against the window. Bridgette and Jake were sacked out in their bucket seats, too. Apparently, Bridgette snored.

Simone faced forward again, lowering the volume on the seemingly endless playlist. The current song was something gentle and slow with a singer who was crooning about wolves and stars and the moon. "Looks like the kids are all tuckered out," she said.

"Yeah." Ray glanced at the rearview with a wistful smile. "You should take a picture. Quietly."

Happy to have a task, Simone twisted in her seat and aimed her phone's camera as best she could, making sure she got everyone's sleepy face in the frame. "Gosh, they're cute when they're like this." She grinned as she thumbed through her snapshots. There was a very good close-up of Petey, complete with his mouth hanging open.

"Let me see," Ray said.

"I don't want to distract you. You should be paying attention to the road."

"We haven't seen another car in five miles. Come on, just hold up your phone next to the wheel. One glance."

Simone sighed. "Fine." She held up her phone for Ray to take a peek.

"Aww," they crooned. "Adorable." Ray's eyes flicked back to the road. "Glad they can relax a bit. They needed a break. Things at work have been . . ." They trailed off, shrugging.

"Rough?" Simone offered.

Ray sighed and made a small adjustment to their A/C vents. "Yeah. For everyone."

Not everyone was getting constantly misgendered by half the staff, but Simone didn't point that out. They drove in silence for a few miles before Simone worked up the nerve to speak again. It might be the only chance they'd have to hash things out in private.

"When you first came out to me, I promised I would try to make things easier on you. I'm sorry I couldn't." She kept her gaze locked on the side window, watching the greenery rushing by. "You made your choice—I get that, I do—but—" She sealed her lips over her teeth. The last thing she needed was a repeat of their last argument. But if nothing had changed between them since then, how could they even begin to talk about it?

"Hey." Ray looked over at Simone for a moment before focusing on their driving again. "I don't like it any more than you do. Chase is a bully, and TDC is a shitty workplace, but right now I just need to grin and bear it."

"But why?" Simone pleaded. "Your videos are so popular; I'm sure you could strike out on your own, or—"

Ray gave her another glance, longer this time. "Simone," they said slowly, like they were thinking long and hard about what to say and whether to say it at all.

"Yes?"

"The thing is—"

Simone's eyes darted to the windshield. "Deer!" she shouted, pointing. A young buck was bounding out of the trees and onto the road in front of them.

"Wha— Oh, *shit*." Ray slammed on the brakes and turned the wheel. Rubber screeched on cement. The sleeping crew in the back seat jolted awake with cries of surprise. Simone shut her eyes and braced for impact, but none came.

She opened her eyes. They were stopped safely on the shoulder of the (thankfully) empty road. They were in one piece.

And Ray's arm was thrown across Simone's middle, as if in that adrenaline-fueled moment, Ray had wanted to make sure she was safe.

And Simone, without even remembering when or how she'd done it, was clutching onto Ray's arm like her life depended on it.

Simone watched as the deer gave them a concerned look before disappearing into the woods.

"Hey, what the fuck?" Jake croaked from the back seat. "Did we crash?"

"I don't think so." Petey rubbed the sleep from his eyes. "Ray?"

Ray swallowed. Their arm didn't move. "Just a deer," they called over their shoulder. "Everyone all right?"

A mumbled collection of affirmatives followed. Simone wasn't listening to them, though. Her gaze was riveted to the woods where the deer had slipped away, cool as you please. Like nothing had happened.

"Simone?" Ray's voice was a soft whisper that jolted Simone back to reality.

"Yes, I'm fine," she said quickly. "I'm all right."

"Good. Uh—can I have my arm back?"

"Oh!" Simone released Ray as swiftly as possible, her hands frozen in midair. "Sorry, I— Just a little shaken, I guess."

"No worries." Then, to the rest of the crew in a louder voice, Ray said, "It's only another hour and change till we get to the brewery. Anyone need to stop for anything?"

While Lin negotiated a stop at the next gas station for what she claimed were very necessary Twizzlers, Simone rubbed at her stomach where Ray's bare arm had been just moments ago. In a moment of crisis, Ray's instinct had been to protect her. That had to mean something, didn't it?

Simone stared at the trees as they once again whizzed by. The logical side of her brain told her it didn't mean much, just that Ray didn't want to see her die, which was really the bare minimum of concern for a fellow human being.

"Need anything?" Ray asked, shaking her from her thoughts.

"Huh?"

"When we stop at the gas station," Ray clarified. "Do you need anything?"

She shook her head. "No, I'm good."

"*Want* anything, then?" Ray pressed, a teasing smile on their lips.

You have no idea. "Not really. Thanks."

She was quiet for the rest of the ride.

By the time they arrived at the Finger Lakes region, Simone was exhausted from sitting in the van all morning. She was more than ready to get out of the passenger seat and take in the surroundings. The brewery was housed in a newish red brick building, built to fit into the rolling hills and farmland. The area around it was breathtaking: the patio deck out back provided a beautiful view of a blue-gray river, and the forested countryside could almost convince Simone they were in some far-flung valley in rural France and not five hours outside of the city. Even the air smelled different, cleaner, crisper, with something like the hint of spring water in it.

They were met by the owner of the brewery, a red-faced gentleman in overalls who immediately became Ray's best friend. Simone assumed she would hang back until they were ready to shoot the Revamp footage, but instead she was ushered along on the tour, giving Ray and the host a chance to show her all the different stages of beer brewing.

"Should I really be appearing in one of the Brew It Up videos?" she asked, even as Ray had her tasting a coffee porter—breakfast beer, the owner had called it.

"It'll be a crossover episode," Ray said, and poured themself another measure of the thick, dark beer.

They took a break between shoots. Lunch was a catered affair, a picnic of local meats, cheeses, breads, pickles, and jams provided by the very accommodating brewery staff. Simone felt a little like a celebrity, what with so many people coming up to her like they knew her, telling her how much they loved her TDC videos. At first it was a little overwhelming, but then she spotted Ray seated in an Adirondack chair under a lovely shade tree, picnic sandwich in one hand, lunch beer in the other, chatting with one of the brewmasters. They seemed so relaxed in this environment, and so excited to be talking about brewing with someone else who knew their stuff. It had been a while since Simone had seen Ray light up like that.

If Ray could take this trip as an opportunity to find a bright spot in an otherwise horrible month, Simone figured she should, too. She bit into a slice of artisan pain de campagne topped with smears of Cayuga Blue cheese, a drizzle of local honey, and a few leaves of crisp arugula, sighing as the flavors danced in her mouth.

Yeah, there were worse ways to spend a workday.

Because they were shooting outside of the test kitchen and away from the near-endless supplies in the TDC pantry, the Recipe Revamp episode had a slightly different format. Instead of trying to reinvent a recipe on the fly, Simone and Ray had brought ready-made food that featured beer as a star ingredient—a tie-in to their brewery visit. It was more of a show-and-tell than anything, with the only real surprise being that they were supposed to keep their food a secret from each other until the cameras started rolling.

It was a cute concept, and it would have worked. Except they'd both brought the same thing.

"Oh, come on," Simone groaned when they lifted the lids off their super-secret chafing dishes. "We both did fondue? Petey, why didn't you tell us?!" She glared at her director-slash-producer, who was standing behind the cameras with a huge smile on his face.

"I thought it would be kind of funny," he said.

"All right, hold on," Ray said above the laughter of the crew and the brewery staff who were watching the shoot. "You brought fondue. I brought beer cheese. They're totally different."

"Not really." Simone pointed to her dish, an elegant mixture of Gruyére, Emmentaler, and garlic with a dry IPA replacing the traditional white wine. "Cheese and beer." She then pointed to Ray's electric-orange offering. "Cheese and beer. It's the same!"

"Isn't there an O. Henry story that's kind of like this?" Jake mused from behind Camera 2.

Simone glared at him. "Petey, edit that part out."

"I don't think I will," Petey said.

Surprisingly, Ray was the one to pull the shoot out of the realm of ridiculous and put it back on track. They looked into Camera 1. "Well, it just proves that beer and cheese go together like . . . wine and cheese? And there's more than one way to get your fix. Here's how I made my version back at the test kitchen." They made a finger-gun gesture at the lens.

"And time stamp here for yesterday's Ray footage," Amir said into one of the mics.

Simone shook her head in disbelief. Their audience was still laughing themselves silly.

"Mona, do your flashback intro and then we'll get to tasting," Petey said.

Simone raised her head with a sigh. "And here's how I made my version of beer fondue, which you, too, can make at home or bring to a dinner party where everyone else will have brought the same thing, causing massive lactose intolerance and decimating the guest list."

The brewmasters were laughing so hard, doubled over with tears in their eyes or slapping their thighs, that it set Ray off into a huge, honking laugh. They ducked behind the table they'd set up on the beautiful brewery lawn for the shoot, trying and failing to calm down. It was one of those moments where nobody could stop laughing, and every time they tried, something else set them off again. The fact that they'd been tasting beer for the last few hours probably didn't help.

"There's no way we can use this footage," Simone said, and although her tone was striving for stern, she couldn't stop her mouth from wobbling into a smile at the sound of everyone cracking up.

"No, it's great," Petey assured her through his giggles. "Amir, time stamp?"

"I can't breathe," Amir wheezed, boom mic drooping.

Bridgette laughed so hard she farted, which meant another riot of hysteria from everyone. This time, Simone actually joined in.

They somehow finished the episode, wrapping up way after their scheduled end time, but no one seemed to mind the long day. Spirits were high as they packed up the van to head to dinner. Ray had chosen a BBQ place that was known for their extensive beer and wine list.

"Don't worry," they told Lin and Amir, "it's not just salads on your side of the menu; they've got a veggie pizza and a wrap, too."

Simone was strangely touched that Ray had thought of the team's dietary restrictions. It wasn't something that was usually considered at TDC, where being an omnivore was practically part of the job description, at least on the editorial side. She wondered how many people had been deterred from joining the company because they kept kosher or halal or didn't eat meat.

She picked at her (extremely tasty) pulled pork and slaw sandwich. Food was supposed to bring people together; she'd always believed that. Yet every time she thought about how The Discerning Chef operated, she found another way it was failing in that mission.

Petey glanced at his watch as everyone was finishing up their meals. "It's getting late. We should get to the motel, get some rest. It's another early start tomorrow. We've got two more brewery tours to film before we head home."

Jake made a back-and-forth gesture between himself and Amir. "We're sharing a room, right?"

"No doubt," Amir said, giving him a fist bump over the table.

Simone frowned. "Sharing? We don't get our own rooms tonight?"

"The budget they gave me was *really* tight," Petey reminded her. She must have looked panicked, because he added, "Don't worry, it's not like we'll have to share beds or anything. Four rooms, two beds apiece, I made sure of it."

Simone was simultaneously relieved and frustrated by this news. The idea of possibly sharing a bed with a coworker was daunting, but the idea that the coworker might be Ray was . . . different.

Lin grinned at Bridgette. "Are we going to braid each other's hair and talk about boys all night?"

"How about we buy a bottle of wine to split back in the room while we bitch about Chase?" Bridgette said.

"Deal." They shook on it.

As everyone began gathering their trash and taking it to the bin by the soda fountain, Simone lingered at the table with Ray. Her hands felt jittery with nerves. "Guess we're sharing, then, huh?" She tried to sound light and casual, but to her ears it came out a little strangled.

Ray sucked the last of their soda from their drinking straw, brows drawing down in confusion. "What? Oh, nah, I'm bunking with Petey," they said.

"Really?" Simone flushed. "I thought maybe—"

Ray set their soda cup on the table with a rattle of ice. They kept their gaze down. "Just because we both have vaginas doesn't mean we have to be roomies, Simone."

Simone gaped. "I wasn't saying that. I just thought, since Petey is kind of the boss, he might want a room to himself," she said. She very carefully did not mention how she might have been hoping for that, anyway. Ray didn't seem to be in a very receptive mood right now. "Sorry, I didn't think how it would sound."

Ray's eyes flicked up at her as if assessing her honesty. They must have found it, because Ray relaxed enough to say, "It's okay. I've been a little on edge lately, I guess. Didn't mean to get so defensive."

"Not your fault," Simone said, and she meant it. She wished Ray knew exactly how much she meant it.

Ray stretched, their long arms going far above their head. "Petey's crashed on my couch before, anyway, so it's not that much different. Besides, I figured you'd want your privacy."

Simone swallowed. She'd known Petey and Ray were good friends outside of work, but she hadn't realized they were having sleepovers after all-night hangouts. The rest of the crew was so close, and Simone was the one standing apart. She thought back to the shouting match she'd had with Ray in the walk-in all those weeks ago. They'd called her a perfect little princess, and here she was, alone in her tower. Her throat went tight.

"Thanks," she forced herself to say. "That's very thoughtful of you."

Lin breezed past the table, waving a bottle of local Riesling she'd purchased at the counter. "Come on," she said, "time to load up."

Chapter 21

The motel was clearly a family-run operation, not at all like one of the bland chains. It was the classic two-story setup with an open walkway connecting the rooms. Huge pots bursting with red geraniums hung from the upper level, and in the field adjoining the parking lot, there was a metal fire pit with a nice blaze already going. A few guests, a family with a young child, were sitting around the fire on rough-hewn benches, bundled up in hoodies and sweatshirts against the chilly night air. Simone stepped out of the van to a chorus of crickets and night birds.

"Cute," Lin said. "Nice pick, boss."

"I got a great rate," Petey said with a hint of braggadocio in his voice. "You all grab the bags; I'll check in."

There was the expected mild chaos as the team unpacked the video equipment from the van to reach their luggage, then the dance of the room key distribution—real keys on real key chains, not swipe cards—and the friendly arguments about who would get the room with the best view of the lake. Finally, Simone claimed her room and bid her coworkers a good night. She shut her door, feeling a bit sad. After an entire day in the company of other people, she should have been ready to enjoy some peace and quiet, but for some reason the silence of her empty motel room just made her restless. It was dark out, but still too early to go to bed. Simone considered reading the book she'd packed or seeing what channels the ancient TV in her room got, but none of that appealed. She checked her phone. There were a couple texts from Luna asking if she'd arrived safely; it was something they usually did with travel, letting each other know when their flights touched down, but Simone had forgotten this time what with the hectic schedule. She sent Luna a belated message and went back and forth with her a few times, telling her a bit about the trip. Then she changed out of her road-wrinkled clothes and into her pajamas just for something to do.

She raised the venetian blinds on the window and stared out into the night. Her room did not have a view of the lake—she'd let Lin and Bridgette win the battle for that—but it did overlook the fire pit. The family had abandoned the benches around it, and the fire was still going strong. It looked inviting, so Simone pulled on her mom's old NYU sweatshirt, tugged on her sneakers without bothering with socks, and headed down.

The fire was nice and warm in contrast to the cold air. Simone could see her breath if she blew hard enough. Funny how different the weather was here; in the city, people were already shedding their light spring jackets, ready for summer. Simone claimed one of the Adirondack chairs near the fire pit, relaxing into the slight recline and propping her feet up on a polished log stool. After a few minutes of soaking up the heat of the fire, she even kicked off her shoes and wiggled her bare toes. There was something soothing about fire. She could watch it dance all night.

"Mind if I join you?" a voice called from the darkness.

Simone twisted around in her chair to see Ray plodding across the grass. They were wearing the zip-up hoodie they'd had on earlier that morning, hood up to keep their half-shaved head warm.

"Petey's taking a shower, and he sings." Ray pulled a face. "Not very well. I needed an escape." They lifted a six-pack. "I brought this, if it helps my case."

Simone smiled and shook her head. "You don't need to make a case. Come on, take a seat."

Ray chose the other Adirondack chair right next to Simone, which pleased her more than it should have. She told herself to calm down. So Ray chose the most comfortable option; it didn't mean anything.

Ray's bottle opener made a loud crack as they opened one of the beers. "Want one? It's a local apricot sour. You like sours, right?"

"You remember what I like?" Simone asked, then, realizing how that sounded, quickly tacked on, "Beer-wise, I mean."

"How could I forget?" Ray held out the open bottle. "It was the first time you ever said anything remotely nice to me."

Simone flushed and accepted the bottle. "That can't be true." She thought hard. "Is that true?"

"Maybe not," Ray said, their eyes crinkling at the corners with suppressed laughter. "You know me. I tend to exaggerate."

"Well." Simone tried to recover. "At least it was memorable."

"Exactly." Ray opened another bottle for themself, and they clinked the bottle necks together before taking the first sip.

Simone rolled the beer around on her tongue. It was funky, only a tiny hint of fruit, and she wasn't sure she would have known it was apricot if Ray hadn't told her.

"Not bad," she said, "but I liked yours better."

"Thanks." Maybe she imagined it, but Ray seemed to smile before taking another drink.

They sat for a while in silence, just the sounds of the fire crackling and the insects humming around them. It wasn't tense, Simone thought, just comfortable. She was loath to break it. It felt like a truce.

Ray started peeling away the label on their bottle with the edge of their thumbnail. The firelight played along the planes of their face. Simone tried not to stare at the shadowed divot right above their upper lip. "Hey, can we talk? About what happened a few weeks ago?"

Simone went rigid in her chair. "A few weeks ago?" she said, as if she didn't remember exactly what Ray meant.

"The day HR sent out that damn email." Ray scrubbed a hand over their face and sighed. "I think I need to apologize for how I acted."

"What?" Simone shot upright and stared at Ray. "No, I'm the one who should apologize. I was way out of line. You're not a coward. I don't know why I said that."

"Yeah, you do," Ray said softly, eyes on the fire. "You weren't wrong. One little bump in the road and back I went into the closet, didn't even put up a fight."

"I'm sure you had your reasons," Simone said, realizing as she said it that it was probably something she should have considered before. "Ray, you keep saying you need this job. Why is that?"

Ray pushed the hood off their head, running an impatient hand through their wild curls. "It's kind of personal," they said. "At the time, I didn't want to get into the whole thing, you know?"

"Sorry. That's— Of course you don't have to tell me."

"No, I want to tell you. I've been meaning to." Ray sighed. They were quiet for a moment, then said, "You know how I'm taking off work for a few weeks next month?"

"Yes, I saw that on the production calendar." Simone's thoughts raced. TDC offered two weeks of paid vacation as part of their benefits package, something you didn't get working at most restaurants. Was that really so important to Ray? "So, two whole weeks off. Where are you going?"

"Uh, nowhere. Except into surgery," Ray said. "The two weeks are my recovery period."

"Oh!" Simone gasped. But Ray was the picture of health! So virile and . . . uh, just really virile. *Stop thinking about the word "virile," Larkspur.* "What's wrong? Is it serious?"

"No, it's— I mean, it is a problem, but the surgery is a good thing. I'm looking forward to it. Have been for years, actually."

Simone frowned. "Years?" Ray had been dealing with some serious health issue for years and it was only being resolved now? "I don't understand."

Ray was all patience. "I'm getting top surgery, Simone."

"Oh." Simone stared blankly, then, realizing this referred to the removal of breast tissue and not some kind of sexually dominant thing, she brightened. "Oh, of course."

Ray cocked an eyebrow. "You do know what that is, right?"

"Well, I have a vague idea. You're getting your"—she flung a hand toward Ray's chest—"top . . . done? Like, *done*-done?"

"Yep. My top half will be officially done-zo," Ray said with a slow-spreading smile.

Simone flushed. "Right! Exciting. Bon voyage to all that." She surreptitiously eyed Ray's broad, hoodie-covered chest again. "Will it hurt?"

"Eh, it won't be a picnic." Ray shrugged. "But the important thing is that my surgeon takes health insurance. Not all of them do."

Simone looked off into the dancing fire, trying to marshal her thoughts. Along with vacation days, TDC had a decent insurance plan, something no restaurant gig ever offered. "Oh my god." Her eyes widened as she turned back to Ray. "That's why you can't risk your job right now."

"Yep." Ray took a long swig. "No health insurance, no surgery. There's no way I'd be able to pay for it all out of pocket. I could barely scrape together the co-pay as it is." They ripped the last of the label away from the bottle, balling it up and throwing it into the fire pit. Simone watched it sizzle into nothing.

"They don't know, do they?" Simone asked. "Anyone at TDC?"

"No." Ray shuddered. "Absolutely not. If the wrong people found out, it could get even worse for me. I don't want to give them one more thing to hold over my head."

"One more thing?" Simone frowned. "Did they threaten you before?"

"Nothing that scary," Ray said quickly. "Just little things, trying to make my life that much harder. Like this trip." They gestured to the van, sitting in the parking lot, and the dark, quiet shape of the motel. "There was a lot of talk about wanting me to formally apologize to Chase and walk back any plans to come out on video and, 'oh, by the way, completely unrelated, but we may not have the budget for that proposed trip upstate, so you might have to fill in the shooting schedule with some of Chase's ideas.'"

"Like the women-in-brewing thing?" Simone guessed.

Ray gave her a salute with their beer bottle. "Bingo. At least this way, the whole crew doesn't get punished." They stuck their empty back in its slot in the six-pack and grabbed a fresh one, which meant they didn't have to maintain eye contact before saying, "They also implied that they were thinking of changing direction on Revamp. That if I didn't do what they wanted, they'd split us up, have just you on the show by yourself."

"What?" Simone's mouth dropped open. "But you're the reason the show works. Why would they even consider doing that?"

Ray shrugged, not meeting her eye. "Maybe they thought I was getting too popular or something. I don't know. I just . . . I didn't want to stop working with you."

"I don't want that either," Simone said, her voice small and quiet. If she were a different kind of person, she would gather up her courage and say it was more than the work, that she didn't want them to be separated at all. But that was a bridge too far.

That green gaze swung to her again, then darted away. Ray sighed. "I wish I could just walk away from the whole damn thing, really." They cracked open the fresh bottle, loud in the quiet night.

Right. Simone swallowed, understanding washing over her. The job was a necessary evil, and though working together was one comparatively bright spot, they wouldn't know each other at all if Ray had a choice in the matter. But this wasn't about Simone or her ego. This was about Ray.

"I get why you can't quit, though," Simone said. She bit her lip. "I—I think you're strong, to do what you're doing." She caught Ray's eye as she said it, trying to feel a fraction of that kind of bravery as she held their gaze.

Ray gave a disbelieving huff. "A stronger person wouldn't need this stupid surgery; they'd just accept their body for what it is and tell the rest of the world to fuck right off."

"Hey, that is not true." Simone sat up straight and then draped over the arm of her chair so she could lean closer and see Ray's forlorn face better in the dark. "Needing surgery isn't weak. You wouldn't tell someone with cancer or—or—or a broken leg to just get over it, would you?"

Ray slumped low in their chair. "It's not the same thing."

"Maybe not the exact same thing, but, Ray, come on." She made a helpless gesture. "You've worked so hard and sacrificed so much for this. You don't do all that without being a total badass."

"Maybe." Ray gave her a fleeting glance. "I guess when you said I was acting like a coward, it brought up a bunch of shit that I thought I'd already dealt with."

Simone leaned closer. "I'm so, so sorry—"

Ray waved her away. "It's fine."

"No, it's not! Listen." She swallowed. What she wanted to say was important, and she wanted to get it right. "You have more dignity and courage in your little finger than the rest of TDC combined. You . . . you amaze me."

Ray's smile returned in degrees. They turned to Simone with a wattage that rivaled the fire. "I do?"

"Totally."

"Thanks, Mona," Ray said. "You're pretty amazing yourself."

Simone smiled back.

They kept smiling at each other. The fire kept crackling. The insects kept humming. Simone thought it was going rather well. Such a nice moment.

Of course, she ruined it by opening her big mouth.

"Lucky for you the surgery won't be that extensive," she said, "since you're already pretty trim up top."

Ray cocked their head. "Oh?" Their eyebrows shot up. "I am, am I?"

Simone flushed hotly. "That is, you have an athletic build! You're not very—um—endowed. In the region in question. Not that I've noticed, really." Oh, Christ. She could feel her face getting redder by the second, so she hid it in her hands. That one beer must have gone straight to her head. "Okay, forget that I said any of that."

"Yeah, don't think I can." Ray laughed. "Not endowed, huh? I don't think anyone's ever applied those words to me in that order."

"I am going to crawl into the fire."

Big, chapped hands took Simone gently by the wrists and pried her hands from her face. Simone looked up miserably at Ray, who wore an amused twist to their lips. "My chest looks flat because I wear a binder every day. Once I get the surgery, I won't need to do that anymore."

"Oh," Simone whispered. "I didn't know."

"You couldn't've. You've never seen me without a binder before. I'm actually pretty big up top. Like, a C-cup."

Simone's eyes widened. "You are?" Her eyes stayed riveted to Ray's face as she fought the urge to glance down at their chest. "Sorry, I don't want to be rude, I just . . . never imagined." Her forehead creased with worry. "That must be really painful, having to wear something so restrictive all the time. No wonder you need this surgery."

Ray looked pleasantly surprised. "Yeah, exactly. Glad you understand."

Simone dredged up a watery smile before realizing how close they still were. She looked down and saw that Ray was still holding her by the wrists, big palms warm on her skin. She tore her gaze away. Eye contact. Eye contact was more polite. Eye contact was normal. But when she met Ray's eyes, they only held hers for a moment before drifting down to her lips.

For one half-second, Simone thought maybe that look meant something.

But only for a half-second.

Then Ray was back in motion, dropping her wrists with a short laugh. They picked up their beer where they'd left it leaning against their chair leg in the grass. "You're a good friend, Mona."

Friends. Simone's heart stuttered. They were still friends.

That was something. Wasn't it?

She watched Ray's profile as they sipped at their beer, the planes and angles of their face bathed in firelight. The green in their eyes looked greener, somehow; their hair softer now that it wasn't shoved under a ball cap. Maybe it was just the beer Simone had drunk, but she felt the urge to reach over and brush a few stray curls from Ray's forehead. To leave her chair behind and sit in Ray's lap instead. To find out if the apricot sour tasted any better from Ray's lips.

Simone sucked in a gasp.

Those were not friendly thoughts. She had to get away before she did something she'd regret. This was too newly mended, the peace between them. She had to preserve it at all costs.

"It's getting late," she said, rising awkwardly from her chair. "I should get to bed."

Ray looked up at her, a twinkle in their eye. "You've been drinking. Need me to tuck you in?"

"No!" Simone sputtered, her face growing hot. "I barely finished the one beer." She held up her bottle for examination. A half-inch of liquid still sloshed at the bottom.

"Relax," Ray laughed. "I was just joking. I know what Drunk Simone looks like."

"Well, you're never meeting her again." Simone tossed back

the last mouthful of beer and handed the empty to Ray. Their fingers brushed, which she resolutely ignored. "See you in the morning," she said, turning toward the motel.

She wasn't even out of the ring of benches around the fire pit before Ray's voice stopped her. "Hey, Mona?"

She turned, her heart in her throat. "Yes?" *Ask me to stay. Ask me if you can come to my room. Ask me anything, please, anything.*

Ray seemed to hesitate before saying, "Sleep well."

"You too." Covering her disappointment, Simone trudged back to her lonely room.

She did not sleep well at all. She spent most of the night staring up at the strange ceiling, listening to the weird non-city night sounds, and trying very hard to fall asleep and not dream of Ray.

Chapter 22

Simone knew on some level that people fell in love all the time. She'd heard about it, anyway. Her parents must have been in love at some point before they got married and subsequently divorced. The couples she saw sharing dessert in restaurants—they had to be in love. (Simone couldn't fathom any other reason for allowing someone to eat half of your nicely composed and well-executed dessert.)

Love happened, if only, she had assumed, to other people.

It would be extremely inconvenient to find herself in that position, and yet she wondered if maybe she *had* ended up there—and with a coworker, no less. A coworker who was, as Luna would say, *going through it* at the moment. The last thing either of them needed, really, was Simone complicating things even further. So on the way back from the Finger Lakes, Simone made a pact with herself: she would not mention these pesky feelings—which may or may not have been love—and she would be the best friend and ally to Ray that she could be. Ray needed support at this critical time, not some simpering, lovesick idiot asking them out to brunch. Perhaps at some future date, when Simone had earned it, she could see if Ray would be interested in more. For now, though, she would Act Normal.

Simone acted as normal as possible, to her credit. She went to work, shot videos with Ray, wrote her articles—despite Mikkah's increasingly draconian deadlines; two days to research and write a longform article on food delivery apps was not cool—and populated her social media feeds like she was supposed to. The atmosphere in the office and test kitchen was still fairly tense. Nobody except her and the video crew used Ray's correct pronouns, unless you counted Gene, who had stammered between *she* and *they* in the kitchen one morning before throwing his hands in the air and saying, "I don't want to make waves, okay? I've got two kids at home." To which Ray had rolled their shoulders and stalked off to find the fresh oregano Gene needed.

At least now Simone knew what was at stake and was able to hold her tongue for Ray's sake. She found small ways to show her support in silence. A slice of spring vegetable frittata wrapped in parchment and left in the pocket of Ray's apron early in the morning, for example, or an extra piece of lemon meringue pie left by their laptop after a video shoot. It was the least she could do, especially when nine times out of ten she came into the test kitchen in the early morning to find that Ray had already set out all the ingredients she would need for the day on her workstation. That kind of efficiency was enough to make anyone's heart beat a little faster, surely.

Simone checked the production calendar regularly for work purposes, of course, but now she kept an eye on the date that Ray's "vacation" was due to begin, making sure it didn't change. The day was fast approaching. Soon, Ray would get their surgery—and then they wouldn't be beholden to their job at TDC. Simone wondered if they would quit right away. She wanted them to be happy, of course, but the idea of coming into the test kitchen every day and not seeing Ray's smile or hearing their weird laugh . . . Simone didn't much like that idea either.

She sighed as she stirred a pot of fragrant broth. If only there was a way to cut out the bad parts of TDC and keep the parts she loved. Like cooking. And baking. And possibly Ray.

Who was apparently standing right at her elbow. "Are you busy?" they asked.

Simone nearly dropped her wooden spoon into the broth. "What? Uh—" She glanced at the pot's bubbling contents. "This needs to simmer for a bit, so I have time. What's up?"

Ray's eyes slid over to the next workstation, where Chase was haranguing Gene about the right way to stand while shooting his next video. "Come take a look at the storage room with me," they said. This was a conversation to be had on the down-low, apparently.

Once they were safely behind the storeroom's closed door, Simone asked in a rush, "Is everything okay?" It was Thursday, and Ray's time off was scheduled to begin Monday. Had something happened to upset Ray's plans?

Ray stuck their hands in their pockets and leaned back against the shut door. "I need to ask you for a favor."

"Of course. Anything." Simone winced. *Sound more desperate*, she berated herself.

"It's kind of a big one. You can totally say no."

"Noted," Simone said, though she'd already made up her mind to do whatever Ray needed. "What is it?"

"I, uh—" Ray cracked their neck side to side. The pops were audible. "So, you know how I'm going into surgery on Monday?"

"Oh, is it that time already?" Simone said, trying for casual. She attempted to lean against a tower of rice sacks, but they shifted dangerously, so she gave up on that and just stood.

"Yeah," Ray said, eyeing her strangely. "Anyway, my friend— uh, ex-girlfriend turned friend, Kelsey—she was going to keep an eye on me while I recovered, but now something's come up for her and she can't be at my place the first night after the surgery. Do you think you could . . . ?"

"Absolutely!" Simone gushed. "However long you need!" She couldn't believe her luck. Ray wasn't asking Petey or Jake or Lin or anyone else for help. They were asking *her*. Finally, a chance to be useful.

Ray blinked, probably a little taken aback by her enthusiasm. "It would just be one night. Kels will be free after that. She's got to travel for work, some last-minute thing."

"Not a problem." Simone shook her head fervently. "Like, at all."

"Great." Ray's smile fell a bit. "The first night is supposed to be pretty rough. Do you think you can handle a little blood? Or are you kind of squeamish?"

"I've butchered whole pigs," Simone said. "I think I can handle a few wounds. What are friends for?"

"Exactly." Was it Simone's imagination, or had Ray gone all tight around the corners of their mouth? Whatever it was passed quickly, and they pulled out their phone. "Here, let me text you all the details. My address, the surgery timeline, all that stuff." They looked up, green eyes soft. "And seriously. Thank you. I was freaking out for a second there. Thought we might have to postpone."

"It's no big deal," Simone assured. "Happy to help." She offered what she hoped was a normal smile, all the while fighting the growing warmth building inside her at the thought of spending more time with Ray outside of work. Sure, Ray would be recovering from surgery, but still. It was something.

They made their plans and parted ways with promises not to mention it again while they were at the office.

Simone arrived at Ray's building after work on Monday carrying a huge insulated cooler bag filled with individual meals frozen in little plastic containers. She had spent most of her weekend prepping them, carefully choosing recipes she knew would freeze well, discarding any that were too rich on account of how they might upset Ray's stomach. She had done some Googling to find the best kinds of foods for post-surgery recoveries, and it was pretty standard: nothing too spicy, nothing too greasy, low in sodium. Simone had opted for healthy comfort food: chicken noodle soup from scratch, lasagna roll-ups with shredded carrot and zucchini in the sauce, shepherd's pie with cauliflower mashed into the potato topping, homemade frozen burritos with a mild bean and cheese filling. There was even a masterful semifreddo, in case Ray was feeling up for some dessert.

Chocolate, of course, Ray's favorite.

The giant bag filled with all these treats sat at Simone's feet while she herself sat on the steps leading up to the building's front door. Simone checked her phone again. Kelsey, Ray's former-girlfriend-now-friend (whatever *that* meant), had texted her nearly forty minutes ago to say they were leaving the hospital and would be there soon. Another resident of the building approached the door and gave Simone a curious look. Simone waved hello and tried to look as non-suspicious as possible.

It was a newer building, and pretty big; Simone had seen an elevator when she'd peeked in the front windows that flanked the lobby door. Most of the people going in and out seemed to be young, diverse, not many in pairs, only one baby stroller that Simone helped to lug up the steps, the mother thanking her in Spanish.

Finally, a car with an Uber sticker in the window pulled up to the curb and a tiny pixie jumped out of the back seat, dressed in workout clothes and with a haircut that Simone felt was too trendy to be real.

Simone hesitated on the sidewalk, unsure if this was the infamous Kels. She called out, "Hello? Are you Kelsey?"

Kelsey didn't even look her way, too busy with going around to the other side of the car. "Can you give me a hand?" She spoke in a clipped, curt way that made it sound like she was angry that Simone hadn't done so already without being asked.

"Oh, sure!" Simone gave her cooler bag an agonized glance before abandoning it momentarily. She made her way around the car, where Kelsey was pulling Ray out of the back seat.

Simone stopped short when she finally saw Ray. They were

wearing their gray hoodie, zipped only halfway with nothing underneath but bandages. Dabs of dried blood and iodine were still on their neck and the hollow of their throat. Their face was ashen and blank, like they were sleeping with their eyes open. It was a shock to see Ray like this, the opposite of their usual lively self.

"Get their other arm," Kelsey snapped. "I can't carry them by myself. At least at the hospital, I had an aide to help me."

"Right. Sorry." Simone moved as quick as she could, wedging herself in the awkward, tiny space they had to maneuver Ray out of the Uber. She took their left hand while Kels took the right, and together they gently coaxed Ray to their feet. They were only wearing socks, Simone noticed, the bright-blue non-slip kind that they give you in hospitals. She winced at the thought of their feet separated from New York City pavement by only a thin layer of cotton.

"What happened to Ray's shoes?" she asked.

Kelsey gave a frustrated grunt. "There's a bag in the back seat. I'm trying to get to it, if you would just handle Ray for one second."

"Okay," Simone said, stung. "I was just asking."

Kelsey left her post on Ray's right side to dig around in the back seat, and Simone nearly buckled under Ray's weight. She only managed to keep them upright by leaning them carefully against the side of the car.

"Do you have to be so tall?" she muttered.

"Oh, hey, Mona," Ray said, their sleepy, roving gaze fastening onto her face for just a moment. "You made it."

Simone managed a smile. "Of course I did. I told you I'd be here, didn't I?"

"You did. Because you're so nice. Very nice to me. All the time." Ray's head lolled.

"I don't know about all the time." Simone laughed weakly, remembering their talk by the fire upstate.

"All the time! But especially now." Ray nodded as if this pronouncement was final. "And Kels is here! Have you met Kelsey? She's nice, too."

Kelsey reappeared at Ray's right side, a backpack slung over one shoulder as she wriggled under Ray's arm. "The anesthesia is still kind of wearing off," she said to Simone.

"Yeah, I figured."

"Come on, sweetie," Kelsey said into Ray's ear. Simone filed that endearment away to think about some other time, when she wasn't responsible for Ray's health. "We've got to go inside now. Can you help us out? Walk a little?"

"I'm great at walking," Ray said, and attempted to prove it with a wobbly step in the direction of the sidewalk.

They made the laborious trek up the walkway toward the lobby door. Simone paused at the steps to grab her cooler bag, slinging it over her shoulder so she could have both hands free to catch Ray if the worst happened and they took a tumble. Kels couldn't seem to hold back a scoff as they all stopped.

"Did you think this was going to be a picnic? Why'd you bring all that?"

Simone struggled under the combined weight of the food and Ray. "They're frozen meals. I thought Ray might not be up to cooking for a while."

"Aw, that was thoughtful of you, Mona. Kels, wasn't that thoughtful?" Ray's head rested briefly on Simone's shoulder before switching to Kelsey's.

"Knowing you, there won't be any space in the freezer for it anyway," Kelsey grumbled.

"I'll make space. Don't worry about it." Simone tried to keep her tone light—for Ray's sake, if nothing else—but it was difficult when Kelsey was being so combative for no reason.

They made their way into the building and up the elevator to Ray's third-floor studio apartment. Kelsey was in charge of the keys, so Simone made sure Ray was propped up against the wall as she negotiated the door locks.

"Hey," Ray drawled, some of their usual light coming back

to their eyes, "this is kind of like that one time, remember? When I carried you home?"

"You did not carry—there was no carrying," Simone said to Kelsey, who was now looking at her with narrowed eyes. Then, to Ray, Simone said, "At least you have an elevator, right?"

"Yeah. And Kels. We didn't have her last time. That would've made things easier."

"Maybe," Simone said, though she doubted it.

"Door's open," Kelsey announced loudly. She dumped the backpack inside and took Ray by the arm. "Let's get this one into bed."

Conveniently, Ray's compact apartment meant they didn't have far to go. It was a straight shot to the modest double bed situated on the far side of the open living space. Simone didn't notice much else; she was too occupied with Ray. She kept a keen eye on them, worried they would slip from her grasp and fall to the floor. As they passed the loveseat, Simone managed to wriggle the strap of her cooler bag and her tote off her arm and set them down on the cushions.

"Okay," Kelsey said, all singsong, as she yanked the covers down. "Slide on in. Remember what the doctor said: on your back at all times. Here, let's take off your jacket."

Simone felt incredibly superfluous as Kelsey handled everything at once. She fluffed the pillows, unzipped Ray's hoodie, and started peeling it off their shoulders. Simone wondered if she should look away for modesty's sake, and something of her confusion must have shown on her face, because Kelsey snorted and said, "You don't have to act like it's a peep show. There's literally nothing to see."

The hoodie fell away, and Simone saw she was right. Ray's entire upper torso was wrapped in thick layers of bandages. A tube protruded from under their right arm, a drainage bulb dangling from the end.

"Kels," Ray muttered, exhaustion making their voice thready, "give her a break. None of us has exactly been through this before." They tried to crawl into bed, but Simone and Kelsey held them fast.

"Flip around," Simone said. "You're supposed to lie on your back."

Ray gave a groan and followed instructions, sliding awkwardly between the sheets, pulling their long legs up after them. Simone caught a glimpse of the soft pajama pants they were wearing. Up close, she could see they had tiny rainbow-colored cupcakes patterned on them.

"Nice jammies," she commented, pulling the sheet up to Ray's waist.

"I like cupcakes," Ray whined. "Everyone acts like cupcakes are girly, but they're not, they're for everyone." Simone couldn't argue with that, and she didn't want to.

"I'll bake you some when you're feeling better," she promised, which earned her a slightly woozy smile.

"Sleep now," Kelsey ordered like a drill sergeant. She produced a pack of wet wipes from her pocket and started scrubbing the dried blood and iodine stains from Ray's neck and collarbone. Simone wished she'd thought to bring something useful like that herself. "I'll be back before you know it. Tomorrow afternoon at the latest."

Ray's eyes were already closed. "I know, I know. Go. Have a good trip."

Kelsey seemed to waver at Ray's bedside, gaze darting to Simone, then back to Ray again. "I can still cancel if you want. It's not too late. My boss would understand; it wouldn't be the end of the world if I'm not in the meeting."

"No, you said it was important, so you should go. We'll be fine, Kels. Seriously." Ray nuzzled against their pillow. "Simone is the most responsible person in the world. She won't let me die."

"That's not funny," Kelsey said.

"Yeah, it's really not." Simone fidgeted with the duvet, smoothing it over Ray's legs.

"Go," Ray insisted. "Boston needs you. Get to the airport."

"Ugh. Fine." Kelsey bent to press a quick kiss to Ray's forehead. Simone looked away at that. "Be good, sweetie. See you tomorrow."

Ray mumbled a goodbye that morphed into a soft snore. Out like a light.

"Hey." Kelsey spoke in a quiet undertone, so as not to wake the patient. She jerked her head toward the kitchen area. "Let's talk for a minute."

Simone nodded and grabbed her cooler bag, thinking to make it a more efficient trip. She stood in Ray's tiny—yet aggressively organized—kitchen, trying not to feel cowed by Ray's equally tiny and aggressive ex-girlfriend. Kelsey had retrieved the backpack from its spot by the door and was emptying it out onto the kitchen counter. A glossy folder bursting with paperwork, a graduated cylinder, a weird blue-and-white plastic thing with tubes and hooks, and about forty thousand orange prescription bottles cascaded onto the lab-engineered stone slab. There wasn't much room for it all; Ray's homebrew equipment was taking up most of the counter space. The huge coffee urn–looking machine and endless coils of tubing were scrubbed clean as whistles, Simone noticed, like they were waiting for their owner's next batch of beer.

"This is everything the doctor gave me," Kelsey said, pointing to her untidy pile. "Ray starts taking the pills tomorrow morning unless they wake up and need the pain meds tonight. I wrote down the schedule." She smacked a piece of paper with a list of times and dosages beside the mountain of stuff. "There's instructions on how to empty the drain, too. Basically, if you see the bulb is full of fluid—"

"I got it," Simone broke in, impatient. "I watched a YouTube video on how to do it."

Kelsey stared at her for a beat, then turned back to the pile. "Okay. Don't forget to measure the fluid when you pour it out.

That's what the little . . . measuring cup thing is for." She picked up the graduated cylinder to show it to Simone.

"And keep a record of how many milliliters and the date and time, yes, I know," Simone said.

Kelsey tossed the plastic cylinder onto the counter with enough force to make a loud clatter. "So I guess you know everything and I should just get out of your hair, huh?" she said. "God, Ray was right. You really are a control freak."

Simone drew back, trying not to let the hurt show on her face. Was that really how Ray saw her? "I'm not trying to be controlling. I just did a little research because I wanted to make sure I could help out as best I can. That's why I'm here, isn't it?"

"I don't know why you're here, honestly," Kelsey seethed. "You shouldn't be. Not after you called Ray a coward."

It took Simone a moment to realize that Kelsey was referring to the argument they'd had in the walk-in before the road trip. "Ray told you about that?"

"I'm their best friend. Of course they told me." Kelsey crossed her arms over her chest and gave Simone a hard look.

"Look, Ray and I talked it over," Simone said. "I've already apologized."

"Yeah?" She looked unimpressed. "Ray's too forgiving. I've told them that a thousand times."

Simone threw her hands up in the air. "Look, I get that you're protective, but they asked me to do this so you've just got to trust she—I mean, they made the right call." She looked away, flustered at her misstep and angry with herself for getting so worked up in the first place.

Kelsey's nostrils flared as she leaned forward into Simone's personal space. "You better not misgender them to their face while you're here."

"I know, I'm sorry. I'm still new to it. I'm trying my best to—"

"Post-surgery is a really delicate time, mental health–wise," Kelsey barreled on. "Some people get super depressed, like the adrenaline's worn off and they start thinking maybe they made a mistake because they're in pain and it sucks. And hearing you say 'she' could do a lot of damage."

"I understand," Simone said. "It won't happen again."

Kelsey didn't look convinced. "At least it's just for one night," she muttered. She turned back to the glossy folder and flicked it open. "If something happens, like if Ray gets feverish or is in a lot of pain or there's bleeding through the bandages, you call this number." She stabbed a neon-painted fingernail at the page. "And tell the doctor. And then you call me, and I'll get on the first flight back."

"That won't happen. Everything is going to be fine."

Kelsey's glare promised murder if it wasn't. She left the kitchen, Simone trailing behind, and grabbed a small roller bag that had been stored near the coat rack. "I've got to get to JFK. You have my number. Text me if anything happens."

"I will," Simone said.

Kelsey stood by the door, phone in hand, doubtless already ordering an Uber. "Don't fuck this up," she said, and with that final, hostile piece of advice, she left Simone alone with only Ray's snoring as company.

Chapter 23

Once Kelsey was gone and Simone had given herself some time to calm down from their encounter, she was able to putter. She loved puttering around her own apartment, tidying up, watering her and Luna's one houseplant, taking stock of the kitchen and making grocery lists. She was very much looking forward to puttering around Ray's studio and, in the process, perhaps learning a little bit more about what made them tick. The neatly made bed had been a shock—a pleasant one—and Simone was curious to see what other surprises Ray's home had in store.

First things first: she put away the frozen meals she'd brought. Kelsey had been right; Ray's freezer was pretty full. It looked like they used it as storage for almost everything. There were squishy ice packs, loaves of bread and bagels, meticulously labeled packets of meat, even blocks of cheese still in their shrink-wrapped packaging. Simone turned these over with a frown.

"Who freezes five pounds of cheddar?" she murmured to herself. Maybe it had been on sale.

She rearranged the freezer to make space for her new additions, trying not to mess too much with what was clearly

Ray's personal organizational system. Once that was done, she turned her attention to tidying—not that there was much to do. Ray kept their small apartment almost as spotless as they did the test kitchen. Mostly, Simone just stacked the papers Kelsey had dumped on the countertop, giving them all a quick read-through as she worked. Then she scooped up all the medications and lined them up on Ray's dresser. She consulted Kelsey's handwritten pill schedule and arranged the prescription bottles in the approximate order in which they needed to be taken. She noticed the pharmacy labels listed the patient's name as Rachel Lyton, and Simone felt a strange surge of anger at that. She found a pen in a cup on the coffee table and scratched them all out, writing RAY above it in neat block letters.

There was a weight bench shoved into one corner of the apartment with stacks of weights beside it. Simone didn't even try to tidy up there, not wanting to move the heavy plates on her own. Instead, she drifted over to the modular bookshelf that served as a divider between the sitting and sleeping portions of the studio, hoping to find out what Ray liked to read, but was disappointed to find it held no books at all, just tchotchkes and framed photographs. Simone picked up a soft plastic monkey, squeezing it experimentally until it gave a piercing squeak. Startled, she turned to check to see if it had woken up Ray, but they were still sleeping soundly, unmoving on the bed. Simone put the monkey back.

Feeling a little like a detective, she turned back to examine the framed pictures, wondering if she could spot any family photos, but she came up with nothing on that front. There were no older people who could have been Ray's parents, no possible siblings who shared Ray's green eyes or pointy chin. *Must all be pictures of friends,* Simone reasoned. It looked like they were mostly taken at parties, entirely candid. She picked up one. Ray looked so young. Their hair was longer, dyed a wild shade of green. Simone replaced the photo, glad that Ray had gone back to their naturally blond curls. Simone was very fond of those curls.

The smile she hadn't realized she had fell from her lips when she spotted Kelsey in several group shots. One photo featured just her and Ray, the two of them drinking out of beer bottles in unison, arms slung around each other. Simone picked up the simple wooden frame that held the photo, as if looking at it more closely would reveal some clue. It was a later photo, just the tips of Ray's hair retaining the green color. Had this been taken when Ray and Kels were still dating? She wasn't sure it was kosher to keep couple-y photos after a breakup, no matter how friendly you remained with your ex. And Kelsey still called Ray *sweetie*. Simone made a face, watching her reflection in the frame's glass. Maybe Kelsey was the type of person who called everyone *sweetie*, but she doubted it.

Ray's gravelly voice nearly made her drop the picture. "How do you like me in green?" they asked. "Think I should dye it again?"

"Hey! You're awake." Simone fumbled the framed photograph back onto the shelf. "How are you feeling?"

Ray made a noise between a grunt and a question. "A little fuzzy. Did Kels leave?"

"Yeah, like four hours ago. Don't you remember?"

"Not really." Ray tipped their head back into their pillow. "Guess the drugs did a real number on me. Was she mean to you, or did I just dream that?"

Simone didn't want to speak ill of Ray's friend, so instead of total honesty, she said, "I think she was a little stressed out, what with her travel plans and everything."

"So she *was* mean to you." Ray gave her a lazy grin. "Trust me, I dated her for over three years; I know how Kels can get."

Simone drifted over to the bed and, lacking anywhere else, sat carefully on the edge of the mattress. "Three years? That's, um—that's a long time."

"Yeah." Ray shifted, eyes drifting to half-shut. "A really long time."

"It's nice that you're still such good friends," Simone said, a bit forced. "She clearly cares for you a lot." That much was true, though Simone left out the part where Kelsey had demonstrated it by practically lifting her leg and marking her territory. Maybe Kelsey still had feelings for Ray? Simone's curiosity finally overwhelmed her sense of propriety. "How come you broke up?"

"Oh, you know," Ray said, lifting a tired hand and giving a brief wave. "Stuff. Getting older. Growing apart." They turned their head toward the kitchen. "Can I have some water?"

Finally, something to do. Simone busied herself with that, returning with the cup of water to find Ray struggling to sit up in bed.

"No, don't move so much, I've got it." Simone sat on the edge of the mattress again and held the glass for Ray, angling the drinking straw so they could sip while mostly flat on their back. As she watched Ray drink, Simone was aware of how close they were. Ray kept their gaze on the water glass, but Simone was free to watch every movement in their face. "Sorry," she said, "I know I shouldn't pry. About Kelsey, I mean. That's your business."

Ray finished drinking and melted back into the bed with a little grunt of pain. "It's fine, really. The truth is, after I figured out all my gender stuff, Kels wasn't really interested in dating me anymore."

Simone nearly spilled the glass of water as she set it on the bedside table. "Really? She said that? And you're still friends with her?" She could feel her face getting hot just thinking about it, angry at Kelsey's hypocrisy.

"It wasn't her fault," Ray said. "Wasn't anyone's fault, really. She wanted to be supportive, but I'm not a woman and Kels is a lesbian. For some queer couples, that might work, but for us it didn't. She felt guilty for not being attracted to me anymore, I felt like shit for making her stay—it was honestly the best thing we could have done, breaking up. Hurt like hell at the time, sure, but—" Ray winced, hand going to their diaphragm. "Ugh. That feels not so great."

"Just to be clear, we're talking current physical pain, right? Not residual breakup pain?"

"Yeah. Can you get me one of the pain pills?" Ray's head tipped at the lineup of orange prescription bottles on the dresser.

"Of course." Simone found the oxy-whatever and pulled out her phone, typing the name into Google just to be certain. "Okay, this is the one. It says you should take it with food. Have you eaten?"

"Believe it or not, the Uber driver wouldn't let us stop at Per Se on the way home for a quick four-course dinner."

"Good to see your sense of humor wasn't surgically removed." Simone rolled her eyes and bustled toward the tiny kitchen. "What are you hungry for? Sandwich? Salad? Ooh," she said, after opening the fridge and seeing a carton of eggs and a plastic clamshell of baby spinach. "I can make a quiche."

"Cereal," Ray pleaded from the bed. "Please, nothing more complicated than cereal."

Simone poked her head out of the kitchen to give Ray an admonishing look. "Just cereal? Are you sure?" She couldn't quite keep the disappointment out of her voice.

Ray groaned and made an abortive move to rub their chest. "I swear, the minute I get my appetite back, you can feed me as much as you want. Right now, I just want to take the damn pills."

"Fine." Simone disappeared back into the kitchen and found some store-brand bagged cereal on top of the fridge. She opened cabinets and drawers until she found a bowl and a spoon. "Your cereal is for children," she called as she poured the brightly colored marshmallow-laden bits into the bowl, where they clinked crisply.

"You're just jealous," Ray called back, but their breath hitched at the end in a pained gasp.

Simone hurried to pour the milk and get back to the bed,

cereal and pain medicine in each hand. "Is it bad?" she asked. Her brow furrowed at the sight of Ray laid out in bed. There was a fine sheen of sweat on their forehead.

"It's not great," Ray admitted, and reached for the cereal bowl. "Thanks."

Simone pulled a little footstool over from the sitting area so she could be at Ray's bedside. They took a few bites, then made a grabby hand motion at the pill bottle Simone still held.

"Right. One every eight hours as needed, it says." She shook one white oblong pill into her palm and held it out to Ray.

"Probably will only need this one, to be honest. At least, I hope so." Ray popped the pill and swallowed it dry before Simone could offer them the glass of water. They made a face. "Bleh. Hate these things. They make me so groggy."

"You've had them before?"

"Once, when I got my wisdom teeth pulled. I think I slept for, like, two days. So be prepared for that exciting adventure, I guess." Ray managed a watery smile.

Simone tapped the rim of the cereal bowl Ray still held awkwardly in one hand. "Eat a little more, okay?"

"Yes, Mom," Ray grumbled, and ate another spoonful. Simone watched them hide a wince as they moved their arm to do so.

"I could do that for you if you'd rather," she said.

"I'm not a baby," Ray said around a mouthful of marshmallow bits. "I can do it myself."

"But you don't *need* to."

"Maybe I *want* to," Ray shot back, then stifled another pained gasp, hand flying to the edge of their bandages. "Fuck."

"Okay, that's it, I'm overriding whatever you want." Simone took the bowl from Ray's lax hand. And not a moment too soon; they probably would have dropped it, as shaky as they looked. "Are you all right?"

"Yeah." Ray's voice shook just like their arm had. "Just need a minute for the pill to kick in." Their eyes were clamped shut, but Simone suspected if they opened, she might see tears. The thought made her heart race. She hated seeing Ray like this. They were supposed to be flitting around, talking everyone's ear off and being the most vibrant person in the room. It was wrong, seeing them pale and sweaty and stuck in bed.

Loading up the spoon with cereal, she tried for a little levity. "Here comes the airplane." She lifted it and did a few swirls in the air. "Vroom vroom."

"Airplanes don't go vroom vroom."

"Okay, fine. Insert jet engine noise here. Now eat."

Ray groaned. "A few more bites, then I'm done," they said, and accepted the spoon into their mouth with a long-suffering sigh. "This is embarrassing," they said as they chewed.

"No, it's not. I'm supposed to be helping you out. You're just letting me do my job. One more?" She gave Ray another mouthful. It was all very Florence Nightingale. She hoped she wasn't turning as red as she felt.

Ray ate the last bite and held up a hand. "I'm good now." They tried to slowly wriggle into a more prone position, and Simone rushed to set down the bowl and help rearrange pillows. Ray seemed to be drooping fast.

"Tired?" she asked.

Ray nodded. "Exhausted." Their eyes drifted closed, then opened again at half-mast. "It wasn't just me, you know."

"What wasn't just you?"

"Me and Kels breaking up." They settled back into their newly fluffed pillows with a small sigh. "It wasn't just me being nonbinary. She's got this picture in her mind of what she wants her future to look like. You know, wife, two kids, a dog, big backyard. Not that I don't like kids," Ray mumbled, eyes fluttering shut again. "Kids are awesome. Just not for me. Does that make sense?"

"Totally," Simone said. "I'm the same way. I love other people's kids." She busied herself with tidying away the pill bottle and dumping the still-half-full cereal bowl into the kitchen sink.

"But that doesn't mean I want my own, necessarily," she called from the kitchen. Children, in Simone's experience, were illogical and sticky. She could never quite picture how they would fit into her carefully ordered life. She figured that if she felt so ambivalent about it, it was probably a sign that she shouldn't have kids. She hastened back to the bed.

"Exactly. See? You get it." Ray yawned hugely. "Kels didn't. And carrying 'em, also not for me. That was the plan, Kelsey's plan. That we'd each have one. Didn't know how to explain to her why I didn't want to be pregnant. That's, like, my nightmare. Literally, it's a whole recurring thing."

Simone, lacking any other little chores to do, came back to sit at Ray's side. "Sorry," she said quietly. "That sounds hard."

"Well, that's what I get for dating a cis person." Ray turned their head into their pillow, nuzzling it like a puppy trying to find the coziest spot. "Won't make that mistake again."

Simone felt the breath leave her lungs in one long punched-out rush. That was certainly information she would have rather not known, if only to avoid feeling . . . however she was feeling now. Was it possible to feel rejected before you'd even made a move? Strange feelings of inadequacy welled up in her belly.

Of course Ray wouldn't be interested in someone like her. Of course there was no chance. Of course their bits of banter didn't mean anything, of course it was just work, of course she shouldn't have given in to daydreams. Stupid, stupid, stupid.

She was also acutely aware that the drugs and the exhaustion might be making Ray a little looser in the tongue than usual (which was really saying something), and perhaps the polite thing to do would be to stop the conversation before they said something even more personal.

"Get some rest," she said thickly, tucking the blankets around Ray's waist, careful not to disturb the bandages. "I'll be here if you need anything."

Ray was already asleep, snoring with their mouth slightly open. Simone watched them for a moment, just to make sure their breathing was even and not pained, and then retreated to the nearby loveseat. She felt the urge to keep puttering around the small studio, maybe clean the bathroom, but didn't want to go too far in case Ray woke up. The sun had set, and the last of the day's light was filtering through the gauzy curtains. They'd said the first night would be the hardest, so all of Simone's nerves were on high alert. Yet Ray was sleeping so deeply. Maybe Ray would be knocked out for the rest of the evening and Simone wouldn't need to do much at all.

She was considering pulling her paperback out of her tote bag and settling in when she heard Ray give a little whimper of pain. Simone vaulted off the couch and rushed to the bed just in time to see Ray, eyes still closed in sleep, trying their best to roll over on their right side, where the drain was sticking out of their skin.

"Okay, nope, we're sleeping on our back tonight, remember?" Simone took Ray by the shoulders—*damn, they were built*—and tried to gently guide them back into the proper position. But Ray was strong, even in sleep, and fought against Simone's grasp.

"Ray, you've got to wake up. Just for a second." Simone patted them gently on the cheek. "Can you open your eyes for me?"

"Nggrk." One green eye opened into a tiny slit. "What?"

"You keep trying to sleep on your side. You can't do that, okay?" Simone was on the bed now, kneeling beside Ray, using her weight to keep them pinned. "You'll pull your stitches."

Ray blinked, slow and miserable. "Sorry. My brain's all—" They tried to make a gesture, but Simone caught their hand before it could be raised too high.

"I know, you're not yourself. Drugs and the leftover anesthesia and exhaustion—just stay like this, okay? Can you do that?"

Ray seemed to have reached their limit on questions. They groaned, pressing their face to the side, into their pillow. "I jus' want to sleep."

"I know," Simone cooed. "I'm sorry, I know this sucks."

She checked the bulb at the end of Ray's drain tube. It was full of pinkish fluid. "Okay, I've got to empty this. Just stay still."

She flew around the apartment, gathering all the things she would need: the measurement tube from the doctor's office, a wad of paper towels, a notebook and pen from the coffee table. Her heart was pounding as she tried to remember every detail of that video she'd watched, but that had been yesterday, which seemed a lifetime ago. To be safe, she grabbed the printout from the doctor that contained step-by-step instructions on how to empty the drain.

"Okay," she murmured, flipping the page over to make sure she had all the steps. "Okay, no problem." She looked up to find Ray now trying to crawl onto their left side. "Hey, none of that!" She dropped the paper onto the floor and moved Ray back into place. "Come on, Ray. You've got to stay here."

As sleepy as they were, Ray still managed to moan out a sound that pierced Simone's heart. Was this normal? Should she call the doctor and ask? She glanced at the clock; it was definitely past business hours. And if she called the doctor, she would be obliged to call Kelsey, and she didn't want Kelsey to think she couldn't handle this.

Her hands shook as she pinched the drain tube where it entered Ray's skin. Ray, head lolling, watched as Simone worked the tube through her fingertips to get as much fluid out as possible.

"Ugh, gross," Ray mumbled, tossing their head back into the pillow. "I'm so gross. Mona, I'm sorry. You shouldn't have to do this. This was a bad idea."

"Shut up," Simone said. "I'm trying to concentrate." Then, because Ray's answering whine made her feel like she'd just yelled at a basket full of kittens, she added, "And you're not gross. You're healing. Don't worry about it."

She managed to work open the bulb and empty it into the measuring tube. Only a few drops dribbled down the side, and she was quick to mop them up with the paper towels. She checked the level on the beaker, then made a quick notation of the amount on the notepad along with the date and time. It was within the normal range, per the doctor's instructions.

"There. Easy," she said with a nod, though it had actually been pretty terrifying. She took the beaker into the bathroom and disposed of the fluid in the toilet, flushing it away. Logically, she knew that Ray had just been through surgery, and it was only normal for the body to bleed and leak and produce all kinds of stuff to try and heal itself, but she didn't like the idea of the blood and junk being Ray's. Ray's blood and junk belonged on the inside.

She came back to the bed and nearly screamed in frustration. Ray was, once again, sleepily rolling over onto their side, the bedsheets all twisted up in their legs.

"You've got to stop doing this," she said, putting the rinsed cylinder back on the dresser with the pill bottles and manhandling Ray into the correct position. "You're going to hurt yourself!"

"'M sorry," Ray said, and they sounded it. "But I never sleep on my back. I'm not trying to do it, I swear, it just happens."

"Okay." Simone thought hard. Ray needed to sleep, but they moved in their sleep. How could she stop them from moving? "I'm going to try something. Sorry, it's not going to be— Sorry." She clambered onto the bed, walking on her knees, and scooted down the mattress so she was below Ray's waist. Swallowing whatever was left of her pride, she wrapped her arms and legs around Ray's legs, using all her weight to keep them pinned in place.

Ray went very still.

"Is this okay?" Simone mumbled against Ray's pajama-covered kneecap. "It's the only thing I could think to do."

"Oh. Uh." Ray's foot twitched against Simone's calf. "Guess we can try it this way." Their hand reached down and patted Simone's head. "Thanks. I'm not normally one for being held down in bed, but I appreciate it."

"Don't try to make me laugh," Simone snapped. "I don't want to jostle you."

"Okay," Ray said, uncharacteristically quiet. "Sorry."

"No need to be sorry. Just go to sleep." She gave Ray's lanky legs a little squeeze, hugging them to her. However Ray felt or did not feel about her, Simone wasn't about to let them down. Even if that meant sleeping in ten- and fifteen-minute fits and starts all night, wrapped around Ray octopus-like, and waking at the slightest motion of Ray's body.

It's what friends do, Simone thought with a tinge of sleep-deprived bitterness. *Just friends, and nothing else.*

Chapter 24

The next morning, Simone didn't wake up so much as muzzily open her eyes for the millionth time. Weak morning light was slanting through the windows on either side of the bed. She untangled herself from Ray as gracefully as she could manage. Ray, for their part, was finally sleeping like a log and didn't appear to be moving anytime soon. It had been a rough night for them both and Simone wanted to let them sleep as long as possible.

Simone slid off the bed with all of her stealth and emptied Ray's drain again. Once that odious task was done, she went to the kitchen in search of breakfast. She ignored Ray's cereal selection in favor of a bowl of oatmeal—not from a packet, of course. She was glad to see Ray was too thrifty for that. Instead, she scooped some quick oats from the labeled container in the cupboard, then added whatever she could find: a lump of brown sugar, a few slivered almonds, a handful of dried cranberries, a drop of vanilla extract (not pure vanilla, Simone noted, but since Ray was not a baker, they could be excused), a pinch of kosher salt. She even added a dab of the protein powder she found sitting on top of Ray's fridge in a fat gallon tub. Mix it up with a little milk, microwave on high for a couple minutes, *et voilà*. A real breakfast.

Simone ate her oatmeal while making a circuit of Ray's studio. She drifted to the window, chewing, and parted the thin linen curtains. Looked like a bleak day outside, all late-spring rainclouds with nary a sunbeam in sight. She let the curtain fall back into place and turned to the living area.

She still couldn't believe Ray didn't keep any books on their bookshelf. Maybe they didn't read. Or maybe they only read e-books; having a tiny apartment would certainly be a reason to go fully digital, Simone supposed. But nothing? Not even a cookbook? Simone herself was swimming in cookbooks, some of them gifts from family members who didn't know what else to get her when Christmas and her birthday rolled around. Mostly, though, they were purchases she could not help but make for herself. A beautiful cookbook with tantalizing photographs and challenging techniques—there was nothing Simone liked more. She owned hardcovers of every single one of Lisette D'Amboise's books, of course, even the ones that were more travel writing than recipes. They lived on the bookcase in her living room, with Luna's true crime collection occupying the higher shelves.

Simone poked around the small modern coffee table, peeking into its many levels and drawers to see if maybe that's where Ray's book collection was hiding. She muffled a cry of triumph when a drawer at last gave up its secrets. Books! Three of them! And yes, they were cookbooks. Of course they were. Simone beamed, happy in the knowledge that, at least in this, she and Ray had something in common. She pulled the books from their drawer to take a look through them, her bowl of oatmeal forgotten for the moment on the coffee table's polished surface.

The covers crinkled under her fingertips. Simone frowned and looked more closely. They were wrapped in stiff plastic. Odd. She flipped the book around.

On the back was a barcode taped to the plastic. And on

the barcode was the logo for the New York Public Library, Fort Washington branch.

Simone had nothing against libraries, and in fact made a point to donate to the NYPL every holiday season, but she had never checked out a cookbook. It seemed strange to do so. What if you wanted to note in the margins that ⅓ cup of butter was better than ¼? She glanced at the titles.

Retro Dinner Party.

A Taste of Midwest Classics.

Quick and Easy Meals for Every Mom! Published—Simone checked the frontispiece—in 1972.

Her brow was now fully furrowed. "But—"

There were bright-pink Post-it notes sticking up from the top of each book. Simone flipped to one of the marked pages. Ray's doctor-scrawl handwriting appeared on the rest of the note. Simone squinted at it, trying to make out the illegible words. "'Picnic'?" she read aloud. "'Some aunt'? What the heck?" Her eyes fell to the recipe title.

It was Yankee Salad.

She tore through the book to get to the other marked pages. Frito Pie. Fried bologna sandwiches. Sloppy Joes. She dropped the first book and went for the next. Hot dish. *Pasta* hot dish (which was subtitled "Homemade Hamburger Helper," Christ). Creamed corn casserole.

"No, no, no," Simone whispered as she opened the final book.

Strawberry pretzel salad.

Fancy, party-ready cheese ball.

Pigs in a blanket. With beer-cheese dip.

Simone let the book fall from her hands to land on the area rug with a soft thump. Every single one of the dishes they'd used in Recipe Revamp, including some that she was sure were marked for future episodes . . . they were all here in these old library books.

She stared into space as her tired brain tried to kick into

gear. Why would Ray need these cookbooks when they had their family recipe box?

The recipe box, which, she now realized, she'd never actually opened.

What in the world was going on?

"Found a good beach read?"

Ray's dry, if groggy, voice was so unexpected, Simone nearly jumped out of her skin. She turned to find Ray awake and watching her with a wry raise of an eyebrow. She looked down at the books she still held. "I just sort of stumbled across them," Simone said needlessly.

The eyebrow arched a little higher. "You stumbled through a drawer?"

"Uh." Simone held the books awkwardly against her chest.

Ray gave a low groan and shifted a little against the pillows. "Well, at least you didn't open the drawer with all the weird sex stuff."

"The—what?"

"Nothing." They gestured to the library books. "So. You found 'em, huh?"

"I was curious," Simone barreled onward, "so I flipped through them, and it looks like—Ray?" She stared down at the topmost book, its cover a burnt-orange throwback to some other era. "What's going on? Why do you have these? Were you . . . doing research or something? Comparing your family recipes to these, maybe?"

Ray exhaled through their nose. "No," they said, sounding very tired. "I mean, it was research, sure. But I wasn't comparing anything."

"I don't understand."

"There's nothing to compare," Ray said, closing their eyes. "There are no Lyton family recipes."

"But your little recipe box—with the flowers all over it—"

"It's a prop, Mona. I found it at Goodwill for, like, a dollar.

It's empty. Well." They waggled their head. "Sometimes I keep bottle caps in it."

"But . . . why?" Simone asked, confusion clouding her voice.

Ray shrugged, then scrunched their face in pain, their shoulders hunching. "Thought it would make for good video. The whole family angle."

"Okay," Simone said, drawing out the word, "but why not tell me it was all just for the show?" She saw how tired Ray still was, how difficult it was for them to form an answer, so she tried injecting a little levity into the conversation. For their sake. "I mean, it would have been a load off my mind if you told me you weren't actually forced to eat this crap as a kid." She gave a weak laugh, holding up the books.

"Oh, no, I did eat that crap." Ray scrubbed a hand over their face. "That part's true, at least."

"But you just said there are no Lyton family recipes."

"I'm not explaining this well." Ray sighed. Chewed their lip. Looked over to their nightstand and began to reach for the water glass that still sat there, half-full.

"Would you just let me—" Simone put the books down on the coffee table with a heavy *thunk* and maneuvered around the bed to do her nursemaid routine, drinking straw and all. As Ray sipped, sullenly staring up at her, Simone felt guilt gnawing away at her belly. Ray was supposed to be taking it easy, and here she was, upsetting them with Twenty Questions.

"I didn't mean to give you the third degree," she said into the silence that had descended. "I just don't get why you went through this whole song and dance."

Ray finished drinking the water and laid back on their pillow, their gaze pinned to the ceiling. "The thing is," they said slowly, "I'm not really in touch with my family. My parents and I don't talk. I have a sister, but it's been years since we last texted. So, yeah, I didn't have the recipes I remembered from way back when. That's why I had to look them up in library books."

Simone set the water glass back on the nightstand. "You couldn't just Google it?"

"I'm old-fashioned. In some ways."

"Right, no Facebook for you." Simone gave Ray a small smile, but it faded when it wasn't returned. Ray still wasn't even looking at her. "Hey, it's no big deal. So you're not close with your family; lots of people are in that situation."

"You're right," Ray said. "It's not a big deal."

More silence entered the room, took a look around, and settled into a comfortable chair in the corner. Simone interrupted it.

"Or maybe it is?" She tilted her head, noticing how tense Ray was.

Ray's lips twitched back and forth. They seemed to come to a decision, and their bright green eyes finally found Simone's. "My folks threw me out of the house when I was fifteen," they said, "but I turned out okay. It wasn't this big, dramatic thing, so I don't really talk about it. Could have been worse."

Simone's lips parted. She sat down on the edge of the bed with great care. "Ray, I know you turned out okay," she said. "You're . . . the okayest person I know."

That got a little smile, at least. "Wow, Mona, you really know how to make me feel special."

"You know what I mean," Simone huffed. "And if you don't want to talk about it, that's fine, but just because it could have been worse doesn't mean it wasn't a shitty thing to do. *Fifteen*? Who does that?" She was getting worked up now. "You couldn't even—even drive!"

"Not legally," Ray conceded.

"You're hoping I take the bait and ask about your misspent youth of unlicensed driving—"

"Mostly pick-up trucks."

"—but it's not going to work. Unless you want me to drop the whole thing," Simone hurried to add, "in which case, consider it dropped. I just don't—" She could feel her hands trembling with rage at these parents. "How could someone not want you in their home?" She sealed her lips shut and looked away before she let loose any other too-poignant opinions. Her eyes felt hot and prickly with tears.

Ray cleared their throat with a soft cough. "I mean, look at me," they said, quiet in the strange, early-morning softness. "I'm six foot one. I can't shut up. I've got this loud laugh—"

"But that's *you*," Simone said.

"Yeah, and it makes it impossible for me to lay low. I can't fly under the radar; I'm not built for it. I couldn't"—Ray made an aborted gesture, their hand falling back to the bed in exhaustion—"dial down the queerness. My parents, my mom especially, they begged me to try to fit in. Said it would be safer. It's a cliché, I know, but small towns are really like that sometimes. And I did try." Ray shrugged. "It just never worked." They looked down and picked at a loose thread at the corner of their bedsheet. "And then you have a few arguments about dating girls, and you can't seem to make anyone happy, and one day you come home and the door's got new locks."

Simone knew her mouth had fallen open in shock, but she couldn't pretend to be unmoved. "That's how they did it? Ray, that is—that is cruel. You were a child."

Ray shrugged again. "It wasn't like I was sleeping in a gutter or anything. I just sort of couch-surfed with friends for a few years, the ones with chill parents. I got by."

"Still," Simone said, "that doesn't excuse what your parents did. Those—those *assholes*, pardon my French."

"And that was them just thinking I was gay," Ray said with a false grin. "Imagine if they'd stuck around to find out about the gender stuff."

Simone didn't think it was very funny. Her face remained hard as stone. "I'm glad they didn't." Her hand found Ray's on the bed and held it tightly. "They don't deserve to have someone as great as you in their life. Seriously, it's their loss. Fuck them."

Ray's eyes went wide. "Oh, you said the bad word. The worst one."

"I save it for important things." She gave Ray's hand a squeeze. In that moment, she actually understood where Kelsey was coming from; who wouldn't be furious at someone who had hurt Ray?

Ray squeezed back, stronger than Simone would have thought possible, given how tired they were.

She considered sitting there all day, holding Ray's hand, but then she remembered how Ray was very clearly not interested in her as anything more than a colleague and friend. Only a horrible cheat would use Ray's momentary vulnerability to get closer, to pretend they could be more. To secretly derive pleasure from the press of their calloused palm.

Simone snatched her hand back, cradling it in her lap as if it had been burned. She didn't know where to look. "So. Meds now?" Her voice was high. "Kelsey left me a list. Let's see what you're due to take."

She floated around the apartment, chattering away to fill the silence. Ray was still tired and far too quiet, so Simone found herself picking up the slack. She talked about the weather, about how nasty Mikkah had been when she'd asked her to approve this Tuesday off, about the recipe for summer berry crepes she'd been working on all week, anything she could think of that didn't involve pain or heartache. Ray took their pills without complaint but wasn't interested in eating anything more than a few bites of cereal again. There was an awkward moment when Ray got up to use the bathroom and asked Simone to dig up some clean clothes so they could change. Simone contemplated the small dresser and tentatively peeked into the top drawer, thankfully not finding any weird sex stuff, just socks and underwear. As it turned out, Ray was partial to boxer briefs, a piece of information that Simone really wished she hadn't learned in this context. She passed a pair of them and some fresh sweatpants through the cracked bathroom door, trying and failing not to blush all the while.

"What do you want to do for the rest of the day?" she asked through the bathroom door. "Do you want to watch some movies or something?" All the research she'd done had said that patients needed to relax, especially the first few days.

"Not sure I'm up for anything that requires more than ten minutes of my attention span," Ray said. The door opened, revealing Ray wearing the new sweatpants Simone had picked out. And, she could only assume, the underwear, although she had no proof of that.

She produced a belated smile. "Looking good."

"Feeling like crap," Ray said. They nodded at the pile of dirty clothes they'd left behind on the bathroom floor. "I couldn't really bend down easily. Would you mind—?"

"Yeah, of course. Let's get you to bed first." Simone took Ray gently by the arm.

Ray made a frustrated sound. "I'm sorry I'm so useless like this," they said as they tottered out of the bathroom.

"You're not useless. Why can't you just accept help when you need it?"

"Guess I'm just not used to it." Ray slid back into bed slowly, careful not to catch their bandages on anything. "Would rather take care of myself."

"Well, you don't have a choice right now. I'm going to get you more fluids," Simone said, guiding their socked feet under the covers, "and then I'm going to make you eat something, even if it's just plain crackers. Then I'm going to put your dirty clothes in the hamper. And then I am going to put on the best thing for someone with a ten-minute attention span to watch."

Ray squinted at Simone in confusion. "Which is?"

Simone couldn't hide her grin now. "Lisette D'Amboise on public access."

Simone made good on all her promises, including loading up the entire back catalog of Lisette's late '90s show, *Classic Kitchen*, on Ray's Netflix account. She moved the TV on its wheeled stand to the foot of the bed and joined Ray in sitting against the headboard. Maybe on any other day, Simone would not have dared sit in Ray's bed while they watched TV together, but she reasoned that they had already spent the night together in said bed, so this wasn't any worse.

Ray watched the TV screen with a sleepy expression. "What is she doing to that chicken?"

"Spatchcocking," Simone gushed.

"Her hair is really something."

"This was her 1998 look. It was the style at the time, I guess. At least in France."

Ray stifled a yawn in their hand. "This is not a judgment on your taste in television, Mona, but I think I might fall asleep."

"That's okay. Lisette D'Amboise is famously soothing. Do you want any more water or crackers before you—?" Simone looked over at Ray only to find they had already nodded off. She watched their face, slack in sleep, for just a moment before muting the TV. There was lots to do before Kelsey arrived from her afternoon flight home. Simone knew she should get up, make herself some lunch, maybe try to catch up on work emails that had surely piled up during her day off. But she was still wiped from a sleepless night, and now that Ray was sleeping, all the adrenaline that had kept Simone going was seeping away, leaving her wrung out.

She'd just wait a few minutes before getting up. Make sure that Ray was well and truly out; less chance to disturb them. Simone relaxed against the headboard and closed her eyes just for a moment.

She was asleep before she knew what hit her.

An alarm woke her hours later. Simone jerked awake and fumbled in her pocket for her phone, staring at it without comprehension for a while. Right, she'd set alerts for Ray's pill times. She also had some texts from Kelsey, saying she was getting on her flight back home. She'd asked for updates no less than four times, getting increasingly demanding as time went on without an answer. Simone grimaced, typing out a quick apology one-handed and letting her know that Ray was doing fine, they were just tired.

Simone rubbed the grains of sleep from her eyes. They both were, she supposed.

A soft sound captured her attention, and she looked over to find that Ray had tipped over slightly to lean against Simone's shoulder. They were still sleeping; Simone could see their eyes moving beneath their eyelids. She hoped it was a good dream.

"Sorry," she whispered, easing her arm out from under Ray's head. "We've got to wake up. You need your meds."

Ray gave a grunt of protest and mashed their face harder against Simone. She could feel their breath through her sleeve. "'M fine right here," they murmured. Their arm reached over as if preparing to wrap Simone up in an embrace, but Simone caught Ray by the wrist before they could twist too much.

"Careful," she said. "You're—you're moving around again. Wake up." She gave Ray's shoulder a little shake with her free hand.

Green eyes blinked open. At first, they were warm and clouded with sleep. Then recognition flooded in, and Simone had to clamp down on the pain in her chest as Ray realized who they'd been reaching for. How quickly Ray pulled away and sat up, clearing their throat.

"Sorry," they said in a gravelly voice. "I didn't—"

"It's okay. You were asleep." Simone tried to project a calm she didn't feel as she floundered her way out of the bed and onto her feet. She smoothed down her hair and tried to force some cheer into her voice. "Okay! Antibiotics and pills for nerve pain, coming right up. Oh, and Kelsey texted me. Her flight should be landing any minute. Soon you'll be back in the care of your real nurse."

"Great," Ray said. They still sounded tired, but Simone knew that was to be expected. She tried not to worry too much, though it was impossible for her not to worry when it came to Ray.

The rest of the afternoon was a blur of pills, then a tiny bit of food—Ray actually agreed to eat some of Simone's chicken and dumplings, a real coup—and more episodes of *Classic Kitchen*. Simone tried to wear a brave face for Ray's sake, but the truth was she was really exhausted. She was too old to go without a good night's sleep. She wondered how Kelsey was planning to manage nearly two full weeks of caretaking without a break. It didn't seem possible.

By the time Kelsey buzzed to be let up, Simone had made up her mind. It was just as well Ray was in the bathroom when she let Kelsey into the apartment; this was a conversation that should be had in private.

"You cannot do this by yourself," she said to Kelsey in lieu of a greeting. "I was up all night with Ray, and every time I think I can get a little rest, it's time for pills or food or a bathroom break. Two weeks is a long time, and I don't think you should do it alone."

"Hello, Kelsey. How was the flight, Kelsey? Isn't Boston beautiful this time of year, Kelsey?" Kelsey muttered as she entered, wheeling her suitcase behind her. "Why, yes, Simone. Thank you, Simone. It's so nice to be back."

"I'm serious." Simone shut the door and locked it. "I think it's a bad idea to put all this responsibility on one person. You're going to burn yourself out."

Kelsey dropped herself onto the loveseat and kicked off her heeled boots. "Well, Ray's insurance doesn't cover a visiting nurse, so what do you propose I do?"

"Let me help," Simone said. "We can work in shifts. You take the days, I can take nights. Maybe we trade weekends."

Kelsey looked up at her, a frown crossing her pretty face. "The first night is usually the worst, right? So it should be smooth sailing from here on out. I don't need your help."

"Maybe." Simone crossed her arms over her chest. "But do you want Ray to have two competent caretakers instead of one sleep-deprived zombie? Do you want their recovery to be as painless as possible? Or do you hate my guts so much that you don't care?"

"I don't hate your guts," Kelsey said, looking away with guilt in her eyes. "I just—Ray's my best friend." She fidgeted with the piping on one of the throw pillows. "What you said all those weeks ago really hurt them. I don't like seeing them get hurt."

"I don't either," Simone said. She spread her hands in offering. "I just want to help. I swear."

Kelsey's lips twisted in thought before she blew out a sigh. "Well, it's up to Ray, of course, but I guess it wouldn't be a bad idea to have you help out at night." She gave Simone a questioning look. "How are you going to manage coming here after a full day at the office? Won't you be running on empty?"

"I can take a couple of half-days if I need to catch up on sleep." Simone shrugged. "I have a ton of vacation time banked that I need to use up, anyway."

Ray's voice came from across the room. "Why am I not surprised."

"Ray!" Simone turned to see them leaning heavily against the wall. "You were supposed to let me know when you were done," she chided, rushing to their side and ducking under their arm to lend some support.

"Wanted to try making it back on my own. Almost had it that time. Hey, Kels, how was Boston?" Ray nodded to her as they plodded by.

"Harbor-esque. Simone wants us to keep you company in shifts. What do you think?"

"Uh, sure. Sounds good. You really don't mind giving up your free time for a while?" This last part was directed at Simone while they went through the careful maneuver of sliding back into bed with Simone's help.

"Not in the least," Simone said, tugging the sheets up to Ray's waist and smoothing them over their lap.

Ray looked wildly over to Kelsey, and the two of them shared a look that Simone could not decipher. She swallowed a sigh. Exes-turned-best-friends probably had their own secret language that Simone could never hope to learn.

"It might be nice for me to have a break once in a while," Kelsey said slowly, "but only if you're cool with it, Ray."

"Yeah, I'm cool." Ray's voice squeaked, and they cleared their throat to try again. "Totally cool."

"It's settled, then." Simone straightened. "Kelsey, I left all the drain output notes here on the dresser with the pills, and I also made some notations on your pill schedule so you know when Ray took their last oxy. Oh, and also—"

"I've got it." Kelsey laughed, waving Simone away. "Go home and get some sleep. I'll see you tomorrow."

Simone wished them both good night and went home to fall face-first and fully clothed into bed, where she stayed until her alarm went off the next morning.

The next few days were a strain, energy-wise, but it was worth a few hours' lost sleep for Simone to go to Ray's at the end of a long workday. They spent the evenings eating Simone's frozen meals and watching bad movies, with episodes of Lisette D'Amboise shows sprinkled in for flavor. Ray's strength returned little by little, and soon they could get out of bed and walk around the apartment without any help. Simone still told Ray to stay in bed and let her get the water glass or the dish of semifreddo, and usually Ray complied with only mild complaining, but even those bickering sessions were precious to Simone.

At night, they still shared a bed. In case Ray started rolling over in their sleep, of course. Neither of them mentioned how Ray hadn't had any issues with that since the first night home. Simone slept on top of the sheets, listening to Ray breathe in the dark. She didn't dare try to cuddle close. She didn't want to end up putting any pressure on Ray's wounds, for one thing. And she doubted Ray would be thrilled to wake up to find Simone was treating them like her own personal body pillow.

She thought about it, though. Dreamt about it more than she cared to admit.

Sometimes she caught herself wishing that Ray never fully healed so she'd have plenty of excuses to hang out with them, and then she felt terrible for even thinking such a thing. Of course she wanted Ray to heal. Once they could return to work, Simone could see them all day long in the test kitchen. But being at the office was not the same as the warm summer nights spent lounging in Ray's bed, watching Lisette make croissants on TV, the box fan turned up as high as it would go, and Ray laughing at some very French thing Lisette had said.

Soon the weekend rolled around, and the one-week mark approached. Ray was scheduled for their first follow-up that Monday, when they would finally get their bandages removed. Kelsey had asked Simone to take the Sunday shift, and Simone had happily agreed. She was looking forward to spending a whole day with Ray.

"Can we go for a walk?" Ray asked the minute she came in the door. "I'm going stir-crazy sitting inside all day."

Simone considered the picture Ray made at the foot of the bed, sweatpants and high-top sneakers already on. They wore a loud button-up shirt patterned all over with fluorescent yellow fish, though it was hanging open and unbuttoned at the moment.

"Did the doctor say you were allowed to leave the house?" she asked.

Ray nodded. "He said a little exercise is fine. No weightlifting yet, but I'm cleared for a short walk. You can call Kelsey if you don't believe me. She just left, like, five minutes ago. Probably isn't even on the subway yet."

"I'll take you at your word," Simone said magnanimously, and stepped forward to grab the panes of Ray's open shirt.

"Here, let me." She buttoned it starting at the bottom, careful not to brush against the bandages that still covered Ray's chest. "How's the pain?"

"It's fine. Looking forward to getting these off tomorrow, though." Ray dipped their chin at the bandages. "And really looking forward to finally taking a damn shower. Sorry if I smell. My little bird baths at the sink are probably not cutting it."

Simone ignored the temptation to assure Ray that their scent, as strong as it was after nearly a week without showering, was not the worst thing Simone's nose had ever encountered. In fact, she'd come to associate that cedar tang of Ray's skin with laughter and good food in the test kitchen. But only a gross weirdo would admit they had not only memorized a friend's smell, but wished it came in some kind of portable version. Like a sachet Simone could inhale when Ray wasn't around.

Yeah, definitely should not say that out loud.

"So where are we walking?" she said instead in a bid to ignore the awkwardness of dressing Ray like a life-sized doll.

Ray's gaze was heavy on Simone's face; she could feel it even though she was concentrating on the movements of her hands. "There's something I'd like to show you. It's not far."

Simone left the top three buttons undone. Enough for just a tiny bit of Ray's collarbones to peek out. "Sounds good to me."

Ray was only a little unsteady on their feet as they left the building. Simone noticed they used the handrails in the elevators and on the short set of steps leading from the front door to the sidewalk. Their legs were probably shaky from so many days spent on bed rest.

"Do you want to hold my arm?" she offered.

"As much as I'd like to promenade with you," Ray said, "I think I'm okay for now."

Simone kept her mouth shut, but hovered close to Ray's side just in case they needed extra support.

Ray led the way down the street and through a small, narrow park. It was very pretty, leafy trees and flower beds bursting to life with summertime colors. They passed by a sloping meadow—Ray mentioned it was where all the neighborhood kids came to go sledding when it snowed—and then out through a set of park gates.

"You don't want to keep walking through here?" Simone asked. The park stretched ahead of them, but Ray was leading them back to the busy street.

"Just a little further. This way," Ray said.

They navigated the crosswalk and made their way up one block to an intersection where the road split. In the triangle that the streets made sat a huge old building, its curved facade dotted with boarded-up windows, bits of graffiti, and a few NO TRES-PASSING signs. Simone didn't really have an eye for architecture, but even she could see the art deco lines of the building and its little fan-shaped embellishments must have once made it a grand structure indeed. Across the top of the facade, just above the third-floor windows, the words BILLINGS MECHANICAL were engraved in letters as tall as Simone. She gazed up at them and wondered why Ray would bring her to see an abandoned building.

"So?" Ray was looking only at Simone, as if gauging her reaction. "What do you think?"

Simone struggled to find a more polite way to phrase it, but in the end could only ask, "What is it?"

"It's an old auto showroom and repair shop from the twenties." Ray's usually wild gestures were somewhat hampered by their bandages, but they pointed as eagerly as possible to the various windows, or what had once been windows. "The new cars were displayed up there, see? So that everybody going by could see the shiny new models. And then below on the first floor, you've got the body shop, and then below that, the base-ment for storing parts and stuff. It's been sitting here empty since, like, 1965."

"I didn't know you were so into classic cars," Simone said, uncertain. "Uh—*are* you into classic cars? Or just old buildings associated with classic cars?"

Ray looked at her. Their cheeks were flushed and their eyes creased at the corners like they were examining Simone as hard as they could.

"If I tell you something," Ray said, "will you promise not to make fun of me?" They shifted on their feet, sneakers squeaking.

Simone could tell this question was serious. This wasn't like Ray's usually carefree joking; they were honestly nervous.

"I swear," Simone said with all the gravity she could muster.

Ray let out a sigh and gazed up at the crumbling building. "For a few years now, ever since I saw this place, I thought maybe—" Their tongue darted out to wet their lower lip. "This would be an amazing place to set up a brewery."

"Really?" Simone looked back at the hulking structure again, trying to picture it. It took some effort, but she could imagine the building becoming something beautiful, something Ray would be at home in. It was a little bittersweet to think of Ray here, far from the familiar world of the test kitchen, but they would be happy. That, Simone could picture clearly. "That would be amazing," she said, and she meant it.

Ray lit up, rounding on her with a huge grin. "Right? There's more than enough space for the brewing operation, maybe even a tasting room." They paced down the sidewalk, staring up at the stone facade. "You could brew a full lineup: IPAs, porter, sours, lagers. You could even have seasonal stuff. And the bars around here, the little mom-and-pop places, you could supply them at a discount once you got a distribution network going. Maybe you could even rent out some floors as event space, put in a rooftop deck if you could get the permits. It would be so perfect."

Simone stared at their profile. She'd never seen them this excited, and Simone had thought she was well-acquainted with the highest levels of Ray's excitement. It was infectious. "It sounds like you've put a lot of thought into this already," she said.

Ray turned back to Simone, and their smile fell from their face in slow degrees. "I mean, it's just a daydream. I know it's never really going to happen. Just one of those things that's, uh."

They ducked their head and scratched at their arm. "Nice to think about, sometimes."

Simone shrugged. "Why couldn't it happen? Seems to me you've already got a great concept."

"Sure, but . . ." Ray flicked a hand toward the empty, silent building. "I'd need to be rich to take on something like this. Even if I could afford to buy the place outright, it would take millions to refurbish it." Ray kicked at a pebble on the sidewalk, and it skittered away into the gutter.

"True," Simone admitted. "But maybe someday . . ."

"Yeah." Ray swallowed. "Maybe someday."

They both stared up at the building for a moment in silence.

"I'm pretty wiped," Ray finally said, turning around. "We should get back before I pass out on the nearest park bench."

Simone caught up with Ray's longer stride, walking at their side. When they reentered the park, she said, "Thank you for showing me your daydream."

Ray gave her an unreadable look. "You're welcome, Mona." They made their way through a narrow point in the path between some shady trees. "What's yours?"

"My what?"

"Your dream," Ray said. They shoved their hands in the pockets of their sweatpants and looked over at Simone with interest. "You must have one."

Simone's tongue felt too thick. For a few moments, it wasn't working properly. She knew she couldn't be completely honest, but she could flirt with the truth.

"My dream was to work at TDC, for all the good that did me. I don't know. I guess I've given up on stuff like that."

"No more big dreams?"

Simone looked at Ray, at their mussed hair that needed a touch-up on the buzzed sides. At the way their collarbones peeked through the neck of their shirt. At their eyes, sad and deep.

"No," she said, turning away. "No more dreams."

They didn't talk the rest of the way home.

Chapter 25

Simone had never in her life fallen asleep at a desk, whether in school or at work. Sleeping in public, in fact, was not a skill she'd ever learned. Her anxiety wouldn't let her, just one of its many fun side effects. All that aside, Simone wondered if today would be the day she broke her lifelong streak, because she was pretty sure she was about to pass out onto her keyboard while trying to write this article about baguettes.

Her hand groped for her coffee cup, and she took another swig, frowning as she tasted it. It had gone stone cold. If Ray were here, Simone might've wheedled a cup of espresso from them, but as it was, Ray was still on leave. Soon, though, Ray would be back at the office. For however long it took them to find a new job, at least.

Simone heaved a sigh. She knew she should be looking for a new position, too, but between Ray's surgery and the extra work Mikkah was piling on her plate, Simone just hadn't found the time.

"Knock, knock."

Simone swiveled in her office chair to find Delilah standing at her cubicle wall, a secret sort of smile on her face.

"Hi. Hello." Simone blinked. She didn't get many visitors at her desk these days, what with Mikkah's icy silence and the office's low morale. And she certainly wasn't expecting the assistant to the editor in chief. "What can I do for you, Delilah?"

"The real question is, do you want to know what I've done for *you*?" Delilah dipped her head at the photo of Lisette D'Amboise pinned to Simone's cube wall. "You're a Lisette fan, right?"

"Oh, absolutely." Simone's hands flew to cover her heart. "I've watched her on TV since I was a little kid. She's the best."

"Well, you know how they say you should never meet your heroes?" Delilah's smile widened. "Prepare for possible disappointment, I guess, because you're going to be joining her on stage at this year's Food Fest."

Simone's mouth dropped open. "What? Why? How did you—"

Delilah held up one finely manicured hand. "Let's just say I made some phone calls. And I know a few people. And someone has to keep TDC running while Pim Gladly is playing croquet or whatever at her beach house." This last was said in a whisper, and Simone stifled her laugh accordingly.

"But Food Fest . . . that's the biggest charity event in the industry," she said. "Every famous chef in the country is going to be there. How the heck did I get an invite?"

"You're one of the big dogs now," Delilah informed her. "Just look at the views on your videos. When I heard the guy from *Chef's Country* magazine wasn't going to make it this year, I figured, why not make some moves? Try to get our people on the big stage? You and Ray are going to be great."

"*Both* of us are going? Oh my god." Simone's excitement was immediately doused, though. "Uh, have you run this by any of the leadership yet? I'm not sure they would go for it."

Delilah looked around the bullpen, which was predictably empty at lunchtime. She dropped her voice anyway, leaning in so she could share her whispers with Simone. "Look, I see all of Pim's emails, you get me? The stuff TDC is doing to Ray—it's bullshit. They don't deserve this nonsense."

Simone's eyes went wide. "You know about that?"

"Yeah, but I can't say anything, obviously. No one listens to me around here. I keep making all these suggestions about how to get our business model in shape, but Pim never takes me seriously. She laughed me out of her office when I told her we really should be selling merch for your show." Delilah shook her head in disgust. "So I may have fudged the details a little bit when explaining Food Fest to the big boss. Said the Fest asked specifically for you and Ray. It wasn't a total lie; they did want you both—after I made the pitch."

"That's amazing," Simone breathed, "but why are you helping us?"

Delilah looked at her funny. "Because someone at this company needs to keep their head out of their ass. Ray's the reason we're in the black for the first time in years. We expand Ray's platform, we get more viewers, we get more money, the company doesn't fold, I keep getting a paycheck. It's simple math."

"Wow." Simone gazed up at her. "I wish you were in charge. You're really good at this stuff."

"I know, right?" Delilah smirked. "So when does Ray get back from vacation? I need to give you both a rundown on the event. Get this: we're going to livestream it." She did a little dance. "Lisette D'Amboise on *our* channel. Our numbers are going to explode!"

Holy crap. Simone's brain tried to catch up. Not only was she going to meet her culinary hero, she was going to do it live for the world to see.

"Uh, I think Ray's back in the office on Monday," she managed to say, as if she hadn't memorized Ray's schedule. "Can we talk then?"

"I'll put it on the calendar." Delilah was already tapping

away at her phone. "Better find a good party dress, Simone. You're going to need it." She flashed her a smile and left.

Even the thought of having to shop for a dress couldn't dampen Simone's mood. She whipped out her phone and sent Ray a text.

You're never going to believe what just happened.

They texted back and forth for the rest of the day, mostly misspelled words and strings of emojis on Ray's part. Simone couldn't seem to stop smiling. She was wide awake now, like the news had given her a second wind.

If you weren't still healing, she texted in a giddy haze, I'd give you a big hug tonight.

She stared at her phone after hitting Send, wondering what had gotten into her. Ray had made it very clear that romantically, they were not interested. Simone was acting like a fool, telling Ray stuff like that, even if it was true.

There was a long silence on Ray's end of the text conversation. Simone stared at the little screen. *Ray is typing*, it said.

Ray is typing.

Ray is still typing.

Then it stopped.

Simone's brow furrowed. Why couldn't she keep her big mouth shut? She started typing again, an apology for making it weird, but Ray's response finally pinged.

I'm healing as fast as I can.

Simone stared at the message. Another ping followed.

☺

A smiley face? What the hell was that supposed to mean? Simone huffed and tossed her phone in her desk drawer. She needed to concentrate on her work, not . . . whatever this was.

When Simone came into the test kitchen the next Monday, her heart almost burst from her chest. There was Ray, leather apron and all, pen stuck between their ear and their cap, puzzling over a stack of grocery invoices at one of the kitchen islands.

Simone took a small plastic container, the disposable kind that her local Chinese place used to deliver soup, and placed it on the counter. "Welcome back," she said. "Good to see you."

Ray gave her an amused glance. "You just saw me last night."

It was true; Simone had come over just to check up on Ray, not that they needed much help. Their recovery had gone smoothly, and the doctor had given the OK for Ray to return to work—with the appropriate amount of caution, of course.

Simone shrugged. "Still. I made you a promise." She indicated the container. "Go ahead."

Ray peeled open the lid and peeked inside. They pulled out a single chocolate cupcake, topped with swirls of rainbow-colored buttercream. "You promised me . . . a gay cupcake?" Ray asked.

Simone's smile fell. "Yeah. Like your pajamas."

Ray's look of confusion did not abate.

"You were joking about it when you got home from the hospital. Don't you remember?" Simone pressed.

"Uh, I was kind of high as a kite right after the surgery." Ray scratched their cheek. "I'm sure I said a lot of weird stuff."

"Oh." Simone deflated.

Ray hurried to say, "Not that I'm ever going to say no to something you baked." They took a huge bite, moaning happily. Their eyes danced. "Thank you, Simone," they said. With their mouth full. "This is the best gay cupcake ever."

"Keep your mouth closed while you're chewing," Simone said on autopilot.

"Yes, Mom," Ray returned, and ate another bite.

Other staff members began trickling in then, and the work-day began ramping up. Simone didn't have much time to speak to Ray again until later that afternoon, when she saw Ray out of the corner of her eye, struggling to lift a huge box onto the top shelf of a baking rack.

"Hey!" She abandoned the dough she'd been kneading and raced over, wiping her hands on her apron as she went. She spoke in a low hiss so Gene and Becca wouldn't overhear from their workstations. "You're not supposed to be doing that yet." She knew from the post-op info packets she'd read that Ray was prohibited from lifting anything above their head for the time being. Otherwise the surgery scars might pull and never heal right.

"It's just this one box," Ray whispered back. "It's not a big deal."

Simone began elbowing Ray out of the way. "Give it to me."

"You're too short."

"Then I'll put it somewhere else. Come on, give it to me."

"Simone." The way Ray hissed her name made her freeze. That was Ray's serious voice. She looked up to see Ray's face pinched in frustration. Their green eyes flickered over to Gene. "If they think I can't do my job," they said quietly, "they'll fire me."

Simone glanced back at Gene, who was oblivious to them, working on rolling out sheets of pasta. "Gene wouldn't—" She bit her tongue. She hadn't thought Mikkah capable of the things she'd said either. She tried again. "You're not just a kitchen manager anymore. You're a star. They won't fire you. And if they did, someone else would snatch you right up."

Ray snorted, but let Simone take the box from their hands. "Not a lot of open positions for 'goofball homebrewing video series host.' I checked."

Simone stored the box on a lower shelf. It didn't exactly fit, but she didn't care. "So, you've been looking for something else so you can get out of here?" She tried to keep her tone neutral. She didn't want Ray to think she was anything but encouraging, but it was hard to think of Ray leaving forever.

"I don't know." Ray lifted their hat and reset it lower on their forehead. "A friend of a friend is hiring for this new restaurant out in Brooklyn. The pay is shit and the commute would be awful, but—" They shrugged. "It's an option. Just not sure I'm ready to take it."

Simone nodded sagely. "You want to heal completely first, I

get it." All the research she'd seen said it would take at least six months for Ray to be back in fighting shape. And working in a real restaurant kitchen meant long hours and more heavy lifting.

"Sure, there's that," Ray said, looking down at their shoes. "But also, as much as this place sucks"—they looked up at Simone, eyes clear and open—"there're some parts that are really good."

Simone frowned. "Like the free food?"

Ray blinked exactly once. "Yeah, Mona. Like the free food."

"Well, I guess there's no reason for you to rush into anything." Simone gave the box one final shove, wedging it in place and dusting off her hands. "Plus, there's Food Fest to look forward to, at least. Do you know what you're going to wear? Delilah said I should get a dress."

Ray leaned against the wall, arms crossed over their chest. "Yeah, I've got this off-the-shoulder ballgown I thought I might dust off for the occasion."

Simone boggled. "Really?" She watched the smile spread across Ray's face and huffed. "Are you making fun of me again?"

"It's just so easy, is the thing."

"Hey!"

They both looked up to see Chase stalking across the test kitchen with the video crew setting up for a shoot behind him. "Are you ladies going to just stand around and chat all day, or can we get to work?"

Simone was about to snap. Food Fest be damned; a chance to meet Lisette be damned, even. She couldn't stand one more minute of this jerk. Her nostrils flared as she raised a finger in the air, ready to tell him off.

But Ray's hand covered hers, dragging her arm back down at her side. "Sure, Chase. Be right there."

Chase gave them one last smug look before going back to the camera setup, where he began bothering Jake about his lenses.

"I can't stand the way he talks to you," Simone whispered as they made their way to the workstation.

"Learn to let it go," Ray said back just as quietly. "I have."

Simone stared at the back of Chase's head, trying and failing to light him on fire with her mind. "You shouldn't have to."

Ray opened their mouth to retort, but then Chase called for places and the cameras started rolling. And it was back to business as usual.

If you could call turning a fried bologna sandwich into something edible "usual."

Chapter 26

The night of Food Fest finally arrived. The event was scheduled to take place on the observation deck of a massive high-rise overlooking the Hudson, with a cocktail hour on the outdoor terrace and the seated dinner and entertainment to follow inside the sprawling dining room. Simone still couldn't believe she was billed as part of said entertainment, her name and Ray's listed right under Lisette D'Amboise in the program.

It was a warm summer night, even with the breeze on the terrace, and Simone felt sweaty and nervous in her layers of floral chiffon. She tugged the flowing hem of her dress back into place and flipped through the program, pretending to read it for the fifteenth time.

People had been coming up to her all evening, asking for photos. One or two had even wanted autographs. Simone didn't see why anyone would want her signature; she was a very minor celebrity in the food world, at best. Ray was the real star— although Simone hadn't seen them arrive yet.

The breeze kicked up again. Simone slapped her hand down against her thigh before the chiffon could fly up and expose her. Why had she agreed to this stupid dress? She'd told Luna it was a bad idea. Simone had wanted to wear something simple and black, like Lisette always did on camera, but Luna had nixed that idea.

"You're the hot new thing," she'd insisted as she'd attacked the displays at Nordstrom Rack. "You're going to want to stand out."

Well, she would do that for sure if everyone got a peek at her underwear. Very memorable, flashing the entire culinary world. She sighed, putting the program away for the moment. At least the dress had pockets. She looked around, desperate to catch the eye of one of the waitstaff. Why did hors d'oeuvres never seem to pass within ten feet of her?

"Wow," a familiar voice on her right said. "Look at you."

Simone turned, a smile already on her lips to greet Ray, but she froze when she saw them standing there by the terrace rail. "Wow yourself." They were wearing a charcoal-gray suit with their white high-top sneakers, a brightly printed shirt open at the collar. "You . . . really clean up well."

"Thanks." Ray rubbed the back of their neck. "You look amazing. Obviously."

Simone tried not to glow at the compliment. Instead, she looked closer and saw the shirt's print was actually tiny purple and orange flowers. "Oh, look, we kind of match," she said, lifting the skirt of her floral dress.

"Yeah, kind of." Ray reached up, maybe to readjust a baseball cap that wasn't there. Realizing their head was bare, they shoved their hand in their trouser pocket instead. "Uh, Luna might have recommended I wear this, actually. So if I look good, it's because of her."

Simone's nose scrunched. "Luna? Why was my roommate—I didn't know you two were friends."

"We're not. Not really. I just gave her my number that night I"—Ray hesitated—"took you home?"

"Oh." Simone flushed, remembering. "Right." Her stomach felt like she'd just swallowed a whole box of pie weights. Ray *had* said they weren't interested in dating cis people. Of course they'd give Luna their phone number. Luna was beautiful and funny and knew what colors went with what. Why wouldn't Ray want to date her?

"In case something happened to you," Ray said in a hurry, "I told her she should get in touch."

"So you've just been texting since then?" Simone couldn't help but ask. Maybe it wasn't her business, but she couldn't believe Luna hadn't said anything.

"Not before last night. She messaged me out of the blue to ask me what I was wearing to this thing." Ray gave a sheepish shrug. "When I told her I hadn't really thought about it, she, uh—insisted on giving me some pointers."

"Pointers?" Simone parroted.

"Yeah." Ray gestured between their shirt and Simone's dress. "She thought it would look good on camera if we sort of coordinated. A matched set, you know?"

Simone snapped her mouth closed, shame and relief swamping her every cell. Of *course* Luna was just trying to help, albeit in her own nosy, meddling way. It was crazy to get so jealous over nothing. What had she been thinking?

She must have been silent for too long, because Ray was starting to look worried. "Or maybe it's creepy that we match. Is it creepy? I can, uh, go find another shirt if you'd rather—"

"No, it's fine," Simone said. "You look fine. Great. You look . . . fine and great." She winced at the sound of her own stupid voice. She turned away to study the milling crowd. "I feel a little bit like a kid playing dress-up, you know? Like any minute now, someone's going to grab me and tell me I'm not allowed to be here."

"I know the feeling." Ray leaned back against the rail, their arm brushing Simone's. "Kind of wild that this is real, huh? We should probably enjoy it."

"Yeah," Simone said. She stared out over the river. "While it lasts."

Ray's hand touched hers. Simone froze.

"Mona," they said, "I—"

"There you two are!" Pim Gladly roared into their cozy bubble like water in a hot pan, sputtering everywhere. She seemed to be wearing a more formal jumpsuit for the occasion, a bizarre collection of sequins with a cape stitched onto the back. "I have been looking high and low for you. You should be getting ready backstage."

Delilah came right behind Pim, breathing hard like she'd been running to keep up. She juggled her phone and a clipboard. "They have about forty minutes before they need to be mic'd up, Ms. Gladly," she said. "We're still ahead of schedule."

Pim ignored her. "Come now, no more dillydallying." She herded Ray and Simone away from the railing, taking each by the elbow and marching them back inside. Simone watched a tray of smoked salmon and crème fraîche canapes pass by on the shoulder of a waiter, her eyes filled with longing.

"Ms. Gladly, I'm sure we can find our way to the right area," she said. "You must want to mingle with the other guests."

Pim gave an aggravated sneer. "I'd rather gargle broken glass. These events are all the same; I've been to a thousand of them. Though this is the first time we have TDC on the main stage." She preened. "That should show those anal-retentive pricks from *Chef's Country*."

Ray's eyes went comically wide as they stared at Simone, but Simone shushed them with a look.

Pim kept talking as she dragged them through the crowd, heedless of Delilah trying to keep up in her high heels. "Now then, have you prepared for this fireside chat or whatever the hell it is you're supposed to do up there with that self-righteous frog?"

Simone objected to that characterization of Lisette, but she bit her tongue.

"Delilah prepped us really well, ma'am," Ray said instead. "We're ready."

It was true. Delilah had spent hours over the past few weeks making sure Simone and Ray knew the format and were comfortable answering the suggested starter questions. It was supposed to be an informal chat among all three of them on the subject of family and food. Since Lisette had hosted about a dozen shows over the decades on home cooking, and Recipe Revamp was ostensibly about family recipes, it was a natural topic. Simone had been wary to agree to it at first, knowing the truth about Ray's background, but Ray had convinced her it was okay.

"It'll be fun," they'd said. "Just the two of us and Lisette, shooting the shit."

Now, Simone wondered, with Pim Gladly's nails digging into her arm, *when would it start getting fun?*

"You had better be ready," Pim muttered. She swept past security leading into the backstage area. "Let me give you some advice before you get up there, hm?" She yanked them into a shadowy corner behind some lighting equipment. Simone felt the hair on the back of her neck stand up. She wished, as ridiculous as it was, that Ray's hand would find hers and give it a quick squeeze. But they couldn't, not under the watchful gaze of Pim Gladly.

The woman seemed to tower over them in her sky-high heels, her teeth clenched as she leaned close to hiss, "You are representing The Discerning Chef on that stage. We are expecting a massive audience for our livestream, not to mention how many potential sponsors will be sitting in that crowd. You are not to do anything that might even remotely besmirch the TDC name."

Simone cleared her throat. "Ma'am, of course we—"

"And *you.*" Pim Gladly ignored Simone and poked a finger right into the center of Ray's chest. "You'd better watch your step, mister. Or madam, or whatever it is you want to call yourself."

Simone didn't even think. She just acted.

She grabbed Pim by the wrist and tore her hand away from

Ray. Their scars were still healing, and who knew what kind of damage those talons might inflict?

"Their *name*," she said, "is Ray. You can call them that, *ma'am*." She dropped Pim's hand like it was a rotten potato.

A/V techs don't always appear exactly when they're needed, but this one did, popping into view with a bouquet of lapel mics dangling from one hand. "Are you here to get mic'd up?" he asked.

"Yes, thanks," Ray said to him over the head of Pim Gladly, who was staring at Simone with murderous intent. Their voice was calm as anything. "We'll be right there. Ms. Gladly, you should take your seat. You don't want to miss the show."

Pim gave the A/V tech a glance of distaste before apparently deciding she didn't want to say anything more in front of a witness. She eyed Simone and Ray one last time before sweeping out of the backstage area, collecting Delilah where she had been held up by security.

"Oh, hold on." The tech examined the boxes on his mics. "I need some fresh batteries. One second," he promised before dashing away.

Simone took the moment of quiet to turn to Ray. Her palm raised of its own volition, as if it wanted to press to Ray's chest to assess the damage, but Simone lowered it before it could make contact. "You okay?"

"Yeah." Ray grinned and rubbed along the line of buttons on their shirt. "She didn't hit any scars. Avoided the nipples, too, thank god. That would've been weird."

A group of stagehands strode by, carrying the armchairs that Simone presumed they'd be sitting in on stage. She waited until they'd gone before speaking again. "Ray, we don't have to do this. We don't have to get up there and pretend everything's okay. This is—this is not okay!"

"The mademoiselle, she is right," a voice said from the shadows. "All is very much not, as you say, okay."

Simone's mouth dropped open. That voice. She turned

around slowly. There she was: Lisette D'Amboise in the flesh, wearing her trademark black sack dress, a small plate of oysters in one hand and a flute of champagne in the other. Despite her tiny size, she seemed to fill up the space. Just like Ray could, Simone thought numbly.

"Madame D'Amboise," she breathed. "You . . . Hi."

"Bonjour." Lisette knocked back the last of her champagne and set the empty flute on one of the many black-and-silver equipment boxes that littered the backstage area. "Am I right in thinking you are les enfants I am to share the stage with tonight?"

"Oui," Simone stammered. She stepped forward to shake the hand Lisette offered and launched into her rusty (but still impressive) high school French: "I am Simone, so very pleased to meet you, madame. I cannot tell you what this means to me. Please allow me to introduce my—" She turned to Ray. She knew the French words for *colleague*, for *collaborator*, for *partner*. But none of those words seemed to do Ray justice. "My Ray," she finally said, gesturing to them.

Lisette lit up. "Ah, they did not tell me you are a French speaker. How wonderful! And so lovely to meet your Ray, of course," she rattled on in French as she shook Ray's hand. "I have seen you on the internet. So funny, the two of you!" She balanced her cocktail plate of oysters on another box, giving Ray her full attention.

"Hey, this is super cool, and I don't want to be rude," Ray said, "but can we speak in English? Or even conversational Spanish? I'm feeling a little lost."

"Ah, yes, my apologies," said Lisette, switching back to English, or at least her version of it. "I must admit, though I did not intend to spy, I overheard Madame Gladly." She gentled her handshake with Ray, turning it into something else, taking their hand in hers and patting it with her other. "What has she been up to, eh?"

Ray shot Simone a wild look. Simone recognized that look

as a plea for help, but she didn't know what to do. Finally, Ray said, "It—it's nothing. Just creative differences." They gave a forced smile. "You know how it is."

Lisette gave a slow nod. "I know Pim. I wish I did not but—" She made an extremely Gallic gesture. "The food world, it is small. May I tell you something?" She took a seat on one of the black gear boxes with more grace than should have been possible and crossed her ankles. She gestured to the other boxes stacked around them. "Come, come, sit, sit."

Simone looked at Ray, who just shrugged and perched on one of the boxes. Simone followed suit, folding her dress around her legs. It felt strangely like children's storytime at the library.

"I have a grandson," Lisette said, "though I did not know I did until last year. You understand what I mean, yes?" She paused, letting that sink in. "When he tells me he is my grandson, I say, 'mon Dieu, your life, how hard it will be!' But he says, 'non, it will be harder to live that other life, the one you think I should have perhaps?' And I tell him, 'my dearest boy, you know yourself better than anyone else. And of course I am proud to have you exactly as you are.'" She very delicately swallowed a single oyster and placed the empty shell back on her plate. "So you see, as old as I am, the dog, she can learn new tricks, no? Madame Gladly could, too, if she cared to try. Her age is not an excuse. She is just a stupid cow."

Simone sat there, blinking. Delilah had warned her about meeting her heroes, but this one—this one was the real deal.

She felt tears welling in her eyes, and she couldn't explain why. It just felt so nice to know somebody out there, someone as powerful and respected as Lisette D'Amboise, could have Ray's back, too.

"Madame," Ray said, and leaned forward to take her wrinkled hand. "You. Are. Awesome." They pressed a kiss to the back of it, making Lisette titter. "Your grandson is lucky to have you."

"Your Ray is a charmer, Simone." She laughed. "Dear me, you are as lovely in person as on your show, eh?"

Simone shook her head. "I can't believe you've seen our videos."

"Every one!" Lisette declared. "My grandson, he made sure I was—how do you say?—subscriber." She fluttered her hands in excitement. "Ah, but I am forgetting the real reason I seek you out before we go onstage!"

"What's that, madame?" Simone asked.

Their newly minted patron saint smiled. "I have a proposition for you."

Ten minutes later, Simone and Ray were frozen in place on their boxes, staring at Lisette with open mouths.

"Are you—are you for real?" Ray asked.

Lisette nodded. "Very real."

"And we'd really be— And we could—?" Simone stammered.

"Yes and yes," Lisette said. She watched them flop like landed fish for a moment more before saying, "It is a lot to consider, non? Please, I do not need an answer right now. Take your time, think it over."

"Mics are ready!" said the tech, popping in at last with his fresh batteries. "Sorry for the delay, ladies."

Lisette held up a hand, stopping him from pinning the mic to her dress. "Not ladies," she said sternly. "You may call us *chefs*."

Ray held up a hand. "Uh, I'm not really a—"

Lisette gave them a look.

"I'm a chef," Ray amended.

"Uh." The A/V guy looked at the three of them. "Okay. Sorry, chefs."

Lisette dropped her hand. "Très bien. Continue," she said,

and leaned back to be fitted with the mic with the ease of someone who'd been mic'd a million times before.

Everything after that was a whirlwind of people getting them ready and getting them in place and making last-minute adjustments. Simone didn't even have time to breathe before she found herself standing in the darkened area off stage left with Ray by her side, listening to some celebrity chef welcome Lisette to the stage. Soon it would be their turn.

Ray's voice was a welcome whisper in her ear. "About what Lisette said—"

"You have to do it." Simone turned to squint at Ray's face in the shadows. "You've got to. It's perfect for you; this is a once-in-a-lifetime chance, Ray."

"Yeah, but—" Ray blew out a breath. "What about you? Would you come with me?"

Anywhere, Simone wanted to say. "Of course I would. But only if you want to do it."

"I only want to do it if *you* want to," Ray countered.

"Well, good, because it sounds like we're both voting yes for Lisette's offer," she said.

"Sounds like." A smile spread across Ray's face. They blinked hard a few times, and Simone could see the tears gathering there. "Christ, is this what relief feels like?"

"Hey, no, don't cry." Simone fumbled a tissue from her pocket—thank god for dresses with pockets—and dabbed at Ray's eyes. She could hear the audience burst into applause as Lisette walked onstage from the other side. "We have to go out there in, like, two minutes."

"I know, I know, I'm good." Ray took a deep, shuddering breath. Their hands came up to cup Simone's bare shoulders. "Mona, if we do this—"

"Things will change. That's okay." The touch made Simone's heart lurch in her chest like a filling trying to escape a poorly constructed ravioli. "That's really, really okay, actually."

"I kind of feel like I want to do something crazy," Ray said. Their eyes were gleaming.

Simone was going to actually die. "Yeah? Like what?"

Ray told her. "Will you do it with me?" they asked.

Now Simone was the one on the verge of tears. "It would be my pleasure."

"And now," said the celebrity chef announcer, "please welcome the stars of the internet sensation Recipe Revamp, Ray Lyton and Simone Larkspur."

"That's your cue," an event coordinator told them, giving them a nudge in the right direction.

Simone had never been the sort of person who loved the spotlight. Her life up to this point had been a private one, concerned only with her work and her cooking. She didn't know what to do as she walked out onstage and saw the sea of faces, the bright lights, the flashes of camera phones. Way back by the audio booth, she could just make out Petey and the rest of the crew shooting for the livestream, with Chase in a slick suit ordering them around with jerky gestures. Ray looked in Petey's direction and made a weird gesture with their hand, like their palm was a plane going for takeoff.

"Is that from *West Wing*?" Simone said into Ray's ear, where their mics wouldn't catch it.

"Petey will get it," Ray whispered back, and sure enough, in the distance Petey repeated the gesture himself.

Simone took a deep breath, trying to concentrate on Ray's presence beside her. They were at home under the bright lights, giving the crowd an easy smile, unbuttoning their suit coat as they prepared to sit down in a chair across from Lisette. Lisette, for her part, rose to greet them both with kisses on their cheeks.

Once the applause died down and they took their seats, Simone could only look at Ray. She couldn't remember ever being this terrified, and she wasn't even scared for herself. She must have looked like a real deer in the headlights, because

Lisette gave her a quizzical look. Simone swallowed and tried to communicate with her eyes that something big was about to happen, and hoped to god her eyes spoke French.

Ray was the first to actually speak, turning to the audience like they were old friends. "Hey, it's so great to see you all here. I want to thank Chef Justin for that introduction. Can we all give him a hand?" They clapped, and everyone joined in with some polite applause. Simone gave a weak series of claps, concentrating on not letting her stomach claw its way out of her throat.

Ray continued, "It's such an honor to be here tonight, and I do appreciate how Justin talked up all our accomplishments"— a short wave of laughter—"but he left out something, through no fault of his own. So, if I could take a moment to introduce myself: my name is Ray. My pronouns are they/them/theirs."

The murmurs from the audience spurred Simone to speak. "And I'm Simone, she/her/hers."

She could see Chase back by the audio booth, having what looked like a fit. He was shouting at Petey, but he was too far away for Simone to make it out. Damn it, was he going to make the crew cut the live feed?

"And I am Chef Lisette D'Amboise." Lisette's voice rang out, silencing the entire room. She sat, tiny and poised, dressed all in black, and surveyed the crowd with a fierce stare. "You may refer to me with the 'she' and with the 'her.' Now Ray, my darling, tell me—" She turned to Ray as if the crowd of people didn't exist any longer. "We are to speak about family and food tonight, eh? What comes to mind when you think of that?"

They had prepped an answer for this weeks ago. But Ray did not give it.

"To be honest, madame, I think of family meals at the restaurants where I've worked. And all the great food Simone here has cooked for me." Ray's hand landed on Simone's knee. And stayed there. "I'm not in touch with my blood relatives anymore, so for me, family means the people I've worked alongside, the folks that really have my back. And I've been lucky to find them."

Simone covered Ray's hand with her own and squeezed. She wasn't sure how they all got through the fireside chat—she was pretty sure she'd just rambled when it was her turn to speak—but somehow it came to an end. She stumbled offstage to a rousing round of clapping and noise, but she wasn't sure if it was the good kind of noise or the bad kind.

"Did we do okay?" she asked.

"I think we did fine." Ray clapped Lisette on her tiny shoulder. "Thanks for the assist out there, madame."

"Oh." She shrugged in her French way, boneless and buttery. "It was, quite literally, the least I could do. Am I right in thinking, though, that this new, ah, development may make things quite difficult for you at *Le Chef Discernant*?"

"Wee," Ray said. "Tray difficult. That's why we should probably talk about the terms of your offer. Sorry, can I borrow this for a second? Thanks." They grabbed a pen and notepad from a beleaguered stagehand, uncapping the pen with their teeth. "Here's what I'm thinking. Number one: we get to bring on our own crew. Number two . . ."

Chapter 27

Simone spent the next day, a Sunday, in her pajamas, sleeping in and definitely not answering emails. She did read them, though. Just like she read the hundreds of comments on her Instagram and the livestream of the event.

Ray had gone viral. Again. The reaction was overwhelmingly positive, she was happy to see. It was all over the food blogs. Ray had even done an interview via Skype with *TasteBuzz*, correct pronouns and all, though it focused mostly on the charities that Food Fest supported.

TDC remained silent on their official social channels, of course. The internet speculated, but Simone knew why. Petey was the only one who knew the passwords, and he wasn't answering emails that weekend either.

The emails sitting in their inboxes were from HR, from Mikkah, from Pim. They all ran along the same lines: *Obviously, TDC has always welcomed a diverse collection of food professionals from numerous kinds of backgrounds, and we couldn't be prouder when our homegrown talent exemplifies exactly the kind of spirit that TDC blah blah blah . . .*

It was just like Chase on a larger scale—they knew which

way the wind was blowing, and they would try to cover their asses, now that the whole world was watching. Once those eyes glanced away, they would be right back at their old tricks. Maybe at some point Simone had believed TDC could change for the better, that she could work hard on the inside to make things less awful for those who came later—but now she saw that was a fool's errand. Only the people at the top could change things, and they'd made it clear over and over again that they didn't want to.

So: fuck them.

Early Monday morning, Simone rode the elevator up to the TDC offices. No one else was in yet. Lights were off, rooms were empty.

Simone walked through the place like a ghost, or a queen.

First, she retrieved her frozen sourdough starter from the walk-in. No way was she leaving that behind. On a whim, she grabbed a single plum, summer ripe, from a crate. She felt a little thrill go through her; she'd never taken so much as a paper clip from any place she'd ever worked, but this time, she considered it fair play.

She then went to her desk in the deserted bullpen and booted up her laptop. As it went through the laborious process of waking up, she methodically removed the postcard picture of Lisette from her wall and placed it in her tote bag with the sourdough starter and the plum. Then came her personal coffee mug, her good pens, and the assorted aspirin and Band-Aids she kept in her desk drawer. Into the tote bag they went.

At last, her laptop was ready. She sat down and stared at the blank window where she was supposed to write a message. There had been a little—very little—argument over the group chat about who should write this email, but in the end Petey reminded Simone that she was the professional writer, so she should be the one to handle it.

It had been the right call. She knew exactly what to say. It took her less than four minutes to type it all out.

Afterward, she checked the test kitchen one last time, just to make sure she hadn't forgotten anything. She considered taking her apron from its hook, but thought it was probably the rightful property of TDC, and anyway, she'd never liked how dowdy it made her look. Ray's leather apron, though, could not be left behind. She took it gently from its peg and folded it into a neat square.

"Oh, hey, sorry, they told me no one else was going to be here this early." A braying laugh chased its way to Simone's ears.

The smile was already on her face before she'd turned around. "Hey, Ray. You got everything?"

"Yep." Ray shut the walk-in door with their shoulder and lifted the two six-packs of homebrew they carried. "The fruits of my labor are coming home with me."

Simone raised the folded apron aloft. "Don't forget this either."

"Aw, dang. Do you have room in your bag for it?" Ray shrugged, indicating their full hands. "I should've thought to bring one, I guess."

"It's okay. I can hold it for you." Simone slipped it into her tote, weirdly pleased to be in charge of it.

The kitchen door creaked open. Delilah stood there, one hand on the jamb, the other on the knob. She looked at Ray, then at Simone.

"We good?"

Simone nodded. "Is Petey—"

Petey appeared right behind Delilah, peeking over her shoulder. "Just finished copying over my personal files." He held up a thumb drive. "The crew's done, too."

"Let's get out of here, then," Ray said.

As they left the test kitchen, Simone gave it one last glance. She wouldn't miss it, exactly, but still. There were a lot of memories in this place.

The four of them exited the building together. They were met in the little park with the fountain by the video crew.

Bridgette, Amir, Jake, and Lin were all carrying bags filled with personal stuff. Amir even had a potted plant tucked in the crook of his arm.

"So is it done?" Lin asked. "Are we officially unemployed?"

"We're not unemployed," Delilah said with a roll of her eyes. "We'll see each other when production starts. And you better not be late to set."

"Okay, Mrs. Hotshot Producer." Jake gave her a playful nudge.

"What's a producer do, anyway?" Amir asked.

"Everything," Simone said. "If anyone should be in charge of the whole enchilada, it's Delilah."

"Damn right," Delilah said. "So, Simone, *is* it official? Did you send the thing?"

"Hold on, I have it saved in my drafts. I wanted to wait until we were all together." She retrieved her phone from her pocket, opening her work email and the unsent message.

She looked around the circle of faces. These were her friends, her partners. Equal partners, actually, in a new venture, a production company that was going to make a new kind of baking competition show, starring Lisette D'Amboise.

The format had been Ray's idea because Ray was good with those kinds of ideas. The contestants would be amateur bakers, but not semi-pro perfectionists. They'd be inexperienced, interested in baking but lacking the equipment or time to learn anything advanced. The show would change that. Simone would be their instructor; Ray would be their encouraging and somewhat goofy host; and Lisette would be the judge who decided who stayed and who left the show. Netflix had already ordered twelve episodes thanks to Lisette's name recognition, but it was a gamble. None of them had ever worked on a real TV show before, but they'd agreed to give it a shot. Together.

Simone swallowed. "Does anyone want to back out? Now's the time to speak up."

"No more backing out or down," Petey said, throwing his arms in the air. "Send that shit, Mona!"

"Okay." Simone tapped the screen. Waited a moment. Then let out a breath. "It's done."

Delilah gave Bridgette a high-five. "Eight simultaneous resignations, effective immediately! Read it and weep, Ms. Pim 'Oh, I'm sincerely sorry but we just don't have a salary increase for you in the budget this year' Gladly!"

"You kept all the stuff about how they treated Ray in there, right?" Jake asked. "And how white that leadership team is?"

"Oh yes," Simone said, "all our grievances are in there. I may have blind-copied some food writers I know on it, too. I'm guessing this will hit *TasteBuzz* in a few minutes, so you might want to turn off your Twitter notifications."

Bridgette giggled. "My mom always said don't burn your bridges, but I've got to say, it feels good."

Simone smiled, then noticed Ray on the edge of their group, strangely quiet with their gaze on the pavement.

"Hey." She touched their arm. "You all right?"

Ray jolted like they'd been torn from some deep thoughts. "What? Yeah. Just tired, I guess. It's been a long couple of days."

"A long week," Lin added.

"A long-ass almost-a-whole *year*," Jake laughed.

"Well, I'm going home and getting some very deserved rest before life gets really wild." Delilah shouldered her purse. "See you all in a few months."

A chorus of goodbyes followed, with everyone exchanging hugs or shaking hands before going their separate ways. Simone watched them all go one by one until she and Ray were left in the park with only the pigeons for company.

"It'll be strange," Simone said, struggling for something to say that would prolong their farewell. "Not seeing you for a while, I mean."

"I'm sure we'll see each other for pre-production meetings, stuff like that." Ray stooped and picked up their beer from the pavement. "It'll fly by. We'll be back to being coworkers before you know it. Like nothing's ever changed."

"Yeah." Simone dropped her gaze to the ground. "Great." It was true, even if she didn't want it to be. She and Ray were still just friends, just coworkers, and nothing would ever change that.

"You, uh—take the local train home, right?" Ray nodded at the subway entrance down the block.

"Yeah." Simone tucked a loose strand of hair behind her ear. "You need the express to get to your place, right?" She wasn't sure why she was asking; she'd been to Ray's place often enough to know how to get there.

Ray made a considering noise. "I can take the local and switch at 168th Street. Might be a better bet than the express this time of day."

"Oh, right." Simone checked her phone. It was no longer early morning, but regular old morning. "It's rush hour."

"Do you mind if I ride with you?" Ray asked.

"I mean, if you're going the same way, it just makes sense—"

"Right, exactly."

They made their way awkwardly to the subway, not speaking as they swiped in and waited side by side on the platform.

"This is weird," Simone said, staring ahead at the downtown platform across the way.

Ray gave her a look. "Having second thoughts?"

"About quitting? No." Simone shook her head. "It's just weird to think—I worked so hard to get a job at TDC. I thought that was the pinnacle."

She thought about how TDC had taken advantage of that—taken advantage of her. Her passion for her work should have been an asset, but Pim Gladly and Mikkah and the whole TDC machine had only seen it as a resource to be tapped. She'd spent some of the best years of her life working long hours for low pay and zero respect, and for what? To line the pockets of the TDC shareholders who probably didn't even know a crouton from a crudité? It almost felt like— Well, Simone hesitated to be overly dramatic about it, but then she remembered what her ex-mentor had said about eschewing drama, and her anger surged all over again. Yes, actually, it felt a lot like leaving an emotionally abusive relationship! And here she was, on the verge of blaming herself for being so stupid and not seeing all the clues earlier, for letting her anxiety get out of control under the pressure, for being so focused on being the best. But she wasn't the one who had turned TDC into a shitty workplace. TDC had done that all on its own. And now she was mourning a thing that hadn't really ever existed: her perfect job.

"I honestly thought that was what I was born to do," Simone said, watching a train leave the station on the downtown track.

Ray hummed. "Maybe you were meant for something else. Something better. There's time to find out what it is. Don't beat yourself up too much, Mona. We'll get there in the end."

Simone flushed, thinking she was nowhere near where she really wanted them to be. "I guess," she mumbled.

The train screeched into the station, and they boarded together. As Simone had suspected, rush hour meant the car was packed to the gills, standing room only. Ray squished between some people so they could grab a pole. The six-packs were placed on the floor between Ray's spread feet. Simone hated using the overhead rail—she was just short enough to make it hard on her shoulder—so she wedged herself in the spot next to them and managed to find a few inches of pole to grab. They stood next to each other, gazes focused on the ad above their heads. Some kind of trade school up in the Bronx. Simone read through the list of offered courses about five times.

If she stopped to think, she would start thinking about Ray. She always seemed to be thinking about Ray these days. And now, standing so close to them in this crowded subway car, she thought about how they smelled, and how they kept their socks rolled in the top drawer, and how their laugh carried across a room, and how much—

How much Simone just wanted to—

"Times Square, Forty-Second Street," said the automated

subway announcement as the train pulled into the station. Simone braced herself as a wave of people trying to leave the car fought against the wave of people trying to get into it. More and more people joined the crush, the combined forces of the bodies shoving her hard. Her fingers slipped from the pole, and she would have fallen over if Ray hadn't caught her around the waist.

"You okay?" they asked.

"Move in, move in," some guy in a hardhat was yelling. More people pressed into the car, knocking Simone off balance again. She yelped and instinctively wrapped her arms around Ray for support.

"Hey, buddy—" Ray snapped at the person who'd almost knocked over Simone.

"I'm fine! It's okay, I'm fine," Simone babbled. She tried to pull away from Ray and reclaim her little piece of subway car, but the crowd had shifted, and the spot had disappeared. She groaned into the softness of Ray's T-shirt, embarrassed to be in such a compromising position. Every inch of her from her knees to the top of her head was trapped against Ray.

"Sorry," she mumbled into Ray's shirt. "I can't seem to move."

"It's all right." Ray's arm tightened around her. "I've got you."

Simone almost let herself relax into the embrace, but then she remembered her face was pretty much mashed against Ray's surgical site. "Oh!" She jerked her head back, nearly knocking it into some tall guy's backpack. "Your scars—I don't want to mess anything up."

"Don't worry. You're not hurting anything." Ray's hand came up and gently—gently—slid into Simone's hair, coaxing her head back to rest against Ray's chest. "You can stay there."

Simone stilled. She could hear Ray's voice as a vibration under her ear; she could feel their heartbeat. Her eyes drifted shut. She couldn't let this go on. She couldn't bear it. She had to let Ray know how she felt. She wouldn't be able to move on to the next phase of her life, a phase that was supposed to include Ray as her business partner, while hiding this secret. She knew Ray wouldn't be happy about the news, but she hoped they would understand so they could move past it.

At least she could hide her face here against Ray, protected by the curtain of her own hair. She wouldn't have to look Ray in the face when she confessed.

"So, I just wanted to say . . ." Simone sighed, a warm puff of air against Ray's chest, and said, very seriously, "There's nothing wrong with having personal preferences, you know? Sometimes a person just isn't interested in a certain kind of person, and that's nobody's fault."

Ray's hand went still in her hair. "That's true," they said, wariness creeping into their voice.

"And, by the same token, some people are drawn to certain people without even realizing it at first, maybe, and when they do it's too late to stop feeling some particular way about them, but that's not anyone's fault either," Simone said, her words falling from her mouth in a rush.

Ray stiffened against Simone. She could feel their spine going rigid under her palms. "Look," Ray said to the top of Simone's head, "if you want me to let you go right now—"

"What?" Simone gasped. "Please don't; I'll fall."

"Well, then what do you want me to do?" Ray's voice was an impatient growl in their chest. "Because I get what you're saying, but I don't understand what you want me to do about it."

Simone clung to them harder, feeling very small. "Just, please, don't hate me," she said.

A beat, and then all of the anger seemed to leave Ray, softening their spine, their touch to Simone's hair. "I don't hate you, Mona," they whispered. "I couldn't. Like you said, it's nobody's fault."

Simone felt tears prick her eyes. She cursed herself; she didn't want to get Ray's shirt damp. "Thank you for understanding," she murmured. "I swear I'll never bring it up again. My feelings for you won't ever get in the way of our work, I promise."

"Wait." Ray went rigid again. "Your what?"

"My feelings," Simone repeated. She hated how juvenile that phrase sounded, but she didn't want to make things even worse by using stronger, potentially more accurate language. "They won't get in the way at all."

"Your feelings . . . for me?" Ray asked slowly.

Simone crushed her eyes shut and buried her face in Ray's chest. "Could you please just give it a rest? It's not funny. Not to me."

"Mona, I'm not joking." Ray's tone carried an edge of panic. "Since when have you— I thought we were talking about how I felt about *you*."

"What?" Now it was Simone's turn to be confused. She raised her head and peered up into Ray's concerned face. "Ray, I know how you feel already. You said it loud and clear: you're not interested in dating cis people."

"I'm— When did I say that?"

"When you got home from surgery," Simone said, getting a little angry now that Ray was dragging her through this again. "You were telling me about how Kelsey broke up with you, and you said—"

"Simone, I could have said I was the Emperor of Bohemia, for all I know! I was out of my mind on pain meds!"

"No." Simone shook her head. "You—you were a little tired maybe, but you definitely said—"

"You're not listening." The train came to a halt in another station, and Ray released the pole to grasp Simone with both hands, one on each elbow so they could look each other in the face. "I'm telling you now, completely sober: there's at least one cis person I can think of that I'd really, really want a chance with." Their green eyes went soft and hopeful. "If she's up for it?"

Simone's mouth opened and closed like a busy oven. "She . . . ? As in, me?"

Ray laughed long and loud in the packed car, heedless of the heads turning their way. "Who else, Mona?"

Red heat suffused Simone's face. "Don't laugh! It's not funny."

"Oh, but it's so easy." Ray smiled. Took Simone by the chin and tilted her face up. "Can I—"

"Yes," Simone breathed.

This was pretty easy, too.

Ray leaned down and pressed a kiss to Simone's parted lips. They tasted just like they smelled, clean and woodsy. Simone had an excellent palate, so she knew what she was talking about.

She wrapped her arms around their neck and hung on for dear life, trusting Ray's hands to be steady at her waist. The train braked hard, and a few people lost their footing, but not Ray. They kept their feet planted firmly on the floor and didn't let Simone waver.

When the kiss ended, Ray didn't pull back, just kept their mouth millimeters from Simone's, like they couldn't stand to leave. "Simone—" they said, quiet against her lips.

Simone didn't believe in wasting time. They'd wasted enough already. She looked Ray right in the eye.

"Take me home with you?" she asked.

A grin spread across Ray's face. "I think we can swing that. As it happens, I have no plans today."

Simone kissed them again, just to see if they tasted any different through a smile.

Neither of them noticed, but they'd already missed Simone's station by two stops, anyway.

A few more stops, and it was time for them to switch to the express train. Simone could hear the announcement for 168th Street, but she was having a hard time tearing herself away from Ray's mouth. A year ago, Simone would have scoffed at the notion of two full-grown adults making out on the subway—in the middle of rush hour, no less—but she found she didn't care about what that other Simone would've thought.

"It's the last stop," Simone said between more kisses. "We should get on the A."

"Okay," Ray groaned, "but I'm not letting you go."

People were filing out of the train all around them. "How are you going to carry your beer, then?" Simone teased.

"Shit. Uh." Ray glanced at the six-packs still sitting on the floor at their feet. "All right. One second, and then I won't let you go." They held up one finger and grabbed the six-packs off the floor. "Hey, man, you drink beer?" Ray asked a bleary-eyed person in scrubs, clearly getting off a long shift.

"Uh, yeah?"

"Great. Mazel tov." Ray pressed one pack into his arms, then turned to a little old lady dressed entirely in purple. "Ma'am, would you like some beer? I made it myself, it's pretty good."

"I wouldn't say no—"

"Then don't! Here you go." They handed over the last pack, which she accepted with a confused smile.

"Well! God bless," she said.

"You too. Bye." Ray grabbed Simone's hand and pulled her onto the platform. "My good deeds are done for the day." They flashed her a smile.

"I hope not," Simone murmured, and kissed them again. "I can't believe you gave away your beer."

"I can always make more beer," Ray said, holding her close. "I can't grow more hands."

Simone made a face, though she kept smiling. "That's a weird thing to say. But still kind of sweet."

"Weird and sweet: that's what you're signing up for, Mona."

She knew. And she didn't mind.

The rest of the trip uptown was a giddy series of subway stops and kisses and laughter that Simone couldn't seem to suppress. She didn't even care that she was drawing stares from the few people left on the subway. And even though the train was no longer crowded, she and Ray were pressed even closer together.

When they finally arrived at Ray's stop, they left the station hand in hand, the novelty of it making Simone's heart flutter. She wanted to tell everyone they saw—the parent pushing the huge baby stroller, the subway attendant in the booth, the guy selling newspapers and gum right outside the turnstiles—*Look! I get to hold their hand! I couldn't do that an hour ago; isn't that amazing?*

They tumbled into the lobby of Ray's building, and Simone made a beeline for the elevator. The faster they got to Ray's apartment, the better. She jammed the call button over and over, willing the elevator to arrive quickly.

"You know, it might be faster to take the stairs," Ray said, pressing up close behind her and kissing the back of her neck. "It's only three flights."

"Oh, that's true. Maybe we should— Hey!" Simone cried out as Ray grabbed hold of her and hoisted her into their arms. "Ray, put me down! You'll hurt yourself."

"I'm cleared to lift weights again, so I don't see why I can't lift you." Ray headed for the stairs, easily carrying Simone up to the first landing. "As long as I don't try to raise you above my head—which, I don't know, I could probably manage it." They lifted Simone up another inch or two, and she clamped her arms around Ray's neck in terror.

"Don't you dare!"

Ray laughed, the echo of it booming through the stairwell as they reached the second floor. "I'm kidding! God, the look on your face."

Simone buried her face against Ray's neck. "I hate you."

Ray's hand cupped the back of her head, and Simone pulled back just enough to look into Ray's dancing eyes.

"No you don't," they said.

"No," she whispered. "I don't. I tried to, but it just didn't stick."

Ray didn't seem to have a joking response for that, because they just stared down at Simone and kissed her.

"Okay, big romantic gesture over," they declared, depositing Simone on her feet. "We're home."

It was true; they were at Ray's door. Simone couldn't hustle them inside fast enough.

Never one to shy away from doing all the work, Simone was on Ray the instant the door was closed and locked. Height difference be damned, she was determined to pin them against the wall and kiss them as much as she wanted.

"Whoa," Ray managed to say between Simone's kisses, "I thought you might be a little feisty, but this is—"

Simone pulled back. "Too much?"

Ray brushed a lock of hair away from her eyes and tucked it behind her ear. "I was going to say 'a really pleasant surprise.'"

Simone flushed with pleasure. "Good." Her gaze fell back to Ray's broad chest, and she faltered.

"I know that face," Ray said, pressing a kiss to Simone's ear. "What's the little anxiety alarm in your head trying to say, Mona?"

She laid her palm atop Ray's sternum, a light touch. She could feel their heartbeat going wild. "I just worry— I mean, your surgery and all," she said. She made a point of looking into Ray's eyes, of not staring at their chest. "I don't want to make you uncomfortable or focus on it too much. Should I not look at it?"

Ray honked with laughter. "I hope you will; I paid a lot of money for this! Someone should enjoy it."

"I'm being serious," Simone snapped.

"So am I." Ray cupped her face in their work-rough hands and kissed her. "God, Simone, for the first time in—*ever*, I am really looking forward to getting naked with someone."

Simone swallowed. "That is a lot of pressure," she mumbled.

"Hey, no. No pressure." Ray's forehead tipped against Simone's and stayed there. Simone kept her eyes open even as Ray's slipped shut. "I'm easy. Seriously. Whatever we do, I get to do it with my whole self. I get to do it with you. That's— It's amazing, okay?" Ray opened their eyes, a soft, honest green. "You're already the best I've ever had."

Simone squirmed under that gaze. Her instinct was to borrow a page from Ray's playbook, to make a joke out of it. *I haven't even gotten your pants off.* But she stopped herself. Ray was being open with her, and she owed them the same in return.

"Okay," she said instead. She tipped her face up to press a kiss to Ray's chin. "Okay," she said again, and pulled them away from the wall and toward the bed.

"How about you, Mona?" they asked. "What do you want?" They leaned in and kissed Simone on her jaw, down her throat. "What do you need?"

She had one answer for both questions. "You," she breathed. "Just you."

They stumbled toward the bed, Simone kissing any part of Ray she could reach while clawing away their denim jacket. Ray's hands were hard at work, too, getting rid of Simone's tank top and bra. Simone tried not to be embarrassed by her clothes; if she had known this was going to happen, she wouldn't have dressed in such slouchy, stay-at-home stuff. Then again, if she had known this was going to happen, she probably would have had a heart attack before she even left the house.

Ray didn't seem to care about her unsexy, mismatched underclothes or the fact that her leggings had a tiny hole on the knee. They were too busy tossing each piece to the floor to comment on it. Simone was still struggling with their shirt, trying and failing to figure out a way to divest Ray of the damn thing without having them lift their arms too high.

"Here, I've got it." Ray pulled the tee over their head and off their arms in an awkward but practical motion. Simone caught sight of their surgical scars for the first time—two shiny, red curves along the bottom of Ray's chest. Long, but healing well. Nothing more than a fact of Ray's body. Not as scary as she thought they might look.

"Well?" Ray held out their arms as if presenting themself to an audience. "What do you think?" They sounded genuinely eager to know. Their face was absolutely glowing from the force of their smile.

Simone tried to find the words. Ray looked . . . wonderful. Perfectly happy. Incredibly alive.

"You look like *you*," she finally managed to say.

Ray's smile curved. "That a good thing?"

Simone nodded. "The best thing."

She pulled Ray down on top of her, coaxing them to press her into the (very competently made) bed. More bare skin was touching than Simone could even process. She stared up at Ray, at the glorious picture they made with their sandy curls hanging in their eyes and their lips flushed red from Simone's kisses.

"This okay?" Ray asked, breathing hard.

Simone held their face in her hands. She wanted to imprint every detail of this into her memory. "More than."

Because it was only fair, Simone made short work of Ray's jeans, laughing when she came up against the pair of tight boxer briefs, this time a light heather gray.

"What's so funny?" Ray asked, nosing along her ear. "It's just my underwear."

"I was really angry at them—I mean, when I was here after your surgery," she tried to explain. "It was like they were mocking me. Do you know how much willpower it takes not to imagine you in them all the time once I know they're there?" She reached boldly for them, palming Ray's ass through the soft fabric and giving it a cheeky little squeeze.

"Why, Ms. Larkspur," Ray gasped, not entirely in jest, arching a little against Simone, "I am shocked you would objectify your very professional colleague in a professional setting, professionally. Highly unprofessional of you."

"You're not listening. I said I exerted my willpower *not* to do that." She gave Ray a pinch on their hip, laughing at the yelp it produced.

"So you wasted all that time *not* picturing me in my underwear?" Ray clicked their tongue against their teeth and caged in Simone's head with their forearms. "Sounds inefficient."

Simone's laugh turned into another sound entirely as Ray bent to kiss her breasts. When was the last time she'd laughed so much in bed? In Simone's experience, sex was a serious enterprise, something of a chore, a long list of boxes to check. She had always been so focused on making sure her partner was pleased and that she looked and sounded sexy, whatever that might mean. It was different here with Ray. Things were weirdly simple.

She'd never been more turned on.

There was no need to calculate the pros and cons in snaking her hand down between their bodies, so she did, urged on by Ray's moan of approval. They were already wet, Simone's fingertips finding the spot on their boxer briefs and pressing there experimentally.

"Good?" Simone breathed.

"More than," Ray whispered, and kissed her lazily, like they had all the time in the world to be like this.

Simone fiddled with the waistband of Ray's briefs. "Can I get rid of these?"

"Permanently?" Ray smirked down at her. They wiggled their hips, helping Simone dislodge them. "I know you're holding a grudge."

"I swear I won't rip them into pieces," Simone said, peeling them away. "Yet." She gave Ray a kiss on the tip of their nose. She'd never done that with someone, she realized. Given them a silly little gesture like that. It made her wonder what other sorts of things she might be up for trying with Ray. "Hey, were you joking when you said you have a drawer filled with weird sex stuff? Or is that a real thing that could happen?"

"That depends." Ray licked their lips, cocking their head to the side. "How weird do you want to get?"

"Well, I do love gadgets," Simone said. She flung the briefs to the floor. Then, more forcefully, "But not uni-taskers.

Something should be useful in more ways than one if it's going to take up space in a drawer."

"Uh—" Ray boggled at her. "Did you just invoke kitchen gear philosophy when we're about to have sex?"

Simone considered this. "Yes?"

"God, you're hot," Ray breathed, and kissed her again.

There was indeed a drawer full of stuff, though Simone wouldn't have called it truly weird. Everything was neatly arranged by color, making a rainbow pattern that brought a smile to Simone's lips. She hung half-off the bed with Ray's arm braced around her waist to keep her steady while she perused the offerings.

"I mean, we do have all day, no job to go to," she said, tucking a strand of hair behind her ear so it wasn't hanging in her eyes. "Maybe I should pick out an assortment."

"How about one for now? Like, right now." Ray's hand roamed up her body to cup her breast. "Like, right this very second, no pressure at all."

Simone smiled, picking up Ray's hand and pressing a kiss to the rough palm. "You're the one who told me to relax and go with the flow."

"Did I?" They kissed her shoulder, then gave it a tiny bite. Simone didn't hide the shiver that gave her. "I was a different person then. You shouldn't listen to that fool."

"It was fifteen minutes ago."

"How about this one?" Ray reached over Simone's shoulder, pressing against her back in a delightfully warm way, and grabbed a tiny egg-shaped toy that Simone had only passed over thus far because she hadn't noticed it among the heftier options. "Can't go wrong with this one, I've found."

Simone took it between her thumb and forefinger, examining it from all angles. It was black and sleek, covered with a pleasantly soft casing with a little controller dangling from a cord at its wide end. She switched it on, jolting at the unexpectedly strong vibration.

She grinned over her shoulder at Ray. "What else does it do?"

"Oh, it has tons of applications." Ray plucked the toy from her hand and dragged her back to the center of the bed by the waist. "Let me show you."

As in so many arenas, Ray proved to be a gracious and entertaining host. They laid Simone down and pressed the little buzzing device first to her ticklish ribs, making her squirm with laughter, then to one nipple, making her sigh, and then lower. Simone wasn't sure how to categorize the sound she made at that, but it was loud.

Though she was very much enjoying herself, Simone managed to voice a thought from her distracted brain. "What about you?" She grasped at Ray's forearm, at the shape of one thigh with its pleasantly crisp hairs. She needed to touch more of Ray; she wanted them to feel what she was feeling.

"Don't worry about me. I'm good. I'm great." Ray gave her a grin that could only be described as feral and rose to their knees above Simone, rearranging limbs and Simone herself like it was nothing. "Fuck, you're so gorgeous." They slotted themself between Simone's legs, moving the vibrator around her clit in deft whorls. Simone could feel how slick she was. Ray was right there, pressing into her, sharing the little toy between them. A shudder ran through them both, and Simone wasn't sure who it had come from first. She supposed it didn't matter.

She looped her arms around Ray's strong neck and pulled them down into a kiss. The long, bare length of Ray's body covered her in delicious heat. Ray lifted a hand—the one not hard at work between them—and dug it into the fall of her hair. A noise like wanting escaped from Simone, but it wasn't that, because she already had what she wanted right here.

She opened her eyes, not sure when she'd closed them, and saw in blurry close-up the little mark on the side of Ray's neck just below their ear. A frisson of proprietary feeling ran through her, and before she could second-guess herself, she was surging up to bite Ray exactly there. The pleased hiss she got in return made her even bolder. She swiped her tongue over the spot before nipping again.

"How did I know you'd be a biter?" Ray groaned, tipping their head back for easier access.

"You sure had a lot of theories about how I'd be in bed." Simone nosed her way behind Ray's ear, laughing against their neck. "How often did you think about this?"

"All the time." The words rumbled against Simone.

She pulled back just enough to see Ray's eyes. "Seriously?"

"Seriously. Constantly." Ray pressed a kiss to the corner of Simone's lips. "Every damn day," they said, and their hand did something very clever between them.

Simone bit her lip. Not that it stopped the noises from escaping.

"Let go," Ray said against her mouth. "Let go for me."

And, for once, Simone did.

Twice, actually.

Not that she was counting.

She felt Ray start to shake apart and pulled herself together to reach down and take hold of the toy just as it began to slip from their grip. She held it steady and watched all the little flickers of surprise and joy wash over Ray's face.

And she knew she would never get enough of that sight.

Good thing they had all day.

Chapter 28

Ray had five pounds of frozen cheddar, but only two eggs.

Simone stood in front of the open fridge and freezer doors, shivering in the chill as she surveyed the appliance's contents. She was wearing nothing but Ray's T-shirt, which fell to mid-thigh on her. The sun wasn't even up yet, but Simone's internal clock was still stuck on her old schedule. She didn't mind; it had been a sweet revelation, waking up in Ray's bed, still wrapped up in Ray's arms. Just like a dream. Simone had left them to sleep while she wrangled breakfast.

Or at least tried to.

Who only kept two eggs in their fridge? You couldn't make anything with two eggs.

"Hey." Strong arms wrapped around Simone's waist. Ray shuffled in close to say in her ear, "What are you doing up so early?"

"I wanted to make breakfast." She tipped her head to the side to let Ray kiss her neck. "It's one of the few perks of dating a trained pastry chef, you know. Might as well enjoy it."

"I can think of plenty of perks when it comes to you," Ray said. They pulled her gently away from the fridge. "But you're not on the clock right now, Mona. Get back in bed. Let me handle it."

"What?" Simone couldn't keep the wounded note from her voice. "Are you sure?" She turned around and saw that Ray was dressed only in a pair of their black boxer briefs. Her hands smoothed down Ray's bare arms of their own accord. "I don't mind cooking for you. I kind of like it, actually."

Ray's smile was lazy and knowing. "I get that. But just this once, let me feed you." They reached past Simone and started taking ingredients out of the fridge: a packet of good local bacon, the two eggs in their near-empty plastic carton, a bottle of milk. "It won't be anything fancy, but—"

Simone cut them off with a kiss, her hand on their jaw to keep them where she wanted them.

"Okay," she said when they finally broke for air. "I will try not to judge your breakfast by professional standards."

"Snob," Ray said, and kissed her on her nose. "Get out of here."

Simone wandered back to Ray's bed, slipping under the sheets and luxuriating in the Ray scent of the pillows. She wasn't used to being waited on. It was kind of strange. She lay there and listened to the clink of pots and pans in the kitchen, the click of a stove burner, the soft sounds of Ray cooking for her.

"What are you making?" she called, unable to contain her curiosity.

"It's a surprise. You'll see soon enough," Ray called back.

Simone frowned to herself. "It can't be an omelet. You don't have enough eggs."

"Just be patient." Simone could hear the hiss of food hitting a hot pan. She sniffed the air. Spices and sugar.

"You're not baking, are you?" she asked in alarm.

"Relax," Ray called to her. "Just trust me, will you?"

Simone settled back into the pillows with a huff. She thought she was genetically incapable of relaxation, but somehow, between the cozy sounds floating in from the kitchen and the warm smell of Ray's sheets, she found herself drifting off. She only came back into hazy awareness when a plate of food appeared before her. She blinked at it.

"Oh," she said, sitting up. It looked amazing.

"Sourdough French toast with a maple glaze and a side of bacon," Ray said. "Bon appétit."

Simone took the plate slowly, glancing between it and Ray. She picked up the fork that lay tucked under the slices of French toast. Her eyes flicked up to Ray, who was still standing beside the bed, watching her intently. Under their eager gaze, she cut herself a piece of toast and bacon, dragged it through the sticky glaze, and brought the forkful to her mouth.

She nearly burst into tears as she chewed. It was sweet, but not cloying, savory without being too heavy. It was perfectly balanced. And someone had cared enough to make it for her.

She moved the plate from her lap to the bedside table. Ray watched her with wide eyes.

"Hey, if you want something else, I can order something from the deli down the—"

Simone grabbed them by their wrist and tugged them down on top of her in bed, kissing them harder than she'd ever kissed anyone. Ray melted against her with a small noise of surprise, eyes drifting shut, mouths content to explore for a moment.

Then Simone pulled away and said, "That is the most delicious thing I've ever eaten."

"I'll make it for you anytime if this is the reaction it gets me," Ray said against her throat. "Aren't you going to eat the rest? It'll go cold if you leave it too long."

Simone kissed the bottom of Ray's chin. "In a minute," she promised, running her hands down over Ray's warm skin.

Some appetites could never be satisfied.

Epilogue

Lisette D'Amboise was a tiny figure in her camel hair coat and intricately knotted scarf, standing on the sidewalk in front of the old, curving building. Her eyes were still sharp and bright as they roamed over the boarded-up windows and graffiti.

"Ah, yes," she said in her typically French way, "she has seen better days. But haven't we all?" She turned to Simone and Ray, who were standing nervously off to the side. Reflexively, Simone's hand sought out Ray's and gave it a squeeze. The Netflix money they'd earned thus far was good money, more than either had ever made at any culinary gig, but a project like this needed very deep pockets. Lisette-deep.

"It may not look like much now—" Ray began. They had a whole pitch ready. Simone had listened to it and critiqued it about a million times.

But Lisette just waved a hand through the air. "Dear child, I have an imagination. Of course I see what she could be if we love her as she should be loved." She paused, gazing up at the stonework with a thoughtful frown. "Perhaps I should not call her 'her.' It is a difficult habit to break, no?"

"Oh, I think she's definitely a her," Ray said. "And I do love her." They squeezed Simone's hand in return. They shared a look that, only a year prior, Simone might have scoffed at as being too mushy and not at all serious.

"So?" Simone turned to Lisette, her breath misting in the air. "What do you think?"

The Frenchwoman gave the building one last measuring look. "Is there space for things besides your brewery, dear Ray?"

"Totally. We could turn some floors into event space, maybe a tasting area—"

"What about a studio?" Lisette turned to them and winked. "We still need a place to make our little show, no?"

Simone's mouth dropped open. Her mind boggled at the possibilities. They could own the entire operation if they shot here at the brewery. "But it would need to be fixed up really fast if we wanted to use it for shooting. Like, immediately."

"Well." Lisette smiled. "Then let's get to work."

Acknowledgments

First things first: thank you, Dana. You're a great friend and a great first reader. You were also extremely shrewd to negotiate for top billing in the acknowledgments. This is all to say, you believed in me so hard. I needed that, bitch.

Thank you to my excellent wife, the best wife, the winner of all wife awards. You listened to me whine about my characters and their problems for months, which qualifies you for sainthood in my book. With you, anything is possible. I love you.

Thanks, Mom! I turned out great. Having you as a parent and English teacher is partly to blame. Thank you for taking care of me, before and after surgery. So, in essence, my entire life.

Thank you to the most tireless and wonderful agent in the business, Larissa Melo Pienkowski and the entire team at Jill Grinberg. You got what I was doing, Larissa, and I couldn't ask for a more supportive person in my corner.

To my editor, Lara, thank you for constantly being on the same wavelength as me, for giving Ray and Simone the perfect home, and for reading my horoscope. My eternal gratitude to everyone at Emily Bestler who made this book possible: Liz Byer,

James Iacobelli, Min Choi, Lexy Alemao, Paige Lytle, Iris Chen, Megan Rudloff, Katelyn Phillips, Karlyn Hixson, and all the rest. Thank you to Colleen Reinhart for bringing my children to life on the cover. Thank you especially to the copy editors, the unsung heroes of the universe, for fixing all my bonkers mistakes. I've probably made several in this paragraph. Sorry.

To all my friends, both meat-based and virtual, thank you for listening to me talk nonstop about this project: Tony, Liz, Dani, Taylor, Lauren, Kaila, and everyone in the group chat. You're worth more than gold.

And to every trans and nonbinary person, out or not, stuck in a soul-sucking job and surrounded by people who don't see you, appreciate you, or respect you: thank you for existing. You're doing the most in a world that is giving you the least. I love you and I cherish every atom of your beautiful being.

If you loved this, don't miss the next
delightfully queer love story . . .

Chef's Choice
TJ Alexander

**Take one fake-dating setup, add a pinch of pining
and a dash of flirtation, then leave to simmer . . .**

When Luna O'Shea is unceremoniously fired from her frustrating
office job, she tries to count her blessings: she's a proud trans
woman who has plenty of friends, a wonderful roommate, and
a good life in New York City. But blessings don't pay the bills.

Enter Jean-Pierre, a laissez-faire trans man and the heir to a huge
culinary empire – which he'll only inherit if he can jump through
the hoops his celebrity-chef grandfather has placed in his path.

First hoop: he needs a girlfriend. Second hoop: they both need
to learn to cook the family's world-renowned, elaborate recipes.

Luna's happy to play the role of devoted girlfriend and chef,
for a price. Never mind the fact she's never even cracked an egg.
Or the pesky feelings she's starting to have for Jean-Pierre . . .

Available in paperback and eBook from 20 July 2023

**SIMON &
SCHUSTER**